COLONIAL HORRORS

COLONIAL HORRORS

Sleepy Hollow and Beyond

EDITED BY

Graeme Davis

PEGASUS BOOKS

NEW YORK LONDON

COLONIAL HORRORS

Pegasus Books Ltd.
148 W 37th Street, 13th Floor
New York, NY 10018

Compilation copyright © 2017 by Graeme Davis

Introduction © 2017 by Graeme Davis

First Pegasus Books cloth edition October 2017

Interior design by Maria Fernandez

Library of Congress Cataloging-in-Publication Data is available.

ISBN: 978-1-68177-529-6

10 9 8 7 6 5 4 3 2 1

Printed in the United States of America
Distributed by W. W. Norton & Company

Dedicated to my wife, best friend, and partner in crime,
Jamie Paige Davis, who understands the love of a good story.

CONTENTS

INTRODUCTION *by Graeme Davis* · ix

THE LEGEND OF SLEEPY HOLLOW *by Washington Irving* · 1

AN ESSAY FOR THE RECORDING OF REMARKABLE PROVIDENCES *by Increase Mather* · 31

WONDERS OF THE INVISIBLE WORLD *by Cotton Mather* · 49

LITHOBOLIA *by R.C.* · 61

WIELAND *by Charles Brockden Brown* · 79

THE MONEY-DIGGERS *by Washington Irving* · 93

RACHEL DYER *by John Neal* · 161

MOLL PITCHER *by John Greenleaf Whittier* · 173

THE BIRTH-MARK *by Nathaniel Hawthorne* · 197

A TALE OF THE RAGGED MOUNTAINS *by Edgar Allan Poe* · 215

THE LAKE GUN *by James Fenimore Cooper* · 227

IN THE PINES *by W. F. Mayer* · 239

THE ROMANCE OF CERTAIN OLD CLOTHES *by Henry James* · 255

AN AUTHENTICATED HISTORY OF THE BELL WITCH
by Martin van Buren Ingram · 275

MYTHS AND LEGENDS OF OUR OWN LAND
by Charles M. Skinner · 319

THE SALEM WOLF *by Howard Pyle* · 335

THE CASE OF CHARLES DEXTER WARD *by H. P. Lovecraft* · 349

ACKNOWLEDGMENTS · 381

INTRODUCTION

by Graeme Davis

From the Salem witch trials to Washington Irving's headless horseman to the shadows that lay thick over Lovecraft Country, the Colonial era is the native soil from which American horror literature first sprang. Where European writers of the Gothic and bizarre evoked ruined castles and crumbling abbeys, their American counterparts looked back to the mysteries and superstitions of the Thirteen Colonies with their inward-looking towns, their stifling religion, and their dark and perilous woods.

Some tales of the Colonial era have gone on to become part of American literary canon and have spread across other media. Washington Irving's "The Legend of Sleepy Hollow," published in 1820, was filmed as early as 1922, presented onstage in multiple forms including a short-lived 1948 Broadway musical, and most recently has inspired a popular television series. The dark and brutal history of the Salem witch hysteria has been revisited in novels, films, and plays—most notably Arthur Miller's *The*

Crucible—and continues to inspire both supernatural fiction and social and political commentary.

To the first colonists, the New World was a strange and threatening place, ruled by native peoples whom the colonists feared and despised as "heathen savages." The Puritans of the Massachusetts Bay Colony believed that the Devil was real and active in all human affairs, and Puritan logic maintained that all who were not Christians (and many of those who were the wrong kind of Christians) actually worshipped the Devil: in his 1684 work *An Essay for the Recording of Illustrious Providences*, the Puritan minister (and later, Salem judge) Increase Mather observes that in "a great Wigwam (i.e. Indian House) at both ends was an Image; here the Indians in the War time were wont to Powaw (i.e. invocate the Devil)." Satan clearly held sway over this newly discovered continent, and would surely attack Christians there with every means at his command. Tales of native barbarism, violence, and cruelty were rife, with each fresh atrocity described in almost salacious detail: unsurprisingly, reports of colonial violence against native communities were briefer and more soberly expressed.

Witches, of course, were the Devil's natural allies and servants even in Europe, where more than a millennium of Christianity and almost two centuries of persecution had, according to some, failed to stamp them out completely. Given Satan's long ascendancy in the New World, they posed an even greater threat, working to weaken the Christian society of the colonies from within while hostile natives attacked from without.

Certain historical events were seized upon as proof that the Devil stalked the New World and would stop at nothing to destroy the souls of good Christians. The mysterious disappearance of the Roanoke Colony in 1590 fuels wild theories that persist to this day. A possible outbreak of ergot poisoning at Salem led to the witch hysteria of 1692-3, and although accused witches had been hanged in New England as early as 1647, the town has been synonymous with witchcraft ever since. A religious feud in New Jersey led to the legend of the Jersey Devil, which has since grown into a pop-culture icon as well as a hunted cryptid.

Early reports of witches, ghosts, and other supernatural terrors were reported as fact by the writers of the seventeenth century, although it has been suggested that a formal division between fiction and nonfiction did not yet exist. At least some of these tales were religious or political allegories, or were intended to have an "improving" effect upon readers, rather than simply to entertain them.

The eighteenth century saw the rise of the novel as a literary form in English, first in Britain and then in the newly independent United States of America. In the second half of the eighteenth century and the early part of the nineteenth, Gothic fiction developed in Europe, and when American writers looked for a homegrown setting to match the ruined castles and crumbling monasteries of the European Gothic, it was natural that they should turn to the troubled and superstitious time of the colonies.

Charles Brockden Brown's *Wieland* was published in 1798, just two years after Matthew Lewis's Gothic classic *The Monk*, and Washington Irving published "The Legend of Sleepy Hollow" two years after Mary Shelley's *Frankenstein*. Although American writers did not entirely ignore the attractions of a European setting, it was the Thirteen Colonies that became the natural home of American horror.

Later writers followed suit. The crumbling towns of New England's backwaters cast a deep shadow over H. P. Lovecraft's stories, many of which dealt with an evil from the past coming horribly into the present. The mere mention of Salem, or any reference to dark deeds in Colonial times, has become something like a certificate of pedigree, invoking the shades of Cotton Mather, Washington Irving, and the rest to attest to a story's American credentials.

Today, the descendants of Salem witches still cavort across the pages of popular fiction, falling in love with Byronic vampires and manly werewolves or simply trying to get by in a hostile world. The various adaptations of "The Legend of Sleepy Hollow" have already been mentioned. The 2004 movie *National Treasure* followed Masonic clues left by the Founding Fathers in a lighthearted answer to Dan Brown's Eurocentric hits *The Da Vinci Code* and *Angels & Demons*. In 2012, the popular video game franchise *Assassin's Creed* set its third installment amid a Templar conspiracy during the Revolutionary War. In 2015, the movie *The VVitch: A New England Folktale* won awards at the Sundance and London Film Festivals, among others. There is even a *Dungeons & Dragons*–style tabletop roleplaying game called *Colonial Gothic*, in which players encounter Masonic plots, witchcraft, monsters from Native American lore, and Lovecraftian horrors from beyond space and time.

The Colonial era is the true birthplace of American horror, and will no doubt continue to host all manner of tales of terror and suspense. The stories in this book—some well-known, others less so—are where it all began.

EDITOR'S NOTE: Because of their antiquity, many of the stories in this collection—which range in year of publication from 1684 to 1927—use archaic spellings and turns of phrase. Even some of the nineteenth-century tales use British-style spelling and grammar. If these stories came from present-day authors, an editor would feel compelled to "correct" the anomalies, but I believe the period language is a vital part of them, and so they are presented as I found them in their original state.

COLONIAL HORRORS

COLONIAL
HORRORS

THE LEGEND OF SLEEPY HOLLOW

Washington Irving

1820

It seems strange that America's best-known and most iconic ghost story was written while its author was living in England. Irving traveled widely throughout his life, and was staying with his sister Sarah and her husband, Henry van Wart, in the English city of Birmingham when he wrote this story and the other stories in his col-lection The Sketch Book of Geoffrey Crayon, Gent.

In America, the collection was published in seven parts between June 1819 and September 1820; a two-volume set was published in London in February and July of 1820, and formed the basis for the first single-volume American edition, published in 1824. "The Legend of Sleepy Hollow" appeared in the sixth American installment and was an immediate success. Sir Walter Scott, one of Irving's literary heroes, called the book "positively beautiful," and the fashionable poet Lord George Byron claimed to have learned it by heart. In Britain, the book not only helped establish Irving's reputation as a writer, but also established American writers in general as being worthy of consideration by British readers, who had previously dismissed all English writing produced outside their own country.

Although the Sketch Book's *other content—with the notable exception of "Rip Van Winkle"—has sunk into obscurity, "The Legend of Sleepy Hollow" is still going strong. The story has been filmed multiple times, starting in 1922. It has spawned stage plays, musicals, operas, and musical suites. Multiple television adaptations include a 2013 series which brings Ichabod Crane's battle with the headless horseman into the present day. Almost two centuries after its original publication, "The Legend of Sleepy Hollow" remains the one Colonial horror story that everyone knows—even if they have never read it in its original form.*

(Found among the papers of the late Diedrich Knickerbocker.)

> *A pleasing land of drowsy-head it was,*
> *Of dreams that wave before the half-shut eye,*
> *And of gay castles in the clouds that pass,*
> *For ever flushing round a summer sky.*
>
> —*Castle of Indolence*

I n the bosom of one of those spacious coves which indent the eastern shore of the Hudson, at that broad expansion of the river denominated by the ancient Dutch navigators the Tappan Zee, and where they always prudently shortened sail and implored the protection of St. Nicholas when they crossed, there lies a small market-town or rural port which by some is called Greensburg, but which is more generally and properly known by the name of Tarry Town. This name was given, we are told, in former days by the good housewives of the adjacent country from the inveterate propensity of their husbands to linger about the village tavern on market days. Be that as it may, I do not vouch for the fact, but merely advert to it for the sake of being precise and authentic. Not far from this village, perhaps about two miles, there is a little valley, or rather lap of land, among high hills, which is one of the quietest places in the whole world. A small brook glides through it, with just murmur enough to lull one to repose, and the occasional whistle of a quail or tapping of a woodpecker is almost the only sound that ever breaks in upon the uniform tranquillity.

I recollect that when a stripling my first exploit in squirrel-shooting was in a grove of tall walnut trees that shades one side of the valley. I had wandered into it at noontime, when all Nature is peculiarly quiet, and was startled by the roar of my own gun as it broke the Sabbath stillness around and was prolonged and reverberated by the angry echoes. If ever I should wish for a retreat whither I might steal from the world and its distractions and dream quietly away the remnant of a troubled life, I know of none more promising than this little valley.

From the listless repose of the place and the peculiar character of its inhabitants, who are descendants from the original Dutch settlers, this sequestered glen has long been known by the name of SLEEPY HOLLOW, and its rustic lads are called the Sleepy Hollow Boys throughout all the neighboring country. A drowsy, dreamy influence seems to hang over the land and to pervade the very atmosphere. Some say that the place was bewitched by a High German doctor during the early days of the settlement; others, that an old Indian chief, the prophet or wizard of his tribe, held his powwows there before the country was discovered by Master Hendrick Hudson. Certain it is, the place still continues under the sway of some witching power that holds a spell over the minds of the good people, causing them to walk in a continual reverie. They are given to all kinds of marvellous beliefs, are subject to trances and visions, and frequently see strange sights and hear music and voices in the air. The whole neighborhood abounds with local tales, haunted spots, and twilight superstitions; stars shoot and meteors glare oftener across the valley than in any other part of the country, and the nightmare, with her whole ninefold, seems to make it the favorite scene of her gambols.

The dominant spirit, however, that haunts this enchanted region, and seems to be commander-in-chief of all the powers of the air, is the apparition of a figure on horseback without a head. It is said by some to be the ghost of a Hessian trooper whose head had been carried away by a cannonball in some nameless battle during the Revolutionary War, and who is ever and anon seen by the country-folk hurrying along in the gloom of night as if on the wings of the wind. His haunts are not confined to the valley, but extend at times to the adjacent roads, and especially to the vicinity of a church at no great distance. Indeed, certain of the most authentic historians of those parts, who have been careful in collecting and collating the floating facts concerning this spectre, allege that the body of the trooper having been buried in the churchyard, the ghost rides forth to the scene of battle in nightly quest of his head, and that the rushing speed with which he sometimes passes along the Hollow, like a midnight blast, is owing to his being belated and in a hurry to get back to the churchyard before daybreak.

Such is the general purport of this legendary superstition, which has furnished materials for many a wild story in that region of shadows; and the spectre is known at all the country firesides by the name of the Headless Horseman of Sleepy Hollow.

It is remarkable that the visionary propensity I have mentioned is not confined to the native inhabitants of the valley, but is unconsciously imbibed by every one who resides there for a time. However wide awake they may have been before they entered that sleepy region, they are sure in a little time to inhale the witching influence of the air and begin to grow imaginative—to dream dreams and see apparitions.

I mention this peaceful spot with all possible laud, for it is in such little retired Dutch valleys, found here and there embosomed in the great State of New York, that population, manners, and customs remain fixed, while the great torrent of migration and improvement, which is making such incessant changes in other parts of this restless country, sweeps by them unobserved. They are like those little nooks of still water which border a rapid stream where we may see the straw and bubble riding quietly at anchor, or slowly revolving in their mimic harbor, undisturbed by the rush of the passing current.

Though many years have elapsed since I trod the drowsy shades of Sleepy Hollow, yet I question whether I should not still find the same trees and the same families vegetating in its sheltered bosom.

In this by-place of Nature there abode, in a remote period of American history—that is to say, some thirty years since—a worthy wight of the name of Ichabod Crane, who sojourned, or, as he expressed it, "tarried", in Sleepy Hollow for the purpose of instructing the children of the vicinity. He was a native of Connecticut, a State which supplies the Union with pioneers for the mind as well as for the forest, and sends forth yearly its legions of frontier woodmen and country schoolmasters. The cognomen of Crane was not inapplicable to his person. He was tall, but exceedingly lank, with narrow shoulders, long arms and legs, hands that dangled a mile out of his sleeves, feet that might have served for shovels, and his whole frame most loosely hung together. His head was small, and flat at top, with huge ears, large green glassy eyes, and a long snip nose, so that it looked like a weathercock perched upon his spindle neck to tell which way the wind blew. To see him striding along the profile of a hill on a windy day, with his clothes bagging and fluttering about him, one might have mistaken him for the genius of Famine descending upon the earth or some scarecrow eloped from a cornfield.

His school-house was a low building of one large room, rudely constructed of logs, the windows partly glazed and partly patched with leaves of old copybooks. It was most ingeniously secured at vacant hours by a withe twisted in the handle of the door and stakes set against the window-shutters, so that, though a thief might get in with perfect ease, he would find some embarrassment in getting out—an idea most probably borrowed by the architect, Yost Van Houten, from the mystery of an eel-pot. The school-house stood in a rather lonely but pleasant situation, just at the foot of a woody hill, with a brook running close by and a formidable birch tree growing at one end of it. From hence the low murmur of his pupils' voices, conning over their lessons, might be heard in a drowsy summer's day like the hum of a bee-hive, interrupted now and then by the authoritative voice of the master in the tone of menace or command, or, peradventure, by the appalling sound of the birch as he urged some tardy loiterer along the flowery path of knowledge. Truth to say, he was a conscientious man, and ever bore in mind the golden maxim, "Spare the rod and spoil the child." Ichabod Crane's scholars certainly were not spoiled.

I would not have it imagined, however, that he was one of those cruel potentates of the school who joy in the smart of their subjects; on the contrary, he administered justice with discrimination rather than severity, taking the burden off the backs of the weak and laying it on those of the strong. Your mere puny stripling, that winced at the least flourish of the rod, was passed by with indulgence; but the claims of justice were satisfied by inflicting a double portion on some little tough, wrong-headed, broad-skirted Dutch urchin, who sulked and swelled and grew dogged and sullen beneath the birch. All this he called "doing his duty by their parents;" and he never inflicted a chastisement without following it by the assurance, so consolatory to the smarting urchin, that "he would remember it and thank him for it the longest day he had to live."

When school-hours were over he was even the companion and playmate of the larger boys, and on holiday afternoons would convoy some of the smaller ones home who happened to have pretty sisters or good housewives for mothers noted for the comforts of the cupboard. Indeed it behooved him to keep on good terms with his pupils. The revenue arising from his school was small, and would have been scarcely sufficient to furnish him with daily bread, for he was a huge feeder, and, though lank, had the dilating powers of an anaconda; but to help out his maintenance he was, according to country custom in those parts, boarded and lodged at the houses of the farmers whose children he instructed. With these he lived successively a week at a time, thus going the rounds of the neighborhood with all his worldly effects tied up in a cotton handkerchief.

That all this might not be too onerous on the purses of his rustic patrons, who are apt to consider the costs of schooling a grievous burden and school-masters as mere drones, he had various ways of rendering himself both useful and agreeable. He assisted the farmers occasionally in the lighter labors of their farms, helped to make hay, mended the fences, took the horses to water, drove the cows from pasture, and cut wood for the winter fire. He laid aside, too, all the dominant dignity and absolute sway with which he lorded it in his little empire, the school, and became wonderfully gentle and ingratiating. He found favor in the eyes of the mothers by petting the children, particularly the youngest; and like the lion bold, which whilom so magnanimously the lamb did hold, he would sit with a child on one knee and rock a cradle with his foot for whole hours together.

In addition to his other vocations, he was the singing-master of the neighborhood and picked up many bright shillings by instructing the young folks in psalmody. It was a matter of no little vanity to him on Sundays to take his station in front of the church-gallery with a band of chosen singers, where, in his own mind, he completely carried away the palm from the parson. Certain it is, his voice resounded far above all the rest of the congregation, and there are peculiar quavers still to be heard in that church, and which may even be heard half a mile off, quite to the opposite side of the mill-pond on a still Sunday morning, which are said to be legitimately descended from the nose of Ichabod Crane. Thus, by divers little makeshifts in that ingenious way which is commonly denominated "by hook and by crook," the worthy pedagogue got on tolerably enough, and was thought, by all who understood nothing of the labor of headwork, to have a wonderfully easy life of it.

The schoolmaster is generally a man of some importance in the female circle of a rural neighborhood, being considered a kind of idle, gentleman-like personage of vastly superior taste and accomplishments to the rough country swains, and, indeed, inferior in learning only to the parson. His appearance, therefore, is apt to occasion some little stir at the tea-table of a farmhouse and the addition of a supernumerary dish of cakes or sweet-meats, or, peradventure, the parade of a silver tea-pot. Our man of letters, therefore, was peculiarly happy in the smiles of all the country damsels. How he would figure among them in the churchyard between services on Sundays, gathering grapes for them from the wild vines that overrun the surrounding trees; reciting for their amusement all the epitaphs on the tombstones; or sauntering, with a whole bevy of them, along the banks of the adjacent mill-pond, while the more bashful country bumpkins hung sheepishly back, envying his superior elegance and address.

From his half-itinerant life, also, he was a kind of travelling gazette, carrying the whole budget of local gossip from house to house, so that his appearance was always greeted with satisfaction. He was, moreover, esteemed by the women as a man of great erudition, for he had read several books quite through, and was a perfect master of Cotton Mather's *History of New England Witchcraft*, in which, by the way, he most firmly and potently believed.

He was, in fact, an odd mixture of small shrewdness and simple credulity. His appetite for the marvellous and his powers of digesting it were equally extraordinary, and both had been increased by his residence in this spellbound region. No tale was too gross or monstrous for his capacious swallow. It was often his delight, after his school was dismissed in the afternoon, to stretch himself on the rich bed of clover bordering the little brook that whimpered by his school-house, and there con over old Mather's direful tales until the gathering dusk of the evening made the printed page a mere mist before his eyes. Then, as he wended his way by swamp and stream and awful woodland to the farmhouse where he happened to be quartered, every sound of Nature at that witching hour fluttered his excited imagination—the moan of the whip-poor-will from the hillside; the boding cry of the tree-toad, that harbinger of storm; the dreary hooting of the screech-owl, or the sudden rustling in the thicket of birds frightened from their roost. The fire-flies, too, which sparkled most vividly in the darkest places, now and then startled him as one of uncommon brightness would stream across his path; and if, by chance, a huge blockhead of a beetle came winging his blundering flight against him, the poor varlet was ready to give up the ghost, with the idea that he was struck with a witch's token. His only resource on such occasions, either to drown thought or drive away evil spirits, was to sing psalm tunes; and the good people of Sleepy Hollow, as they sat by their doors of an evening, were often filled with awe at hearing his nasal melody, "in linked sweetness long drawn out," floating from the distant hill or along the dusky road.

Another of his sources of fearful pleasure was to pass long winter evenings with the old Dutch wives as they sat spinning by the fire, with a row of apples roasting and spluttering along the hearth, and listen to their marvellous tales of ghosts and goblins, and haunted fields, and haunted brooks, and haunted bridges, and haunted houses, and particularly of the headless horseman, or Galloping Hessian of the Hollow, as they sometimes called him. He would delight them equally by his anecdotes of witchcraft and of the direful omens and portentous sights and sounds in the air which prevailed in the earlier times of Connecticut, and would frighten them woefully with speculations upon comets and shooting stars, and with the alarming fact that the world did absolutely turn round and that they were half the time topsy-turvy.

But if there was a pleasure in all this while snugly cuddling in the chimney-corner of a chamber that was all of a ruddy glow from the crackling wood-fire, and where, of course, no spectre dared to show its face, it was dearly purchased by the terrors of his subsequent walk homewards. What fearful shapes and shadows beset his path amidst the dim and ghastly glare of a snowy night! With what wistful look did he eye every trembling ray of light streaming across the waste fields from some distant window! How often was he appalled by some shrub covered with snow, which, like a sheeted spectre, beset his very path! How often did he shrink with curdling awe at the sound of his own steps on the frosty crust beneath his feet, and dread to look over his shoulder, lest he should behold some uncouth being tramping close behind him! And how often was he thrown into complete dismay by some rushing blast howling among the trees, in the idea that it was the Galloping Hessian on one of his nightly scourings!

All these, however, were mere terrors of the night, phantoms of the mind that walk in darkness; and though he had seen many spectres in his time, and been more than once beset by Satan in divers shapes in his lonely perambulations, yet daylight put an end to all these evils; and he would have passed a pleasant life of it, in despite of the devil and all his works, if his path had not been crossed by a being that causes more perplexity to mortal man than ghosts, goblins, and the whole race of witches put together, and that was—a woman.

Among the musical disciples who assembled one evening in each week to receive his instructions in psalmody was Katrina Van Tassel, the daughter and only child of a substantial Dutch farmer. She was a blooming lass of fresh eighteen, plump as a partridge, ripe and melting and rosy-cheeked as one of her father's peaches, and universally famed, not merely for her beauty, but her vast expectations. She was withal a little of a coquette, as might be perceived even in her dress, which was a mixture of ancient and modern fashions, as most suited to set off her charms. She wore the ornaments of pure yellow gold which her great-great-grandmother had brought over from Saardam, the tempting stomacher of the olden time, and withal a provokingly short petticoat to display the prettiest foot and ankle in the country round.

Ichabod Crane had a soft and foolish heart towards the sex, and it is not to be wondered at that so tempting a morsel soon found favor in his eyes, more especially after he had visited her in her paternal mansion. Old Baltus Van Tassel was a perfect picture of a thriving, contented, liberal-hearted farmer. He seldom, it is true, sent either his eyes or his thoughts beyond the boundaries of his own farm, but within those everything was snug, happy, and well-conditioned. He was satisfied with his wealth but not proud of it, and piqued himself upon the hearty abundance, rather than the style, in which he lived. His stronghold was situated on the banks of the Hudson, in one of those green, sheltered, fertile nooks in which the Dutch farmers are so fond of nestling. A great elm tree spread its broad branches over it, at the foot of which bubbled up a spring of the softest and sweetest water in a little well formed of a barrel, and then stole sparkling away through the grass to a neighboring brook that bubbled along among alders and dwarf willows. Hard by the farmhouse was a vast barn, that might have served for a church, every window and crevice of which seemed bursting forth with the treasures of the farm; the flail was busily resounding within it from morning to night; swallows and martins skimmed twittering about the eaves; and rows of pigeons, some with one eye turned up, as if watching the weather, some with their heads under their wings or buried in their bosoms, and others, swelling, and cooing, and bowing about their dames, were enjoying the sunshine on the roof. Sleek, unwieldy porkers were grunting in the repose and abundance of their pens, whence sallied forth, now and then, troops of sucking pigs as if to snuff the air. A stately squadron of snowy geese were riding in an adjoining pond, convoying whole fleets of ducks; regiments of turkeys were gobbling through the farmyard, and guinea-fowls fretting about it, like ill-tempered housewives, with their peevish, discontented cry. Before the barn-door strutted the gallant cock, that pattern of a husband, a warrior, and a fine gentleman, clapping his burnished wings and crowing in the pride and gladness of his heart—sometimes tearing up the earth with his feet, and then generously calling his ever-hungry family of wives and children to enjoy the rich morsel which he had discovered.

The pedagogue's mouth watered as he looked upon this sumptuous promise of luxurious winter fare. In his devouring mind's eye he pictured to himself every roasting-pig running about with a pudding in his belly and an apple in his mouth; the pigeons were snugly put to bed in a comfortable pie and tucked in with a coverlet of crust; the geese were swimming in their own gravy; and the ducks pairing cosily in dishes, like snug married couples, with a decent competency of onion sauce. In the porkers he saw carved out the future sleek side of bacon and juicy relishing ham; not a turkey but he beheld daintily trussed up, with its gizzard under its wing, and, peradventure, a necklace of savory sausages; and even bright Chanticleer himself lay sprawling on his back in a side-dish, with uplifted claws, as if craving that quarter which his chivalrous spirit disdained to ask while living.

As the enraptured Ichabod fancied all this, and as he rolled his great green eyes over the fat meadow-lands, the rich fields of wheat, of rye, of buckwheat, and Indian corn, and the orchards burdened with ruddy fruit, which surrounded the warm tenement of Van Tassel, his heart yearned after the damsel who was to inherit these domains, and his imagination expanded with the idea how they might be readily turned into cash and the money invested in immense tracts of wild land and shingle palaces in the wilderness. Nay, his busy fancy already realized his hopes, and presented to him the blooming Katrina, with a whole family of children, mounted on the top of a wagon loaded with household trumpery, with pots and kettles dangling beneath, and he beheld himself bestriding a pacing mare, with a colt at her heels, setting out for Kentucky, Tennessee, or the Lord knows where.

When he entered the house the conquest of his heart was complete. It was one of those spacious farmhouses with high-ridged but lowly-sloping roofs, built in the style handed down from the first Dutch settlers, the low projecting eaves forming a piazza along the front capable of being closed up in bad weather. Under this were hung flails, harness, various utensils of husbandry, and nets for fishing in the neighboring river. Benches were built along the sides for summer use, and a great spinning-wheel at one end and a churn at the other showed the various uses to which this important porch might be devoted. From this piazza the wondering Ichabod entered the hall, which formed the centre of the mansion and the place of usual residence. Here rows of resplendent pewter, ranged on a long dresser, dazzled his eyes. In one corner stood a huge bag of wool ready to be spun; in another a quantity of linsey-woolsey just from the loom; ears of Indian corn and strings of dried apples and peaches hung in gay festoons along the walls, mingled with the gaud of red peppers; and a door left ajar gave him a peep into the best parlor, where the claw-footed chairs and dark mahogany tables shone like mirrors; andirons, with their accompanying shovel and tongs, glistened from their covert of asparagus tops; mock-oranges and conch-shells decorated the mantelpiece; strings of various-colored birds' eggs were suspended above it; a great ostrich egg was hung from the centre of the room, and a corner cupboard, knowingly left open, displayed immense treasures of old silver and well-mended china.

From the moment Ichabod laid his eyes upon these regions of delight the peace of his mind was at an end, and his only study was how to gain the affections of the peerless daughter of Van Tassel. In this enterprise, however, he had more real difficulties than generally fell to the lot of a knight-errant of yore, who seldom had anything but giants, enchanters, fiery dragons, and such-like easily-conquered adversaries to contend with, and had to make his way merely through gates of iron and brass and walls of adamant to the castle keep, where the lady of his heart was confined; all which he achieved as easily as a man would carve his way to the centre of a Christmas pie, and then the lady gave him her hand as a matter of course. Ichabod, on the contrary, had to win his way to the heart of a country coquette beset with a labyrinth of whims and caprices, which were forever presenting new difficulties and impediments, and he had to encounter a host of fearful adversaries of real flesh and blood, the numerous rustic admirers who beset every portal to her heart, keeping a watchful and angry eye upon each other, but ready to fly out in the common cause against any new competitor.

Among these the most formidable was a burly, roaring, roistering blade of the name of Abraham—or, according to the Dutch abbreviation, Brom—Van Brunt, the hero of the country round, which rang with his feats of strength and hardihood. He was broad-shouldered and double-jointed, with short curly black hair and a bluff but not unpleasant countenance, having a mingled air of fun and arrogance. From his Herculean frame and great powers of limb, he had received the nickname of BROM BONES, by which he was universally known. He was famed for great knowledge and skill in horsemanship, being as dexterous on horseback as a Tartar. He was foremost at all races and cockfights, and, with the ascendancy which bodily strength acquires in rustic life, was the umpire in all disputes, setting his hat on one side and giving his decisions with an air and tone admitting of no gainsay or appeal. He was always ready for either a fight or a frolic, but had more mischief than ill-will in his composition; and with all his overbearing roughness there was a strong dash of waggish good-humor at bottom. He had three or four boon companions who regarded him as their model, and at the head of whom he scoured the country, attending every scene of feud or merriment for miles around. In cold weather he was distinguished by a fur cap surmounted with a flaunting fox's tail; and when the folks at a country gathering descried this well-known crest at a distance, whisking about among a squad of hard riders, they always stood by for a squall. Sometimes his crew would be heard dashing along past the farm-houses at midnight with whoop and halloo, like a troop of Don Cossacks, and the old dames, startled out of their sleep, would listen for a moment till the hurry-scurry had clattered by, and then exclaim, "Ay, there goes Brom Bones and his gang!" The neighbors looked upon him with a mixture of awe, admiration, and good-will, and when any madcap prank or rustic brawl occurred in the vicinity always shook their heads and warranted Brom Bones was at the bottom of it.

This rantipole hero had for some time singled out the blooming Katrina for the object of his uncouth gallantries, and, though his amorous toyings were something like the gentle caresses and endearments of a bear, yet it was whispered that she did not altogether discourage his hopes. Certain it is, his advances were signals for rival candidates to retire who felt no inclination to cross a line in his amours; insomuch, that when his horse was seen tied to Van Tassel's paling on a Sunday night, a sure sign that his master was courting—or, as it is termed, "sparking"—within, all other suitors passed by in despair and carried the war into other quarters.

Such was the formidable rival with whom Ichabod Crane had to contend, and, considering all things, a stouter man than he would have shrunk from the competition and a wiser man would have despaired. He had, however, a happy mixture of pliability and perseverance in his nature; he was in form and spirit like a supple-jack—yielding, but although; though he bent, he never broke and though he bowed beneath the slightest pressure, yet the moment it was away—jerk!—he was as erect and carried his head as high as ever.

To have taken the field openly against his rival would have been madness: for he was not man to be thwarted in his amours, any more than that stormy lover, Achilles. Ichabod, therefore, made his advances in a quiet and gently insinuating manner. Under cover of his character of singing-master, he made frequent visits at the farm-house; not that he had anything to apprehend from the meddlesome interference of parents, which is so often a stumbling-block in the path of lovers. Balt Van Tassel was an easy, indulgent soul; he loved his daughter better even than his pipe, and, like a reasonable man and an excellent father, let her have her way in everything. His notable little wife, too, had enough to do to attend to her housekeeping and manage her poultry for, as she sagely observed, ducks and geese are foolish things and must be looked after, but girls can take care of themselves. Thus while the busy dame bustled about the house or plied her spinning-wheel at one end of the piazza, honest Balt would sit smoking his evening pipe at the other, watching the achievements of a little wooden warrior who, armed with a sword in each hand, was most valiantly fighting the wind on the pinnacle of the barn. In the meantime, Ichabod would carry on his suit with the daughter by the side of the spring under the great elm, or sauntering along in the twilight, that hour so favorable to the lover's eloquence.

I profess not to know how women's hearts are wooed and won. To me they have always been matters of riddle and admiration. Some seem to have but one vulnerable point, or door of access, while others have a thousand avenues and may be captured in a thousand different ways. It is a great triumph of skill to gain the former, but still greater proof of generalship to maintain possession of the latter, for the man must battle for his fortress at every door and window. He who wins a thousand common hearts is therefore entitled to some renown, but he who keeps undisputed sway over the heart of a coquette is indeed a hero. Certain it is, this was not the case with the redoubtable Brom Bones; and from the moment Ichabod Crane made his advances, the interests of the former evidently declined; his horse was no longer seen tied at the palings on Sunday nights, and a deadly feud gradually arose between him and the preceptor of Sleepy Hollow.

Brom, who had a degree of rough chivalry in his nature, would fain have carried matters to open warfare, and have settled their pretensions to the lady according to the mode of those most concise and simple reasoners, the knights-errant of yore—by single combat; but Ichabod was too conscious of the superior might of his adversary to enter the lists against him: he had overheard a boast of Bones, that he would "double the schoolmaster up and lay him on a shelf of his own school-house;" and he was too wary to give him an opportunity. There was something extremely provoking in this obstinately pacific system; it left Brom no alternative but to draw upon the funds of rustic waggery in his disposition and to play off boorish practical jokes upon his rival. Ichabod became the object of whimsical persecution to Bones and his gang of rough riders. They harried his hitherto peaceful domains; smoked out his singing school by stopping up the chimney; broke into the schoolhouse at night in spite of its formidable fastenings of withe and window stakes, and turned everything topsy-turvy; so that the poor schoolmaster began to think all the witches in the country held their meetings there. But, what was still more annoying, Brom took all opportunities of turning him into ridicule in presence of his mistress, and had a scoundrel dog whom he taught to whine in the most ludicrous manner, and introduced as a rival of Ichabod's, to instruct her in psalmody.

In this way, matters went on for some time without producing any material effect on the relative situation of the contending powers. On a fine autumnal afternoon Ichabod, in pensive mood, sat enthroned on the lofty stool whence he usually watched all the concerns of his little literary realm. In his hand he swayed a ferule, that sceptre of despotic power; the birch of justice reposed on three nails behind the throne, a constant terror to evildoers; while on the desk before him might be seen sundry contraband articles and prohibited weapons detected upon the persons of idle urchins, such as half-munched apples, popguns, whirligigs, fly-cages, and whole legions of rampant little paper gamecocks. Apparently there had been some appalling act of justice recently inflicted, for his scholars were all busily intent upon their books or slyly whispering behind them with one eye kept upon the master, and a kind of buzzing stillness reigned throughout the school-room. It was suddenly interrupted by the appearance of a negro in tow-cloth jacket and trowsers, a round-crowned fragment of a hat like the cap of Mercury, and mounted on the back of a ragged, wild, half-broken colt, which he managed with a rope by way of halter. He came clattering up to the school door with an invitation to Ichabod to attend a merry-making or "quilting frolic" to be held that evening at Mynheer Van Tassel's; and, having delivered his message with that air of importance and effort at fine language which a negro is apt to display on petty embassies of the kind, he dashed over the brook, and was seen scampering away up the hollow, full of the importance and hurry of his mission.

All was now bustle and hubbub in the late quiet school-room. The scholars were hurried through their lessons without stopping at trifles; those who were nimble skipped over half with impunity, and those who were tardy had a smart application now and then in the rear to quicken their speed or help them over a tall word. Books were flung aside without being put away on the shelves, inkstands were overturned, benches thrown down, and the whole school was turned loose an hour before the usual time, bursting forth like a legion of young imps, yelping and racketing about the green in joy at their early emancipation.

The gallant Ichabod now spent at least an extra half hour at his toilet, brushing and furbishing up his best, and indeed only, suit of rusty black, and arranging his locks by a bit of broken looking-glass that hung up in the school-house. That he might make his appearance before his mistress in the true style of a cavalier, be borrowed a horse from the farmer with whom he was domiciliated, a choleric old Dutchman of the name of Hans Van Ripper, and, thus gallantly mounted, issued forth like a knight-errant in quest of adventures. But it is meet I should, in the true spirit of romantic story, give some account of the looks and equipments of my hero and his steed. The animal he bestrode was a broken-down plough-horse that had outlived almost everything but his viciousness. He was gaunt and shagged, with a ewe neck and a head like a hammer; his rusty mane and tail were tangled and knotted with burrs; one eye had lost its pupil and was glaring and spectral, but the other had the gleam of a genuine devil in it. Still, he must have had fire and mettle in his day, if we may judge from the name he bore of Gunpowder. He had, in fact, been a favorite steed of his master's, the choleric Van Ripper, who was a furious rider, and had infused, very probably, some of his own spirit into the animal; for, old and broken down as he looked, there was more of the lurking devil in him than in any young filly in the country.

Ichabod was a suitable figure for such a steed. He rode with short stirrups, which brought his knees nearly up to the pommel of the saddle; his sharp elbows stuck out like grasshoppers'; he carried his whip perpendicularly in his hand like a sceptre; and as his horse jogged on the motion of his arms was not unlike the flapping of a pair of wings. A small wool hat rested on the top of his nose, for so his scanty strip of forehead might be called, and the skirts of his black coat fluttered out almost to his horse's tail. Such was the appearance of Ichabod and his steed as they shambled out of the gate of Hans Van Ripper, and it was altogether such an apparition as is seldom to be met with in broad daylight.

It was, as I have said, a fine autumnal day, the sky was clear and serene, and Nature wore that rich and golden livery which we always associate with the idea of abundance. The forests had put on their sober brown and yellow, while some trees of the tenderer kind had been nipped by the frosts into brilliant dyes of orange, purple, and scarlet. Streaming files of wild-ducks began to make their appearance high in the air; the bark of the squirrel might be heard from the groves of beech and hickory nuts, and the pensive whistle of the quail at intervals from the neighboring stubble-field.

The small birds were taking their farewell banquets. In the fulness of their revelry they fluttered, chirping and frolicking, from bush to bush and tree to tree, capricious from the very profusion and variety around them. There was the honest cock robin, the favorite game of stripling sportsmen, with its loud querulous note; and the twittering blackbirds, flying in sable clouds; and the golden-winged woodpecker, with his crimson crest, his broad black gorget, and splendid plumage; and the cedar-bird, with its red-tipt wings and yellow-tipt tail and its little monteiro cap of feathers; and the blue jay, that noisy coxcomb, in his gay light-blue coat and white underclothes, screaming and chattering, bobbing and nodding and bowing, and pretending to be on good terms with every songster of the grove.

As Ichabod jogged slowly on his way his eye, ever open to every symptom of culinary abundance, ranged with delight over the treasures of jolly Autumn. On all sides he beheld vast store of apples—some hanging in oppressive opulence on the trees, some gathered into baskets and barrels for the market, others heaped up in rich piles for the cider-press. Farther on he beheld great fields of Indian corn, with its golden ears peeping from their leafy coverts and holding out the promise of cakes and hasty pudding; and the yellow pumpkins lying beneath them, turning up their fair round bellies to the sun, and giving ample prospects of the most luxurious of pies; and anon he passed the fragrant buckwheat-fields, breathing the odor of the beehive, and as he beheld them soft anticipations stole over his mind of dainty slapjacks, well buttered and garnished with honey or treacle by the delicate little dimpled hand of Katrina Van Tassel.

Thus feeding his mind with many sweet thoughts and "sugared suppositions," he journeyed along the sides of a range of hills which look out upon some of the goodliest scenes of the mighty Hudson. The sun gradually wheeled his broad disk down into the west. The wide bosom of the Tappan Zee lay motionless and glassy, excepting that here and there a gentle undulation waved and prolonged the blue shadow of the distant mountain. A few amber clouds floated in the sky, without a breath of air to move them. The horizon was of a fine golden tint, changing gradually into a pure apple green, and from that into the deep blue of the mid-heaven. A slanting ray lingered on the woody crests of the precipices that overhung some parts of the river, giving greater depth to the dark-gray and purple of their rocky sides. A sloop was loitering in the distance, dropping slowly down with the tide, her sail hanging uselessly against the mast, and as the reflection of the sky gleamed along the still water it seemed as if the vessel was suspended in the air.

It was toward evening that Ichabod arrived at the castle of the Heer Van Tassel, which he found thronged with the pride and flower of the adjacent country—old farmers, a spare leathern-faced race, in homespun coats and breeches, blue stockings, huge shoes, and magnificent pewter buckles; their brisk withered little dames, in close crimped caps, long-waisted shortgowns, homespun petticoats, with scissors and pincushions and gay calico pockets hanging on the outside; buxom lasses, almost as antiquated as their mothers, excepting where a straw hat, a fine ribbon, or perhaps a white frock, gave symptoms of city innovation; the sons, in short square-skirted coats with rows of stupendous brass buttons, and their hair generally queued in the fashion of the times, especially if they could procure an eel-skin for the purpose, it being esteemed throughout the country as a potent nourisher and strengthener of the hair.

Brom Bones, however, was the hero of the scene, having come to the gathering on his favorite steed Daredevil—a creature, like himself full of metal and mischief, and which no one but himself could manage. He was, in fact, noted for preferring vicious animals, given to all kinds of tricks, which kept the rider in constant risk of his neck, for he held a tractable, well-broken horse as unworthy of a lad of spirit.

Fain would I pause to dwell upon the world of charms that burst upon the enraptured gaze of my hero as he entered the state parlor of Van Tassel's mansion. Not those of the bevy of buxom lasses with their luxurious display of red and white, but the ample charms of a genuine Dutch country tea-table in the sumptuous time of autumn. Such heaped-up platters of cakes of various and almost indescribable kinds, known only to experienced Dutch housewives! There was the doughty doughnut, the tenderer oily koek, and the crisp and crumbling cruller; sweet cakes and short cakes, ginger cakes and honey cakes, and the whole family of cakes. And then there were apple pies and peach pies and pumpkin pies; besides slices of ham and smoked beef; and moreover delectable dishes of preserved plums and peaches and pears and quinces; not to mention broiled shad and roasted chickens; together with bowls of milk and cream—all mingled higgledy-piggledy, pretty much as I have enumerated them, with the motherly teapot sending up its clouds of vapor from the midst. Heaven bless the mark! I want breath and time to discuss this banquet as it deserves, and am too eager to get on with my story. Happily, Ichabod Crane was not in so great a hurry as his historian, but did ample justice to every dainty.

He was a kind and thankful creature, whose heart dilated in proportion as his skin was filled with good cheer, and whose spirits rose with eating as some men's do with drink. He could not help, too, rolling his large eyes round him as he ate, and chuckling with the possibility that he might one day be lord of all this scene of almost unimaginable luxury and splendor.

Then, he thought, how soon he'd turn his back upon the old school-house, snap his fingers in the face of Hans Van Ripper and every other niggardly patron, and kick any itinerant pedagogue out of doors that should dare to call him comrade!

Old Baltus Van Tassel moved about among his guests with a face dilated with content and good-humor, round and jolly as the harvest moon. His hospitable attentions were brief, but expressive, being confined to a shake of the hand, a slap on the shoulder, a loud laugh, and a pressing invitation to "fall to and help themselves."

And now the sound of the music from the common room, or hall, summoned to the dance. The musician was an old gray-headed negro who had been the itinerant orchestra of the neighborhood for more than half a century. His instrument was as old and battered as himself. The greater part of the time he scraped on two or three strings, accompanying every movement of the bow with a motion of the head, bowing almost to the ground and stamping with his foot whenever a fresh couple were to start.

Ichabod prided himself upon his dancing as much as upon his vocal powers. Not a limb, not a fibre about him was idle; and to have seen his loosely hung frame in full motion and clattering about the room you would have thought Saint Vitus himself, that blessed patron of the dance, was figuring before you in person. He was the admiration of all the negroes, who, having gathered, of all ages and sizes, from the farm and the neighborhood, stood forming a pyramid of shining black faces at every door and window, gazing with delight at the scene, rolling their white eyeballs, and showing grinning rows of ivory from ear to ear. How could the flogger of urchins be otherwise than animated and joyous? The lady of his heart was his partner in the dance, and smiling graciously in reply to all his amorous oglings, while Brom Bones, sorely smitten with love and jealousy, sat brooding by himself in one corner.

When the dance was at an end Ichabod was attracted to a knot of the sager folks, who, with old Van Tassel, sat smoking at one end of the piazza gossiping over former times and drawing out long stories about the war.

This neighborhood, at the time of which I am speaking, was one of those highly favored places which abound with chronicle and great men. The British and American line had run near it during the war; it had therefore been the scene of marauding and infested with refugees, cow-boys, and all kinds of border chivalry. Just sufficient time had elapsed to enable each storyteller to dress up his tale with a little becoming fiction, and in the indistinctness of his recollection to make himself the hero of every exploit.

There was the story of Doffue Martling, a large blue-bearded Dutchman, who had nearly taken a British frigate with an old iron nine-pounder from a mud breastwork, only that his gun burst at the sixth discharge. And there was an old gentleman who shall be nameless, being too rich a mynheer to be lightly mentioned, who, in the battle of Whiteplains, being an excellent master of defence, parried a musket-ball with a small sword, insomuch that he absolutely felt it whiz round the blade and glance off at the hilt: in proof of which he was ready at any time to show the sword, with the hilt a little bent. There were several more that had been equally great in the field, not one of whom but was persuaded that he had a considerable hand in bringing the war to a happy termination.

But all these were nothing to the tales of ghosts and apparitions that succeeded. The neighborhood is rich in legendary treasures of the kind. Local tales and superstitions thrive best in these sheltered, long-settled retreats but are trampled under foot by the shifting throng that forms the population of most of our country places. Besides, there is no encouragement for ghosts in most of our villages, for they have scarcely had time to finish their first nap and turn themselves in their graves before their surviving friends have travelled away from the neighborhood; so that when they turn out at night to walk their rounds they have no acquaintance left to call upon. This is perhaps the reason why we so seldom hear of ghosts except in our long-established Dutch communities.

The immediate causes however, of the prevalence of supernatural stories in these parts, was doubtless owing to the vicinity of Sleepy Hollow. There was a contagion in the very air that blew from that haunted region; it breathed forth an atmosphere of dreams and fancies infecting all the land. Several of the Sleepy Hollow people were present at Van Tassel's, and, as usual, were doling out their wild and wonderful legends. Many dismal tales were told about funeral trains and mourning cries and wailings heard and seen about the great tree where the unfortunate Major Andre was taken, and which stood in the neighborhood. Some mention was made also of the woman in white that haunted the dark glen at Raven Rock, and was often heard to shriek on winter nights before a storm, having perished there in the snow. The chief part of the stories, however, turned upon the favorite spectre of Sleepy Hollow, the headless horseman, who had been heard several times of late patrolling the country, and, it was said, tethered his horse nightly among the graves in the churchyard.

The sequestered situation of this church seems always to have made it a favorite haunt of troubled spirits. It stands on a knoll surrounded by locust trees and lofty elms, from among which its decent whitewashed walls shine modestly forth, like Christian purity beaming through the shades of retirement. A gentle slope descends from it to a silver sheet of water bordered by high trees, between which peeps may be caught at the blue hills of the Hudson. To look upon its grass-grown yard, where the sunbeams seem to sleep so quietly, one would think that there at least the dead might rest in peace. On one side of the church extends a wide woody dell, along, which raves a large brook among broken rocks and trunks of fallen trees. Over a deep black part of the stream, not far from the church, was formerly thrown a wooden bridge; the road that led to it and the bridge itself were thickly shaded by overhanging trees, which cast a gloom about it even in the daytime, but occasioned a fearful darkness at night. Such was one of the favorite haunts of the headless horseman, and the place where he was most frequently encountered. The tale was told of old Brouwer, a most heretical disbeliever in ghosts, how he met the horseman returning from his foray into Sleepy Hollow, and was obliged to get up behind him; how they galloped over bush and brake, over hill and swamp, until they reached the bridge, when the horseman suddenly turned into a skeleton, threw old Brouwer into the brook, and sprang away over the tree-tops with a clap of thunder.

This story was immediately matched by a thrice-marvellous adventure of Brom Bones, who made light of the galloping Hessian as an arrant jockey. He affirmed that on returning one night from the neighboring village of Sing-Sing he had been over taken by this midnight trooper; that he had offered to race with him for a bowl of punch, and should have won it too, for Daredevil beat the goblin horse all hollow, but just as they came to the church bridge the Hessian bolted and vanished in a flash of fire.

All these tales, told in that drowsy undertone with which men talk in the dark, the countenances of the listeners only now and then receiving a casual gleam from the glare of a pipe, sank deep in the mind of Ichabod. He repaid them in kind with large extracts from his invaluable author, Cotton Mather, and added many marvellous events that had taken place in his native state of Connecticut and fearful sights which he had seen in his nightly walks about Sleepy Hollow.

The revel now gradually broke up. The old farmers gathered together their families in their wagons, and were heard for some time rattling along the hollow roads and over the distant hills. Some of the damsels mounted on pillions behind their favorite swains, and their light-hearted laughter, mingling with the clatter of hoofs, echoed along the silent woodlands, sounding fainter and fainter until they gradually died away, and the late scene of noise and frolic was all silent and deserted. Ichabod only lingered behind, according to the custom of country lovers, to have a tête-à-tête with the heiress, fully convinced that he was now on the high road to success. What passed at this interview I will not pretend to say, for in fact I do not know. Something, however, I fear me, must have gone wrong, for he certainly sallied forth, after no very great interval, with an air quite desolate and chop-fallen. Oh these women! these women! Could that girl have been playing off any of her coquettish tricks? Was her encouragement of the poor pedagogue all a mere sham to secure her conquest of his rival? Heaven only knows, not I! Let it suffice to say, Ichabod stole forth with the air of one who had been sacking a hen-roost, rather than a fair lady's heart. Without looking to the right or left to notice the scene of rural wealth on which he had so often gloated, he went straight to the stable, and with several hearty cuffs and kicks roused his steed most uncourteously from the comfortable quarters in which he was soundly sleeping, dreaming of mountains of corn and oats and whole valleys of timothy and clover.

It was the very witching time of night that Ichabod, heavy-hearted and crestfallen, pursued his travel homewards along the sides of the lofty hills which rise above Tarry Town, and which he had traversed so cheerily in the afternoon. The hour was as dismal as himself. Far below him the Tappan Zee spread its dusky and indistinct waste of waters, with here and there the tall mast of a sloop riding quietly at anchor under the land. In the dead hush of midnight he could even hear the barking of the watch-dog from the opposite shore of the Hudson; but it was so vague and faint as only to give an idea of his distance from this faithful companion of man. Now and then, too, the long-drawn crowing of a cock, accidentally awakened, would sound far, far off, from some farm-house away among the hills; but it was like a dreaming sound in his ear. No signs of life occurred near him, but occasionally the melancholy chirp of a cricket, or perhaps the guttural twang of a bull-frog from a neighboring marsh, as if sleeping uncomfortably and turning suddenly in his bed.

All the stories of ghosts and goblins that he had heard in the afternoon now came crowding upon his recollection. The night grew darker and darker; the stars seemed to sink deeper in the sky, and driving clouds occasionally had them from his sight. He had never felt so lonely and dismal. He was, moreover, approaching the very place where many of the scenes of the ghost-stories had been laid. In the centre of the road stood an enormous tulip tree which towered like a giant above all the other trees of the neighborhood and formed a kind of landmark. Its limbs were gnarled and fantastic, large enough to form trunks for ordinary trees, twisting down almost to the earth and rising again into the air. It was connected with the tragical story of the unfortunate Andre, who had been taken prisoner hard by, and was universally known by the name of Major Andre's tree. The common people regarded it with a mixture of respect and superstition, partly out of sympathy for the fate of its ill-starred namesake, and partly from the tales of strange sights and doleful lamentations told concerning it.

As Ichabod approached this fearful tree he began to whistle: he thought his whistle was answered; it was but a blast sweeping sharply through the dry branches. As he approached a little nearer he thought he saw something white hanging in the midst of the tree: he paused and ceased whistling, but on looking more narrowly perceived that it was a place where the tree had been scathed by lightning and the white wood laid bare. Suddenly he heard a groan: his teeth chattered and his knees smote against the saddle; it was but the rubbing of one huge bough upon another as they were swayed about by the breeze. He passed the tree in safety, but new perils lay before him.

About two hundred yards from the tree a small brook crossed the road and ran into a marshy and thickly-wooded glen known by the name of

Wiley's Swamp. A few rough logs, laid side by side, served for a bridge over this stream. On that side of the road where the brook entered the wood a group of oaks and chestnuts, matted thick with wild grape-vines, threw a cavernous gloom over it. To pass this bridge was the severest trial. It was at this identical spot that the unfortunate Andre was captured, and under the covert of those chestnuts and vines were the sturdy yeomen concealed who surprised him. This has ever since been considered a haunted stream, and fearful are the feelings of the schoolboy who has to pass it alone after dark.

As he approached the stream his heart began to thump; he summoned up, however, all his resolution, gave his horse half a score of kicks in the ribs, and attempted to dash briskly across the bridge; but instead of starting forward, the perverse old animal made a lateral movement and ran broadside against the fence. Ichabod, whose fears increased with the delay, jerked the reins on the other side and kicked lustily with the contrary foot: it was all in vain; his steed started, it is true, but it was only to plunge to the opposite side of the road into a thicket of brambles and alder bushes. The schoolmaster now bestowed both whip and heel upon the starveling ribs of old Gunpowder, who dashed forward, snuffing and snorting, but came to a stand just by the bridge with a suddenness that had nearly sent his rider sprawling over his head. Just at this moment a plashy tramp by the side of the bridge caught the sensitive ear of Ichabod. In the dark shadow of the grove on the margin of the brook he beheld something huge, misshapen, black, and towering. It stirred not, but seemed gathered up in the gloom, like some gigantic monster ready to spring upon the traveller.

The hair of the affrighted pedagogue rose upon his head with terror. What was to be done? To turn and fly was now too late; and besides, what chance was there of escaping ghost or goblin, if such it was, which could ride upon the wings of the wind? Summoning up, therefore, a show of courage, he demanded in stammering accents, "Who are you?" He received no reply. He repeated his demand in a still more agitated voice. Still there was no answer. Once more he cudgelled the sides of the inflexible Gunpowder, and, shutting his eyes, broke forth with involuntary fervor into a psalm tune. Just then the shadowy object of alarm put itself in motion, and with a scramble and a bound stood at once in the middle of the road. Though the night was dark and dismal, yet the form of the unknown might now in some degree be ascertained. He appeared to be a horseman of large dimensions and mounted on a black horse of powerful frame. He made no offer of molestation or sociability, but kept aloof on one side of the road, jogging along on the blind side of old Gunpowder, who had now got over his fright and waywardness.

Ichabod, who had no relish for this strange midnight companion, and bethought himself of the adventure of Brom Bones with the Galloping Hessian, now quickened his steed in hopes of leaving him behind. The stranger, however, quickened his horse to an equal pace. Ichabod pulled up, and fell into a walk, thinking to lag behind; the other did the same. His heart began to sink within him; he endeavored to resume his psalm tune, but his parched tongue clove to the roof of his mouth and he could not utter a stave. There was something in the moody and dogged silence of this pertinacious companion that was mysterious and appalling. It was soon fearfully accounted for. On mounting a rising ground, which brought the figure of his fellow-traveller in relief against the sky, gigantic in height and muffled in a cloak, Ichabod was horror-struck on perceiving that he was headless!—but his horror was still more increased on observing that the head, which should have rested on his shoulders, was carried before him on the pommel of the saddle. His terror rose to desperation, he rained a shower of kicks and blows upon Gunpowder, hoping by a sudden movement to give his companion the slip; but the spectre started full jump with him. Away, then, they dashed through thick and thin, stones flying and sparks flashing at every bound. Ichabod's flimsy garments fluttered in the air as he stretched his long lank body away over his horse's head in the eagerness of his flight.

They had now reached the road which turns off to Sleepy Hollow; but Gunpowder, who seemed possessed with a demon, instead of keeping up it, made an opposite turn and plunged headlong down hill to the left. This road leads through a sandy hollow shaded by trees for about a quarter of a mile, where it crosses the bridge famous in goblin story, and just beyond swells the green knoll on which stands the whitewashed church.

As yet the panic of the steed had given his unskillful rider an apparent advantage in the chase; but just as he had got halfway through the hollow the girths of the saddle gave away and he felt it slipping from under him.

He seized it by the pommel and endeavored to hold it firm, but in vain, and had just time to save himself by clasping old Gunpowder round the neck, when the saddle fell to the earth, and he heard it trampled under foot by his pursuer. For a moment the terror of Hans Van Ripper's wrath passed across his mind, for it was his Sunday saddle; but this was no time for petty fears; the goblin was hard on his haunches, and (unskilled rider that he was) he had much ado to maintain his seat, sometimes slipping on one side, sometimes on another, and sometimes jolted on the high ridge of his horse's back-bone with a violence that he verily feared would cleave him asunder.

An opening in the trees now cheered him with the hopes that the church bridge was at hand. The wavering reflection of a silver star in the bosom of the brook told him that he was not mistaken. He saw the walls of the church dimly glaring under the trees beyond. He recollected the place where Brom Bones' ghostly competitor had disappeared. "If I can but reach that bridge," thought Ichabod, "I am safe." Just then he heard the black steed panting and blowing close behind him; he even fancied that he felt his hot breath. Another convulsive kick in the ribs, and old Gunpowder sprang upon the bridge; he thundered over the resounding planks; he gained the opposite side; and now Ichabod cast a look behind to see if his pursuer should vanish, according to rule, in a flash of fire and brimstone. Just then he saw the goblin rising in his stirrups, and in the very act of hurling his head at him. Ichabod endeavored to dodge the horrible missile, but too late. It encountered his cranium with a tremendous crash; he was tumbled headlong into the dust, and Gunpowder, the black steed, and the goblin rider passed by like a whirlwind.

The next morning the old horse was found, without his saddle and with the bridle under his feet, soberly cropping the grass at his master's gate. Ichabod did not make his appearance at breakfast; dinner-hour came, but no Ichabod. The boys assembled at the school-house and strolled idly about the banks of the brook but no schoolmaster. Hans Van Ripper now began to feel some uneasiness about the fate of poor Ichabod and his saddle. An inquiry was set on foot, and after diligent investigation they came upon his traces. In one part of the road leading to the church was found the saddle trampled in the dirt; the tracks of horses' hoofs, deeply dented in the road and evidently at furious speed, were traced to the bridge, beyond which, on the bank of a broad part of the brook, where the water ran deep and black, was found the hat of the unfortunate Ichabod, and close beside it a spattered pumpkin.

The brook was searched, but the body of the schoolmaster was not to be discovered. Hans Van Ripper, as executor of his estate, examined the bundle which contained all his worldly effects. They consisted of two shirts and a half, two stocks for the neck, a pair or two of worsted stockings, an old pair of corduroy small-clothes, a rusty razor, a book of psalm tunes full of dog's ears, and a broken pitch-pipe. As to the books and furniture of the school-house, they belonged to the community, excepting Cotton Mather's *History of Witchcraft*, a New England Almanac, and a book of dreams and fortune-telling; in which last was a sheet of foolscap much scribbled and blotted in several fruitless attempts to make a copy of verses in honor of the heiress of Van Tassel. These magic books and the poetic scrawl were forthwith consigned to the flames by Hans Van Ripper, who from that time forward determined to send his children no more to school, observing that he never knew any good come of this same reading and writing. Whatever money the schoolmaster possessed—and he had received his quarter's pay but a day or two before—he must have had about his person at the time of his disappearance.

The mysterious event caused much speculation at the church on the following Sunday. Knots of gazers and gossips were collected in the church-yard, at the bridge, and at the spot where the hat and pumpkin had been found. The stories of Brouwer, of Bones, and a whole budget of others were called to mind, and when they had diligently considered them all, and compared them with the symptoms of the present case, they shook their heads and came to the conclusion that Ichabod had been carried off by the galloping Hessian. As he was a bachelor and in nobody's debt, nobody troubled his head any more about him, the school was removed to a different quarter of the hollow and another pedagogue reigned in his stead.

It is true an old farmer, who had been down to New York on a visit several years after, and from whom this account of the ghostly adventure was received, brought home the intelligence that Ichabod Crane was still alive; that he had left the neighborhood, partly through fear of the goblin and Hans Van Ripper, and partly in mortification at having been suddenly dismissed by the heiress; that he had changed his quarters to a distant part of the country, had kept school and studied law at the same time, had been admitted to the bar, turned politician, electioneered, written for the newspapers, and finally had been made a justice of the Ten Pound Court. Brom Bones too, who shortly after his rival's disappearance conducted the blooming Katrina in triumph to the altar, was observed to look exceedingly knowing whenever the story of Ichabod was related, and always burst into a hearty laugh at the mention of the pumpkin; which led some to suspect that he knew more about the matter than he chose to tell.

The old country wives, however, who are the best judges of these matters, maintain to this day that Ichabod was spirited away by supernatural means; and it is a favorite story often told about the neighborhood round the winter evening fire. The bridge became more than ever an object of superstitious awe, and that may be the reason why the road has been altered of late years, so as to approach the church by the border of the mill-pond. The schoolhouse, being deserted, soon fell to decay, and was reported to be haunted by the ghost of the unfortunate pedagogue; and the plough-boy, loitering homeward of a still summer evening, has often fancied his voice at a distance chanting a melancholy psalm tune among the tranquil solitudes of Sleepy Hollow.

POSTSCRIPT

(Found in the handwriting of Mr. Knickerbocker.)

The preceding tale is given almost in the precise words in which I heard it related at a Corporation meeting of the ancient city of Manhattoes, at which were present many of its sagest and most illustrious burghers. The narrator was a pleasant, shabby, gentlemanly old fellow in pepper-and-salt clothes, with a sadly humorous face, and one whom I strongly suspected of being poor, he made such efforts to be entertaining. When his story was concluded there was much laughter and approbation, particularly from two or three deputy aldermen who had been asleep the greater part of the time.

There was, however, one tall, dry-looking old gentleman, with beetling eyebrows, who maintained a grave and rather severe face throughout, now and then folding his arms, inclining his head, and looking down upon the floor, as if turning a doubt over in his mind. He was one of your wary men, who never laugh but upon good grounds—when they have reason and the law on their side. When the mirth of the rest of the company had subsided and silence was restored, he leaned one arm on the elbow of his chair, and sticking the other akimbo, demanded, with a slight but exceedingly sage motion of the head and contraction of the brow, what was the moral of the story and what it went to prove.

The story-teller, who was just putting a glass of wine to his lips as a refreshment after his toils, paused for a moment, looked at his inquirer with an air of infinite deference, and, lowering the glass slowly to the table, observed that the story was intended most logically to prove—

"That there is no situation in life but has its advantages and pleasures—provided we will but take a joke as we find it;

"That, therefore, he that runs races with goblin troopers is likely to have rough riding of it.

"Ergo, for a country schoolmaster to be refused the hand of a Dutch heiress is a certain step to high preferment in the state."

The cautious old gentleman knit his brows tenfold closer after this explanation, being sorely puzzled by the ratiocination of the syllogism, while methought the one in pepper-and-salt eyed him with something of a triumphant leer. At length he observed that all this was very well, but still he thought the story a little on the extravagant—there were one or two points on which he had his doubts.

"Faith, sir," replied the story-teller, "as to that matter, I don't believe one-half of it myself."

D. K.

AN ESSAY FOR THE RECORDING OF REMARKABLE PROVIDENCES

Increase Mather

1684

Today, Increase Mather is best known as the father of Cotton Mather, whose work will be found later in this book. A first-generation American, Mather was born in 1639 in Dorchester, in what was then the Massachusetts Bay Colony. He was the youngest of six brothers born to Rev. Richard Mather and Katherine Holt Mather, who had left the England of King Charles I as part of the great Puritan migration to the New World.

Like his father and three of his brothers, Mather set his sights on a career in the church. He received a B.A. from Harvard College (as it was then) and traveled to Trinity College, Dublin, for his M.A. While in Ireland, he was licensed as a Commonwealth Minister by Oliver Cromwell. After graduating in 1659, he served as a garrison chaplain in the Channel Islands, but Cromwell's death and the restoration of the English monarchy prompted him to return to Massachusetts and marry.

Mather became minister of Boston's North Church and president of Harvard, and was recognized as one of the most influential political and religious thinkers in Massachusetts. As the Salem witch hysteria unfolded, Mather gave a number of sermons pleading for calm but failed to speak out against the use of so-called "spectral" evidence, based on dreams and visions—one of the most controversial aspects of the trials at the time.

The bulk of Mather's writing was on religious and political themes. He wrote two books prompted by the Salem witch trials, Cases of Conscience Concerning Evil Spirits *and* A Further Account of the Tryals of the New-England Witches *(both 1693), as well as a history of the Native American conflict known as King Philip's War, and scientific papers on comets and earthquakes.*

Published eight years before Mather was called upon to act as a judge at the notorious Salem witch trials, An Essay for the Recording of Illustrious Providences *is one of the earliest accounts of the wonders of the New World, both natural and supernatural. Although it was published as nonfiction, its influence on subsequent American horror fiction is plain to see. Chapter V, reproduced here, recounts a number of supernatural incidents. The text has not been altered from Mather's original.*

Concerning things preternatural which have hapned in New-England. A Remarkable Relation about Ann Cole of Hartford. Concerning several Witches in that Colony. Of the Possessed Maid at Groton. An account of the House in Newberry lately troubled with a Daemon. A parallel Story of an House at Tedworth in England. Concerning another in Hartford. And of one in Portsmouth in New-England lately disquieted by Evil Spirits. The Relation of a Woman at Barwick in New-England molested with Apparitions, and sometimes tormented by invisible Agents.

I nasmuch as things which are praeternatural, and not accomplished without diabolical operation, do more rarely happen, it is pity but that they should be observed. Several Accidents of that kind have hapned in New-England; which I shall here faithfully Relate so far as I have been able to come unto the knowledge of them.

Very Remarkable was that Providence wherein Ann Cole of Hartford in New-England was concerned. She was, and is accounted a person of real Piety and Integrity. Nevertheless, in the Year 1662, then living in her Father's House (who has likewise been esteemed a godly Man) She was taken with very strange Fits, wherein her Tongue was improved by a Daemon to express things which she her self knew nothing of. Sometimes the Discourse would hold for a considerable time. The general purpose of which was, that such and such persons (who were named in the Discourse which passed from her) were consulting how they might carry on mischievous designs against her and several others, mentioning sundry wayes they should take for that end, particularly that they would afflict her Body, spoil her Name, &c. The general answer made amongst the Daemons, was, *She runs to the Rock.* This having been continued some hours, the Daemons said, *Let us confound her Language, that she may tell no more tales.* She uttered matters unintelligible. And then the Discourse passed into a Dutch-tone (a Dutch Family then lived in the Town) and therein an account was given of some afflictions that had befallen divers; amongst others, what had befallen a Woman that lived next Neighbour to the Dutch Family, whose Arms had been strangely pinched in the night, declaring by whom and for what cause that course had been taken with her. The Reverend Mr. Stone (then Teacher of the Church in Hartford) being by, when the Discourse hapned, declared, that he thought it impossible for one not familiarly acquainted with the Dutch (which Ann Cole had not in the least been) should so exactly imitate the Dutch-tone in the pronunciation of English. Several Worthy Persons, (viz. Mr. Iohn Whiting, Mr. Samuel Hooker, and Mr. Ioseph Hains) wrote the intelligible sayings expressed by Ann Cole, whilest she was thus amazingly handled. The event was that one of the persons (whose Name was Greensmith) being a lewd and ignorant Woman, and then in Prison on suspicion for Witch-craft) mentioned in the Discourse as active in the mischiefs done and designed, was by the Magistrate sent for;

Mr. Whiting and Mr. Haines read what they had written; and the Woman being astonished thereat, confessed those things to be true, and that she and other persons named in this preternatural Discourse, had had familiarity with the Devil: Being asked whether she had made an express Covenant with him; she answered, she had not, only as she promised to go with him when he called, which accordingly she had sundry times done; and that the Devil told her that at Christmass they would have a merry Meeting, and then the Covenant between them should be subscribed. The next day she was more particularly enquired of concerning her Guilt respecting the Crime she was accused with. She then acknowledged, that though when Mr. Hains began to read what he had taken down in Writing, her rage was such that she could have torn him in pieces, and was as resolved as might be to deny her guilt (as she had done before) yet after he had read awhile, she was (to use her own expression) as if her flesh had been pulled from her bones, and so could not deny any longer: She likewise declared, that the Devil first appeared to her in the form of a Deer or Fawn, skipping about her, where with she was not much affrighted, and that by degrees he became very familiar, and at last would talk with her. Moreover, she said that the Devil had frequently the carnal knowledge of her Body. And that the Witches had Meetings at a place not far from her House; and that some appeared in one shape, and others in another; and one came flying amongst them in the shape of a Crow. Upon this Confession, with other concurrent Evidence, the Woman was Executed; so likewise was her Husband, though he did not acknowledge himself guilty. Other persons accused in the Discourse made their escape. Thus doth the Devil use to serve his Clients. After the suspected Witches were either executed or fled, Ann Cole was restored to health, and has continued well for many years, approving her self a serious Christian.

There were some that had a mind to try whither the Stories of Witches not being able to sink under water, were true; and accordingly a Man and Woman mentioned in Ann Cole's Dutch-toned discourse, had their hands and feet tyed, and so were cast into the water, and they both apparently swam after the manner of a Buoy, part under, part above the Water. A by-stander imagining that any person bound in that posture would be so born up, offered himself for trial, but being in the like manner gently laid on the

the Water, he immediately sunk right down. This was no legal Evidence against the suspected persons; nor were they proceeded against on any such account; However doubting that an Halter would choak them, though the Water would not; they very fairly took their flight, not having been seen in that part of the World since. Whether this experiment were lawful, or rather Superstitious and Magical, we shall enquire afterwards.

Another thing which caused a noise in the Countrey, and wherein Satan had undoubtedly a great influence, was, that which hapned at Groton. There was a Maid in that Town (one Elizabeth Knap) who in the Moneth of October, Anno. 1671, was taken after a very strange manner, sometimes weeping, sometimes laughing, sometimes roaring hideously, with violent motions and agitations of her body, crying out Money, Money, &c. In November following, her Tongue for many hours together was drawn like a semicircle up to the roof of her Mouth, not to be removed, though some tried with their fingers to do it. Six Men were scarce able to hold her in some of her fits, but she would skip about the House yelling and looking with a most frightful Aspect. *December 17.* Her Tongue was drawn out of her mouth to an extraordinary length; and now a Daemon began manifestly to speak in her. Many words were uttered wherein are the Labial Letters, without any motion of her Lips, which was a clear demonstration that the voice was not her own. Sometimes Words were spoken seeming to proceed out of her throat, when her Mouth was shut. Sometimes with her Mouth wide open, without the use of any of the Organs of speech. The things then uttered by the Devil were chiefly Railings and Revilings of Mr. Willard (who was at that time a Worthy and Faithful Pastor to the Church in Groton.) Also the Daemon belched forth most horrid and nefandous Blasphemies, exalting himself above the most High. After this she was taken speechless for some time. One thing more is worthy of Remark concerning this miserable creature. She cried out in some of her Fits, that a Woman, (one of her Neighbours) appeared to her, and was the cause of her Affliction. The Person thus accused was a very sincere, holy Woman, who did hereupon with the Advice of Friends visit the poor Wretch; and though she was in one of her Fits, having her Eyes shut, when the innocent person impeached by her came in; yet could she (so powerful were Satan's Operations upon her) declare who was there, and could tell the touch of that Woman from any ones else. But the gracious Party thus accused and abused by a malicious Devil, Prayed earnestly with and for the Possessed creature; after which she confessed that Satan had deluded her; making her believe evil of her good Neighbour without any cause. Nor did she after that complain of any Apparition or Disturbance from such an one. Yea, she said, that the Devil had himself in the likeness and shape of divers tormented her, and then told her it was not he but they that did it.

As there have been several Persons vexed with evil Spirits, so divers Houses have been wofully Haunted by them. In the Year 1679, the House of William Morse in Newberry in New-England, was strangely disquieted by a Daemon. After those troubles began, he did by the Advice of Friends write down the particulars of those unusual Accidents. And the Account which he giveth thereof is as followeth;

On December 3. in the night time, he and his Wife heard a noise upon the roof of their House, as if Sticks and Stones had been thrown against it with great violence; whereupon he rose out of his Bed, but could see nothing. Locking the Doors fast, he returned to Bed again. About midnight they heard an Hog making a great noise in the House, so that the Man rose again, and found a great Hog in the house, the door being shut, but upon the opening of the door it ran out.

On December 8. in the Morning, there were five great Stones and Bricks by an invisible hand thrown in at the west end of the house while the Man's Wife was making the Bed, the Bedstead was lifted up from the floor, and the Bedstaff flung out of the Window, and a Cat was hurled at her; a long Staff danced up and down in the Chimney; a burnt Brick, and a piece of a weatherboard were thrown in at the Window: The Man at his going to Bed put out his Lamp, but in the Morning found that the Saveall of it was taken away, and yet it was unaccountably brought into its former place. On the same day, the long Staff but now spoken of, was hang'd up by a line, and swung to and fro, the Man's Wife laid it in the fire, but she could not hold it there, inasmuch as it would forcibly fly out; yet after much ado with joynt strength they made it to burn. A shingle flew from the Window, though no body near it, many sticks came in at the same place, only one of these was so scragged that it could enter the hole but a little way, whereupon the

Man pusht it out, a great Rail likewise was thrust in at the Window, so as to break the Glass.

At another time an Iron Crook that was hanged on a Nail, violently flew up and down also a Chair flew about, and at last lighted on the Table where Victuals stood ready for them to eat, and was likely to spoil all, only by a nimble catching they saved some of their Meal with the loss of the rest, and the overturning of their Table.

People were sometimes Barricado'd out of doors, when as yet there was no body to do it: and a Chest was removed from place to place, no hand touching it. Their Keys being tied together, one was taken from the rest, & the remaining two would fly about making a loud noise by knocking against each other. But the greatest part of this Devil's feats were his mischievous ones, wherein indeed he was sometimes Antick enough too, and therein the chief sufferers were, the Man and his Wife, and his Grand-Son. The Man especially had his share in these Diabolical Molestations. For one while they could not eat their Suppers quietly, but had the Ashes on the Hearth before their eyes thrown into their Victuals; yea, and upon their heads and Clothes, insomuch that they were forced up into their Chamber, and yet they had no rest there; for one of the Man's Shoes being left below, 'twas filled with Ashes and Coals, and thrown up after them. Their Light was beaten out, and they being laid in their Bed with their little Boy between them, a great stone (from the Floor of the Loft) weighing above three pounds was thrown upon the man's stomach, and he turning it down upon the floor, it was once more thrown upon him. A Box, and a Board were likewise thrown upon them all. And a Bag of Hops was taken out of their Chest, wherewith they were beaten, till some of the Hops were scattered on the floor, where the Bag was then laid, and left.

In another Evening, when they sat by the fire, the Ashes were so whirled at them, that they could neither eat their Meat, nor endure the House. A Peel struck the Man in the face. An Apron hanging by the fire, was flung upon it, and singed before they could snatch it off. The Man being at Prayer with his Family, a Beesom gave him a blow on his head behind, and fell down before his face.

On another day, when they were Winnowing of Barley, some hard dirt was thrown in, hitting the Man on the Head, and both the Man and his

Wife on the back; and when they had made themselves clean, they essayed to fill their half Bushel but the foul Corn was in spite of them often cast in amongst the clean, and the Man being divers times thus abused was forced to give over what he was about.

On January 23 (in particular) the Man had an iron Pin twice thrown at him, and his Inkhorn was taken away from him while he was writing, and when by all his seeking it he could not find it, at last he saw it drop out of the Air, down by the fire: a piece of Leather was twice thrown at him; and a shoe was laid upon his shoulder, which he catching at, was suddenly rapt from him. An handful of Ashes was thrown at his face, and upon his clothes: and the shoe was then clapt upon his head, and upon it he clapt his hand, holding it so fast, that somewhat unseen pulled him with it backward on the floor.

On the next day at night, as they were going to Bed, a lost Ladder was thrown against the Door, and their Light put out; and when the Man was a bed, he was beaten with an heavy pair of Leather Breeches, and pull'd by the Hair of his Head and Beard, Pinched and Scratched, and his Bed-board was taken away from him; yet more in the next night, when the Man was likewise in Bed; his Bed-board did rise out of its place, notwithstanding his putting forth all his strength to keep it in; one of his Awls was brought out of the next room into his Bed and did prick him; the clothes wherewith he hoped to save his head from blows were violently pluckt from thence. Within a night or two after, the Man and his Wife received both of them a blow upon their heads, but it was so dark that they could not see the stone which gave it; the Man had his Cap pulled off from his head while he sat by the fire.

The night following, they went to bed undressed, because of their late disturbances, and the Man, Wife, Boy, presently felt themselves pricked, and upon search found in the Bed a Bodkin, a knitting Needle, and two sticks picked at both ends. He received also a great blow, as on his Thigh, so on his Face, which fetched blood: and while he was writing a Candlestick was twice thrown at him, and a great piece of Bark fiercely smote him, and a pail of Water turned up without hands. On the 28 of the mentioned Moneth, frozen clods of Cow-dung were divers times thrown at the man out of the house in which they were; his Wife went to milk the Cow, and received a blow on her head, and sitting down at her Milking-work had Cow-dung divers times thrown into her Pail, the Man tried to save the Milk, by holding a Piggin side-wayes under the Cowes belly, but the Dung would in for all, and the Milk was only made fit for Hogs. On that night ashes were thrown into the porridge which they had made ready for their Supper, so as that they could not eat it; Ashes were likewise often thrown into the Man's Eyes, as he sat by the fire. And an iron Hammer flying at him, gave him a great blow on his back; the Man's Wife going into the Cellar for Beer, a great iron Peel flew and fell after her through the trap-door of the Cellar; and going afterwards on the same Errand to the same place, the door shut down upon her, and the Table came and lay upon the door, and the man was forced to remove it ere his Wife could be released from where she was; on the following day while he was Writing, a dish went out of its place, leapt into the pale, and cast Water upon the Man, his Paper, his Table, and disappointed his procedure in what he was about; his Cap jumpt off from his head, and on again, and the Pot-lid leapt off from the Pot into the Kettle on the fire.

February 2. While he and his Boy were eating of Cheese, the pieces which he cut were wrested from them, but they were afterwards found upon the Table under an Apron, and a pair of Breeches: And also from the fire arose little sticks and Ashes, which flying upon the Man and his Boy, brought them into an uncomfortable pickle; But as for the Boy which the last passage spoke of, there remains much to be said concerning him, and a principal sufferer in these afflictions: For on the 18. of December, he sitting by his Grandfather, was hurried into great motions and the Man thereupon took him, and made him stand between his Legs, but the Chair danced up and down, and had like to have cast both Man and Boy into the fire: and the Child was afterwards flung about in such a manner, as that they feared that his Brains would have been beaten out; and in the evening he was tossed as afore, and the Man tried the project of holding him, but ineffectually. The Lad was soon put to Bed, and they presently heard an huge noise, and demanded what was the matter? and he answered that his Bed-stead leaped up and down: and they (i.e. the Man and his Wife) went up, and at first found all quiet, but before they had been there long, they saw the Board by his Bed trembling by him, and the Bed-clothes flying off him, the latter they laid on immediately, but they were no sooner on than off; so they took him out of his Bed for quietness.

December 29. The Boy was violently thrown to and fro, only they carried him to the house of a Doctor in the Town, and there he was free from disturbances, but returning home at night, his former trouble began and the Man taking him by the hand they were both of them almost tript into the fire. They put him to bed, and he was attended with the same iterated loss of his clothes, shaking off his Bed-board, and Noises, that he had in his last conflict; they took him up, designing to sit by the fire, but the doors clattered, and the Chair was thrown at him, wherefore they carried him to the Doctors house, and so for that night all was well. The next morning he came home quiet, but as they were doing somewhat, he cried out that he was prickt on the back, they looked, and found a three-tin'd Fork sticking strangely there; which being carried to the Doctors house, not only the Doctor himself said that it was his, but also the Doctors Servant affirmed it was seen at home after the Boy was gone. The Boys vexations continuing, they left him at the Doctors, where he remained well till awhile after, and then he complained he was pricked, they looked and found an iron Spindle sticking below his back; he complained he was pricked still, they looked, and found Pins in a Paper sticking to his skin; he once more complained of his Back, they looked, and found there a long Iron, a bowl of a Spoon, and a piece of a Pansheard. They lay down by him on the Bed, with the Light burning, but he was twice thrown from them, and the second time thrown quite under the Bed; in the Morning the Bed was tossed about with such a creaking noise, as was heard to the Neighbours; in the afternoon their knives were one after another brought, and put into his back, but pulled out by the Spectators; only one knife which was missing seemed to the standers by to come out of his Mouth: he was bidden to read his Book, was taken and thrown about several times, at last hitting the Boys Grandmother on the head. Another time he was thrust out of his Chair and rolled up and down with out cries, that all things were on fire; yea, he was three times very dangerously thrown into the fire, and preserved by his Friends with much ado. The Boy also made for a long time together a noise like a Dog, and like an Hen with her Chickens, and could not speak rationally.

Particularly, on December 26. He barked like a Dog, and clock't like an Hen, and after long distraining to speak, said, there's Powel, I am pinched; his Tongue likewise hung out of his mouth, so as that it could by no means be forced in till his Fit was over, and then he said 'twas forced out by Powel. He & the house also after this had rest till the ninth of Ianuary: at which time because of his intolerable ravings, and because the Child lying between the Man and his Wife, was pulled out of Bed, and knockt so vehemently against the Bed-stead Boards, in a manner very perillous and amazing. In the Day time he was carried away beyond all possibility of their finding him. His Grandmother at last saw him creeping on one side, and drag'd him in, where he lay miserable lame, but recovering his speech, he said, that he was carried above the Doctor's house, and that Powel carried him, and that the said Powel had him into the Barn, throwing him against the Cart-wheel there, and then thrusting him out at an hole; and accordingly they found some of the Remainders of the Threshed Barley which was on the Barn-floor hanging to his Clothes.

At another time he fell into a Swoon, they forced somewhat Refreshing into his mouth, and it was turned out as fast as they put it in; e're long he came to himself, and expressed some willingness to eat, but the Meat would forcibly fly out of his mouth; and when he was able to speak, he said Powel would not let him eat: Having found the Boy to be best at a Neighbour's house, the Man carried him to his Daughters, three miles from his own. The Boy was growing antick as he was on the Journey, but before the end of it he made a grievous hollowing, and when he lighted, he threw a great stone at a Maid in the house, and fell on eating of Ashes. Being at home afterwards, they had rest awhile, but on the 19 of Ianuary in the Morning he swooned, and coming to himself, he roared terribly, and did eat Ashes, Sticks, Rug-yarn. The Morning following, there was such a racket with the Boy, that the Man and his Wife took him to Bed to them. A Bed-staff was thereupon thrown at them, and a Chamber pot with its Contents was thrown upon them, and they were severely pinched. The Man being about to rise, his Clothes were divers times pulled from them, himself thrust out of his Bed, and his Pillow thrown after him. The Lad also would have his clothes plucked off from him in these Winter Nights, and was wofully dogg'd with such fruits of Devilish spite, till it pleased God to shorten the Chain of the wicked Daemon.

All this while the Devil did not use to appear in any visible shape, only they would think they had hold of the Hand that sometimes scratched them; but it would give them the slip. And once the Man was discernably beaten by a Fist, and an Hand got hold of his Wrist which he saw, but could not catch; and the likeness of a Blackmore Child did appear from under the Rugg and Blanket, where the Man lay, and it would rise up, fall down, nod & slip under the clothes when they endeavoured to clasp it, never speaking any thing.

Neither were there many Words spoken by Satan all this time, only once having put out their Light, they heard a scraping on the Boards, and then a Piping and Drumming on them, which was followed with a Voice, singing Revenge! Revenge! Sweet is Revenge! And they being well terrified with it, called upon God; the issue of which was, that suddenly with a mournful Note, there were six times over uttered such expressions as Alas! Alas! me knock no more! me knock no more! and now all ceased.

The Man does moreover affirm, that a Seaman (being a Mate of a Ship) coming often to visit him, told him that they wronged his Wife who suspected her to be guilty of Witchcraft; and that the Boy (his Grandchild) was the cause of this trouble; and that if he would let him have the Boy one day, he would warrant him his house should be no more troubled as it had been; to which motion he consented. The Mate came the next day betimes, and the Boy was with him until night; after which his house he saith was not for some time molested with evil Spirits.

Thus far is the Relation concerning the Daemon at William Morse his House in Newbery. The true Reason of these strange disturbances is as yet not certainly known: some (as has been hinted) did suspect Morse's Wife to be guilty of Witchcraft.

One of the Neighbours took Apples which were brought out of that house and put them into the fire; upon which they say, their houses were much disturbed. Another of the Neighbours, caused an Horse-shoe to be nailed before the doors, & as long as it remained so, they could not perswade the suspected person to go into the house; but when the Horse-shoe was gone, she presently visited them. I shall not here inlarge upon the vanity and superstition of those Experiments, reserving that for another place: All that I shall say at present is, that the Daemons whom the blind Gentiles of old worshipped, told their Servants, that such things as these would very much affect them; yea, and that certain Characters, Signs and Charms would render their power ineffectual; and accordingly they would become subject, when their own directions were obeyed. It is sport to the Devils when they see silly Men thus deluded and made fools of by them. Others were apt to think that a Seaman by some suspected to be a Conjurer, set the Devil on work thus to disquiet Morse's Family. Or it may be some other thing as yet kept hid in the secrets of providence might be the true original of all this Trouble.

A Disturbance not much unlike to this hapned above twenty years ago, at an house in Tedworth, in the County of Wilts in England, which was by wise men judged to proceed from Conjuration.

Mr. Mompesson of Tedworth being in March 1661 at Lungershall, and hearing a Drum beat there, he demanded of the Bailiff of the Town what it meant, who told him, they had for some dayes been troubled with an idle Drummer, pretending Authority, and a Pass under the hands of some Gentlemen. Mr. Mompesson reading his Pass, and knowing the hands of those Gentlemen, whose Names were pretended to be subscribed, discovered the Cheat, and commanded the Vagrant to put off his Drum, and ordered a Constable to secure him: but not long after he got clear of the Constable.

In April following, Mr. Momposson's house was much disturbed with Knockings, and with Drummings; for an hour together a Daemon would beat Round-heads and Cuckolds, the Tattoo and several other points of War as well as any Drummer. On November 5. The Daemon made a great noise in the House, and caused some Boards therein to move to and fro in the day time when there was an whole room full of People present. At his departure, he left behind him a Sulphurous smell, which was very offensive. The next night, Chairs walked up and down the Room; the Childrens Shoes were hurled over their heads. The Minister of the Town being there, a Bedstaff was thrown at him, and hit him on the Leg, but without the least hurt. In the latter end of December, 1662. They heard a noise like the jingling of Money, the occasion of which was thought to be, some words spoken the night before, by one in the Family; who said that Faires used to leave money behind them, and they wished it might be so now. In Ianuary Lights were seen in the House, which seemed blue and glimmering, and caused a great stiffness in the eyes of them that saw them. One in the room (by what Authority I cannot tell) said, Satan, if the Drummer set thee a work give three knocks and no more, which was done accordingly. Once when it was very sharp severe Weather, the room was suddenly filled with a Noisome smell, and was very hot though without fire. This Daemon would play some nasty and many ludicrous foolish tricks. It would empty Chamberpots into the Beds; and fill Porringers with Ashes. Sometimes it would not suffer any light to be in the room, but would carry them away up the Chimney. Mr. Mompesson coming one morning into his Stable, found his Horse on the ground, having one of his hinder legs in his mouth, and so fastened there, that it was difficult for several men with a Leaver to get it out. A Smith lodging in the House, heard a noise in the room, as if one had been shoeing an Horse, and somewhat come as it were with a Pincers snipping at the Smith's Nose, most part of the night. The Drummer was under vehement suspicion for a Conjurer. He was condemned to Transportation. All the time of his restraint and absence, the House was quiet. See Mr. Glanvil's *Collection of Modern Relations*, p. 71. &c.

But I proceed to give an account of some other things lately hapning in New-England, which were undoubtedly praeternatural, and not without Diabolical operation. The last year did afford several Instances, not unlike unto those which have been mentioned. For then Nicholas Desborough of Hartford in New-England, was strangely molested by stones, pieces of earth, cobs of Indian Corn, &c. falling upon and about him, which sometimes came in through the door, sometimes through the Window, sometimes down the Chimney, at other times they seemed to fall from the floor of the Chamber, which yet was very close; sometimes he met with them in his Shop, the Yard, the Barn, and in the Field at work. In the House, such things hapned frequently, not only in the night but in the day time, if the Man himself was at home, but never when his Wife was at home alone. There was no great violence in the motion, though several persons of the Family, and others also were struck with the things that were thrown by an invisible hand, yet they were not hurt thereby. Only the Man himself had once his Arm somewhat pained by a blow given him; and at another time, blood was drawn from one of his Legs by a scratch given it. This molestation began soon after a Controversie arose between Desborough and another person, about a Chest of Clothes which the other said that Desberough did unrighteously retain: and so it continued for some Moneths (though with several intermissions.) In the latter end of the last year, when also the Man's Barn was burned with the Corn in it; but by what means it came to pass is not known. Not long after, some to whom the matter was referred, ordered Desberough to restore the Clothes to the Person who complained of wrong; since which he hath not been troubled as before. Some of the stones hurled were of considerable bigness; one of them weighed four pounds, but generally the stones were not great, but very small ones. One time a piece of Clay came down the Chimney, falling on the Table which stood at some distance from the Chimney. The People of the House threw it on the Hearth, where it lay a considerable time: they went to their Supper, and whilest at their Supper, the piece of Clay was lifted up by an invisible hand, and fell upon the Table; taking it up, they found it hot, having lain so long before the fire, as to cause it to be hot.

Another Providence no less Remarkable than this last mentioned, hapned at Portsmouth in New-England, about the same time: concerning which I have received the following account from a Worthy hand.

On Iune 11. 1682. Being the Lords Day, at night showers of stones were thrown both against the sides and roof of the house of George Walton: some of the People went abroad, found the Gate at some distance from the house, wrung off the Hinges, and stones came thick about them: sometimes falling down by them, sometimes touching them without any hurt done to them, though they seemed to come with great force, yet did no more but softly touch them; Stones flying about the room the Doors being shut. The Glass-Windows shattered to pieces by stones that seemed to come not from without but within; the Lead of the Glass Casements, Window-Bars, &c. being driven forcibly outwards, and so standing bent. While the Secretary was walking in the room a great Hammer came brusling along against the Chamber floor that was over his head, and fell down by him. A Candlestick beaten off the Table. They took up nine of the stones and marked them, and laid them on the Table, some of them being as hot as if they came out of the fire; but some of those mark't stones were found flying about again. In this manner, about four hours space that night: The Secretary then went to bed, but a stone came and broke up his Chamber-door, being put to (not lockt) a Brick was sent upon the like Errand. The abovesaid Stone the Secretary lockt up in his Chamber, but it was fetched out, and carried with great noise into the next Chamber. The Spit was carried up Chimney, and came down with the point forward, and stuck in the Back-log, and being removed by one of the Company to one side of the Chimney, was by an unseen hand thrown out at Window. This trade was driven on the next day, and so from Day to Day, now and then there would be some intermission, and then to it again. The stones were most frequent where the Master of the house was, whether in the Field or Barn, &c. A black Cat was seen once while the Stones came, and was shot at, but she was too nimble for them. Some of the Family say, that they once saw the appearance of an hand put forth at the Hall Window, throwing stones towards the Entry, though there was no body in the Hall the while: sometimes a dismal hollow whistling would be heard; sometimes the noise of the trotting of an horse, and snorting, but nothing seen. The Man went up the great Bay in his Boat to a Farm he had there, and while haling Wood or Timber to the Boat he was disturbed by the Stones as before at home. He carried a stirrup iron from the house down to the Boat, and there left it; but while he was going up to the house, the iron came jingling after him through the Woods, and returned to the house, and so again, and at last went away, and was heard of no more. Their Anchor leapt over-board several times as they were going home and stopt the boat. A Cheese hath been taken out of the Press and crumbled all over the floor. A piece of Iron with which they weighed up the Cheese-press stuck into the Wall, and a Kittle hung up thereon. Several Cocks of English-hay mowed near the house, were taken and hung upon Trees; and some made into small whisps, and put all up and down the Kitchin, *Cum multis aliis*, &c. After this manner, have they been treated ever since at times; it were endless to particularize. Of late they thought the bitterness of Death had been past, being quiet for sundry dayes and nights: but last week were some Returnings again; and this week (Aug. 2. 1682) as bad or worse than ever. The Man is sorely hurt with some of the Stones that came on him, and like to feel the effects of them for many dayes. Thus far is that Relation.

I am moreover informed, that the Daemon was quiet all the last Winter, but in the Spring he began to play some ludicrous tricks, carrying away some Axes that were locked up safe. This last Summer he has not made such disturbances as formerly. But of this no more at present.

There have been strange and true Reports concerning a Woman now living near the Salmon Falls in Barwick (formerly called Kittery) unto whom Evil Spirits have sometimes visibly appeared; and she has sometimes been sorely tormented by invisible hands: Concerning all which, an Intelligent Person has sent me the following Narrative.

A Brief Narrative of sundry Apparitions of Satan unto and Assaults at sundry times and places upon the Person of Mary the Wife of Antonio Hortado, dwelling near the Salmon Falls: Taken from her own mouth, Aug. 13. 1683.

In Iune 1682. (the day forgotten) at Evening, the said Mary heard a voice at the door of her Dwelling, saying, What do you here? about an hour after, standing at the Door of her House, she had a blow on her Eye that settled her head near to the Doorpost, and two or three dayes after, a Stone, as she judged about half a pound or a pound weight was thrown along the house within into the Chimney, and going to take it up it was gone; all the Family was in the house, and no hand appearing which might be instrumental in throwing the stone. About two hours after, a Frying-pan then hanging in the Chimney was heard to ring so loud, that not only those in the house heard it, but others also that lived on the other side of the River near an hundred Rods distant or more. Whereupon the said Mary and her Husband going in a Cannoo over the River, they saw like the head of a man new-shorn, and the tail of a white Cat about two or three foot distance from each other, swimming over before the Cannoo, but no body appeared to joyn head and tail together; and they returning over the River in less than an hour's time, the said Apparition followed their Cannoo back again, but disappeared at Landing. A day or two after, the said Mary was stricken on her head (as she judged) with a stone, which caused a Swelling and much soreness on her head, being then in the yard by her house, and she presently entring into her house was bitten on both Arms black and blue, and one of her Breasts scratched; the impressions of the Teeth being like Man's Teeth, were plainly seen by many: Whereupon deserting their House to sojourn at a Neighbours on the other side of the River, there appeared to said Mary in the house of her sojourning, a Woman clothed with a green Safeguard, a short blue Cloak, and a white Cap, making a profer to strike her with a Fire-brand, but struck her not. The Day following the same shape appeared again to her, but now arrayed with a gray Gown, white Apron, and white Head-clothes, in appearance laughing several times, but no voice heard. Since when said Mary has been freed from those Satanical Molestations.

But the said Antonio being returned in March last with his Family, to dwell again in his own house, and on his entrance there, hearing the noise of a Man walking in his Chamber, and seeing the boards buckle under his feet as he walked, though no man to be seen in the Chamber (for they went on purpose to look) he returned with his Family to dwell on the other side of the River; yet planting his Ground though he forsook his House, he hath had five Rods of good Log-fence thrown down at once, the feeting of Neat Cattle plainly to be seen almost between every Row of Corn in the Field yet no Cattle seen there, nor any damage done to his Corn, not so much as any of the Leaves of the Corn cropt.

Thus far is that Narrative.

I am further informed, that some (who should have been wiser) advised the poor Woman to stick the House round with Bayes, as an effectual preservative against the power of Evil Spirits. This Counsel was followed. And as long as the Bayes continued green, she had quiet; but when they began to wither, they were all by an unseen hand carried away, and the Woman again tormented.

It is observable, that at the same time three Houses in three several Towns should be molested by Daemons, as has now been related.

WONDERS OF THE INVISIBLE WORLD

Cotton Mather

1693

The son of Increase Mather, Cotton Mather (1663-1728) was an equally influential Puritan minister who authored a number of religious works aimed at improving and promoting religious life in the New England colonies. Works published in his lifetime include Marginalia Christi Americana *(1702),* Corderius Americanus: A Discourse on the Good Education of Children *(1708), and* Americana: An Essay on the Golden Street of the Holy City *(1710). His great* Biblia Americana, *a massive commentary on the Bible intended as his masterwork, remained unfinished at his death.*

Mather is best known today for his support of the Salem witch trials of 1692, and for his book Wonders of the Invisible World *(1693), which begins with some observations upon the Christian virtue of the New England colonies, and the Devil's plans for regaining control of a land which had been his before those colonies were planted. Mathers goes on to report "Some Accounts of the Grievous Molestations, by*

DÆMONS and WITCHCRAFTS, which have lately annoy'd the Countrey; and the Trials of some eminent Malefactors Executed upon occasion thereof; with several Remarkable Curiosities therein occurring"—including accounts of witchcraft and witch trials at Salem, along with some advice for would-be witch hunters.

Published in the year that the Salem witch trials ended, Wonders of the Invisible World *provides an insight into the Puritan mind-set and its response to the unexplained. Before beginning his famous description of the Salem witch trials, Mather reports on two incidents which took place in New England a few years earlier. Once again, the text has not been altered from Mather's original.*

AN EXTRACT

A NARRATIVE OF AN APPARITION WHICH A GENTLEMAN IN BOSTON, HAD OF HIS BROTHER, JUST THEN MURTHERED IN LONDON.

It was on the Second of *May* in the Year 1687, that a most ingenious, accomplished and well-disposed Gentleman, Mr. *Joseph Beacon,* by Name, about Five a Clock in the Morning, as he lay, whether Sleeping or Waking he could not say, (but judged the latter of them) had a View of his Brother then at *London,* altho he was now himself at Our *Boston,* distanced from him a thousand Leagues. This his Brother appear'd unto him, in the Morning about Five a Clock at *Boston,* having on him a *Bengal* Gown, which he usually wore, with a Napkin tyed about his Head; his Countenance was very Pale, Gastly, Deadly, and he had a bloody Wound on one side of his Fore-head. *Brother!* says the Affrighted *Joseph. Brother!* Answered the Apparition. Said *Joseph, What's the matter Brother? How came you here!* The Apparition replied, *Brother, I have been most barbarously and injuriously Butchered, by a Debauched Drunken Fellow, to whom I never did any wrong in my Life.* Whereupon he gave a particular Description of the Murderer; adding, *Brother, This Fellow changing his Name, is attempting to come over unto New-England, in Foy, or Wild; I would pray you on the first Arrival of either of these, to get an Order from the Governor, to Seize the Person, whom I have now described; and then do you Indict him for the Murder of me your Brother: I'll stand by you and prove the Indictment.* And so he Vanished. Mr. *Beacon* was extreamly astonished at what he had seen and hear'd; and the People of the Family not only observed an extraordinary Alteration upon him, for the Week following, but have also given me under their Hands a full Testimony, that he then gave them an Account of this Apparition.

All this while, Mr. *Beacon* had no advice of any thing amiss attending his Brother then in *England*; but about the latter end of *June* following, he understood by the common ways of Communication, that the *April* before, his Brother going in haste by Night to call a Coach for a Lady, met a Fellow then in Drink, with his *Doxy* in his Hand: Some way or other the Fellow thought himself Affronted with the hasty passage of this *Beacon*, and immediately ran into the Fire-side of a Neighbouring Tavern, from whence he fetch'd out a Fire-fork, wherewith he grievously wounded *Beacon* in the Skull; even in that very part where the Apparition show'd his Wound. Of this Wound he Languished until he Dyed on the Second of *May*, about five of the Clock in the Morning at *London*. The Murderer it seems was endeavouring to Escape, as the Apparition affirm'd, but the Friends of the Deceased *Beacon*, Seized him; and Prosecuting him at Law, he found the help of such Friends as brought him off without the loss of his Life; since which, there has no more been heard of the Business.

This History I received of Mr. *Joseph Beacon* himself; who a little before his own Pious and hopeful Death, which follow'd not long after, gave me the Story written and signed with his own Hand, and attested with the Circumstances I have already mentioned.

But I shall no longer detain my Reader, from his expected Entertainment, in a brief account of the Tryals which have passed upon some of the Malefactors lately Executed at *Salem*, for the *Witchcrafts* whereof they stood Convicted. For my own part, I was not present at any of them; nor ever had I any Personal prejudice at the Persons thus brought upon the Stage; much less at the Surviving Relations of those Persons, with and for whom I would be as hearty a Mourner as any Man living in the World: *The Lord Comfort them!* But having received a Command so to do, I can do no other than shortly relate the chief *Matters of Fact*, which occurr'd in the Tryals of some that were Executed, in an Abridgment Collected out of the *Court-Papers*, on this occasion put into my hands. You are to take the Truth, just as it was; and the *Truth* will hurt no good Man. There might have been more of these, if my Book would not thereby have swollen too big; and if some other worthy hands did not perhaps intend something further in these *Collections*; for which cause I have only singled out Four or Five, which may serve to illustrate the way of Dealing, wherein *Witchcrafts* use to be concerned; and I report matters not as an *Advocate*, but as an *Historian*.

They were some of the Gracious Words inserted in the Advice, which many of the Neighbouring Ministers, did this Summer humbly lay before our Honorable Judges, *We cannot but with all thankfulness, acknowledge the success which the Merciful God has given unto the Sedulous and Assiduous endeavours of Our Honourable Rulers, to detect the abominable Witchcrafts which have been committed in the Country; Humbly Praying, that the discovery of those mysterious and mischievous wickednesses, may be Perfected.* If in the midst of the many Dissatisfactions among us, the Publication of these Tryals, may promote such a Pious Thankfulness unto God, for Justice being so far executed among us, I shall Rejoice that God is Glorified; and pray, that no wrong steps of ours may ever sully any of his Glorious Works. But we will begin with,

A MODERN INSTANCE OF WITCHES, DISCOVERED AND CONDEMNED IN A TRYAL, BEFORE THAT CELEBRATED JUDGE, SIR MATTHEW HALE.

It may cast some Light upon the Dark things now in *America*, if we just give a glance upon the *like things* lately happening in *Europe*. We may see the *Witchcrafts* here most exactly resemble the *Witchcrafts* there; and we may learn what sort of Devils do trouble the World.

The Venerable *Baxter* very truly says, *Judge Hale was a Person, than whom, no Man was more Backward to Condemn a Witch, without full Evidence.*

Now, one of the latest Printed Accounts about a *Tryal of Witches*, is of what was before him, and it ran on this wise. And it is here the rather mentioned, because it was a Tryal, much considered by the Judges of *New England.*

I

Rose Cullender and *Amy Duny*, were severally Indicted, for Bewitching *Elizabeth Durent, Ann Durent, Jane Bocking, Susan Chandler, William Durent, Elizabeth* and *Deborah Pacy.* And the Evidence whereon they were Convicted, stood upon divers particular Circumstances.

II

Ann Durent, Susan Chandler, and *Elizabeth Pacy,* when they came into the Hall, to give Instructions for the drawing the Bills of Indictments, they fell into strange and violent Fits, so that they were unable to give in their Depositions, not only then, but also during the whole Assizes. *William Durent* being an Infant, his Mother Swore, That *Amy Duny* looking after her Child one Day in her absence, did at her return confess, that she had *given suck to the Child:* (tho' she were an Old Woman:) Whereat, when *Durent* expressed her displeasure, *Duny* went away with Discontents and Menaces.

The Night after, the Child fell into strange and sad Fits, wherein it continued for Divers Weeks. One Doctor *Jacob* advised her to hang up the Childs Blanket, in the Chimney Corner all Day, and at Night, when she went to put the Child into it, if she found any Thing in it then to throw it without fear into the Fire. Accordingly, at Night, there fell a great Toad out of the Blanket, which ran up and down the Hearth. A Boy catch't it, and held it in the Fire with the Tongs: where it made an horrible Noise, and Flash'd like to Gun-Powder, with a report like that of a Pistol: Whereupon the Toad was no more to be seen. The next Day a Kinswoman of *Duny's*, told the Deponent, that her Aunt was all grievously scorch'd with the Fire, and the Deponent going to her House, found her in such a Condition. *Duny* told her, she might thank her for it; but she should live to see some of her Children Dead, and her self upon Crutches. But after the Burning of the Toad, this Child Recovered.

This Deponent further Testifi'd, That Her Daughter *Elizabeth*, being about the Age of Ten Years, was taken in like manner, as her first Child was, and in her Fits complained much of *Amy Duny*, and said, that she did appear to Her, and afflict her in such manner as the former. One Day she found *Amy Duny* in her House, and thrusting her out of Doors, *Duny* said, *You need not be so Angry, your Child won't live long.* And within three Days the Child Died. The Deponent added, that she was Her self, not long after taken with such a Lameness, in both her Legs, that she was forced to go upon Crutches; and she was now in Court upon them. [It was Remarkable, that immediately upon the Juries bringing in *Duny* Guilty, *Durent* was restored unto the use of her Limbs, and went home without her Crutches.]

III

As for *Elizabeth* and *Deborah Pacy*, one Aged Eleven Years, the other Nine; the elder, being in Court, was made utterly senseless, during all the time of the Trial: or at least speechless. By the direction of the Judg, *Duny* was privately brought to *Elizabeth Pacy*, and she touched her Hand: whereupon the Child, without so much as seeing her, suddenly leap'd up and flew upon the Prisoner; the younger was too ill, to be brought unto the Assizes. But *Samuel Pacy*, their Father, testifi'd, that his Daughter *Deborah* was taken with a sudden Lameness; and upon the grumbling of *Amy Duny*, for being denied something, where this Child was then sitting, the Child was taken with an extream pain in her stomach, like the pricking of Pins; and shrieking at a dreadful manner, like a Whelp, rather than a Rational Creature. The Physicians could not conjecture the cause of the Distemper; but *Amy Duny* being a Woman of ill Fame, and the Child in Fits crying out of *Amy Duny*, as affrighting her with the Apparition of her Person, the

Deponent suspected her, and procured her to be set in the stocks. While she was there, she said in the hearing of Two Witnesses, *Mr. Pacy keeps a great stir about his Child, but let him stay till he has done as much by his Children, as I have done by mine*: And being Asked, What she had done to her Children, she Answered, *She had been fain to open her Childs Mouth with a Tap to give it Victuals*. The Deponent added, that within Two Days, the Fits of his Daughters were such, that they could not preserve either Life or Breath, without the help of a Tap. And that the Children Cry'd out of *Amy Duny*, and of *Rose Cullender*, as afflicting them with their Apparitions.

IV

The Fits of the Children were various. They would sometimes be Lame on one side; sometimes on t'other. Sometimes very sore; sometimes restored unto their Limbs, and then Deaf, or Blind, or Dumb, for a long while together. Upon the Recovery of their Speech, they would Cough extreamly; and with much Flegm, they would bring up Crooked Pins; and one time, a Two-penny Nail, with a very broad Head. Commonly at the end of every Fit, they would cast up a Pin. When the Children Read, they could not pronounce the Name of, *Lord*, or *Jesus*, or *Christ*, but would fall into Fits; and say, Amy Duny *says, I must not use that Name*. When they came to the Name of *Satan*, or *Devil*, they would clap their Fingers on the Book, crying out, *This bites, but it makes me speak right well!* The Children in their Fits would often Cry out, *There stands* Amy Duny, or *Rose Cullender*; and they would afterwards relate, *That these Witches appearing before them, threatned them, that if they told what they saw or heard, they would Torment them ten times more than ever they did before.*

V

Margaret Arnold, the Sister of Mr. *Pacy*, Testifi'd unto the like Sufferings being upon the Children, at her House, whither her Brother had Removed them. And that sometimes, the Children (*only*) would see things like Mice, run about the House; and one of them suddenly snap'd one with the Tongs, and threw it into the Fire, where it screeched out like a Rat. At another time, a thing like a Bee, flew at the Face of the younger Child; the Child fell into a Fit; and at last Vomited up a *Two-penny Nail*, with a Broad Head; affirming, *That the Bee brought this Nail, and forced it into her Mouth.* The Child would in like manner be assaulted with Flies, which brought Crooked Pins, unto her, and made her first swallow them, and then Vomit them. She one Day caught an Invisible *Mouse*, and throwing it into the Fire, it Flash'd like to Gun-Powder. None besides the Child saw the *Mouse*, but every one saw the *Flash*. She also declared, out of her Fits, that in them, *Amy Duny* much tempted her to destroy her self.

VI

As for *Ann Durent*, her Father Testified, That upon a Discontent of *Rose Cullender*, his Daughter was taken with much Illness in her Stomach and great and sore Pains, like the Pricking of Pins: and then Swooning Fits, from which Recovering, she declared, *She had seen the Apparition of* Rose Cullender, *Threatning to Torment her.* She likewise Vomited up diverse Pins. The Maid was Present at Court, but when *Cullender* look'd upon her, she fell into such Fits, as made her utterly unable to declare any thing.

   Ann Baldwin deposed the same.

VII

Jane Bocking, was too weak to be at the Assizes. But her Mother Testifi'd, that her Daughter having formerly been Afflicted with Swooning Fits, and Recovered of them; was now taken with a great Pain in her Stomach; and New Swooning Fits. That she took little Food, but every Day Vomited Crooked Pins. In her first Fits, she would Extend her Arms, and use Postures, as if she catched at something, and when her Clutched Hands were forced open, they would find several Pins diversely Crooked, unaccountably lodged there. She would also maintain a Discourse with some that were

Invisibly present, when casting abroad her Arms, she would often say, *I will not have it!* but at last say, *Then I will have it!* and closing her Hand, which when they presently after opened, a Lath-Nail was found in it. But her great Complaints were of being Visited by the shapes of *Amy Duny,* and *Rose Cullender.*

VIII

As for *Susan Chandler,* her Mother Testified, That being at the search of *Rose Cullender,* they found on her Belly a thing like a Teat, of an Inch long; which the *said Rose* ascribed to a strain. But near her Privy-parts, they found Three more, that were smaller than the former. At the end of the long Teat, there was a little Hole, which appeared, as if newly Sucked; and upon straining it, a white Milky matter issued out. The Deponent further said, That her Daughter being one Day concerned at *Rose Cullenders* taking her by the Hand, she fell very sick, and at Night cry'd out, *That* Rose Cullender *would come to Bed unto her.* Her Fits grew violent, and in the Intervals of them, she declared, *That she saw* Rose Cullender *in them, and once having of a great Dog with her.* She also Vomited up Crooked Pins; and when she was brought into Court, she fell into her Fits. She Recovered her self in some Time, and was asked by the Court, whether she was in a Condition to take an Oath, and give Evidence. She said, she could; but having been Sworn, she fell into her Fits again, and, *Burn her! Burn her!* were all the words that she could obtain power to speak. Her Father likewise gave the same Testimony with her Mother; as to all but the Search.

IX

Here was the Sum of the Evidence: Which Mr. Serjeant *Keeling,* thought not sufficient to Convict the Prisoners. For admitting the Children were Bewitched, yet, said he, it can never be Apply'd unto the Prisoners, upon the Imagination only of the Parties Afflicted; inasmuch as no person whatsoever could then be in Safety.

Dr. *Brown*, a very Learned Person then present, gave his Opinion, that these Persons were Bewitched. He added, That in *Denmark*, there had been lately a great Discovery of Witches; who used the very same way of Afflicting people, by Conveying Pins and Nails into them. His Opinion was, that the Devil in Witchcrafts, did Work upon the Bodies of Men and Women, upon a *Natural Foundation*; and that he did Extraordinarily afflict them, with such Distempers as their Bodies were most subject unto.

X

The Experiment about the *Usefulness*, yea, or *Lawfulness* whereof Good Men have sometimes disputed, was divers Times made, That tho' the Afflicted were utterly deprived of all sense in their Fits, yet upon the *Touch* of the Accused, they would so screech out, and fly up, as not upon any other persons. And yet it was also found that once upon the touch of an innocent person, the like effect follow'd, which put the whole Court unto a stand: altho' a small Reason was at length attempted to be given for it.

XI

However, to strengthen the Credit of what had been already produced against the Prisoners, One *John Soam* Testifi'd, That bringing home his Hay in Three Carts, one of the Carts wrenched the Window of *Rose Cullenders* House, whereupon she flew out, with violent Threatenings against the Deponent. The other Two Carts, passed by Twice, Loaded, that Day afterwards; but the Cart which touched *Cullenders* House, was Twice or Thrice that Day overturned. Having again Loaded it, as they brought it thro' the Gate which Leads out of the Field, the Cart stuck so fast in the Gates Head, that they could not possibly get it thro', but were forced to cut down the Post of the Gate, to make the Cart pass thro', altho' they could not perceive that the Cart did of either side touch the Gate-Post. They afterwards, did with much Difficulty get it home to the Yard; but could not for their Lives get the Cart near the place, where they should unload.

They were fain to unload at a great Distance; and when they were Tired, the Noses of them that came to Assist them, would burst forth a Bleeding; so they were fain to give over till next morning; and then they unloaded without any difficulty.

XII

Robert Sherringham also Testifi'd, That the Axle-Tree of his Cart, happening in passing, to break some part of *Rose Cullenders* House, in her Anger at it, she vehemently threatned him, *His Horses should suffer for it.* And within a short time, all his Four Horses dy'd; after which he sustained many other Losses in the sudden Dying of his Cattle. He was also taken with a Lameness in his Limbs; and so vexed with Lice of an extraordinary Number and Bigness, that no Art could hinder the Swarming of them, till he burnt up two Suits of Apparel.

XIII

As for *Amy Duny*, 'twas Testifi'd by one *Richard Spencer* that he heard her say, *The Devil would not let her Rest; until she were Revenged on the Wife of Cornelius Sandswel.* And that *Sandswel* testifi'd, that her Poultry dy'd suddenly, upon *Amy Dunys* threatning of them; and that her Husbands Chimney fell, quickly after *Duny* had spoken of such a disaster. And a Firkin of Fish could not be kept from falling into the Water, upon suspicious words of *Duny's.*

XIV

The Judge told the Jury, they were to inquire now, first, whether these Children were Bewitched; and secondly, Whether the Prisoners at the Bar were guilty of it. He made no doubt, there were such Creatures as Witches; for the Scriptures affirmed it; and the Wisdom of all Nations had provided

Laws against such persons. He pray'd the God of Heaven to direct their Hearts in the weighty thing they had in hand; for, *To Condemn the Innocent, and let the Guilty go free, were both an Abomination to the Lord.*

The Jury in half an hour brought them in *Guilty* upon their several Indictments, which were Nineteen in Number.

The next Morning, the Children with their Parents, came to the Lodgings of the Lord Chief Justice, and were in as good health as ever in their Lives; being Restored within half an Hour after the Witches were Convicted.

The Witches were Executed; and *Confessed* nothing; which indeed will not be wondred by them, who Consider and Entertain the Judgment of a Judicious Writer, *That the Unpardonable Sin, is most usually Committed by Professors of the Christian Religion, falling into Witchcraft.*

LITHOBOLIA

R.C.

1698

According to a footnote in the New England Historical and Genealogical Register *(Vol. 24, 1870), "R.C." stands for Richard Chamberlayne (sometimes spelled Chamberlain), who was Secretary of the Province of New Hampshire in 1682, when his signature appears on several legal documents. Chamberlayne is not known to have published anything else.*

The event Chamberlayne describes would be categorized today as a serious poltergeist haunting. It is also reported by Increase Mather, whose account was reproduced earlier in this book. Thereby hangs a tale: it seems that Mather heard that Chamberlayne was preparing an account of the incident, and wrote to a New Hampshire contact, one Joshua Moody of Portsmouth, asking him to obtain a copy.

Apparently Mather did not know that Moody was the wrong person to send to Chamberlayne for a favor, because the previous year, Chamberlayne had prosecuted Moody for failing to conduct his services according to the English (i.e., Church of England) Prayer Book—in other words, for conducting Congregationalist services in the Puritan manner—and the case had resulted in Moody being imprisoned for three months. Chamberlayne being no friend of Puritans in general or Moody in particular, Mather's request went unanswered, leaving him to piece together his own account from whatever secondhand sources he could find.

Chamberlayne claims to have witnessed the haunting at first hand, making his the more authoritative account, at least in theory. Although it is framed as nonfiction, Chamberlayne's account is regarded in some quarters as one of the first examples of horror fiction to be written in North America. It was first published in London in 1698.

*L*ithobolia: or, the Stone-Throwing Devil. Being an Exact and True Account (by way of Journal) of the various Actions of Infernal Spirits, or (Devils Incarnate) Witches, or both; and the great Disturbance and Amazement they gave to George Waltons Family, at a place call'd Great Island in the Province of New-Hantshire in New-England, chiefly in Throwing about (by an Invisible hand) Stone, Bricks, and Brick-bats of all Sizes, with several other things, as Hammers, Mauls, Iron-Crows, Spits, and other Domestick Utensils, as came into their Hellish Minds, and this for the space of a Quarter of a Year.

By R. C. Esq; who was a Sojourner in the same Family the whole time, and an Ocular Witness of these Diabolick Inventions.

The Contents hereof being manifestly known to the Inhabitants of that Province, and Persons of other Provinces, and is upon Record in his Majesties Council-Court held for that Province.

London, Printed, and are to be Sold by E. Whitlook near Stationers-Hall, 1698.

To The much Honoured Mart. Lumley, Esq;

Sir,

As the subsequent Script deserves not to be called a Book, so these precedent Lines presume not to a Dedication: But, Sir, it is an occasion that I am ambitious to lay hold on, to discover to You by this Epitome (as it were) the propension and inclination I have to give a more full and perfect demonstration of the Honour, Love, and Service, I own (as I think my self oblig'd) to have for You. To a Sober, Judicious, and well Principled Person, such as your Self, plain Truths are much more agreeable than the most charming and surprising Romance or Novel, with all the strange turns and events. That this is of the first sort, (as I have formerly upon Record attested) I do now aver and protest; yet neither is it less strange than true, and so may be capable of giving you some Diversion for an hour: For this interruption of your more serious ones, I cannot doubt your candor and clemency, in pardoning it, that so well know (and do most sensibly acknowledge) your high Worth and Goodness; and that the Relation I am Dignified with, infers a mutual Patronization.

Sir, I am

Your most Humble Servant,

R.C.

To the much Honoured R. F. Esq;

To tell strange feats of Daemons, here I am;
Strange, but most true they are, ev'n to a Dram,
Tho' Sadduceans cry, 'tis all a Sham.
Here's Stony Arg'uments of persuasive Dint,
They'll not believe it, told, nor yet in Print:
What should the Reason be? The Devil's in't.
And yet they wish to be convinc'd by Sight,
Assur'd by Apparition of a Sprite;

But Learned Brown doth state the matter right:
Satan will never Instrumental be
Of so much Good, to' Appear to them; for he
Hath them sure by their Infidelity.
But you, my Noble Friend, know better things;
Your Faith, mounted on Religions Wings,
Sets you above the Clouds whence Error springs.
Your Soul reflecting on this lower Sphear,
Of froth and vanity, joys oft to hear
The Sacred Ora'cles, where all Truths appear
Which will Conduct out of this Labyrinth of Night,
And lead you to the source of Intellect'ual Light.
Which is the Hearty Prayer of
Your most faithful Humble Servant,
R.C.

Lithobolia: or, the Stone-throwing Devil, etc.

Such is the Sceptical Humour of this Age for Incredulity, (not to say Infidelity,) That I wonder they do not take up and profess, in terms, the Pyrrhonian Doctrine of disbelieving their very Senses. For that which I am going to relate happening to cease in the Province of New-Hampshire in America, just upon that Governour's Arrival and Appearance at the Council there, who was informed by my self, and several other Gentlemen of the Council, and other considerable Persons, of the true and certain Reality hereof, yet he continued tenacious in the Opinion that we were all imposed upon by the waggery of some unlucky Boys; which, considering the Circumstances and Passages hereafter mentioned, was altogether impossible.

I have a Wonder to relate; for such (I take it) is so to be termed whatsoever is Praeternatural, and not assignable to, or the effect of, Natural Causes: It is a *Lithobolia*, or Stone-throwing, which happened by Witchcraft (as was supposed) and maliciously perpetrated by an Elderly Woman, a Neighbour suspected, and (I think) formerly detected for such kind of Diabolical Tricks and Practises; and the wicked Instigation did arise upon the account of some small quantity of Land in her Field, which she pretended was unjustly taken into the Land of the Person where the Scene of this Matter lay, and was her Right; she having been often very clamorous about that Affair, and heard to say, with much Bitterness, that her Neighbour (*innuendo* the fore-mentioned Person, his Name George Walton) should never quietly injoy that piece of Ground. Which, as it has confirm'd my self and others in the Opinion that there are such things as Witches, and the Effects of Witchcraft, or at least of the mischievous Actions of Evil Spirits; which some do as little give Credit to, as in the Case of Witches, utterly rejecting both their Operations and their Beings, we having been Eye-Witnesses of this Matter almost every Day for a quarter of a Year together; so it may be a means to rectifie the depraved Judgment and Sentiments of other disbelieving Persons, and absolutely convince them of their Error, if they please to hear, without prejudice, the plain, but most true Narration of it; which was thus.

Some time ago being in America (in His then Majesty's Service) I was lodg'd in the said George Walton's House, a Planter there, and on a Sunday Night, about Ten a Clock, many Stones were heard by my self, and the rest of the Family, to be thrown, and (with Noise) hit against the top and all sides of the House, after the said Walton had been at his Fence-Gate, which was between him and his Neighbour one John Amazeen an Italian, to view it; for it was again, as formerly it had been (the manner how being unknown) wrung off the Hinges, and cast upon the Ground; and in his being there, and return home with several Persons of (and frequenting) his family and House, about a flight shot distant from the Gate, they were all assaulted with a peal of Stones, (taken, we conceive, from the Rocks hard by the House) and this by unseen Hands or Agents. For by this time I was come down to them, having risen out of my Bed at this strange Alarm of all that were in the House, and do know that they all look'd out as narrowly as I did, or any Person could (it being a bright Moon-light Night), but cou'd make no Discovery. Thereupon, and because there came many Stones, and those pretty great ones, some as big as my Fist, into the Entry or Porch of the House, we withdrew into the next Room to the Porch, no Person having receiv'd any Hurt, (praised be Almighty Providence, for certainly the infernal Agent, constant Enemy to Mankind, had he not been over-ruled, intended no less than Death or Maim) save only that two Youths were lightly hit, one on the Leg, the other on the Thigh, notwithstanding the Stones came so thick, and so forcibly against the sides of so narrow a Room. Whilst we stood amazed at this Accident, one of the Maidens imagined she saw them come from the Hall, next to that we were in, where searching, (and in the Cellar, down out of the Hall,) and finding no Body, another and my self observed two little Stones in a short space successively to fall on the Floor, coming as from the Ceiling close by us, and we concluded it must necessarily be done by means extraordinary and praeternatural. Coming again into the Room where we first were (next the Porch), we had many of these lapidary Salutations, but unfriendly ones; for, shutting the door, it was no small Surprise to me to have a good big Stone come with great force and noise (just by my Head) against the Door on the inside; and then shutting the other Door, next the Hall, to have the like Accident; so going out again, upon a necessary Occasion, to have another very near my Body, clattering against the Board-wall of the House; but it was a much greater, to be so near the danger of having my Head broke with a Maul, or great Hammer brushing along the top or roof of the Room from the other end, as I was walking in it, and lighting down by me; but it fell so, that my Landlord had the greatest damage, his Windows (especially those of the first mention'd Room) being with many Stones miserably and strangely batter'd, most of the Stones giving the Blow on the inside, and forcing the Bars, Lead, and hasps of the Casements outwards, and yet falling back (sometimes a Yard or two) into the Room; only one little Stone we took out of the glass of the Window, where it lodg'd its self in the breaking it, in a Hole exactly fit for the Stone. The Pewter and Brass were frequently pelted, and sometimes thrown down upon the Ground; for the Evil Spirit seemed then to affect variety of Mischief, and diverted himself at this end after he had done so much Execution at the other. So were two Candlesticks, after many hittings, at last struck off the Table where they stood, and likewise a large Pewter Pot, with the force of these Stones. Some of them were taken up hot, and (it seems) immediately coming out of the Fire; and some (which is not unremarkable) having been laid by me upon the Table along by couples, and numbred, were found missing; that is, two of them, as we return'd immediately to the Table, having turn'd our backs only to visit and view some new Stone-charge or Window-breach; and this Experiment was four or five times repeated, and I still found one or two missing of the Number, which we all mark'd, when I did but just remove the Light from off the Table, and step to the Door, and back again.

After this had continued in all the parts and sides of the first Room (and down the Chimney) for above four hours, I, weary of the Noise, and sleepy, went to Bed, and was no sooner fallen asleep, but was awakened with the unwelcome disturbance of another Battery of a different sort, it issuing with so prodigious a Noise against the thin Board-wall of my Chamber (which was within another) that I could not imagine it less than the fracture and downfall of great part of the Chamber, or at least of the Shelves, Books, Pictures, and other things, placed on that side, and on the Partition-Wall between the Anti-Chamber and the Door of mine. But the Noise immediately bringing up the Company below, they assured me no Mischief of that nature was done, and shewed me the biggest Stone that had as yet been made use of in this unaccountable Accident, weighing eight pound and an half, that had burst open my Chamber Door with a rebound from the Floor, as by the Dent and Bruise in it near the Door I found next Morning, done, probably, to make the greater Noise, and give the more Astonishment, which would sooner be effected by three Motions, and consequently three several Sounds, *viz*, one on the Ground, the next to and on the Door, and the last from it again to the Floor, then if it had been one single Blow upon the Door only; which ('tis probable) wou'd have split the Door, which was not permitted, nor so much as a square of the Glass-Window broken or crack'd (at that time) in all the Chamber. Glad thereof, and desiring them to leave me, and the Door shut, as it was before, I endeavoured once more to take my Rest, and was once more prevented by the like passage, with another like offensive Weapon, it being a whole Brick that lay in the anti-Chamber Chimney, and used again to the same malicious purpose as before, and in the same manner too, as by the mark in the Floor, whereon was some of the dust of the Brick, broken a little at the end, apparant next Morning, the Brick it self lying just at the Door. However, after I had lain a while, harkning to their Adventures below, I drop'd asleep again, and receiv'd no further Molestation that Night.

In the Morning (*Monday* Morning) I was inform'd by several of the Domesticks of more of the same kind of Trouble; among which the most signal was, the Vanishing of the Spit which stood in the Chimney Corner, and the sudden coming of it again down the same Chimney, sticking of it in a Log that lay in the Fireplace or Hearth; and then being by one of the Family set by on the other side of the Chimney, presently cast out of the Window into the Back-side. Also a pressing-Iron lying on the ledge of the Chimney back, was convey'd invisibly into the Yard. I should think it (too) not unworthy the Relation, that, discoursing then with some of the Family, and others, about what had past, I said, I thought it necessary to take and keep the great Stone, as a Proof and Evidence, for they had taken it down from my Chambers; and so I carried it up, laid it on my Table in my Chamber, and lock'd my Door, and going out upon occasions, and soon returning, I was told by my Landlady that it was, a little while after my going forth, removed again, with a Noise, which they all below heard, and was thrown into the anti-Chamber, and there I found it lying in the middle of it; thereupon I the second time carried it up, and laid it on the Table, and had it in my Custody a long time to show, for the Satisfaction of the Curious.

There were many more Stones thrown about in the House that Morning, and more in the Fields that Day, where the Master of the House was, and the Men at Work. Some more Mr. Woodbridge, a Minister, and my self, in the Afternoon did see (but could not any Hand throwing them) lighting near, and jumping and tumbling on the Grass: So did one Mrs. Clark, and her Son, and several others; and some of them felt them too. One Person would not be perswaded but that the Boys at Work might throw them, and strait her little Boy standing by her was struck with a Stone on the Back, which caused him to fall a crying, and her (being convinc'd) to carry him away forth-with.

In the Evening, as soon as I had sup'd in the outer Room before mine, I took a little Musical-Instrument, and began to touch it (the Door indeed was then set open for Air), and a good big Stone came rumbling in, and as it were to lead the Dance, but upon a much different account than in the days of Old, and of old fabulous Inchantments, my Musick being none of the best. The Noise of this brought up the Deputy-President's Wife, and many others of the Neighbourhood that were below, who wonder'd to see this Stone followed (as it were) by many others, and a Pewter Spoon among the rest, all which fell strangely into the Room in their Presence, and were taken up by the Company. And beside all this, there was seen by two Youths in the Orchard and Fields, as they said, a black Cat, at the time the Stones were toss'd about, and it was shot at, but missed, by its changing Places, and being immediately at some distance, and then out of sight, as they related: Agreeable to which, it may not be improper to insert, what was observed by two Maids, Grand-Children of Mr. Walton, on the Sunday Night, the beginning of this *Lithoboly*. They did affirm, that as they were standing in the Porch-Chamber Window, they saw, as it were, a Person putting out a Hand out of the Hall Window, as throwing Stones toward the Porch or Entry; and we all know no Person was in the Hall except, at that instant, my self and another, having search'd diligently there, and wondring whence those should come that were about the same time drop'd near us; so far we were from doing it our selves, or seeing any other there to do it.

On *Monday* Night, about the Hour it first began, there were more Stones thrown in the Kitchin, and down the Chimney, one Captain Barefoot, of the Council for that Province, being present, with others; and also (as I was going up to Bed) in an upper Chamber, and down those Stairs.

Upon *Tuesday* Night, about Ten, some five or six Stones were severally thrown into the Maid's Chamber near the Kitchin, and the Glass-Windows broke in three new places, and one of the Maids hit as she lay. At the same time was heard by them, and two young Men in the House, an odd, dismal sort of Whistling, and thereupon the Youths ran out, with intent to take the suppos'd Thrower of Stones, if possible; and on the back-side near the Window they heard the Noise (as they said) of something stepping a little way before them, as it were the trampling of a young Colt, as they fancied, but saw nothing; and going on, could discover nothing but that the Noise of the stepping or trampling was ceas'd, and then gone on a little before.

On *Saturday* Morning I found two Stones more on the Stairs; and so some were on Sunday Night convey'd into the Room next the Kitchin.

Upon *Monday* following Mr. Walton going (with his Men) by Water to some other Land, in a place called the Great Bay, arid to a House where his Son was placed, they lay there that Night, and the next Morning had this Adventure. As the Men were all at work in the Woods, felling Wood, they were visited with another set of Stones, and they gathered up near upon a Hat-full, and put them between two Trees near adjoining, and returning from carrying Wood, to the Boat, the Hat and its contents (the Stones) were gone, and the Stones were presently after thrown about again, as before; and after search, found the Hat press'd together, and lying under a square piece of Timber at some distance from thence. They had them again at young Walton's House, and half a Brick thrown into a Cradle, out of which his young Child was newly taken up.

Here it may seem most proper to inform the Reader of a parallel passage, (*viz.*) what happened another time to my Landlord in his Boat; wherein going up to the same place (the Great Bay) and loading it with Hay for his use at his own House, about the mid-way in the River (Pascataqua) he found his Boat began to be in a sinking Condition, at which being much surpriz'd, upon search, he discover'd the cause to be the pulling out a Plug or Stopple in the bottom of the Boat, being fixed there for the more convenient letting out of the Rain-Water that might fall into it; a Contrivance and Combination of the old Serpent and the old Woman, or some other Witch or Wizard (in Revenge or innate Enmity) to have drown'd both my good Landlord and his Company.

On *Wednesday*, as they were at work again in the Woods, on a sudden they heard something gingle like Glass, or Metal, among the Trees, as it was falling, and being fallen to the Ground, they knew it to be a Stirrup which Mr. Walton had carried to the Boat, and laid under some Wood; and this being again laid by him in that very Boat, it was again thrown after him. The third time, he having put it upon his Girdle or Belt he wore about his Waste, buckled together before, but at that instant taken off because of the Heat of the Weather, and laid there again buckled, it was fetch'd away, and no more seen. Likewise the Graper, or little Anchor of the Boat, cast over-board, which caus'd the Boat to wind up; so staying and obstructing their Passage. Then the setting-Pole was divers times cast into the River, as they were coming back from the Great Bay, which put them to the trouble of Padling, that is, rowing about for it as often to retrieve it.

Being come to his own House, this Mr. Walton was charg'd again with a fresh Assault in the out-Houses; but we heard of none within doors until Friday after, when, in the Kitchin, were 4 or 5 Stones (one of them hot) taken out of the Fire, as I conceive, and so thrown about. I was then present, being newly come in with Mr. Walton from his middle Field (as he call'd it), where his Servants had been Mowing, and had six or seven of his old troublesome Companions, and I had one fall'n down by me there, and another thin flat Stone hit me on the Thigh with the flat side of it, so as to make me just feel, and to smart a little. In the same Day's Evening, as I was walking out in the Lane by the Field before-mentioned, a great Stone made a rusling Noise in the Stone-Fence between the Field and the Lane, which seem'd to me (as it caus'd me to cast my Eye that way by the Noise) to come out of the Fence, as it were pull'd out from among those Stones loose, but orderly laid close together, as the manner of such Fences in that Country is, and so fell down upon the Ground. Some Persons of Note being then in the Field (whose Names are here under-written) to visit Mr. Walton there, are substantial Witnesses of this same Stonery, both in the Field, and afterward in the House that Night, *viz*, one Mr. Hussey, Son of a Counsellour there. He took up one that having first alighted On the Ground, with rebound from thence hit him on the Heel; and he keeps it to show. And Captain Barefoot, mentioned above, has that which (among other Stones) flew into the Hall a little before Supper; which my self also saw as it first came in at the upper part of the Door into the middle of the Room; and then (tho' a good flat Stone, yet) was seen to rowl over and over, as if trundled, under a Bed in the same Room. In short, these Persons, being wonderously affected with the Strangeness of these Passages, offer'd themselves (desiring me to take them) as Testimonies; I did so, and made a Memorandum, by way of Record, thereof, to this effect. *Viz*.

These Persons under-written do hereby Attest the Truth of their being Eye-Witnesses of at least half a score Stones that Evening thrown invisibly into the Field, and in the Entry of the House, Hall, and one of the Chambers of George Walton's. Viz.

Samuel Jenings, Esq; Governour of West-Jarsey.
Walter Clark, Esq; Deputy-Governour of Road-Island.
Mr. Arthur Cook
Mr. Matt. Borden of Road-Island.

Mr. Oliver Hooton of Barbados, Merchant.
Mr. T. Maul of Salem in New-England, Merchant.
Captain Walter Barefoot
Mr. John Hussey
And the Wife of the said Mr. Hussey.

On *Saturday, July* 24, One of the Family, at the usual hour at Night, observ'd some few (not above half a dozen) of these natural (or rather unnatural) Weapons to fly into the Kitchin, as formerly; but some of them in an unusual manner lighting gently on him, or coming toward him so easily, as that he took them before they fell to the Ground. I think there was not any thing more that Night remarkable. But as if the malicious Daemon had laid up for Sunday and Monday, then it was that he began (more furiously than formerly) with a great Stone in the Kitchin, and so continued with throwing down the Pewter-Dishes, etc. great part of it all at once coming clattering down, without the stroke of a Stone, little or great, to move it. Then about Midnight this impious Operation not ceasing, but trespassing with very great Stones, weighing above 30 pound a piece (that used to lye in the Kitchin, in or near the Chimny) were in the former, wonted, rebounding manner, let fly against my Door and Wall in the ante-Chamber, but with some little distance of time. This thundring Noise must needs bring up the Men from below, as before, (I need not say to wake me) to tell me the Effect, which was the beating down several Pictures, and displacing abundance of things about my Chamber: but the Repetition of this Cannon-Play by these great rumbling Engines, now ready at hand for the purpose, and the like additional disturbance by four Bricks that lay in the outer-Room Chimney (one of which having been so imploy'd the first Sunday Night, as has been said) made me despair of taking Rest, and so forced me to rise from my Bed. Then finding my Door burst open, I also found many Stones, and great pieces of Bricks, to fly in, breaking the Glass-Windows, and a Paper-Light, sometimes inwards, sometimes outwards: So hitting the Door of my Chamber as I came through from the ante-Chamber, lighting very near me as I was fetching the Candlestick, and afterward the Candle being struck out, as I was going to light it again. So a little after, coming up for another Candle, and being at the Stare-foot door, a wooden Mortar with great Noise struck against the Floor, and was just at my Feet, only not touching me, moving from the other end of the Kitchin where it used to lye. And when I came up my self, and two more of the same House, we heard a Whistling, as it were near us in the outer Room, several times. Among the rest of the Tools made use of to disturb us, I found an old Card for dressing Flax in my Chamber. Now for *Monday* Night, (*June* 26) one of the severest. The disturbance began in the Kitchin with Stones; then as I was at Supper above in the ante-Chamber, the Window near which I sate at Table was broke in 2 or 3 parts of it inwards, and one of the Stones that broke it flew in, and I took it up at the further end of the Room. The manner is observable; for one of the squares was broke into 9 or 10 small square pieces, as if it had been regularly mark'd out into such even squares by a Workman, to the end some of these little pieces might fly in my Face (as they did) and give me a surprize, but without any hurt. In the mean time it went on in the Kitchin, whither I went down, for Company, all or most of the Family, and a Neighbour, being there; where many Stones (some great ones) came thick and threefold among us, and an old howing Iron, from a Room hard by, where such Utensils lay. Then, as if I had been the design'd Object for that time, most of the Stones that came (the smaller I mean) hit me (sometimes pretty hard) to the number of above 20, near 30, as I remember, and whether I remov'd, sit, or walk'd, I had them, and great ones sometimes lighting gently on me, and in my Hand and Lap as I sate, and falling to the Ground, and sometimes thumping against the Wall, as near as could be to me, without touching me. Then was a Room over the Kitchin infested, that had not been so before, and many Stones greater than usual lumbring there over our Heads, not only to ours, but to the great Disturbance and Affrightment of some Children that lay there. And for Variety, there were sometimes three great, distinct Knocks, sometimes five such sounds as with a great Maul, reiterated divers times.

On *Tuesday* Night (*June* 28) we were quiet; but not so on *Wednesday*, when the Stones were play'd about in the House. And on *Thursday* Morning I found some things that hung on Nails on the Wall in my Chamber, *viz*, a Spherical Sun-Dial, etc. lying on the Ground, as knock'd down by some Brick or Stone in the ante-Chamber. But my Landlord had the worst of that Day, tho' he kept the Field, being there invisibly hit above 40 times, as he affirm'd to me, and he receiv'd some shrowd hurtful Blows on the Back, and other Parts, which he much complained of, and said he thought he should have reason to do, even to his dying day; and I observ'd that he did so, he being departed this Life since.

Besides this, Plants of Indian Corn were struck up by the Roots almost, just as if they had been cut with some edged Instrument, whereas *re vera* they were seen to be eradicated, or rooted up with nothing but the very Stones, altho' the injurious Agent was altogether unseen. And a sort of Noise, like that of Snorting and Whistling, was heard near the Men at Work in the Fields many times, many whereof I my self, going thither, and being there, was a Witness of; and parting thence I receiv'd a pretty hard Blow with a Stone on the Calf of my Leg. So it continued that day in two Fields, where they were severally at Work: and my Landlord told me, he often heard likewise a humming Noise in the Air by him, as of a Bullet discharg'd from a Gun; and so said a Servant of his that work'd with him.

Upon *Saturday* (*July* 1), as I was going to visit my Neighbour Capt. Barefoot, and just at his Door, his Man saw, as well as my self, 3 or 4 Stones fall just by us in the Field, or Close, where the House stands, and not any other Person near us. At Night a great Stone fell in the Kitchin, as I was going to Bed, and the Pewter was thrown down; many Stones flew about, and the Candles by them put out 3 or 4 times, and the Snorting heard; a Negro Maid hit on the Head in the Entry between the Kitchin and Hall with a Porringer from the Kitchin: also the pressing-Iron clattered against the Partition Wall between the Hall and a Chamber beyond it, where I lay, and Mr. Randolph, His Majesty's Officer for the Customs, etc.

Some few Stones we had on *Sunday* Morning, (*July* 2) none at Night. But on *Monday* Morning (the 3d) both Mr. Walton, and 5 or 6 with him in the Field, were assaulted with them, and their Ears with the old Snorting and Whistling. In the Afternoon Mr. Walton was hit on the Back with Stones very grievously, as he was in his Boat that lay at a Cove side by his House. It was a very odd prank that was practis'd by the Devil a little while after this. One Night the Cocks of Hay, made the Day before in the Orchard, was spread all abroad, and some of the Hay thrown up into the Trees, and some of it brought into the House, and scatter'd. Two Logs that lay at the Door, laid, one of them by the Chimny in the Kitchin; the other set against the Door of the Room where Mr. Walton then lay, as on purpose to confine him therein: A Form that stood in the Entry (or Porch) was set along by the Fire side, and a joint Stool upon that, with a Napking spread thereon, with two Pewter Pots, and two Candlesticks: A Cheese-Press likewise having a Spit thrust into one of the holes of it, at one end; and at the other end of the Spit hung an Iron Kettle; and a Cheese was taken out, and broke to pieces. Another time, I full well remember 'twas on a Sunday at Night, my Window was all broke with a violent shock of Stones and Brick-bats, which scarce miss'd my self: among these one huge one made its way through the great square or shash of a Casement, and broke a great hole in it, throwing down Books by the way, from the Window to a Picture over-against it, on the other side of the Chamber, and tore a hole quite through it about half a foot long, and the piece of the Cloth hung by a little part of it, on the back-side of the Picture.

After this we were pretty quiet, saving now and then a few Stones march'd about for Exercise, and to keep (as it were) the Diabolical hand in use, till July 28, being Friday, when about 40 Stones flew about, abroad, and in the House and Orchard, and among the Trees therein, and a Window broke before, was broke again, and one Room where they never used before.

August 1. On Wednesday the Window in my ante-Chamber was broke again, and many Stones were plaid about, abroad, and in the House, in the Day-time, and at Night. The same Day in the Morning they tried this Experiment; they did set on the Fire a Pot with Urin, and crooked Pins in it, with design to have it boil, and by that means to give Punishment to the Witch, or Wizard (that might be the wicked Procurer or Contriver of this Stone Affliction) and take off their own as they had been advised. This was the Effect of it: As the Liquor begun to grow hot, a Stone came and broke the top or mouth of it, and threw it down, and spilt what was in it; which being made good again, another Stone, as the Pot grew hot again, broke the handle off; and being recruited and fill'd the third time, was then with a third Stone quite broke to pieces and split; and so the Operation became frustrate and fruitless.

On *August* 2, two Stones in the Afternoon I heard and saw my self in the House and Orchard; and another Window in the Hall was broke. And as I was entring my own Chamber a great square of a Casement, being a foot square, was broke with the Noise as of a big Stone, and pieces of the Glass flew into the Room, but no Stone came in then, or could be found within or without. At Night, as I, with others, were in the Kitchin, many more came in; and one great Stone that lay on a Spinning-Wheel to keep it steady, was thrown to the other side of the Room. Several Neighbours then present were ready to testifie this Matter.

Upon *August* 3, On *Thursday* the Gate between my said Landlord and his Neighbour John Amazeen was taken off again, and thrown into Amazeen's Field, who heard it fall and averr'd it then made a Noise like a great Gun.

On *Friday* the *4th*, the Fence against Mr. Walton's Neighbour's Door, (the Woman of whom formerly there was great Suspicion, and thereupon Examination had, as appears upon Record;) this Fence being maliciously pull'd down to let in their Cattel into his Ground; he and his Servants were pelted with above 40 Stones as they went to put it up again; for she had often threatned that he should never injoy his House and Land. Mr. Walton was hit divers times, and all that Day in the Field, as they were Reaping, it ceas'd not, and their fell (by the Mens Computation) above an hundred Stones. A Woman helping to Reap (among the rest) was hit 9 or 10 times, and hurt to that degree, that her left Arm, Hip, Thigh, and Leg, were made black and blue therewith; which she showd to the Woman, Mrs. Walton, and others. Mr. Wood-bridge, a Divine, coming to give me a Visit, was hit about the Hip, and one Mr. Jefferys a Merchant, who was with him, on the Leg. A Window in the Kitchin that had been much batter'd before, was now quite broke out, and unwindow'd, no Glass or Lead at all being left: a Glass Bottle broke to pieces, and the Pewter Dishes (about 9 of them) thrown down, and bent.

On *Saturday* the *5th*, as they were Reaping in the Field, three Sickles were crack'd and broke by the force of these lapidary Instruments of the Devil, as the Sickles were in the Reapers hands, on purpose (it seems) to obstruct their Labour, and do them Injury and Damage. And very many Stones were cast about that Day; insomuch, that some that assisted at that Harvest-Work, being struck with them, by reason of that Disturbance left the Field, but were follow'd by their invisible Adversaries to the next House.

On *Sunday*, being the 6th, there fell nothing considerable, nor on *Monday*, *(7th)* save only one of the Children hit with a Stone on the Back.

We were quiet to *Tuesday* the 8th. But on *Wednesday (9th)* above 100 Stones (as they verily thought) repeated the Reapers Disquiet in the Corn-Field, whereof some were affirm'd by Mr. Walton to be great ones indeed, near as big as a Man's Head; and Mrs. Walton, his Wife being by Curiosity led thither, with intent also to make some Discovery by the most diligent and vigilant Observation she could use, to obviate the idle Incredulity some inconsiderate Persons might irrationally entertain concerning this venefi- cial Operation; or at least to confirm her own Sentiments and Belief of it. Which she did, but to her Cost; for she received an untoward Blow (with a Stone) on her Shoulder. There were likewise two Sickles bent, crack'd, and disabled with them, beating them violently out of their Hands that held them, and this reiterated three times successively.

After this we injoy'd our former Peace and Quiet, unmolested by these stony Disturbances, that whole month of August, excepting some few times; and the last of all in the Month of September, (the beginning thereof) wherein Mr. Walton himself only (the Original perhaps of this strange Adventure, as has been declared) was the designed concluding Sufferer; and going in his Canoo (or Boat) from the Great Island, where he dwelt, to Portsmouth, to attend the Council, who had taken Cognizance of this Matter, he being Summoned thither, in order to his and the Suspect's Examination, and the Courts taking Order thereabout, he was sadly hit with three pebble Stones as big as ones Fist; one of which broke his Head, which I saw him show to the President of the Council; the others gave him that Pain on the Back, of which (with other like Strokes) he complained then, and afterward to his Death.

Who, that peruses these praeternatural Occurences, can possibly be so much an Enemy to his own Soul, and irrefutable Reason, as obstinately to oppose himself to, or confusedly fluctuate in, the Opinion and Doctrine of Daemons, or Spirits, and Witches? Certainly he that do's so, must do two things more: He must temariously unhinge, or undermine the Fun- damentals of the best Religion in the World; and he must disingenuously quit and abandon that of the Three Theologick Virtues or Graces, to which the great Doctor of the Gentils gave the Precedence, Charity, through his Unchristian and Uncharitable Incredulity.

WIELAND

Charles Brockden Brown

1798

Born into a Philadelphia Quaker family in 1771, Charles Brockden Brown was one of the first generation of American novelists. He abandoned a career in the law to follow his literary ambitions, and after a few shorter publications in the 1780s and 1790s he wrote seven novels between 1798 and 1801. He also edited two New York–based literary periodicals, The Monthly Magazine and American Review *and* The American Review and Literary Journal, *from 1799 to 1802.*

Among other works, Brown wrote four novels that are normally regarded as belonging to the Gothic genre. Sky-Walk; or, The Man Unknown to Himself *was completed but lost, apart from an excerpt published in* The Weekly Magazine *in March 1798. From what is known of the book, sleep-walking seems to have been its main theme.* Wieland: or, The Transformation: An American Tale *(1798) is a tale of psychological horror set between the French and Indian War and the Revolutionary War. In* Arthur Mervyn: or, Memoirs of the Year 1793 *(1799–1800) yellow fever is the source of the horror which stalks the protagonist's life.* Edgar Huntly: or, Memoirs of a Sleep-Walker *(1799) revisits the theme of the lost* Sky-Walk *and adds a frightening encounter with a hostile Lenni Lenape band.*

Academics regard Charles Brockden Brown as a pioneer of the American novel. Although he is sometimes characterized as a Gothic author, his work is more wide-ranging. However, Wieland *is fully deserving of a place in Gothic canon.*

In his later career, Brown turned away from the Gothic. He wrote a number of political pamphlets and contributed to various periodicals, writing on science, history, philosophy, and other topics. He also wrote various works of historical fiction that were published posthumously under the title Historical Sketches.

Wieland *tells the tale of a family plagued by many misfortunes, some of which appear to be supernatural in nature. In the opening chapters, the family's patriarch, a German immigrant who has founded his own religion, suffers a horrific fate in his homemade temple.*

CHAPTER I

I feel little reluctance in complying with your request. You know not fully the cause of my sorrows. You are a stranger to the depth of my distresses. Hence your efforts at consolation must necessarily fail. Yet the tale that I am going to tell is not intended as a claim upon your sympathy. In the midst of my despair, I do not disdain to contribute what little I can to the benefit of mankind. I acknowledge your right to be informed of the events that have lately happened in my family. Make what use of the tale you shall think proper. If it be communicated to the world, it will inculcate the duty of avoiding deceit. It will exemplify the force of early impressions, and show the immeasurable evils that flow from an erroneous or imperfect discipline.

My state is not destitute of tranquillity. The sentiment that dictates my feelings is not hope. Futurity has no power over my thoughts. To all that is to come I am perfectly indifferent. With regard to myself, I have nothing more to fear. Fate has done its worst. Henceforth, I am callous to misfortune.

I address no supplication to the Deity. The power that governs the course of human affairs has chosen his path. The decree that ascertained the condition of my life, admits of no recall. No doubt it squares with the maxims of eternal equity. That is neither to be questioned nor denied by me. It suffices that the past is exempt from mutation. The storm that tore up our happiness, and changed into dreariness and desert the blooming scene of our existence, is lulled into grim repose; but not until the victim was transfixed and mangled; till every obstacle was dissipated by its rage; till every remnant of good was wrested from our grasp and exterminated.

How will your wonder, and that of your companions, be excited by my story! Every sentiment will yield to your amazement. If my testimony were without corroborations, you would reject it as incredible. The experience of no human being can furnish a parallel: That I, beyond the rest of mankind, should be reserved for a destiny without alleviation, and without example! Listen to my narrative, and then say what it is that has made me deserve to be placed on this dreadful eminence, if, indeed, every faculty be not suspended in wonder that I am still alive, and am able to relate it. My father's ancestry was noble on the paternal side; but his mother was the daughter of a merchant. My grand-father was a younger brother, and a native of Saxony. He was placed, when he had reached the suitable age, at a German college. During the vacations, he employed himself in traversing the neighbouring territory. On one occasion it was his fortune to visit Hamburg. He formed an acquaintance with Leonard Weise, a merchant of that city, and was a frequent guest at his house. The merchant had an only daughter, for whom his guest speedily contracted an affection; and, in spite of parental menaces and prohibitions, he, in due season, became her husband.

By this act he mortally offended his relations. Thenceforward he was entirely disowned and rejected by them. They refused to contribute any thing to his support. All intercourse ceased, and he received from them merely that treatment to which an absolute stranger, or detested enemy, would be entitled.

He found an asylum in the house of his new father, whose temper was kind, and whose pride was flattered by this alliance. The nobility of his birth was put in the balance against his poverty. Weise conceived himself, on the whole, to have acted with the highest discretion, in thus disposing of his child. My grand-father found it incumbent on him to search out some mode of independent subsistence. His youth had been eagerly devoted to literature and music. These had hitherto been cultivated merely as sources of amusement. They were now converted into the means of gain. At this period there were few works of taste in the Saxon dialect. My ancestor may be considered as the founder of the German Theatre. The modern poet of the same name is sprung from the same family, and, perhaps, surpasses but little, in the fruitfulness of his invention, or the soundness of his taste, the elder Wieland. His life was spent in the composition of sonatas and dramatic pieces. They were not unpopular, but merely afforded him a scanty subsistence. He died in the bloom of his life, and was quickly followed to the grave by his wife. Their only child was taken under the protection of the merchant. At an early age he was apprenticed to a London trader, and passed seven years of mercantile servitude.

My father was not fortunate in the character of him under whose care he was now placed. He was treated with rigor, and full employment was provided for every hour of his time. His duties were laborious and mechanical. He had been educated with a view to this profession, and, therefore, was not tormented with unsatisfied desires. He did not hold his present occupations in abhorrence, because they withheld him from paths more flowery and more smooth, but he found in unintermitted labour, and in the sternness of his master, sufficient occasions for discontent. No opportunities of recreation were allowed him. He spent all his time pent up in a gloomy apartment, or traversing narrow and crowded streets. His food was coarse, and his lodging humble. His heart gradually contracted a habit of morose and gloomy reflection. He could not accurately define what was wanting to his happiness. He was not tortured by comparisons drawn between his own situation and that of others. His state was such as suited his age and his views as to fortune. He did not imagine himself treated with extraordinary or unjustifiable rigor. In this respect he supposed the condition of others, bound like himself to mercantile service, to resemble his own; yet every engagement was irksome, and every hour tedious in its lapse.

In this state of mind he chanced to light upon a book written by one of the teachers of the Albigenses, or French Protestants. He entertained no relish for books, and was wholly unconscious of any power they possessed to delight or instruct. This volume had lain for years in a corner of his garret, half buried in dust and rubbish. He had marked it as it lay; had thrown it, as his occasions required, from one spot to another; but had felt no inclination to examine its contents, or even to inquire what was the subject of which it treated.

One Sunday afternoon, being induced to retire for a few minutes to his garret, his eye was attracted by a page of this book, which, by some accident, had been opened and placed full in his view. He was seated on the edge of his bed, and was employed in repairing a rent in some part of his clothes. His eyes were not confined to his work, but occasionally wandering, lighted at length upon the page. The words "Seek and ye shall find," were those that first offered themselves to his notice. His curiosity was roused by these so far as to prompt him to proceed. As soon as he finished his work, he took up the book and turned to the first page. The further he read, the more inducement he found to continue, and he regretted the decline of the light which obliged him for the present to close it.

The book contained an exposition of the doctrine of the sect of Camissards, and an historical account of its origin. His mind was in a state peculiarly fitted for the reception of devotional sentiments. The craving which had haunted him was now supplied with an object. His mind was at no loss for a theme of meditation. On days of business, he rose at the dawn, and retired to his chamber not till late at night. He now supplied himself with candles, and employed his nocturnal and Sunday hours in studying this book. It, of course, abounded with allusions to the Bible. All its conclusions were deduced from the sacred text. This was the fountain, beyond which it was unnecessary to trace the stream of religious truth; but it was his duty to trace it thus far.

A Bible was easily procured, and he ardently entered on the study of it. His understanding had received a particular direction. All his reveries were fashioned in the same mould. His progress towards the formation of his creed was rapid. Every fact and sentiment in this book were viewed through a medium which the writings of the Camissard apostle had suggested. His constructions of the text were hasty, and formed on a narrow scale. Every thing was viewed in a disconnected position. One action and one precept were not employed to illustrate and restrict the meaning of another. Hence arose a thousand scruples to which he had hitherto been a stranger. He was alternately agitated by fear and by ecstasy. He imagined himself beset by the snares of a spiritual foe, and that his security lay in ceaseless watchfulness and prayer.

His morals, which had never been loose, were now modelled by a stricter standard. The empire of religious duty extended itself to his looks, gestures, and phrases. All levities of speech, and negligences of behaviour, were proscribed. His air was mournful and contemplative. He laboured to keep alive a sentiment of fear, and a belief of the awe-creating presence of the Deity. Ideas foreign to this were sedulously excluded. To suffer their intrusion was a crime against the Divine Majesty inexpiable but by days and weeks of the keenest agonies.

No material variation had occurred in the lapse of two years. Every day confirmed him in his present modes of thinking and acting. It was to be expected that the tide of his emotions would sometimes recede, that intervals of despondency and doubt would occur; but these gradually were more rare, and of shorter duration; and he, at last, arrived at a state considerably uniform in this respect.

His apprenticeship was now almost expired. On his arrival of age he became entitled, by the will of my grand-father, to a small sum. This sum would hardly suffice to set him afloat as a trader in his present situation, and he had nothing to expect from the generosity of his master. Residence in England had, besides, become almost impossible, on account of his religious tenets. In addition to these motives for seeking a new habitation, there was another of the most imperious and irresistable necessity. He had imbibed an opinion that it was his duty to disseminate the truths of the gospel among the unbelieving nations. He was terrified at first by the perils and hardships to which the life of a missionary is exposed. This cowardice made him diligent in the invention of objections and excuses; but he found it impossible wholly to shake off the belief that such was the injunction of his duty. The belief, after every new conflict with his passions, acquired new strength; and, at length, he formed a resolution of complying with what he deemed the will of heaven.

The North-American Indians naturally presented themselves as the first objects for this species of benevolence. As soon as his servitude expired, he converted his little fortune into money, and embarked for Philadelphia. Here his fears were revived, and a nearer survey of savage manners once more shook his resolution. For a while he relinquished his purpose, and purchasing a farm on Schuylkill, within a few miles of the city, set himself down to the cultivation of it. The cheapness of land, and the service of African slaves, which were then in general use, gave him who was poor in Europe all the advantages of wealth. He passed fourteen years in a thrifty and laborious manner. In this time new objects, new employments, and new associates appeared to have nearly obliterated the devout impressions of his youth. He now became acquainted with a woman of a meek and quiet disposition, and of slender acquirements like himself. He proffered his hand and was accepted.

His previous industry had now enabled him to dispense with personal labour, and direct attention to his own concerns. He enjoyed leisure, and was visited afresh by devotional contemplation. The reading of the scriptures, and other religious books, became once more his favorite employment. His ancient belief relative to the conversion of the savage tribes, was revived with uncommon energy. To the former obstacles were now added the pleadings of parental and conjugal love. The struggle was long and vehement; but his sense of duty would not be stifled or enfeebled, and finally triumphed over every impediment.

His efforts were attended with no permanent success. His exhortations had sometimes a temporary power, but more frequently were repelled with insult and derision. In pursuit of this object he encountered the most imminent perils, and underwent incredible fatigues, hunger, sickness, and solitude. The licence of savage passion, and the artifices of his depraved countrymen, all opposed themselves to his progress. His courage did not forsake him till there appeared no reasonable ground to hope for success. He desisted not till his heart was relieved from the supposed obligation to persevere. With his constitution somewhat decayed, he at length returned to his family. An interval of tranquillity succeeded. He was frugal, regular, and strict in the performance of domestic duties. He allied himself with no sect, because he perfectly agreed with none. Social worship is that by which they are all distinguished; but this article found no place in his creed. He rigidly interpreted that precept which enjoins us, when we worship, to retire into solitude, and shut out every species of society. According to him devotion was not only a silent office, but must be performed alone. An hour at noon, and an hour at midnight were thus appropriated.

At the distance of three hundred yards from his house, on the top of a rock whose sides were steep, rugged, and encumbered with dwarf cedars and stony asperities, he built what to a common eye would have seemed a summer-house. The eastern verge of this precipice was sixty feet above the river which flowed at its foot. The view before it consisted of a transparent current, fluctuating and rippling in a rocky channel, and bounded by a rising scene of cornfields and orchards. The edifice was slight and airy. It was no more than a circular area, twelve feet in diameter, whose flooring was the rock, cleared of moss and shrubs, and exactly levelled, edged by twelve Tuscan columns, and covered by an undulating dome. My father furnished the dimensions and outlines, but allowed the artist whom he employed to complete the structure on his own plan. It was without seat, table, or ornament of any kind.

This was the temple of his Deity. Twice in twenty-four hours he repaired hither, unaccompanied by any human being. Nothing but physical inability to move was allowed to obstruct or postpone this visit. He did not exact from his family compliance with his example. Few men, equally sincere in their faith, were as sparing in their censures and restrictions, with respect to the conduct of others, as my father. The character of my mother was no less devout; but her education had habituated her to a different mode of worship. The loneliness of their dwelling prevented her from joining any established congregation; but she was punctual in the offices of prayer, and in the performance of hymns to her Saviour, after the manner of the disciples of Zinzendorf. My father refused to interfere in her arrangements. His own system was embraced not, accurately speaking, because it was the best, but because it had been expressly prescribed to him. Other modes, if practised by other persons, might be equally acceptable.

His deportment to others was full of charity and mildness. A sadness perpetually overspread his features, but was unmingled with sternness or discontent. The tones of his voice, his gestures, his steps were all in tranquil unison. His conduct was characterised by a certain forbearance and humility, which secured the esteem of those to whom his tenets were most obnoxious. They might call him a fanatic and a dreamer, but they could not deny their veneration to his invincible candour and invariable integrity. His own belief of rectitude was the foundation of his happiness. This, however, was destined to find an end.

Suddenly the sadness that constantly attended him was deepened. Sighs, and even tears, sometimes escaped him. To the expostulations of his wife he seldom answered any thing. When he designed to be communicative, he hinted that his peace of mind was flown, in consequence of deviation from his duty. A command had been laid upon him, which he had delayed to perform. He felt as if a certain period of hesitation and reluctance had been allowed him, but that this period was passed. He was no longer permitted to obey. The duty assigned to him was transferred, in consequence of his disobedience, to another, and all that remained was to endure the penalty.

He did not describe this penalty. It appeared to be nothing more for some time than a sense of wrong. This was sufficiently acute, and was aggravated by the belief that his offence was incapable of expiation. No one could contemplate the agonies which he seemed to suffer without the deepest compassion. Time, instead of lightening the burthen, appeared to add to it. At length he hinted to his wife, that his end was near. His imagination did not prefigure the mode or the time of his decease, but was fraught with an incurable persuasion that his death was at hand. He was likewise haunted by the belief that the kind of death that awaited him was strange and terrible. His anticipations were thus far vague and indefinite; but they sufficed to poison every moment of his being, and devote him to ceaseless anguish.

CHAPTER II

Early in the morning of a sultry day in August, he left Mettingen, to go to the city. He had seldom passed a day from home since his return from the shores of the Ohio. Some urgent engagements at this time existed, which would not admit of further delay. He returned in the evening, but appeared to be greatly oppressed with fatigue. His silence and dejection were likewise in a more than ordinary degree conspicuous. My mother's brother, whose profession was that of a surgeon, chanced to spend this night at our house. It was from him that I have frequently received an exact account of the mournful catastrophe that followed.

As the evening advanced, my father's inquietudes increased. He sat with his family as usual, but took no part in their conversation. He appeared fully engrossed by his own reflections. Occasionally his countenance exhibited tokens of alarm; he gazed steadfastly and wildly at the ceiling; and the exertions of his companions were scarcely sufficient to interrupt his reverie. On recovering from these fits, he expressed no surprise; but pressing his hand to his head, complained, in a tremulous and terrified tone, that his brain was scorched to cinders. He would then betray marks of insupportable anxiety.

My uncle perceived, by his pulse, that he was indisposed, but in no alarming degree, and ascribed appearances chiefly to the workings of his mind. He exhorted him to recollection and composure, but in vain. At the hour of repose he readily retired to his chamber. At the persuasion of my mother he even undressed and went to bed. Nothing could abate his restlessness. He checked her tender expostulations with some sternness. "Be silent," said he, "for that which I feel there is but one cure, and that will shortly come. You can help me nothing. Look to your own condition, and pray to God to strengthen you under the calamities that await you." "What am I to fear?" she answered. "What terrible disaster is it that you think of?" "Peace—as yet I know it not myself, but come it will, and shortly." She repeated her inquiries and doubts; but he suddenly put an end to the discourse, by a stern command to be silent.

She had never before known him in this mood. Hitherto all was benign in his deportment. Her heart was pierced with sorrow at the contemplation of this change. She was utterly unable to account for it, or to figure to herself the species of disaster that was menaced.

Contrary to custom, the lamp, instead of being placed on the hearth, was left upon the table. Over it against the wall there hung a small clock, so contrived as to strike a very hard stroke at the end of every sixth hour. That which was now approaching was the signal for retiring to the fane at which he addressed his devotions. Long habit had occasioned him to be always awake at this hour, and the toll was instantly obeyed.

Now frequent and anxious glances were cast at the clock. Not a single movement of the index appeared to escape his notice. As the hour verged towards twelve his anxiety visibly augmented. The trepidations of my mother kept pace with those of her husband; but she was intimidated into silence. All that was left to her was to watch every change of his features, and give vent to her sympathy in tears.

At length the hour was spent, and the clock tolled. The sound appeared to communicate a shock to every part of my father's frame. He rose immediately, and threw over himself a loose gown. Even this office was performed with difficulty, for his joints trembled, and his teeth chattered with dismay. At this hour his duty called him to the rock, and my mother naturally concluded that it was thither he intended to repair. Yet these incidents were so uncommon, as to fill her with astonishment and foreboding. She saw him leave the room, and heard his steps as they hastily descended the stairs. She half resolved to rise and pursue him, but the wildness of the scheme quickly suggested itself. He was going to a place whither no power on earth could induce him to suffer an attendant.

The window of her chamber looked toward the rock. The atmosphere was clear and calm, but the edifice could not be discovered at that distance through the dusk. My mother's anxiety would not allow her to remain where she was. She rose, and seated herself at the window. She strained her sight to get a view of the dome, and of the path that led to it. The first painted itself with sufficient distinctness on her fancy, but was undistinguishable by the eye from the rocky mass on which it was erected. The second could be imperfectly seen; but her husband had already passed, or had taken a different direction.

What was it that she feared? Some disaster impended over her husband or herself. He had predicted evils, but professed himself ignorant of what nature they were. When were they to come? Was this night, or this hour to witness the accomplishment? She was tortured with impatience, and uncertainty. All her fears were at present linked to his person, and she gazed at the clock, with nearly as much eagerness as my father had done, in expectation of the next hour.

An half hour passed away in this state of suspense. Her eyes were fixed upon the rock; suddenly it was illuminated. A light proceeding from the edifice, made every part of the scene visible. A gleam diffused itself over the intermediate space, and instantly a loud report, like the explosion of a mine, followed. She uttered an involuntary shriek, but the new sounds that greeted her ear, quickly conquered her surprise. They were piercing shrieks, and uttered without intermission. The gleams which had diffused themselves far and wide were in a moment withdrawn, but the interior of the edifice was filled with rays.

The first suggestion was that a pistol was discharged, and that the structure was on fire. She did not allow herself time to meditate a second thought, but rushed into the entry and knocked loudly at the door of her brother's chamber. My uncle had been previously roused by the noise, and instantly flew to the window. He also imagined what he saw to be fire. The loud and vehement shrieks which succeeded the first explosion, seemed to be an invocation of succour. The incident was inexplicable; but he could not fail to perceive the propriety of hastening to the spot. He was unbolting the door, when his sister's voice was heard on the outside conjuring him to come forth.

He obeyed the summons with all the speed in his power. He stopped not to question her, but hurried down stairs and across the meadow which lay between the house and the rock. The shrieks were no longer to be heard; but a blazing light was clearly discernible between the columns of the temple. Irregular steps, hewn in the stone, led him to the summit. On three sides, this edifice touched the very verge of the cliff. On the fourth side, which might be regarded as the front, there was an area of small extent, to which the rude staircase conducted you. My uncle speedily gained this spot. His strength was for a moment exhausted by his haste. He paused to rest himself. Meanwhile he bent the most vigilant attention towards the object before him.

Within the columns he beheld what he could no better describe, than by saying that it resembled a cloud impregnated with light. It had the brightness of flame, but was without its upward motion. It did not occupy the whole area, and rose but a few feet above the floor. No part of the building was on fire. This appearance was astonishing. He approached the temple. As he went forward the light retired, and, when he put his feet within the apartment, utterly vanished. The suddenness of this transition increased the darkness that succeeded in a tenfold degree. Fear and wonder rendered him powerless. An occurrence like this, in a place assigned to devotion, was adapted to intimidate the stoutest heart.

His wandering thoughts were recalled by the groans of one near him. His sight gradually recovered its power, and he was able to discern my father stretched on the floor. At that moment, my mother and servants arrived with a lanthorn, and enabled my uncle to examine more closely this scene. My father, when he left the house, besides a loose upper vest and slippers, wore a shirt and drawers. Now he was naked, his skin throughout the greater part of his body was scorched and bruised. His right arm exhibited marks as of having been struck by some heavy body. His clothes had been removed, and it was not immediately perceived that they were reduced to ashes. His slippers and his hair were untouched.

He was removed to his chamber, and the requisite attention paid to his wounds, which gradually became more painful. A mortification speedily shewed itself in the arm, which had been most hurt. Soon after, the other wounded parts exhibited the like appearance.

Immediately subsequent to this disaster, my father seemed nearly in a state of insensibility. He was passive under every operation. He scarcely opened his eyes, and was with difficulty prevailed upon to answer the questions that were put to him. By his imperfect account, it appeared, that while engaged in silent orisons, with thoughts full of confusion and anxiety, a faint gleam suddenly shot athwart the apartment. His fancy immediately pictured to itself, a person bearing a lamp. It seemed to come from behind. He was in the act of turning to examine the visitant, when his right arm received a blow from a heavy club. At the same instant, a very bright spark was seen to light upon his clothes. In a moment, the whole was reduced to ashes. This was the sum of the information which he chose to give. There was somewhat in his manner that indicated an imperfect tale. My uncle was inclined to believe that half the truth had been suppressed.

Meanwhile, the disease thus wonderfully generated, betrayed more terrible symptoms. Fever and delirium terminated in lethargic slumber, which, in the course of two hours, gave place to death. Yet not till insupportable exhalations and crawling putrefaction had driven from his chamber and the house every one whom their duty did not detain.

Such was the end of my father. None surely was ever more mysterious. When we recollect his gloomy anticipations and unconquerable anxiety; the security from human malice which his character, the place, and the condition of the times, might be supposed to confer; the purity and cloudlessness of the atmosphere, which rendered it impossible that lightning was the cause; what are the conclusions that we must form?

The prelusive gleam, the blow upon his arm, the fatal spark, the explosion heard so far, the fiery cloud that environed him, without detriment to the structure, though composed of combustible materials, the sudden vanishing of this cloud at my uncle's approach—what is the inference to be drawn from these facts? Their truth cannot be doubted. My uncle's testimony is peculiarly worthy of credit, because no man's temper is more sceptical, and his belief is unalterably attached to natural causes.

I was at this time a child of six years of age. The impressions that were then made upon me, can never be effaced. I was ill qualified to judge respecting what was then passing; but as I advanced in age, and became more fully acquainted with these facts, they oftener became the subject of my thoughts. Their resemblance to recent events revived them with new force in my memory, and made me more anxious to explain them. Was this the penalty of disobedience? This the stroke of a vindictive and invisible hand? Is it a fresh proof that the Divine Ruler interferes in human affairs, meditates an end, selects, and commissions his agents, and enforces, by unequivocal sanctions, submission to his will? Or, was it merely the irregular expansion of the fluid that imparts warmth to our heart and our blood, caused by the fatigue of the preceding day, or flowing, by established laws, from the condition of his thoughts?*

---

* A case, in its symptoms exactly parallel to this, is published in one of the *Journals of Florence.* See, likewise, similar cases reported by Messrs. Merille and Muraire, in the *Journal de Medicine,* for February and May, 1783. The researches of Maffei and Fontana have thrown some light upon this subject.

THE MONEY-DIGGERS

Washington Irving

1824

The son of Scots-English immigrants, Irving was born in Manhattan on April 3, 1783. That same week, news reached New York of the cease-fire that brought the Revolutionary War to an end. He was named after George Washington, whom he met at the age of six. While several of his brothers became successful New York merchants, his family did not oppose Irving's literary aspirations: indeed, his brothers often supported him financially.

In 1798, an outbreak of yellow fever in New York prompted the family to send the fourteen-year-old Irving to the healthier climes of Tarrytown, where he first encountered the landscape he made familiar in Rip Van Winkle *and* The Legend of Sleepy Hollow. *He made several other trips up the Hudson in the years that followed, becoming familiar with the region, its Dutch culture, and its folk tales.*

In 1802, Irving began writing social commentaries on New York life for the Morning Chronicle, *under the pseudonym Jonathan Oldstyle. These came to the attention of Aaron Burr, the* Chronicle's *co-publisher, and Charles Brockden Brown recruited Irving for a Philadlephia literary magazine he was editing.*

From 1804 to 1806, Irving took an extended trip to Europe, and on his return he studied law, barely passing the bar in 1806. He founded a satirical magazine, Salmagundi, *in which he was the first to dub New York "Gotham," from an Anglo-Saxon root meaning "town of goats." He also created the persona of New York–Dutch historian Diedrich Knickerbocker, whose alleged disappearance from a New York hotel caused a minor sensation—and a great deal of publicity for Irving's works—in 1809.*

Irving traveled widely in Europe, and wrote a number of humorous sketches and travelogues which were collected in The Sketch Book of Geoffrey Crayon, Gent. *(1819),* Bracebridge Hall *(1822), and* Tales of a Traveller *(1824). He also wrote a biography of Christopher Columbus and various other material inspired by his visit to Spain in from 1828 to 1829. He returned to serve as American minister to Spain from 1842 to 1846.*

The author of two of America's best-known tales of the uncanny, Rip Van Winkle *(1819) and* The Legend of Sleepy Hollow *(1820), Irving wrote with a warm humanity and wry humor that differed from the prevailing fashion for Gothic gloom. Published in his collection* Tales of a Traveller, *this cycle of supernatural tales shows Irving at his humorous and humanistic best as his protagonists encounter a number of supernatural situations.*

Found among the Papers of the Late Diedrich Knickerbocker

Now I remember those old women's words
Who in my youth would tell me winter's tales;
And speak of spirits and ghosts that glide by night
About the place where treasure had been hid.
                          —Marlow's Jew Of Malta

HELL GATE

About six miles from the renowned city of the Manhattoes, and in that Sound, or arm of the sea, which passes between the main land and Nassau or Long Island, there is a narrow strait, where the current is violently compressed between shouldering promontories, and horribly irritated and perplexed by rocks and shoals. Being at the best of times a very violent, hasty current, its takes these impediments in mighty dudgeon; boiling in whirlpools; brawling and fretting in ripples and breakers; and, in short, indulging in all kinds of wrong-headed paroxysms. At such times, woe to any unlucky vessel that ventures within its clutches.

This termagant humor is said to prevail only at half tides. At low water it is as pacific as any other stream. As the tide rises, it begins to fret; at half tide it rages and roars as if bellowing for more water; but when the tide is full it relapses again into quiet, and for a time seems almost to sleep as soundly as an alderman after dinner. It may be compared to an inveterate hard drinker, who is a peaceable fellow enough when he has no liquor at all, or when he has a skin full, but when half seas over plays the very devil.

This mighty, blustering, bullying little strait was a place of great Difficulty and danger to the Dutch navigators of ancient days; hectoring their tub-built barks in a most unruly style; whirling them about, in a manner to make any but a Dutchman giddy, and not unfrequently stranding them upon rocks and reefs. Whereupon out of sheer spleen they denominated it Hellegat (literally Hell Gut) and solemnly gave it over to the devil. This appellation has since been aptly rendered into English by the name of Hell Gate; and into nonsense by the name of Hurl Gate, according to certain foreign intruders who neither understood Dutch nor English. May St. Nicholas confound them!

From this strait to the city of the Manhattoes the borders of the Sound are greatly diversified; in one part, on the eastern shore of the island of Manhata and opposite Blackwell's Island, being very much broken and indented by rocky nooks, overhung with trees which give them a wild and romantic look.

The flux and reflux of the tide through this part of the Sound is extremely rapid, and the navigation troublesome, by reason of the whirling eddies and counter currents. I speak this from experience, having been much of a navigator of these small seas in my boyhood, and having more than once run the risk of shipwreck and drowning in the course of divers holiday voyages, to which in common with the Dutch urchins I was rather prone.

In the midst of this perilous strait, and hard by a group of rocks called "the Hen and Chickens," there lay in my boyish days the wreck of a vessel which had been entangled in the whirlpools and stranded during a storm. There was some wild story about this being the wreck of a pirate, and of some bloody murder, connected with it, which I cannot now recollect. Indeed, the desolate look of this forlorn hulk, and the fearful place where it lay rotting, were sufficient to awaken strange notions concerning it. A row of timber heads, blackened by time, peered above the surface at high water; but at low tide a considerable part of the hull was bare, and its great ribs or timbers, partly stripped of their planks, looked like the skeleton of some sea monster. There was also the stump of a mast, with a few ropes and blocks swinging about and whistling in the wind, while the sea gull wheeled and screamed around this melancholy carcass.

The stories connected with this wreck made it an object of great awe to my boyish fancy; but in truth the whole neighborhood was full of fable and romance for me, abounding with traditions about pirates, hobgoblins, and buried money. As I grew to more mature years I made many researches after the truth of these strange traditions; for I have always been a curious investigator of the valuable, but obscure branches of the history of my native province. I found infinite difficulty, however, in arriving at any precise information. In seeking to dig up one fact it is incredible the number of fables which I unearthed; for the whole course of the Sound seemed in my younger days to be like the straits of Pylorus of yore, the very region of fiction. I will say nothing of the Devil's Stepping Stones, by which that arch fiend made his retreat from Connecticut to Long Island, seeing that the subject is likely to be learnedly treated by a worthy friend and contemporary historian whom I have furnished with particulars thereof. Neither will I say anything of the black man in a three-cornered hat, seated in the stern of a jolly boat who used to be seen about Hell Gate in stormy weather; and who went by the name of the Pirate's Spuke, or Pirate's Ghost, because I

never could meet with any person of stanch credibility who professed to have seen this spectrum; unless it were the widow of Manus Conklin, the blacksmith of Frog's Neck, but then, poor woman, she was a little purblind, and might have been mistaken; though they said she saw farther than other folks in the dark. All this, however, was but little satisfactory in regard to the tales of buried money about which I was most curious; and the following was all that I could for a long time collect that had anything like an air of authenticity.

KIDD THE PIRATE

In old times, just after the territory of the New Netherlands had been wrested from the hands of their High Mightinesses, the Lords States General of Holland, by Charles the Second, and while it was as yet in an unquiet state, the province was a favorite resort of adventurers of all kinds, and particularly of buccaneers. These were piratical rovers of the deep, who made sad work in times of peace among the Spanish settlements and Spanish merchant ships. They took advantage of the easy access to the harbor of the Manhattoes, and of the laxity of its scarcely-organized government, to make it a kind of rendezvous, where they might dispose of their ill-gotten spoils, and concert new depredations. Crews of these desperadoes, the runagates of every country and clime, might be seen swaggering, in open day, about the streets of the little burgh; elbowing its quiet Mynheers; trafficking away their rich outlandish plunder, at half price, to the wary merchant, and then squandering their gains in taverns; drinking, gambling, singing, swearing, shouting, and astounding the neighborhood with sudden brawl and ruffian revelry.

At length the indignation of government was aroused, and it was determined to ferret out this vermin brood from, the colonies. Great consternation took place among the pirates on finding justice in pursuit of them, and their old haunts turned to places of peril. They secreted their money and jewels in lonely out-of-the-way places; buried them about the wild shores of the rivers and sea-coast, and dispersed themselves over the face of the country.

Among the agents employed to hunt them by sea was the renowned Captain Kidd. He had long been a hardy adventurer, a kind of equivocal borderer, half trader, half smuggler, with a tolerable dash of the pickaroon. He had traded for some time among the pirates, lurking about the seas in a little rakish, musquito-built vessel, prying into all kinds of odd places, as busy as a Mother Carey's chicken in a gale of wind.

This nondescript personage was pitched upon by government as the very man to command a vessel fitted out to cruise against the pirates, since he knew all their haunts and lurking-places: acting upon the shrewd old maxim of "setting a rogue to catch a rogue." Kidd accordingly sailed from New York in the Adventure galley, gallantly armed and duly commissioned, and steered his course to the Madeiras, to Bonavista, to Madagascar, and cruised at the entrance of the Red Sea. Instead, however, of making war upon the pirates, he turned pirate himself: captured friend or foe; enriched himself with the spoils of a wealthy Indiaman, manned by Moors, though commanded by an Englishman, and having disposed of his prize, had the hardihood to return to Boston, laden with wealth, with a crew of his comrades at his heels.

His fame had preceded him. The alarm was given of the reappearance of this cut-purse of the ocean. Measures were taken for his arrest; but he had time, it is said, to bury the greater part of his treasures. He even attempted to draw his sword and defend himself when arrested; but was secured and thrown into prison, with several of his followers. They were carried to England in a frigate, where they were tried, condemned, and hanged at Execution Dock. Kidd died hard, for the rope with which he was first tied up broke with his weight, and he tumbled to the ground; he was tied up a second time, and effectually; from whence arose the story of his having been twice hanged.

Such is the main outline of Kidd's history; but it has given birth to an innumerable progeny of traditions. The circumstance of his having buried great treasures of gold and jewels after returning from his cruising set the brains of all the good people along the coast in a ferment. There were rumors on rumors of great sums found here and there; sometimes in one part of the country, sometimes in another; of trees and rocks bearing mysterious marks; doubtless indicating the spots where treasure lay hidden; of coins found with Moorish characters, the plunder of Kidd's eastern prize, but which the common people took for diabolical or magic inscriptions.

Some reported the spoils to have been buried in solitary unsettled places about Plymouth and Cape Cod; many other parts of the Eastern coast, also, and various places in Long Island Sound, have been gilded by these rumors, and have been ransacked by adventurous money-diggers.

In all the stories of these enterprises the devil played a conspicuous part. Either he was conciliated by ceremonies and invocations, or some bargain or compact was made with him. Still he was sure to play the money-diggers some slippery trick. Some had succeeded so far as to touch the iron chest which contained the treasure, when some baffling circumstance was sure to take place. Either the earth would fall in and fill up the pit or some direful noise or apparition would throw the party into a panic and frighten them from the place; and sometimes the devil himself would appear and bear off the prize from their very grasp; and if they visited the place on the next day, not a trace would be seen of their labors of the preceding night.

Such were the vague rumors which for a long time tantalized without gratifying my curiosity on the interesting subject of these pirate traditions. There is nothing in this world so hard to get at as truth. I sought among my favorite sources of authentic information, the oldest inhabitants, and particularly the old Dutch wives of the province; but though I flatter myself I am better versed than most men in the curious history of my native province, yet for a long time my inquiries were unattended with any substantial result.

At length it happened, one calm day in the latter part of summer, that I was relaxing myself from the toils of severe study by a day's amusement in fishing in those waters which had been the favorite resort of my boyhood. I was in company with several worthy burghers of my native city. Our sport was indifferent; the fish did not bite freely; and we had frequently changed our fishing ground without bettering our luck. We at length anchored close under a ledge of rocky coast, on the eastern side of the island of Manhata. It was a still, warm day. The stream whirled and dimpled by us without a wave or even a ripple, and every thing was so calm and quiet that it was almost startling when the kingfisher would pitch himself from the branch of some dry tree, and after suspending himself for a moment in the air to take his aim, would souse into the smooth water after his prey. While we were lolling in our boat, half drowsy with the warm stillness of the day and the dullness of our sport, one of our party, a worthy alderman, was overtaken by a slumber, and, as he dozed, suffered the sinker of his drop-line to lie upon the bottom of the river. On waking, he found he had caught something of importance, from the weight; on drawing it to the surface, we were much surprised to find a long pistol of very curious and outlandish fashion, which, from its rusted condition, and its stock being worm-eaten and covered with barnacles, appeared to have been a long time under water. The unexpected appearance of this document of warfare occasioned much speculation among my pacific companions. One supposed it to have fallen there during the revolutionary war. Another, from the peculiarity of its fashion, attributed it to the voyagers in the earliest days of the settlement; perchance to the renowned Adrian Block, who explored the Sound and discovered Block Island, since so noted for its cheese. But a third, after regarding it for some time, pronounced it to be of veritable Spanish workmanship.

"I'll warrant," said he, "if this pistol could talk it would tell strange stories of hard fights among the Spanish Dons. I've not a doubt but it's a relique of the buccaneers of old times."

"Like enough," said another of the party. "There was Bradish the pirate, who at the time Lord Bellamont made such a stir after the buccaneers, buried money and jewels somewhere in these parts or on Long-Island; and then there was Captain Kidd—"

"Ah, that Kidd was a daring dog," said an iron-faced Cape Cod whaler. "There's a fine old song about him, all to the tune of:

'My name is Robert Kidd,
As I sailed, as I sailed.'

And it tells how he gained the devil's good graces by burying the Bible:

'I had the Bible in my hand,
As I sailed, as I sailed,
And I buried it in the sand,
As I sailed.'

"Egad, if this pistol had belonged to him I should set some store by it out of sheer curiosity. Ah, well, there's an odd story I have heard about one Tom Walker, who, they say, dug up some of Kidd's buried money; and as the fish don't seem to bite at present, I'll tell it to you to pass away time."

THE DEVIL AND TOM WALKER

A few miles from Boston, in Massachusetts, there is a deep inlet winding several miles into the interior of the country from Charles Bay, and terminating in a thickly-wooded swamp, or morass. On one side of this inlet is a beautiful dark grove; on the opposite side the land rises abruptly from the water's edge, into a high ridge on which grow a few scattered oaks of great age and immense size. It was under one of these gigantic trees, according to old stories, that Kidd the pirate buried his treasure. The inlet allowed a facility to bring the money in a boat secretly and at night to the very foot of the hill. The elevation of the place permitted a good look-out to be kept that no one was at hand, while the remarkable trees formed good landmarks by which the place might easily be found again. The old stories add, moreover, that the devil presided at the hiding of the money, and took it under his guardianship; but this, it is well-known, he always does with buried treasure, particularly when it has been ill gotten. Be that as it may, Kidd never returned to recover his wealth; being shortly after seized at Boston, sent out to England, and there hanged for a pirate.

About the year 1727, just at the time when earthquakes were prevalent in New England, and shook many tall sinners down upon their knees, there lived near this place a meagre miserly fellow of the name of Tom Walker. He had a wife as miserly as himself; they were so miserly that they even conspired to cheat each other. Whatever the woman could lay hands on she hid away; a hen could not cackle but she was on the alert to secure the new-laid egg. Her husband was continually prying about to detect her secret hoards, and many and fierce were the conflicts that took place about what ought to have been common property. They lived in a forlorn-looking house, that stood alone and had an air of starvation. A few straggling savin trees, emblems of sterility, grew near it; no smoke ever curled from its chimney; no traveller stopped at its door. A miserable horse, whose ribs were as articulate as the bars of a gridiron, stalked about a field where a thin carpet of moss, scarcely covering the ragged beds of pudding-stone, tantalized and balked his hunger; and sometimes he would lean his head over the fence, looked piteously at the passer-by, and seem to petition deliverance from this land of famine.

The house and its inmates had altogether a bad name. Tom's wife was a tall termagant, fierce of temper, loud of tongue, and strong of arm. Her voice was often heard in wordy warfare with her husband; and his face sometimes showed signs that their conflicts were not confined to words. No one ventured, however, to interfere between them; the lonely wayfarer shrunk within himself at the horrid clamor and clapper-clawing; eyed the den of discord askance, and hurried on his way, rejoicing, if a bachelor, in his celibacy.

One day that Tom Walker had been to a distant part of the neighborhood, he took what he considered a short cut homewards through the swamp. Like most short cuts, it was an ill-chosen route. The swamp was thickly grown with great gloomy pines and hemlocks, some of them ninety feet high; which made it dark at noon-day, and a retreat for all the owls of the neighborhood. It was full of pits and quagmires, partly covered with weeds and mosses; where the green surface often betrayed the traveller into a gulf of black smothering mud; there were also dark and stagnant pools, the abodes of the tadpole, the bull-frog, and the water-snake, and where trunks of pines and hemlocks lay half drowned, half rotting, looking like alligators, sleeping in the mire.

Tom had long been picking his way cautiously through this treacherous forest; stepping from tuft to tuft of rushes and roots which afforded precarious footholds among deep sloughs; or pacing carefully, like a cat, among the prostrate trunks of trees; startled now and then by the sudden screaming of the bittern, or the quacking of a wild duck, rising on the wing from some solitary pool. At length he arrived at a piece of firm ground, which ran out like a peninsula into the deep bosom of the swamp. It had been one of the strongholds of the Indians during their wars with the first colonists. Here they had thrown up a kind of fort which they had looked upon as almost impregnable, and had used as a place of refuge for their squaws and children. Nothing remained of the Indian fort but a few embankments gradually sinking to the level of the surrounding earth, and already overgrown in part by oaks and other forest trees, the foliage of which formed a contrast to the dark pines and hemlocks of the swamp.

It was late in the dusk of evening that Tom Walker reached the old fort, and he paused there for a while to rest himself. Any one but he would have felt unwilling to linger in this lonely, melancholy place, for the common people had a bad opinion of it from the stories handed down from the time of the Indian wars; when it was asserted that the savages held incantations here and made sacrifices to the evil spirit. Tom Walker, however, was not a man to be troubled with any fears of the kind.

He reposed himself for some time on the trunk of a fallen hemlock, listening to the boding cry of the tree-toad, and delving with his walking-staff into a mound of black mould at his feet. As he turned up the soil unconsciously, his staff struck against something hard. He raked it out of the vegetable mould, and lo! a cloven skull with an Indian tomahawk buried deep in it, lay before him. The rust on the weapon showed the time that had elapsed since this death blow had been given. It was a dreary memento of the fierce struggle that had taken place in this last foothold of the Indian warriors.

"Humph!" said Tom Walker, as he gave the skull a kick to shake the dirt from it.

"Let that skull alone!" said a gruff voice.

Tom lifted up his eyes and beheld a great black man, seated directly opposite him on the stump of a tree. He was exceedingly surprised, having neither seen nor heard any one approach, and he was still more perplexed on observing, as well as the gathering gloom would permit, that the stranger was neither negro nor Indian. It is true, he was dressed in a rude, half Indian garb, and had a red belt or sash swathed round his body, but his face was neither black nor copper color, but swarthy and dingy and begrimed with soot, as if he had been accustomed to toil among fires and forges. He had a shock of coarse black hair, that stood out from his head in all directions; and bore an axe on his shoulder.

He scowled for a moment at Tom with a pair of great red eyes.

"What are you doing in my grounds?" said the black man, with a hoarse growling voice.

"Your grounds?" said Tom, with a sneer; "no more your grounds than mine: they belong to Deacon Peabody."

"Deacon Peabody be d——d," said the stranger, "as I flatter myself he will be, if he does not look more to his own sins and less to his neighbor's. Look yonder, and see how Deacon Peabody is faring."

Tom looked in the direction that the stranger pointed, and beheld one of the great trees, fair and flourishing without, but rotten at the core, and saw that it had been nearly hewn through, so that the first high wind was likely to blow it down. On the bark of the tree was scored the name of Deacon Peabody. He now looked round and found most of the tall trees marked with the names of some great men of the colony, and all more or less scored by the axe. The one on which he had been seated, and which had evidently just been hewn down, bore the name of Crowninshield; and he recollected a mighty rich man of that name, who made a vulgar display of wealth, which it was whispered he had acquired by buccaneering.

"He's just ready for burning!" said the black man, with a growl of triumph. "You see I am likely to have a good stock of firewood for winter."

"But what right have you," said Tom, "to cut down Deacon Peabody's timber?"

"The right of prior claim," said the other. "This woodland belonged to me long before one of your white-faced race put foot upon the soil."

"And pray, who are you, if I may be so bold?" said Tom.

"Oh, I go by various names. I am the Wild Huntsman in some countries; the Black Miner in others. In this neighborhood I am known by the name of the Black Woodsman. I am he to whom the red men devoted this spot, and now and then roasted a white man by way of sweet-smelling sacrifice. Since the red men have been exterminated by you white savages, I amuse myself by presiding at the persecutions of quakers and anabaptists; I am the great patron and prompter of slave dealers, and the grand master of the Salem witches."

"The upshot of all which is, that, if I mistake not," said Tom, sturdily, "you are he commonly called Old Scratch."

"The same at your service!" replied the black man, with a half civil nod.

Such was the opening of this interview, according to the old story, though it has almost too familiar an air to be credited. One would think that to meet with such a singular personage in this wild, lonely place, would have shaken any man's nerves; but Tom was a hard-minded fellow, not easily daunted, and he had lived so long with a termagant wife, that he did not even fear the devil.

It is said that after this commencement they had a long and earnest Conversation together, as Tom returned homewards. The black man told him of great sums of money which had been buried by Kidd the pirate, under the oak trees on the high ridge not far from the morass. All these were under his command and protected by his power, so that none could find them but such as propitiated his favor. These he offered to place within Tom Walker's reach, having conceived an especial kindness for him: but they were to be had only on certain conditions. What these conditions were, may easily be surmised, though Tom never disclosed them publicly. They must have been very hard, for he required time to think of them, and he was not a man to stick at trifles where money was in view. When they had reached the edge of the swamp the stranger paused.

"What proof have I that all you have been telling me is true?" said Tom.

"There is my signature," said the black man, pressing his finger on Tom's forehead. So saying, he turned off among the thickets of the swamp, and seemed, as Tom said, to go down, down, down, into the earth, until nothing but his head and shoulders could be seen, and so on until he totally disappeared.

When Tom reached home he found the black print of a finger burnt, as it were, into his forehead, which nothing could obliterate.

The first news his wife had to tell him was the sudden death of Absalom Crowninshield, the rich buccaneer. It was announced in the papers with the usual flourish, that "a great man had fallen in Israel."

Tom recollected the tree which his black friend had just hewn down, and which was ready for burning. "Let the freebooter roast," said Tom, "who cares!" He now felt convinced that all he had heard and seen was no illusion.

He was not prone to let his wife into his confidence; but as this was an uneasy secret, he willingly shared it with her. All her avarice was awakened at the mention of hidden gold, and she urged her husband to comply with the black man's terms and secure what would make them wealthy for life. However Tom might have felt disposed to sell himself to the devil, he was determined not to do so to oblige his wife; so he flatly refused out of the mere spirit of contradiction. Many and bitter were the quarrels they had on the subject, but the more she talked the more resolute was Tom not to be damned to please her. At length she determined to drive the bargain on her own account, and if she succeeded, to keep all the gain to herself.

Being of the same fearless temper as her husband, she sat off for the old Indian fort towards the close of a summer's day. She was many hour's absent. When she came back she was reserved and sullen in her replies. She spoke something of a black man whom she had met about twilight, hewing at the root of a tall tree. He was sulky, however, and would not come to terms; she was to go again with a propitiatory offering, but what it was she forebore to say.

The next evening she sat off again for the swamp, with her apron heavily laden. Tom waited and waited for her, but in vain: midnight came, but she did not make her appearance; morning, noon, night returned, but still she did not come. Tom now grew uneasy for her safety; especially as he found she had carried off in her apron the silver tea pot and spoons and every portable article of value. Another night elapsed, another morning came; but no wife. In a word, she was ever heard of more.

What was her real fate nobody knows, in consequence of so many pretending to know. It is one of those facts that have become confounded by a variety of historians. Some asserted that she lost her way among the tangled mazes of the swamp and sunk into some pit or slough; others, more uncharitable, hinted that she had eloped with the household booty, and made off to some other province; while others assert that the tempter had decoyed her into a dismal quagmire, on top of which her hat was found lying. In confirmation of this, it was said a great black man with an axe on his shoulder was seen late that very evening coming out of the swamp, carrying a bundle tied in a check apron, with an air of surly triumph.

The most current and probable story, however, observes that Tom Walker grew so anxious about the fate of his wife and his property that he sat out at length to seek them both at the Indian fort. During a long summer's afternoon he searched about the gloomy place, but no wife was to be seen. He called her name repeatedly, but she was no where to be heard. The bittern alone responded to his voice, as he flew screaming by;

or the bull-frog croaked dolefully from a neighboring pool. At length, it is said, just in the brown hour of twilight, when the owls began to hoot and the bats to flit about, his attention was attracted by the clamor of carrion crows that were hovering about a cypress tree. He looked and beheld a bundle tied in a check apron and hanging in the branches of a tree; with a great vulture perched hard by, as if keeping watch upon it. He leaped with joy, for he recognized his wife's apron, and supposed it to contain the household valuables.

"Let us get hold of the property," said he consolingly to himself, "and we will endeavor to do without the woman."

As he scrambled up the tree the vulture spread its wide wings, and sailed off screaming into the deep shadows of the forest. Tom seized the check apron, but, woful sight! found nothing but a heart and liver tied up in it.

Such, according to the most authentic old story, was all that was to be found of Tom's wife. She had probably attempted to deal with the black man as she had been accustomed to deal with her husband; but though a female scold is generally considered a match for the devil, yet in this instance she appears to have had the worst of it. She must have died game, however: from the part that remained unconquered. Indeed, it is said Tom noticed many prints of cloven feet deeply stamped about the tree, and several hand-fuls of hair that looked as if they had been plucked from the coarse black shock of the woodsman. Tom knew his wife's prowess by experience. He shrugged his shoulders as he looked at the signs of a fierce clapper-clawing. "Egad," said he to himself, "Old Scratch must have had a tough time of it!"

Tom consoled himself for the loss of his property by the loss of his wife; for he was a little of a philosopher. He even felt something like gratitude towards the black woodsman, who he considered had done him a kindness. He sought, therefore, to cultivate a farther acquaintance with him, but for some time without success; the old black legs played shy, for whatever people may think, he is not always to be had for calling for; he knows how to play his cards when pretty sure of his game.

At length, it is said, when delay had whetted Tom's eagerness to the quick, and prepared him to agree to any thing rather than not gain the promised treasure, he met the black man one evening in his usual woodman dress, with his axe on his shoulder, sauntering along the edge of the swamp, and humming a tune. He affected to receive Tom's advance with great indifference, made brief replies, and went on humming his tune.

By degrees, however, Tom brought him to business, and they began to haggle about the terms on which the former was to have the pirate's treasure. There was one condition which need not be mentioned, being generally understood in all cases where the devil grants favors; but there were others about which, though of less importance, he was inflexibly obstinate. He insisted that the money found through his means should be employed in his service. He proposed, therefore, that Tom should employ it in the black traffic; that is to say, that he should fit out a slave ship. This, however, Tom resolutely refused; he was bad enough, in all conscience; but the devil himself could not tempt him to turn slave dealer.

Finding Tom so squeamish on this point, he did not insist upon it, but proposed instead that he should turn usurer; the devil being extremely anxious for the increase of usurers, looking upon them as his peculiar people.

To this no objections were made, for it was just to Tom's taste.

"You shall open a broker's shop in Boston next month," said the black man.

"I'll do it to-morrow, if you wish," said Tom Walker.

"You shall lend money at two per cent a month."

"Egad, I'll charge four!" replied Tom Walker.

"You shall extort bonds, foreclose mortgages, drive the merchant to bankruptcy—"

"I'll drive him to the d—l," cried Tom Walker, eagerly.

"You are the usurer for my money!" said the black legs, with delight. "When will you want the rhino?"

"This very night."

"Done!" said the devil.

"Done!" said Tom Walker.—So they shook hands and struck a bargain.

A few days' time saw Tom Walker seated behind his desk in a counting house in Boston. His reputation for a ready-moneyed man, who would lend money out for a good consideration, soon spread abroad. Every body remembers the days of Governor Belcher, when money was particularly scarce. It was a time of paper credit. The country had been deluged with government bills; the famous Land Bank had been established; there had been a rage for speculating; the people had run mad with schemes for new settlements; for building cities in the wilderness; land jobbers went about with maps of grants, and townships, and Eldorados, lying nobody knew where, but which every body was ready to purchase. In a word, the great speculating fever which breaks out every now and then in the country, had raged to an alarming degree, and every body was dreaming of making sudden fortunes from nothing. As usual, the fever had subsided; the dream had gone off, and the imaginary fortunes with it; the patients were left in doleful plight, and the whole country resounded with the consequent cry of "hard times."

At this propitious time of public distress did Tom Walker set up as a usurer in Boston. His door was soon thronged by customers. The needy and the adventurous; the gambling speculator; the dreaming land jobber; the thriftless tradesman; the merchant with cracked credit; in short, every one driven to raise money by desperate means and desperate sacrifices, hurried to Tom Walker.

Thus Tom was the universal friend of the needy, and he acted like a "friend in need;" that is to say, he always exacted good pay and good security. In proportion to the distress of the applicant was the hardness of his terms. He accumulated bonds and mortgages; gradually squeezed his customers closer and closer; and sent them, at length, dry as a sponge from his door.

In this way he made money hand over hand; became a rich and mighty man, and exalted his cocked hat upon 'change. He built himself, as usual, a vast house, out of ostentation; but left the greater part of it unfinished and unfurnished out of parsimony. He even set up a carriage in the fullness of his vain-glory, though he nearly starved the horses which drew it; and as the ungreased wheels groaned and screeched on the axle trees, you would have thought you heard the souls of the poor debtors he was squeezing.

As Tom waxed old, however, he grew thoughtful. Having secured the good things of this world, he began to feel anxious about those of the next. He thought with regret on the bargain he had made with his black friend, and set his wits to work to cheat him out of the conditions. He became, therefore, all of a sudden, a violent church-goer. He prayed loudly and strenuously as if heaven were to be taken by force of lungs. Indeed, one might always tell when he had sinned most during the week, by the clamor of his Sunday devotion. The quiet Christians who had been modestly and steadfastly travelling Zion-ward, were struck with self-reproach at seeing themselves so suddenly outstripped in their career by this new-made convert. Tom was as rigid in religious, as in money matters; he was a stern supervisor and censurer of his neighbors, and seemed to think every sin entered up to their account became a credit on his own side of the page. He even talked of the expediency of reviving the persecution of quakers and anabaptists. In a word, Tom's zeal became as notorious as his riches.

Still, in spite of all this strenuous attention to forms, Tom had a Lurking dread that the devil, after all, would have his due. That he might not be taken unawares, therefore, it is said he always carried a small Bible in his coat pocket. He had also a great folio Bible on his counting-house desk, and would frequently be found reading it when people called on business; on such occasions he would lay his green spectacles on the book, to mark the place, while he turned round to drive some usurious bargain.

Some say that Tom grew a little crack-brained in his old days, and that fancying his end approaching, he had his horse new shod, saddled and bridled, and buried with his feet uppermost; because he supposed that at the last day the world would be turned upside down; in which case he should find his horse standing ready for mounting, and he was determined at the worst to give his old friend a run for it. This, however, is probably a mere old wives' fable. If he really did take such a precaution it was totally superfluous; at least so says the authentic old legend, which closes his story in the following manner:

On one hot afternoon in the dog days, just as a terrible black thunder-gust was coming up, Tom sat in his counting-house in his white linen cap and India silk morning-gown. He was on the point of foreclosing a mortgage, by which he would complete the ruin of an unlucky land speculator for whom he had professed the greatest friendship. The poor land jobber begged him to grant a few months' indulgence. Tom had grown testy and irritated and refused another day.

"My family will be ruined and brought upon the parish," said the land jobber.

"Charity begins at home," replied Tom, "I must take care of myself in these hard times."

"You have made so much money out of me," said the speculator.

Tom lost his patience and his piety—"The devil take me," said he, "if I have made a farthing!"

Just then there were three loud knocks at the street door. He stepped out to see who was there. A black man was holding a black horse which neighed and stamped with impatience.

"Tom, you're come for!" said the black fellow, gruffly. Tom shrunk back, but too late. He had left his little Bible at the bottom of his coat pocket, and his big Bible on the desk buried under the mortgage he was about to foreclose: never was sinner taken more unawares. The black man whisked him like a child astride the horse and away he galloped in the midst of a thunder-storm. The clerks stuck their pens behind their ears and stared after him from the windows. Away went Tom Walker, dashing down the street; his white cap bobbing up and down; his morning-gown fluttering in the wind, and his steed striking fire out of the pavement at every bound. When the clerks turned to look for the black man he had disappeared.

Tom Walker never returned to foreclose the mortgage. A countryman who lived on the borders of the swamp, reported that in the height of the thunder-gust he had heard a great clattering of hoofs and a howling along the road, and that when he ran to the window he just caught sight of a figure, such as I have described, on a horse that galloped like mad across the fields, over the hills and down into the black hemlock swamp towards the old Indian fort; and that shortly after a thunder-bolt fell in that direction which seemed to set the whole forest in a blaze.

The good people of Boston shook their heads and shrugged their shoulders, but had been so much accustomed to witches and goblins and tricks of the devil in all kinds of shapes from the first settlement of the colony, that they were not so much horror-struck as might have been expected. Trustees were appointed to take charge of Tom's effects. There was nothing, however, to administer upon. On searching his coffers all his bonds and mortgages were found reduced to cinders. In place of gold and silver, his iron chest was filled with chips and shavings; two skeletons lay in his stable instead of his half-starved horses, and the very next day his great house took fire and was burnt to the ground.

Such was the end of Tom Walker and his ill-gotten wealth. Let all griping money-brokers lay this story to heart. The truth of it is not to be doubted. The very hole under the oak trees, from whence he dug Kidd's money, is to be seen to this day; and the neighboring swamp and old Indian fort is often haunted in stormy nights by a figure on horseback, in a morning-gown and white cap, which is doubtless the troubled spirit of the usurer. In fact, the story has resolved itself into a proverb, and is the origin of that popular saying prevalent throughout New-England, of "The Devil and Tom Walker."

Such, as nearly as I can recollect, was the tenor of the tale told by the Cape Cod whaler. There were divers trivial particulars which I have omitted, and which whiled away the morning very pleasantly, until the time of tide favorable for fishing being passed, it was proposed that we should go to land, and refresh ourselves under the trees, until the noontide heat should have abated.

We accordingly landed on a delectable part of the island of Mannahatta, in that shady and embowered tract formerly under dominion of the ancient family of the Hardenbrooks. It was a spot well known to me in the course of the aquatic expeditions of my boyhood. Not far from where we landed, was an old Dutch family vault, in the side of a bank, which had been an object of great awe and fable among my schoolboy associates. There were several mouldering coffins within; but what gave it a fearful interest with us, was its being connected in our minds with the pirate wreck which lay among the rocks of Hell Gate. There were also stories of smuggling connected with it, particularly during a time that this retired spot was owned by a noted burgher called Ready Money Prevost; a man of whom it was whispered that he had many and mysterious dealings with parts beyond seas. All these things, however, had been jumbled together in our minds in that vague way in which such things are mingled up in the tales of boyhood.

While I was musing upon these matters my companions had spread a repast, from the contents of our well-stored pannier, and we solaced ourselves during the warm sunny hours of mid-day under the shade of a broad chestnut, on the cool grassy carpet that swept down to the water's edge. While lolling on the grass I summoned up the dusky recollections of my boyhood respecting this place, and repeated them like the imperfectly remembered traces of a dream, for the entertainment of my companions. When I had finished, a worthy old burgher, John Josse Vandermoere, the same who once related to me the adventures of Dolph Heyliger, broke silence and observed, that he recollected a story about money-digging which occurred in this very neighborhood. As we knew him to be one of the most authentic narrators of the province we begged him to let us have the particulars, and accordingly, while we refreshed ourselves with a clean long pipe of Blase Moore's tobacco, the authentic John Josse Vandermoere related the following tale.

WOLFERT WEBBER; OR, GOLDEN DREAMS

In the year of grace one thousand seven hundred and—blank—for I do not remember the precise date; however, it was somewhere in the early part of the last century, there lived in the ancient city of the Manhattoes a worthy burgher, Wolfert Webber by name. He was descended from old Cobus Webber of the Brille in Holland, one of the original settlers, famous for introducing the cultivation of cabbages, and who came over to the province during the protectorship of Oloffe Van Kortlandt, otherwise called the Dreamer. The field in which Cobus Webber first planted himself and his cabbages had remained ever since in the family, who continued in the same line of husbandry, with that praiseworthy perseverance for which our Dutch burghers are noted. The whole family genius, during several generations was devoted to the study and development of this one noble vegetable; and to this concentration of intellect may doubtless be ascribed the prodigious size and renown to which the Webber cabbages attained.

The Webber dynasty continued in uninterrupted succession; and never did a line give more unquestionable proofs of legitimacy. The eldest son succeeded to the looks, as well as the territory of his sire; and had the portraits of this line of tranquil potentates been taken, they would have presented a row of heads marvellously resembling in shape and magnitude the vegetables over which they reigned.

The seat of government continued unchanged in the family mansion:— a Dutch-built house, with a front, or rather gable-end of yellow brick, tapering to a point, with the customary iron weathercock at the top. Every thing about the building bore the air of long-settled ease and security. Flights of martins peopled the little coops nailed against the walls, and swallows built their nests under the eaves; and every one knows that these house-loving birds bring good luck to the dwelling where they take up their abode. In a bright sunny morning in early summer, it was delectable to hear their cheerful notes, as they sported about in the pure, sweet air, chirping forth, as it were, the greatness and prosperity of the Webbers.

Thus quietly and comfortably did this excellent family vegetate under the shade of a mighty button-wood tree, which by little and little grew so great as entirely to overshadow their palace. The city gradually spread its suburbs round their domain. Houses sprung up to interrupt their prospects. The rural lanes in the vicinity began to grow into the bustle and populousness of streets; in short, with all the habits of rustic life they began to find themselves the inhabitants of a city.

Still, however, they maintained their hereditary character, and Hereditary possessions, with all the tenacity of petty German princes in the midst of the Empire. Wolfert was the last of the line, and succeeded to the patriarchal bench at the door, under the family tree, and swayed the sceptre of his fathers, a kind of rural potentate in the midst of a metropolis.

To share the cares and sweets of sovereignty, he had taken unto himself a help-mate, one of that excellent kind called stirring women; that is to say, she was one of those notable little housewives who are always busy when there is nothing to do. Her activity however, took one particular direction; her whole life seemed devoted to intense knitting; whether at home or abroad; walking or sitting, her needles were continually in motion, and it is even affirmed that by her unwearied industry she very nearly supplied her household with stockings throughout the year. This worthy couple were blessed with one daughter, who was brought up with great tenderness and care; uncommon pains had been taken with her education, so that she could stitch in every variety of way; make all kinds of pickles and preserves, and mark her own name on a sampler. The influence of her taste was seen also in the family garden, where the ornamental began to mingle with the useful; whole rows of fiery marigolds and splendid hollyhocks bordered the cabbage-beds; and gigantic sunflowers lolled their broad, jolly faces over the fences, seeming to ogle most affectionately the passers-by.

Thus reigned and vegetated Wolfert Webber over his paternal acres, peaceably and contentedly. Not but that, like all other sovereigns, he had his occasional cares and vexations. The growth of his native city sometimes caused him annoyance. His little territory gradually became hemmed in by streets and houses, which intercepted air and sunshine. He was now and then subject to the irruptions of the border population, that infest the streets of a metropolis, who would sometimes make midnight forays into his dominions, and carry off captive whole platoons of his noblest subjects. Vagrant swine would make a descent, too, now and then, when the gate was left open, and lay all waste before them; and mischievous urchins would often decapitate the illustrious sunflowers, the glory of the garden, as they lolled their heads so fondly over the walls. Still all these were petty grievances, which might now and then ruffle the surface of his mind, as a summer breeze will ruffle the surface of a mill-pond; but they could not disturb the deep-seated quiet of his soul. He would seize a trusty staff, that stood behind the door, issue suddenly out, and anoint the back of the aggressor, whether pig or urchin, and then return within doors, marvellously refreshed and tranquillized.

The chief cause of anxiety to honest Wolfert, however, was the growing prosperity of the city. The expenses of living doubled and trebled; but he could not double and treble the magnitude of his cabbages; and the number of competitors prevented the increase of price; thus, therefore, while every one around him grew richer, Wolfert grew poorer, and he could not, for the life of him, perceive how the evil was to be remedied.

This growing care which increased from day to day, had its gradual effect upon our worthy burgher; insomuch, that it at length implanted two or three wrinkles on his brow; things unknown before in the family of the Webbers; and it seemed to pinch up the corners of his cocked hat into an expression of anxiety, totally opposite to the tranquil, broad-brimmed, low-crowned beavers of his illustrious progenitors.

Perhaps even this would not have materially disturbed the serenity of his mind had he had only himself and his wife to care for; but there was his daughter gradually growing to maturity; and all the world knows when daughters begin to ripen no fruit or flower requires so much looking after. I have no talent at describing female charms, else fain would I depict the progress of this little Dutch beauty. How her blue eyes grew deeper and deeper, and her cherry lips redder and redder; and how she ripened and ripened, and rounded and rounded in the opening breath of sixteen summers, until, in her seventeenth spring, she seemed ready to burst out of her bodice like a half-blown rose-bud.

Ah, well-a-day! could I but show her as she was then, tricked out on a Sunday morning in the hereditary finery of the old Dutch clothes-press, of which her mother had confided to her the key. The wedding dress of her grandmother, modernized for use, with sundry ornaments, handed down as heirlooms in the family. Her pale brown hair smoothed with buttermilk in flat waving lines on each side of her fair forehead. The chain of yellow virgin gold, that encircled her neck; the little cross, that just rested at the entrance of a soft valley of happiness, as if it would sanctify the place. The—but pooh!—it is not for an old man like me to be prosing about female beauty: suffice it to say, Amy had attained her seventeenth year. Long since had her sampler exhibited hearts in couples desperately transfixed with arrows, and true lovers' knots worked in deep blue silk; and it was evident she began to languish for some more interesting occupation than the rearing of sunflowers or pickling of cucumbers.

At this critical period of female existence, when the heart within a damsel's bosom, like its emblem, the miniature which hangs without, is apt to be engrossed by a single image, a new visitor began to make his appearance under the roof of Wolfert Webber. This was Dirk Waldron, the only son of a poor widow, but who could boast of more fathers than any lad in the province; for his mother had had four husbands, and this only child, so that though born in her last wedlock, he might fairly claim to be the tardy fruit of a long course of cultivation. This son of four fathers united the merits and the vigor of his sires. If he had not a great family before him, he seemed likely to have a great one after him; for you had only to look at the fresh gamesome youth, to see that he was formed to be the founder of a mighty race.

This youngster gradually became an intimate visitor of the family. He talked little, but he sat long. He filled the father's pipe when it was empty, gathered up the mother's knitting-needle, or ball of worsted when it fell to the ground; stroked the sleek coat of the tortoise-shell cat, and replenished the teapot for the daughter from the bright copper kettle that sung before the fire. All these quiet little offices may seem of trifling import, but when true love is translated into Low Dutch, it is in this way that it eloquently expresses itself. They were not lost upon the Webber family. The winning youngster found marvellous favor in the eyes of the mother; the tortoise-shell cat, albeit the most staid and demure of her kind, gave indubitable signs of approbation of his visits, the tea-kettle seemed to sing out a cheering note of welcome at his approach, and if the sly glances of the daughter might be rightly read, as she sat bridling and dimpling, and sewing by her mother's side, she was not a wit behind Dame Webber, or grimalkin, or the tea-kettle in good-will.

Wolfert alone saw nothing of what was going on. Profoundly wrapt up in meditation on the growth of the city and his cabbages, he sat looking in the fire, and puffing his pipe in silence. One night, however, as the gentle Amy, according to custom, lighted her lover to the outer door, and he, according to custom, took his parting salute, the smack resounded so vigorously through the long, silent entry as to startle even the dull ear of Wolfert. He was slowly roused to a new source of anxiety. It had never entered into his head, that this mere child, who, as it seemed but the other day, had been climbing about his knees, and playing with dolls and baby-houses, could all at once be thinking of love and matrimony. He rubbed his eyes, examined into the fact, and really found that while he had been dreaming of other matters, she had actually grown into a woman, and what was more, had fallen in love. Here were new cares for poor Wolfert. He was a kind father, but he was a prudent man. The young man was a very stirring lad; but then he had neither money or land. Wolfert's ideas all ran in one channel, and he saw no alternative in case of a marriage, but to portion off the young couple with a corner of his cabbage garden, the whole of which was barely sufficient for the support of his family.

Like a prudent father, therefore, he determined to nip this passion in the bud, and forbade the youngster the house, though sorely did it go against his fatherly heart, and many a silent tear did it cause in the bright eye of his daughter. She showed herself, however, a pattern of filial piety and obedience. She never pouted and sulked; she never flew in the face of parental authority; she never fell into a passion, or fell into hysterics, as many romantic novel-read young ladies would do. Not she, indeed! She was none such heroical rebellious trumpery, I warrant ye. On the contrary, she acquiesced like an obedient daughter; shut the street-door in her lover's face, and if ever she did grant him an interview, it was either out of the kitchen window, or over the garden fence.

Wolfert was deeply cogitating these things in his mind, and his brow wrinkled with unusual care, as he wended his way one Saturday afternoon to a rural inn, about two miles from the city. It was a favorite resort of the Dutch part of the community from being always held by a Dutch line of landlords, and retaining an air and relish of the good old times. It was a Dutch-built house, that had probably been a country seat of some opulent burgher in the early time of the settlement. It stood near a point of land, called Corlears Hook, which stretches out into the Sound, and against which the tide, at its flux and reflux, sets with extraordinary rapidity. The venerable and somewhat crazy mansion was distinguished from afar, by a grove of elms and sycamores that seemed to wave a hospitable invitation, while a few weeping willows with their dank, drooping foliage, resembling falling waters, gave an idea of coolness, that rendered it an attractive spot during the heats of summer.

Here, therefore, as I said, resorted many of the old inhabitants of the Manhattoes, where, while some played at the shuffle-board and quoits and ninepins, others smoked a deliberate pipe, and talked over public affairs.

It was on a blustering autumnal afternoon that Wolfert made his visit to the inn. The grove of elms and willows was stripped of its leaves, which whirled in rustling eddies about the fields.

The ninepin alley was deserted, for the premature chilliness of the day had driven the company within doors. As it was Saturday afternoon, the habitual club was in session, composed principally of regular Dutch burghers, though mingled occasionally with persons of various character and country, as is natural in a place of such motley population.

Beside the fire-place, and in a huge leather-bottomed armchair, sat the dictator of this little world, the venerable Rem, or, as it was pronounced, Ramm Rapelye.

He was a man of Walloon race, and illustrious for the antiquity of his line, his great grandmother having been the first white child born in the province. But he was still more illustrious for his wealth and dignity: he had long filled the noble office of alderman, and was a man to whom the governor himself took off his hat. He had maintained possession of the leathern-bottomed chair from time immemorial; and had gradually waxed in bulk as he sat in his seat of government, until in the course of years he filled its whole magnitude. His word was decisive with his subjects; for he was so rich a man, that he was never expected to support any opinion by argument. The landlord waited on him with peculiar officiousness; not that he paid better than his neighbors, but then the coin of a rich man seems always to be so much more acceptable. The landlord had always a pleasant word and a joke, to insinuate in the ear of the august Ramm. It is true, Ramm never laughed, and, indeed, maintained a mastiff-like gravity, and even surliness of aspect, yet he now and then rewarded mine host with a token of approbation; which, though nothing more nor less than a kind of grunt, yet delighted the landlord more than a broad laugh from a poorer man.

"This will be a rough night for the money-diggers," said mine host, as a gust of wind howled round the house, and rattled at the windows.

"What, are they at their works again?" said an English half-pay captain, with one eye, who was a frequent attendant at the inn.

"Aye, are they," said the landlord, "and well may they be. They've had luck of late. They say a great pot of money has been dug up in the field, just behind Stuyvesant's orchard. Folks think it must have been buried there in old times by Peter Stuyvesant, the Dutch Governor."

"Fudge!" said the one-eyed man of war, as he added a small portion of water to a bottom of brandy.

"Well, you may believe, or not, as you please," said mine host, somewhat nettled; "but every body knows that the old governor buried a great deal of his money at the time of the Dutch troubles, when the English red-coats seized on the province. They say, too, the old gentleman walks; aye, and in the very Same dress that he wears in the picture which hangs up in the family house."

"Fudge!" said the half-pay officer.

"Fudge, if you please!—But didn't Corney Van Zandt see him at midnight, stalking about in the meadow with his wooden leg, and a drawn sword in his hand, that flashed like fire? And what can he be walking for, but because people have been troubling the place where he buried his money in old times?"

Here the landlord was interrupted by several guttural sounds from Ramm Rapelye, betokening that he was laboring with the unusual production of an idea. As he was too great a man to be slighted by a prudent publican, mine host respectfully paused until he should deliver himself. The corpulent frame of this mighty burgher now gave all the symptoms of a volcanic mountain on the point of an eruption. First, there was a certain heaving of the abdomen, not unlike an earthquake; then was emitted a cloud of tobacco smoke from that crater, his mouth; then there was a kind of rattle in the throat, as if the idea were working its way up through a region of phlegm; then there were several disjointed members of a sentence thrown out, ending in a cough; at length his voice forced its way in the slow, but absolute tone of a man who feels the weight of his purse, if not of his ideas; every portion of his speech being marked by a testy puff of tobacco smoke.

"Who talks of old Peter Stuyvesant's walking?—*puff*—Have people no respect for persons?—*puff*—*puff*—Peter Stuyvesant knew better what to do with his money than to bury it—*puff*—I know the Stuyvesant family—*puff*—every one of them—*puff*—not a more respectable family in the province—*puff*—old standers—*puff*—warm householders—*puff*—none of your upstarts—*puff*—*puff*—*puff*.—Don't talk to me of Peter Stuyvesant's walking—*puff*—*puff*—*puff*—*puff*."

Here the redoubtable Ramm contracted his brow, clasped up his mouth, till it wrinkled at each corner, and redoubled his smoking with such vehemence, that the cloudly volumes soon wreathed round his head, as the smoke envelopes the awful summit of Mount Etna.

A general silence followed the sudden rebuke of this very rich man. The subject, however, was too interesting to be readily abandoned. The conversation soon broke forth again from the lips of Peechy Prauw Van Hook, the chronicler of the club, one of those narrative old men who seem to grow incontinent of words, as they grow old, until their talk flows from them almost involuntarily.

Peechy, who could at any time tell as many stories in an evening as his hearers could digest in a month, now resumed the conversation, by affirming that, to his knowledge, money had at different times been dug up in various parts of the island. The lucky persons who had discovered them had always dreamt of them three times beforehand, and what was worthy of remark, these treasures had never been found but by some descendant of the good old Dutch families, which clearly proved that they had been buried by Dutchmen in the olden time.

"Fiddle-stick with your Dutchmen!" cried the half-pay officer. "The Dutch had nothing to do with them. They were all buried by Kidd, the pirate, and his crew."

Here a key-note was touched that roused the whole company. The name of Captain Kidd was like a talisman in those times, and was associated with a thousand marvellous stories.

The half-pay officer was a man of great weight among the peaceable members of the club, by reason of his military character, and of the gun-powder scenes which, by his own account, he had witnessed.

The golden stories of Kidd, however, were resolutely rivalled by the tales of Peechy Prauw, who, rather than suffer his Dutch progenitors to be eclipsed by a foreign freebooter, enriched every spot in the neighborhood with the hidden wealth of Peter Stuyvesant and his contemporaries.

Not a word of this conversation was lost upon Wolfert Webber. He returned pensively home, full of magnificent ideas of buried riches. The soil of his native island seemed to be turned into gold-dust; and every field teemed with treasure. His head almost reeled at the thought how often he must have heedlessly rambled over places where countless sums lay, scarcely covered by the turf beneath his feet. His mind was in a vertigo with this whirl of new ideas. As he came in sight of the venerable mansion of his forefathers, and the little realm where the Webbers had so long and so contentedly flourished, his gorge rose at the narrowness of his destiny.

"Unlucky Wolfert!" exclaimed he, "others can go to bed and dream themselves into whole mines of wealth; they have but to seize a spade in the morning, and turn up doubloons like potatoes; but thou must dream of hardship, and rise to poverty—must dig thy field from year's end to year's end, and—and yet raise nothing but cabbages!"

Wolfert Webber went to bed with a heavy heart; and it was long before the golden visions that disturbed his brain, permitted him to sink into repose. The same visions, however, extended into his sleeping thoughts, and assumed a more definite form. He dreamt that he had discovered an immense treasure in the centre of his garden. At every stroke of the spade he laid bare a golden ingot; diamond crosses sparkled out of the dust; bags of money turned up their bellies, corpulent with pieces of eight, or venerable doubloons; and chests, wedged close with moidores, ducats, and pistareens, yawned before his ravished eyes, and vomited forth their glittering contents.

Wolfert awoke a poorer man than ever. He had no heart to go about his daily concerns, which appeared so paltry and profitless; but sat all day long in the chimney-corner, picturing to himself ingots and heaps of gold in the fire. The next night his dream was repeated. He was again in his garden, digging, and laying open stores of hidden wealth. There was something very singular in this repetition. He passed another day of reverie, and though it was cleaning-day, and the house, as usual in Dutch households, completely topsy-turvy, yet he sat unmoved amidst the general uproar.

The third night he went to bed with a palpitating heart. He put on his red nightcap, wrong side outwards for good luck. It was deep midnight before his anxious mind could settle itself into sleep. Again the golden dream was repeated, and again he saw his garden teeming with ingots and money-bags.

Wolfert rose the next morning in complete bewilderment. A dream three times repeated was never known to lie; and if so, his fortune was made.

In his agitation he put on his waistcoat with the hind part before, and this was a corroboration of good luck. He no longer doubted that a huge store of money lay buried somewhere in his cabbage-field, coyly waiting to be sought for, and he half repined at having so long been scratching about the surface of the soil, instead of digging to the centre.

He took his seat at the breakfast-table full of these speculations; asked his daughter to put a lump of gold in to his tea, and on handing his wife a plate of slap-jacks, begging her to help herself to a doubloon.

His grand care now was how to secure this immense treasure without it being known. Instead of working regularly in his grounds in the day-time, he now stole from his bed at night, and with spade and pickaxe, went to work to rip up and dig about his paternal acres, from one end to the other. In a little time the whole garden, which had presented such a goodly and regular appearance, with its phalanx of cabbages, like a vegetable army in battle array, was reduced to a scene of devastation, while the relentless Wolfert, with nightcap on head, and lantern and spade in hand, stalked through the slaughtered ranks, the destroying angel of his own vegetable world.

Every morning bore testimony to the ravages of the preceding night in cabbages of all ages and conditions, from the tender sprout to the full-grown head, piteously rooted from their quiet beds like worthless weeds, and left to wither in the sunshine. It was in vain Wolfert's wife remonstrated; it was in vain his darling daughter wept over the destruction of some favorite marygold. "Thou shalt have gold of another guess-sort," he would cry, chucking her under the chin; "thou shalt have a string of crooked ducats for thy wedding-necklace, my child." His family began really to fear that the poor man's wits were diseased. He muttered in his sleep at night of mines of wealth, of pearls and diamonds and bars of gold. In the day-time he was moody and abstracted, and walked about as if in a trance. Dame Webber held frequent councils with all the old women of the neighborhood, not omitting the parish dominie; scarce an hour in the day but a knot of them might be seen wagging their white caps together round her door, while the poor woman made some piteous recital. The daughter, too, was fain to seek for more frequent consolation from the stolen interviews of her favored swain, Dirk Waldron. The delectable little Dutch songs with which she used to dulcify the house grew less and less frequent, and she would forget her sewing and look wistfully in her father's face as he sat pondering by the fireside.

Wolfert caught her eye one day fixed on him thus anxiously, and for a moment was roused from his golden reveries—"Cheer up, my girl," said he, exultingly, "why dost thou droop?—thou shalt hold up thy head one day with the—and the Schenaerhorns, the Van Hornes, and the Van Dams— the patroon himself shall be glad to get thee for his son!"

Amy shook her head at this vain-glorious boast, and was more than ever in doubt of the soundness of the good man's intellect.

In the meantime Wolfert went on digging, but the field was extensive, and as his dream had indicated no precise spot, he had to dig at random.

The winter set in before one-tenth of the scene of promise had been explored. The ground became too frozen and the nights too cold for the labors of the spade. No sooner, however, did the returning warmth of spring loosen the soil, and the small frogs begin to pipe in the meadows, but Wolfert resumed his labors with renovated zeal. Still, however, the hours of industry were reversed. Instead of working cheerily all day, planting and setting out his vegetables, he remained thoughtfully idle, until the shades of night summoned him to his secret labors. In this way he continued to dig from night to night, and week to week, and month to month, but not a stiver did he find. On the contrary, the more he digged the poorer he grew. The rich soil of his garden was digged away, and the sand and gravel from beneath were thrown to the surface, until the whole field presented an aspect of sandy barrenness.

In the meantime the seasons gradually rolled on. The little frogs that had piped in the meadows in early spring, croaked as bull-frogs in the brooks during the summer heats, and then sunk into silence. The peach tree budded, blossomed, and bore its fruit. The swallows and martins came, twittered about the roof, built their nests, reared their young, held their congress along the eaves, and then winged their flight in search of another spring. The caterpillar spun its winding-sheet, dangled in it from the great buttonwood tree that shaded the house, turned into a moth, fluttered with the last sunshine of summer, and disappeared; and finally the leaves of the buttonwood tree turned yellow, then brown, then rustled one by one to the ground, and whirling about in little eddies of wind and dust, whispered that winter was at hand.

Wolfert gradually awoke from his dream of wealth as the year declined. He had reared no crop to supply the wants of his household during the sterility of winter. The season was long and severe, and for the first time the family was really straightened in its comforts. By degrees a revulsion of thought took place in Wolfert's mind, common to those whose golden dreams have been disturbed by pinching realities. The idea gradually stole upon him that he should come to want. He already considered himself one of the most unfortunate men in the province, having lost such an incalculable amount of undiscovered treasure, and now, when thousands of pounds had eluded his search, to be perplexed for shillings and pence was cruel in the extreme.

Haggard care gathered about his brow; he went about with a money-seeking air, his eyes bent downwards into the dust, and carrying his hands in his pockets, as men are apt to do when they have nothing else to put into them. He could not even pass the city almshouse without giving it a rueful glance, as if destined to be his future abode.

The strangeness of his conduct and of his looks occasioned much speculation and remark. For a long time he was suspected of being crazy, and then every body pitied him; at length it began to be suspected that he was poor, and then every body avoided him.

The rich old burghers of his acquaintance met him, outside of the door when he called, entertained him hospitably on the threshold, pressed him warmly by the hand on parting, shook their heads as he walked away, with the kind-hearted expression of "poor Wolfert," and turned a corner nimbly, if by chance they saw him approaching as they walked the streets. Even the barber and cobbler of the neighborhood, and a tattered tailor in an alley hard by, three of the poorest and merriest rogues in the world, eyed him with that abundant sympathy which usually attends a lack of means, and there is not a doubt but their pockets would have been at his command, only that they happened to be empty.

Thus every body deserted the Webber mansion, as if poverty were contagious, like the plague; every body but honest Dirk Waldron, who still kept up his stolen visits to the daughter, and indeed seemed to wax more affectionate as the fortunes of his mistress were on the wane.

Many months had elapsed since Wolfert had frequented his old resort, the rural inn. He was taking a long lonely walk one Saturday afternoon, musing over his wants and disappointments, when his feet took instinctively their wonted direction, and on awaking out of a reverie, he found himself before the door of the inn. For some moments he hesitated whether to enter, but his heart yearned for companionship; and where can a ruined man find better companionship than at a tavern, where there is neither sober example nor sober advice to put him out of countenance?

Wolfert found several of the old frequenters of the tavern at their usual posts, and seated in their usual places; but one was missing, the great Ramm Rapelye, who for many years had filled the chair of state. His place was supplied by a stranger, who seemed, however, completely at home in the chair and the tavern. He was rather under-size, but deep-chested, square, and muscular. His broad shoulders, double joints, and bow-knees, gave tokens of prodigious strength. His face was dark and weather-beaten; a deep scar, as if from the slash of a cutlass, had almost divided his nose, and made a gash in his upper lip, through which his teeth shone like a bull-dog's. A mass of iron gray hair gave a grizzly finish to his hard-favored visage. His dress was of an amphibious character. He wore an old hat edged with tarnished lace, and cocked in martial style, on one side of his head; a rusty blue military coat with brass buttons, and a wide pair of short petticoat trousers, or rather breeches, for they were gathered up at the knees. He ordered every body about him with an authoritative air; talked in a brattling voice, that sounded like the crackling of thorns under a pot; damned the landlord and servants with perfect impunity, and was waited upon with greater obsequiousness than had ever been shown to the mighty Ramm himself.

Wolfert's curiosity was awakened to know who and what was this stranger who had thus usurped absolute sway in this ancient domain. He could get nothing, however, but vague information. Peechy Prauw took him aside, into a remote corner of the hall, and there in an under-voice, and with great caution, imparted to him all that he knew on the subject. The inn had been aroused several months before, on a dark stormy night, by repeated long shouts, that seemed like the howlings of a wolf. They came from the water-side; and at length were distinguished to be hailing the house in the seafaring manner. "House-a-hoy!" The landlord turned out with his head-waiter, tapster, hostler, and errand boy—that is to say with his old negro Cuff. On approaching the place from whence the voice proceeded, they found this amphibious-looking personage at the water's edge, quite alone, and seated on a great oaken sea-chest. How he came there, whether he had been set on shore from some boat, or had floated to land on his chest, nobody could tell, for he did not seem disposed to answer questions, and there was something in his looks and manners that put a stop to all questioning. Suffice it to say, he took possession of a corner room of the inn, to which his chest was removed with great difficulty. Here he had remained ever since, keeping about the inn and its vicinity. Sometimes, it is true, he disappeared for one, two, or three days at a time, going and returning without giving any notice or account of his movements. He always appeared to have plenty of money, though often of very strange, outlandish coinage; and he regularly paid his bill every evening before turning in.

He had fitted up his room to his own fancy, having slung a hammock from the ceiling instead of a bed, and decorated the walls with rusty pistols and cutlasses of foreign workmanship. A great part of his time was passed in this room, seated by the window, which commanded a wide view of the Sound, a short old-fashioned pipe in his mouth, a glass of rum toddy at his elbow, and a pocket telescope in his hand, with which he reconnoitred every boat that moved upon the water. Large square-rigged vessels seemed to excite but little attention; but the moment he descried any thing with a shoulder-of-mutton sail, or that a barge, or yawl, or jolly boat hove in sight, up went the telescope, and he examined it with the most scrupulous attention.

All this might have passed without much notice, for in those times the province was so much the resort of adventurers of all characters and climes that any oddity in dress or behavior attracted but little attention. But in a little while this strange sea monster, thus strangely cast up on dry land, began to encroach upon the long-established customs and customers of the place; to interfere in a dictatorial manner in the affairs of the ninepin alley and the bar-room, until in the end he usurped an absolute command over the little inn. It was in vain to attempt to withstand his authority. He was not exactly quarrelsome, but boisterous and peremptory, like one accustomed to tyrannize on a quarter deck; and there was a dare-devil air about every thing he said and did, that inspired a wariness in all bystanders. Even the half-pay officer, so long the hero of the club, was soon silenced by him; and the quiet burghers stared with wonder at seeing their inflammable man of war so readily and quietly extinguished.

And then the tales that he would tell were enough to make a peaceable man's hair stand on end. There was not a sea fight, or marauding or free-booting adventure that had happened within the last twenty years but he seemed perfectly versed in it. He delighted to talk of the exploits of the buccaneers in the West-Indies and on the Spanish Main. How his eyes would glisten as he described the waylaying of treasure ships, the desperate fights, yard arm and yard arm—broadside and broad side—the boarding and capturing of large Spanish galleons! with what chuckling relish would he describe the descent upon some rich Spanish colony; the rifling of a church; the sacking of a convent! You would have thought you heard some gormandizer dilating upon the roasting a savory goose at Michaelmas as he described the roasting of some Spanish Don to make him discover his treasure—a detail given with a minuteness that made every rich old burgher present turn uncomfortably in his chair. All this would be told with infinite glee, as if he considered it an excellent joke; and then he would give such a tyrannical leer in the face of his next neighbor, that the poor man would be fain to laugh out of sheer faint-heartedness. If any one, however, pretended to contradict him in any of his stories he was on fire in an instant. His very cocked hat assumed a momentary fierceness, and seemed to resent the contradiction.—"How the devil should you know as well as I! I tell you it was as I say!" and he would at the same time let slip a broadside of thundering oaths and tremendous sea phrases, such as had never been heard before within those peaceful walls.

Indeed, the worthy burghers began to surmise that he knew more of these stories than mere hearsay. Day after day their conjectures concerning him grew more and more wild and fearful. The strangeness of his manners, the mystery that surrounded him, all made him something incomprehensible in their eyes. He was a kind of monster of the deep to them—he was a merman—he was behemoth—he was leviathan—in short, they knew not what he was.

The domineering spirit of this boisterous sea urchin at length grew quite intolerable. He was no respecter of persons; he contradicted the richest burghers without hesitation; he took possession of the sacred elbow chair, which time out of mind had been the seat of sovereignty of the illustrious Ramm Rapelye. Nay, he even went so far in one of his rough jocular moods, as to slap that mighty burgher on the back, drink his toddy and wink in his face, a thing scarcely to be believed. From this time Ramm Rapelye appeared no more at the inn; his example was followed by several of the most eminent customers, who were too rich to tolerate being bullied out of their opinions, or being obliged to laugh at another man's jokes. The landlord was almost in despair, but he knew not how to get rid of this sea monster and his sea-chest, which seemed to have grown like fixtures, or excrescences on his establishment.

Such was the account whispered cautiously in Wolfert's ear, by the narrator, Peechy Prauw, as he held him by the button in a corner of the hall, casting a wary glance now and then towards the door of the bar-room, lest he should be overheard by the terrible hero of his tale.

Wolfert took his seat in a remote part of the room in silence; impressed with profound awe of this unknown, so versed in freebooting history. It was to him a wonderful instance of the revolutions of mighty empires, to find the venerable Ramm Rapelye thus ousted from the throne; a rugged tarpaulin dictating from his elbow chair, hectoring the patriarchs, and filling this tranquil little realm with brawl and bravado.

The stranger was on this evening in a more than usually communicative mood, and was narrating a number of astounding stories of plunderings and burnings upon the high seas. He dwelt upon them with peculiar relish, heightening the frightful particulars in proportion to their effect on his peaceful auditors. He gave a long swaggering detail of the capture of a Spanish merchantman. She was laying becalmed during a long summer's day, just off from an island which was one of the lurking places of the pirates. They had reconnoitred her with their spy-glasses from the shore, and ascertained her character and force. At night a picked crew of daring fellows set off for her in a whale boat. They approached with muffled oars, as she lay rocking idly with the undulations of the sea and her sails flapping against the masts. They were close under her stern before the guard on deck was aware of their approach. The alarm was given; the pirates threw hand grenades on deck and sprang up the main chains sword in hand.

The crew flew to arms, but in great confusion some were shot down, others took refuge in the tops; others were driven overboard and drowned, while others fought hand to hand from the main deck to the quarter deck, disputing gallantly every inch of ground. There were three Spanish gentlemen on board with their ladies, who made the most desperate resistance; they defended the companion-way, cut down several of their assailants, and fought like very devils, for they were maddened by the shrieks of the ladies from the cabin. One of the Dons was old and soon despatched. The other two kept their ground vigorously, even though the captain of the pirates was among their assailants. Just then there was a shout of victory from the main deck. "The ship is ours!" cried the pirates.

One of the Dons immediately dropped his sword and surrendered; the other, who was a hot-headed youngster, and just married, gave the captain a slash in the face that laid all open. The captain just made out to articulate the words "no quarter."

"And what did they do with their prisoners?" said Peechy Prauw, eagerly.

"Threw them all overboard!" said the merman.

A dead pause followed this reply. Peechy Prauw shrunk quietly back like a man who had unwarily stolen upon the lair of a sleeping lion. The honest burghers cast fearful glances at the deep scar slashed across the visage of the stranger, and moved their chairs a little farther off. The seaman, however, smoked on without moving a muscle, as though he either did not perceive or did not regard the unfavorable effect he had produced upon his hearers.

The half-pay officer was the first to break the silence; for he was Continually tempted to make ineffectual head against this tyrant of the seas, and to regain his lost consequence in the eyes of his ancient companions. He now tried to match the gunpowder tales of the stranger by others equally tremendous. Kidd, as usual, was his hero, concerning whom he had picked up many of the floating traditions of the province. The seaman had always evinced a settled pique against the red-faced warrior. On this occasion he listened with peculiar impatience. He sat with one arm a-kimbo, the other elbow on a table, the hand holding on to the small pipe he was pettishly puffing; his legs crossed, drumming with one foot on the ground and casting every now and then the side glance of a basilisk at the prosing captain. At length the latter spoke of Kidd's having ascended the Hudson with some of his crew, to land his plunder in secrecy.

"Kidd up the Hudson!" burst forth the seaman, with a tremendous oath; "Kidd never was up the Hudson!"

"I tell you he was," said the other. "Aye, and they say he buried a quantity of treasure on the little flat that runs out into the river, called the Devil's Dans Kammer."

"The Devil's Dans Kammer in your teeth!" cried the seaman. "I tell you Kidd never was up the Hudson—what the plague do you know of Kidd and his haunts?"

"What do I know?" echoed the half-pay officer; "why, I was in London at the time of his trial, aye, and I had the pleasure of seeing him hanged at Execution Dock."

"Then, sir, let me tell you that you saw as pretty a fellow hanged as ever trod shoe leather. Aye!" putting his face nearer to that of the officer, "and there was many a coward looked on, that might much better have swung in his stead."

The half-pay officer was silenced; but the indignation thus pent up in his bosom glowed with intense vehemence in his single eye, which kindled like a coal.

Peechy Prauw, who never could remain silent, now took up the word and in a pacifying tone observed that the gentleman certainly was in the right. Kidd never did bury money up the Hudson, nor indeed in any of those parts, though many affirm the fact. It was Bradish and others of the buccaneers who had buried money, some said in Turtle Bay, others in Long-Island, others in the neighborhood of Hell Gate. Indeed, added he, recollect an adventure of Mud Sam, the negro fisherman, many years ago which some think had something to do with the buccaneers. As we are all friends here, and as it will go no farther, I'll tell it to you.

"Upon a dark night many years ago, as Sam was returning from fishing Hell Gate—"

Here the story was nipped in the bud by a sudden movement from the unknown, who, laying his iron fist on the table, knuckles downward, with a quiet force that indented the very boards, and looking grimly over shoulder, with the grin of an angry bear. "Heark'ee, neighbor," said he, with significant nodding of the head, "you'd better let the buccaneers and their money alone—they're not for old men and old women to meddle with. They fought hard for their money, they gave body and soul for it, and wherever lies buried, depend upon it he must have a tug with the devil who gets

This sudden explosion was succeeded by a blank silence throughout the room. Peechy Prauw shrunk within himself, and even the red-faced officer turned pale. Wolfert, who, from a dark corner of the room, had listened with intense eagerness to all this talk about buried treasure, looked with mingled awe and reverence on this bold buccaneer, for such he really suspected him to be. There was a chinking of gold and a sparkling of jewels

in all his stories about the Spanish Main that gave a value to every period, and Wolfert would have given any thing for the rummaging of the ponderous sea-chest, which his imagination crammed full of golden chalices and crucifixes and jolly round bags of doubloons.

The dead stillness that had fallen upon the company was at length interrupted by the stranger, who pulled out a prodigious watch of curious and ancient workmanship, and which in Wolferts' eyes had a decidedly Spanish look. On touching a spring it struck ten o'clock; upon which the sailor called for his reckoning, and having paid it out of a handful of outlandish coin, he drank off the remainder of his beverage, and without taking leave of any one, rolled out of the room, muttering to himself as he stamped up-stairs to his chamber.

It was some time before the company could recover from the silence into which they had been thrown. The very footsteps of the stranger, which were heard now and then as he traversed his chamber, inspired awe.

Still the conversation in which they had been engaged was too interesting not to be resumed. A heavy thunder-gust had gathered up unnoticed while they were lost in talk, and the torrents of rain that fell forbade all thoughts of setting off for home until the storm should subside. They drew nearer together, therefore, and entreated the worthy Peechy Prauw to continue the tale which had been so discourteously interrupted. He readily complied, whispering, however, in a tone scarcely above his breath, and drowned occasionally by the rolling of the thunder, and he would pause every now and then, and listen with evident awe, as he heard the heavy footsteps of the stranger pacing overhead.

The following is the purport of his story.

THE ADVENTURE OF SAM, THE BLACK FISHERMAN, COMMONLY DENOMINATED MUD SAM.

Every body knows Mud Sam, the old negro fisherman who has fished about the Sound for the last twenty or thirty years. Well, it is now many years since that Sam, who was then a young fellow, and worked on the farm of Killian Suydam on Long Island, having finished his work early, was fishing,

one still summer evening, just about the neighborhood of Hell Gate. He was in a light skiff, and being well acquainted with the currents and eddies, he had been able to shift his station with the shifting of the tide, from the Hen and Chickens to the Hog's back, and from the Hog's back to the Pot, and from the Pot to the Frying-pan; but in the eagerness of his sport Sam did not see that the tide was rapidly ebbing; until the roaring of the whirl-pools and rapids warned him of his danger, and he had some difficulty in shooting his skiff from among the rocks and breakers, and getting to the point of Blackwell's Island. Here he cast anchor for some time, waiting the turn of the tide to enable him to return homewards.

As the night set in it grew blustering and gusty. Dark clouds came bundling up in the west; and now and then a growl of thunder or a flash of lightning told that a summer storm was at hand. Sam pulled over, there-fore, under the lee of Manhattan Island, and coasting along came to a snug nook, just under a steep beetling rock, where he fastened his skiff to the root of a tree that shot out from a cleft and spread its broad branches like a canopy over the water. The gust came scouring along; the wind threw up the river in white surges; the rain rattled among the leaves, the thunder bellowed worse than that which is now bellowing, the lightning seemed to lick up the surges of the stream; but Sam, snugly sheltered under rock and tree, lay crouched in his skiff, rocking upon the billows, until he fell asleep. When he awoke all was quiet. The gust had passed away, and only now and then a faint gleam of lightning in the east showed which way it had gone. The night was dark and moonless; and from the state of the tide Sam concluded it was near midnight. He was on the point of making loose his skiff to return homewards, when he saw a light gleaming along the water from a distance, which seemed rapidly approaching. As it drew near he perceived that it came from a lanthorn in the bow of a boat which was gliding along under shadow of the land. It pulled up in a small cove, close to where he was. A man jumped on shore, and searching about with the lanthorn exclaimed, "This is the place—here's the Iron ring." The boat was then made fast, and the man returning on board, assisted his comrades in conveying something heavy on shore. As the light gleamed among them, Sam saw that they were five stout, desperate-looking fellows, in red woollen caps, with a leader in a three-cornered hat, and that some of them were armed with dirks, or long knives, and pistols. They talked low to one another, and occasionally in some outlandish tongue which he could not understand.

On landing they made their way among the bushes, taking turns to relieve each other in lugging their burthen up the rocky bank. Sam's curiosity was now fully aroused, so leaving his skiff he clambered silently up the ridge that overlooked their path. They had stopped to rest for a moment, and the leader was looking about among the bushes with his lanthorn. "Have you brought the spades?" said one. "They are here," replied another, who had them on his shoulder. "We must dig deep, where there will be no risk of discovery," said a third.

A cold chill ran through Sam's veins. He fancied he saw before him a gang of murderers, about to bury their victim. His knees smote together. In his agitation he shook the branch of a tree with which he was supporting himself as he looked over the edge of the cliff.

"What's that?" cried one of the gang. "Some one stirs among the bushes!"

The lanthorn was held up in the direction of the noise. One of the redcaps cocked a pistol, and pointed it towards the very place where Sam was standing. He stood motionless—breathless; expecting the next moment to be his last. Fortunately, his dingy complexion was in his favor, and made no glare among the leaves.

"'Tis no one," said the man with the lanthorn. "What a plague! you would not fire off your pistol and alarm the country."

The pistol was uncocked; the burthen was resumed, and the party slowly toiled up the bank. Sam watched them as they went; the light sending back fitful gleams through the dripping bushes, and it was not till they were fairly out of sight that he ventured to draw breath freely. He now thought of getting back to his boat, and making his escape out of the reach of such dangerous neighbors; but curiosity was all-powerful with poor Sam. He hesitated and lingered and listened. By and bye he heard the strokes of spades.

"They are digging the grave!" said he to himself; the cold sweat started upon his forehead. Every stroke of a spade, as it sounded through the silent groves, went to his heart; it was evident there was as little noise made as possible; every thing had an air of mystery and secrecy. Sam had a great relish for the horrible—a tale of murder was a treat for him; and he was a constant attendant at executions. He could not, therefore, resist an impulse, in spite of every danger, to steal nearer, and overlook the villains at their work. He crawled along cautiously, therefore, inch by inch; stepping with the utmost care among the dry leaves, lest their rustling should betray him. He came at length to where a steep rock intervened between him and the gang; he saw the light of their lanthorn shining up against the branches of the trees on the other side. Sam slowly and silently clambered up the surface of the rock, and raising his head above its naked edge, beheld the villains immediately below him, and so near that though he dreaded discovery, he dared not withdraw lest the least movement should be heard. In this way he remained, with his round black face peering over the edge of the rock, like the sun just emerging above the edge of the horizon, or the round-cheeked moon on the dial of a clock.

The red-caps had nearly finished their work; the grave was filled up, and they were carefully replacing the turf. This done, they scattered dry leaves over the place. "And now," said the leader, "I defy the devil himself to find it out."

"The murderers!" exclaimed Sam involuntarily.

The whole gang started, and looking up, beheld the round black head of Sam just above them. His white eyes strained half out of their orbits; his white teeth chattering, and his whole visage shining with cold perspiration.

"We're discovered!" cried one.

"Down with him!" cried another.

Sam heard the cocking of a pistol, but did not pause for the report. He scrambled over rock and stone, through bush and briar; rolled down banks like a hedgehog; scrambled up others like a catamount. In every direction he heard some one or other of the gang hemming him in. At length he reached the rocky ridge along the river; one of the red-caps was hard behind him. A steep rock like a wall rose directly in his way; it seemed to cut off all retreat, when he espied the strong cord-like branch of a grape-vine reaching half way down it. He sprang at it with the force of a desperate man, seized it with both hands, and being young and agile, succeeded in swinging himself to the summit of the cliff. Here he stood in full relief against the sky, when the red-cap cocked his pistol and fired. The ball whistled by Sam's head.

With the lucky thought of a man in an emergency, he uttered a yell, fell to the ground, and detached at the same time a fragment of the rock, which tumbled with a loud splash into the river.

"I've done his business," said the red-cap, to one or two of his comrades as they arrived panting. "He'll tell no tales, except to the fishes in the river."

His pursuers now turned off to meet their companions. Sam sliding silently down the surface of the rock, let himself quietly into his skiff, cast loose the fastening, and abandoned himself to the rapid current, which in that place runs like a mill-stream, and soon swept him off from the neighborhood. It was not, however, until he had drifted a great distance that he ventured to ply his oars; when he made his skiff dart like an arrow through the strait of Hell Gate, never heeding the danger of Pot, Frying-pan, or Hog's-back itself; nor did he feel himself thoroughly secure until safely nestled in bed in the cockloft of the ancient farm-house of the Suydams.

Here the worthy Peechy paused to take breath and to take a sip of the gossip tankard that stood at his elbow. His auditors remained with open mouths and outstretched necks, gaping like a nest of swallows for an additional mouthful.

"And is that all?" exclaimed the half-pay officer.

"That's all that belongs to the story," said Peechy Prauw.

"And did Sam never find out what was buried by the redcaps?" said Wolfert, eagerly; whose mind was haunted by nothing but ingots and doubloons.

"Not that I know of; he had no time to spare from his work; and to tell the truth, he did not like to run the risk of another race among the rocks. Besides, how should he recollect the spot where the grave had been digged? every thing would look different by daylight. And then, where was the use of looking for a dead body, when there was no chance of hanging the murderers?"

"Aye, but are you sure it was a dead body they buried?" said Wolfert.

"To be sure," cried Peechy Prauw, exultingly. "Does it not haunt in the neighborhood to this very day?"

"Haunts!" exclaimed several of the party, opening their eyes still wider and edging their chairs still closer.

"Aye, haunts," repeated Peechy; "has none of you heard of father red-cap that haunts the old burnt farm-house in the woods, on the border of the Sound, near Hell Gate?"

"Oh, to be sure, I've heard tell of something of the kind, but then I took it for some old wives' fable."

"Old wives' fable or not," said Peechy Prauw, "that farmhouse stands hard by the very spot. It's been unoccupied time out of mind, and stands in a wild, lonely part of the coast; but those who fish in the neighborhood have often heard strange noises there; and lights have been seen about the wood at night; and an old fellow in a red cap has been seen at the windows more than once, which people take to be the ghost of the body that was buried there. Once upon a time three soldiers took shelter in the building for the night, and rummaged it from top to bottom, when they found old father red-cap astride of a cider-barrel in the cellar, with a jug in one hand and a goblet in the other. He offered them a drink out of his goblet, but just as one of the soldiers was putting it to his mouth—Whew! a flash of fire blazed through the cellar, blinded every mother's son of them for several minutes, and when they recovered their eye-sight, jug, goblet, and red-cap had vanished, and nothing but the empty cider-barrel remained."

Here the half-pay officer, who was growing very muzzy and sleepy, and nodding over his liquor, with half-extinguished eye, suddenly gleamed up like an expiring rushlight.

"That's all humbug!" said he, as Peechy finished his last story.

"Well, I don't vouch for the truth of it myself," said Peechy Prauw, "though all the world knows that there's something strange about the house and grounds; but as to the story of Mud Sam, I believe it just as well as if it had happened to myself."

The deep interest taken in this conversation by the company, had made them unconscious of the uproar that prevailed abroad, among the elements, when suddenly they were all electrified by a tremendous clap of thunder. A lumbering crash followed instantaneously that made the building shake to its foundation. All started from their seats, imagining it the shock of an earthquake, or that old father red-cap was coming among them in all his terrors. They listened for a moment, but only heard the rain pelting against the windows, and the wind howling among the trees. The explosion was soon explained by the apparition of an old negro's bald head thrust in at the door, his white goggle eyes contrasting with his jetty poll, which was wet with rain and shone like a bottle. In a jargon but half intelligible he announced that the kitchen chimney had been struck with lightning.

A sullen pause of the storm, which now rose and sunk in gusts, produced a momentary stillness. In this interval the report of a musket was heard, and a long shout, almost like a yell, resounded from the shore. Every one crowded to the window; another musket shot was heard, and another long shout, that mingled wildly with a rising blast of wind. It seemed as if the cry came up from the bosom of the waters; for though incessant flashes of lightning spread a light about the shore, no one was to be seen.

Suddenly the window of the room overhead was opened, and a loud halloo uttered by the mysterious stranger. Several hailings passed from one party to the other, but in a language which none of the company in the bar-room could understand; and presently they heard the window closed, and a great noise overhead as if all the furniture were pulled and hauled about the room. The negro servant was summoned, and shortly after was seen assisting the veteran to lug the ponderous sea-chest down stairs.

The landlord was in amazement. "What, you are not going on the water in such a storm?"

"Storm!" said the other, scornfully, "do you call such a sputter of weather a storm?"

"You'll get drenched to the skin—You'll catch your death!" said Peechy Prauw, affectionately.

"Thunder and lightning!" exclaimed the merman, "don't preach about weather to a man that has cruised in whirlwinds and tornadoes."

The obsequious Peechy was again struck dumb. The voice from the water was again heard in a tone of impatience; the bystanders stared with redoubled awe at this man of storms, which seemed to have come up out of the deep and to be called back to it again. As, with the assistance of the negro, he slowly bore his ponderous sea-chest towards the shore, they eyed it with a superstitious feeling; half doubting whether he were not really about to embark upon it, and launch forth upon the wild waves. They followed him at a distance with a lanthorn.

"Douse the light!" roared the hoarse voice from the water. "No one wants light here!"

"Thunder and lightning!" exclaimed the veteran; "back to the house with you!"

Wolfert and his companions shrunk back is dismay. Still their curiosity would not allow them entirely to withdraw. A long sheet of lightning now flickered across the waves, and discovered a boat, filled with men, just under a rocky point, rising and sinking with the heavy surges, and swashing the water at every heave. It was with difficulty held to the rocks by a boat hook, for the current rushed furiously round the point. The veteran hoisted one end of the lumbering sea-chest on the gunwale of the boat; he seized the handle at the other end to lift it in, when the motion propelled the boat from the shore; the chest slipped off from the gunwale, sunk into the waves, and pulled the veteran headlong after it. A loud shriek was uttered by all on shore, and a volley of execrations by those on board; but boat and man were hurried away by the rushing swiftness of the tide. A pitchy darkness succeeded; Wolfert Webber indeed fancied that He distinguished a cry for help, and that he beheld the drowning man beckoning for assistance; but when the lightning again gleamed along the water all was drear and void. Neither man nor boat was to be seen; nothing but the dashing and weltering of the waves as they hurried past.

The company returned to the tavern, for they could not leave it before the storm should subside. They resumed their seats and gazed on each other with dismay. The whole transaction had not occupied five minutes and not a dozen words had been spoken. When they looked at the oaken chair they could scarcely realize the fact that the strange being who had so lately tenanted it, full of life and Herculean vigor, should already be a corpse. There was the very glass he had just drunk from; there lay the ashes from the pipe which he had smoked as it were with his last breath. As the worthy burghers pondered on these things, they felt a terrible conviction of the uncertainty of human existence, and each felt as if the ground on which he stood was rendered less stable by this awful example.

As, however, the most of the company were possessed of that valuable philosophy which enables a man to bear up with fortitude against the misfortunes of his neighbors, they soon managed to console themselves for the tragic end of the veteran. The landlord was happy that the poor dear man had paid his reckoning before he went.

"He came in a storm, and he went in a storm; he came in the night, and he went in the night; he came nobody knows from whence, and he has gone nobody knows where. For aught I know he has gone to sea once more on his chest and may land to bother some people on the other side of the world! Though it's a thousand pities," added the landlord, "if he has gone to Davy Jones that he had not left his sea-chest behind him."

"The sea-chest! St. Nicholas preserve us!" said Peechy Prauw. "I'd not have had that sea-chest in the house for any money; I'll warrant he'd come racketing after it at nights, and making a haunted house of the inn. And as to his going to sea on his chest, I recollect what happened to Skipper Onderdonk's ship on his voyage from Amsterdam.

"The boatswain died during a storm, so they wrapped him up in a sheet, and put him in his own sea-chest, and threw him overboard; but they neglected in their hurry-skurry to say prayers over him—and the storm raged and roared louder than ever, and they saw the dead man seated in his chest, with his shroud for a sail, coming hard after the ship; and the sea breaking before him in great sprays like fire, and there they kept scudding day after day and night after night, expecting every moment to go to wreck; and every night they saw the dead boatswain in his sea-chest trying to get up with them, and they heard his whistle above the blasts of wind, and he seemed to send great seas mountain high after them, that would have swamped the ship if they had not put up the dead lights. And so it went on till they lost sight of him in the fogs of Newfoundland, and supposed he had veered ship and stood for Dead Man's Isle. So much for burying a man at sea without saying prayers over him."

The thunder-gust which had hitherto detained the company was now at an end. The cuckoo clock in the hall struck midnight; every one pressed to depart, for seldom was such a late hour trespassed on by these quiet burghers. As they sallied forth they found the heavens once more serene. The storm which had lately obscured them had rolled aways and lay piled up in fleecy masses on the horizon, lighted up by the bright crescent of the moon, which looked like a silver lamp hung up in a palace of clouds.

The dismal occurrence of the night, and the dismal narrations they had made, had left a superstitious feeling in every mind. They cast a fearful glance at the spot where the buccaneer had disappeared, almost expecting to see him sailing on his chest in the cool moonshine. The trembling rays glittered along the waters, but all was placid; and the current dimpled over the spot where he had gone down. The party huddled together in a little crowd as they repaired homewards; particularly when they passed a lonely field where a man had been murdered; and he who had farthest to go and had to complete his journey alone, though a veteran sexton, and accustomed, one would think to ghosts and goblins, yet went a long way round, rather than pass by his own church-yard.

Wolfert Webber had now carried home a fresh stock of stories and notions to ruminate upon. His mind was all of a whirl with these freebooting tales; and then these accounts of pots of money and Spanish treasures, buried here and there and every where about the rocks and bays of this wild shore, made him almost dizzy.

"Blessed St. Nicholas!" ejaculated he, half aloud, "is it not possible to come upon one of these golden hoards, and so make one's self rich in a twinkling. How hard that I must go on, delving and delving, day in and day out, merely to make a morsel of bread, when one lucky stroke of a spade might enable me to ride in my carriage for the rest of my life!"

As he turned over in his thoughts all that he had been told of the singular adventure of the black fisherman, his imagination gave a totally different complexion to the tale. He saw in the gang of redcaps nothing but a crew of pirates burying their spoils, and his cupidity was once more awakened by the possibility of at length getting on the traces of some of this lurking wealth. Indeed, his infected fancy tinged every thing with gold. He felt like the greedy inhabitant of Bagdad, when his eye had been greased with the magic ointment of the dervise, that gave him to see all the treasures of the earth. Caskets of buried jewels, chests of ingots, bags of outlandish coins, seemed to court him from their concealments, and supplicate him to relieve them from their untimely graves.

On making private inquiries about the grounds said to be haunted by father red-cap, he was more and more confirmed in his surmise. He learned that the place had several times been visited by experienced money-diggers, who had heard Mud Sam's story, though none of them had met with success. On the contrary, they had always been dogged with ill luck of some kind or other, in consequence, as Wolfert concluded, of their not going to work at the proper time, and with the proper ceremonials. The last attempt had been made by Cobus Quackenbos, who dug for a whole night and met with incredible difficulty, for as fast as he threw one shovel full of earth out of the hole, two were thrown in by invisible hands. He succeeded so far, however, as to uncover an iron chest, when there was a terrible roaring, and ramping, and raging of uncouth figures about the hole, and at length a shower of blows, dealt by invisible cudgels, that fairly belabored him off the forbidden ground. This Cobus Quackenbos had declared on his death-bed, so that there could not be any doubt of it. He was a man that had devoted many years of his life to money-digging, and it was thought would have ultimately succeeded, had he not died suddenly of a brain fever in the alms-house.

Wolfert Webber was now in a worry of trepidation and impatience; fearful lest some rival adventurer should get a scent of the buried gold. He determined privately to seek out the negro fisherman and get him to serve as guide to the place where he had witnessed the mysterious scene of interment. Sam was easily found; for he was one of those old habitual beings that live about a neighborhood until they wear themselves a place in the public mind, and become, in a manner, public characters. There was not an unlucky urchin about the town that did not know Mud Sam the fisherman, and think that he had a right to play his tricks upon the old negro. Sam was an amphibious kind of animal, something more of a fish than a man; he had led the life of an otter for more than half a century, about the shores of the bay, and the fishing grounds of the Sound. He passed the greater part of his time on and in the water, particularly about Hell Gate; and might have been taken, in bad weather, for one of the hobgoblins that used to haunt that strait. There would he be seen, at all times, and in all weathers; sometimes in his skiff, anchored among the eddies, or prowling, like a shark about some wreck, where the fish are supposed to be most abundant. Sometimes seated on a rock from hour to hour, looming through mist and drizzle, like a solitary heron watching for its prey. He was well acquainted with every hole and corner of the Sound; from the Wallabout to Hell Gate, and from Hell Gate even unto the Devil's Stepping Stones; and it was even affirmed that he knew all the fish in the river by their Christian names.

Wolfert found him at his cabin, which was not much larger than a tolerable dog-house. It was rudely constructed of fragments of wrecks and drift-wood, and built on the rocky shore, at the foot of the old fort, just about what at present forms the point of the Battery. A "most ancient and fish-like smell" pervaded the place. Oars, paddles, and fishing-rods were leaning against the wall of the fort; a net was spread on the sands to dry; a skiff was drawn up on the beach, and at the door of his cabin lay Mud Sam himself, indulging in a true negro's luxury—sleeping in the sunshine.

Many years had passed away since the time of Sam's youthful adventure, and the snows of many a winter had grizzled the knotty wool upon his head. He perfectly recollected the circumstances, however, for he had often been called upon to relate them, though in his version of the story he differed in many points from Peechy Prauw; as is not unfrequently the case with authentic historians. As to the subsequent researches of money-diggers, Sam knew nothing about them; they were matters quite out of his line; neither did the cautious Wolfert care to disturb his thoughts on that point. His only wish was to secure the old fisherman as a pilot to the spot, and this was readily effected. The long time that had intervened since his nocturnal adventure had effaced all Sam's awe of the place, and the promise of a trifling reward roused him at once from his sleep and his sunshine.

The tide was adverse to making the expedition by water, and Wolfert was too impatient to get to the land of promise, to wait for its turning; they set off, therefore, by land. A walk of four or five miles brought them to the edge of a wood, which at that time covered the greater part of the eastern side of the island. It was just beyond the pleasant region of Bloomen-dael. Here they struck into a long lane, straggling among trees and bushes, very much overgrown with weeds and mullein stalks as if but seldom used, and so completely overshadowed as to enjoy but a kind of twilight. Wild vines entangled the trees and flaunted in their faces; brambles and briars caught their clothes as they passed; the garter-snake glided across their path; the spotted toad hopped and waddled before them, and the restless cat-bird mewed at them from every thicket. Had Wolfert Webber been deeply read in romantic legend he might have fancied himself entering upon forbidden, enchanted ground; or that these were some of the guardians set to keep a watch upon buried treasure. As it was, the loneliness of the place, and the wild stories connected with it, had their effect upon his mind.

On reaching the lower end of the lane they found themselves near the shore of the Sound, in a kind of amphitheatre, surrounded by forest tree. The area had once been a grass-plot, but was now shagged with briars and rank weeds. At one end, and just on the river bank, was a ruined building, little better than a heap of rubbish, with a stack of chimneys rising like a solitary tower out of the centre. The current of the Sound rushed along just below it, with wildly-grown trees drooping their branches into its waves.

Wolfert had not a doubt that this was the haunted house of father red-cap, and called to mind the story of Peechy Prauw. The evening was approaching, and the light falling dubiously among these places, gave a melancholy tone to the scene, well calculated to foster any lurking feeling of awe or superstition. The night-hawk, wheeling about in the highest regions of the air, emitted his peevish, boding cry. The woodpecker gave a lonely tap now and then on some hollow tree, and the firebird (*Orchard Oreole-ed.*) as he streamed by them with his deep-red plumage, seemed like some genius flitting about this region of mystery.

They now came to an enclosure that had once been a garden. It extended along the foot of a rocky ridge, but was little better than a wilderness of weeds, with here and there a matted rose-bush, or a peach or plum tree grown wild and ragged, and covered with moss. At the lower end of the garden they passed a kind of vault in the side of the bank, facing the water. It had the look of a root-house. The door, though decayed, was still strong, and appeared to have been recently patched up. Wolfert pushed it open. It gave a harsh grating upon its hinges, and striking against something like a box, a rattling sound ensued, and a skull rolled on the floor. Wolfert drew back shuddering, but was reassured on being informed by Sam that this was a family vault belonging to one of the old Dutch families that owned this estate; an assertion which was corroborated by the sight of coffins of various sizes piled within. Sam had been familiar with all these scenes when a boy, and now knew that he could not be far from the place of which they were in quest.

They now made their way to the water's edge, scrambling along ledges of rocks, and having often to hold by shrubs and grape-vines to avoid slipping into the deep and hurried stream. At length they came to a small cove, or rather indent of the shore. It was protected by steep rocks and overshadowed by a thick copse of oaks and chestnuts, so as to be sheltered and almost concealed. The beach sloped gradually within the cove, but the current swept deep and black and rapid along its jutting points. Sam paused; raised his remnant of a hat, and scratched his grizzled poll for a moment, as he regarded this nook: then suddenly clapping his hands, he stepped exultingly forward, and pointing to a large iron ring, stapled firmly in the rock, just where a broad shelve of stone furnished a commodious landing-place. It was the very spot where the red-caps had landed. Years had changed the more perishable features of the scene; but rock and iron yield slowly to the influence of time. On looking more narrowly, Wolfert remarked three crosses cut in the rock just above the ring, which had no doubt some mysterious signification. Old Sam now readily recognized the overhanging rock under which his skiff had been sheltered during the thunder-gust. To follow up the course which the midnight gang had taken, however, was a harder task. His mind had been so much taken up on that eventful occasion by the persons of the drama, as to pay but little attention to the scenes; and places looked different by night and day. After wandering about for some time, however, they came to an opening among the trees which Sam thought resembled the place. There was a ledge of rock of moderate height like a wall on one side, which Sam thought might be the very ridge from which he overlooked the diggers. Wolfert examined it narrowly, and at length described three crosses similar to those above the iron ring, cut deeply into the face of the rock, but nearly obliterated by the moss that had grown on them. His heart leaped with joy, for he doubted not but they were the private marks of the buccaneers, to denote the places where their treasure lay buried. All now that remained was to ascertain the precise spot; for otherwise he might dig at random without coming upon the spoil, and he has already had enough of such profitless labor. Here, however, Sam was perfectly at a loss, and, indeed, perplexed him by a variety of opinions; for his recollections were all confused. Sometimes he declared it must have been at the foot of a mulberry tree hard by; then it was just beside a great white stone; then it must have been under a small green knoll, a short distance from the ledge of rock: until at length Wolfert became as bewildered as himself.

The shadows of evening were now spreading themselves over the woods, and rock and tree began to mingle together. It was evidently too late to attempt anything farther at present; and, indeed, Wolfert had come unprepared with implements to prosecute his researches. Satisfied, therefore, with having ascertained the place, he took note of all its landmarks, that he might recognize it again, and set out on his return homeward, resolved to prosecute this golden enterprise without delay.

The leading anxiety which had hitherto absorbed every feeling being now in some measure appeased, fancy began to wander, and to conjure up a thousand shapes and chimeras as he returned through this haunted region. Pirates hanging in chains seemed to swing on every tree, and he almost expected to see some Spanish Don, with his throat cut from ear to ear, rising slowly out of the ground, and shaking the ghost of a money-bag.

Their way back lay through the desolate garden, and Wolfert's nerves had arrived at so sensitive a state that the flitting of a bird, the rustling of a leaf, or the falling of a nut was enough to startle him. As they entered the confines of the garden, they caught sight of a figure at a distance advancing slowly up one of the walks and bending under the weight of a burthen. They paused and regarded him attentively. He wore what appeared to be a woollen cap, and still more alarming, of a most sanguinary red. The figure moved slowly on, ascended the bank, and stopped at the very door of the sepulchral vault. Just before entering he looked around. What was the horror of Wolfert when he recognized the grizzly visage of the drowned buccaneer. He uttered an ejaculation of horror. The figure slowly raised his iron fist and shook it with a terrible menace. Wolfert did not pause to see more, but hurried off as fast as his legs could carry him, nor was Sam slow in following at his heels, having all his ancient terrors revived. Away, then, did they scramble, through bush and brake, horribly frightened at every bramble that tagged at their skirts, nor did they pause to breathe, until they had blundered their way through this perilous wood and had fairly reached the high-road to the city.

Several days elapsed before Wolfert could summon courage enough to prosecute the enterprise, so much had he been dismayed by the apparition, whether living dead, of the grizzly buccaneer. In the meantime, what a conflict of mind did he suffer! He neglected all his concerns, was moody and restless all day, lost his appetite; wandered in his thoughts and words, and committed a thousand blunders. His rest was broken; and when he fell asleep, the nightmare, in shape of a huge money-bag, sat squatted upon his breast. He babbled about incalculable sums; fancied himself engaged in money digging; threw the bed-clothes right and left, in the idea that he was shovelling among the dirt, groped under the bed in quest of the treasure, and lugged forth, as he supposed, an inestimable pot of gold.

Dame Webber and her daughter were in despair at what they conceived a returning touch of insanity. There are two family oracles, one or other of which Dutch housewives consult in all cases of great doubt and perplexity: the dominie and the doctor. In the present instance they repaired to the doctor. There was at that time a little, dark, mouldy man of medicine famous among the old wives of the Manhattoes for his skill not only in the healing art, but in all matters of strange and mysterious nature. His name was Dr. Knipperhausen, but he was more commonly known by the appellation of the High German doctor. To him did the poor women repair for counsel and assistance touching the mental vagaries of Wolfert Webber.

They found the doctor seated in his little study, clad in his dark camblet robe of knowledge, with his black velvet cap, after the manner of Boorhaave, Van Helmont, and other medical sages: a pair of green spectacles set in black horn upon his clubbed nose, and poring over a German folio that seemed to reflect back the darkness of his physiognomy. The doctor listened to their statement of the symptoms of Wolfert's malady with profound attention; but when they came to mention his raving about buried money, the little man pricked up his ears. Alas, poor women! they little knew the aid they had called in.

Dr. Knipperhausen had been half his life engaged in seeking the short cuts to fortune, in quest of which so many a long lifetime is wasted. He had passed some years of his youth in the Harz Mountains of Germany, and had derived much valuable instruction from the miners, touching the mode of seeking treasure buried in the earth. He had prosecuted his studies also under a travelling sage who united all the mysteries of medicine with magic and legerdemain. His mind, therefore, had become stored with all kinds of mystic lore: he had dabbled a little in astrology, alchemy, and divination; knew how to detect stolen money, and to tell where springs of water lay hidden; in a word, by the dark nature of his knowledge he had acquired the name of the High German doctor, which is pretty nearly equivalent to that of necromancer. The doctor had often heard rumors of treasure being buried in various parts of the island, and had long been anxious to get on the traces of it. No sooner were Wolfert's waking and sleeping vagaries confided to him, than he beheld in them the confirmed symptoms of a case of money-digging, and lost no time in probing it to the bottom. Wolfert had long been sorely depressed in mind by the golden secret, and as a family physician is a kind of father confessor, he was glad of the opportunity of unburthening himself. So far from curing, the doctor caught the malady from his patient. The circumstances unfolded to him awakened all his cupidity; he had not a doubt of money being buried somewhere in the neighborhood of the mysterious crosses, and offered to join Wolfert in the search. He informed him that much secrecy and caution must be observed in enterprises of the kind; that money is only to be digged for at night; with certain forms and ceremonies; the burning of drugs; the repeating of mystic words, and above all, that the seekers must be provided with a divining rod, which had the wonderful property of pointing to the very spot on the surface of the earth under which treasure lay hidden. As the doctor had given much of his mind to these matters, he charged himself with all the necessary preparations, and, as the quarter of the moon was propitious, he undertook to have the divining rod ready by a certain night.

[Footnote: The following note was found appended to this paper in the handwriting of Mr. Knickerbocker. "There has been much written against the divining rod by those light minds who are ever ready to scoff at the mysteries of nature, but I fully join with Dr. Knipperhausen in giving it my faith. I shall not insist upon its efficacy in discovering the concealment of stolen goods, the boundary-stones of fields, the traces of robbers and murderers, or even the existence of subterraneous springs and streams of water; albeit, I think these properties not easily to be discredited; but of its potency in discovering vein of precious metal, and hidden sums of money and jewels, I have not the least doubt. Some said that the rod turned only in the hands of persons who had been born in particular months of the year; hence astrologers had recourse to planetary influence when they would procure a talisman. Others declared that the properties of the rod were either an effect of chance, or the fraud of the holder, or the work of the devil. Thus sayeth the reverend Father Gaspard Schott in his Treatise on Magic. 'Propter haec et similia argumenta audacter ego pronuncio vim conversivam virgulae befurcatae nequaquam naturalem esse, sed vel casa vel fraude virgulam tractantis vel ope diaboli,' etc.

"Georgius Agricula also was of opinion that it was a mere delusion of the devil to inveigle the avaricious and unwary into his clutches, and in his treatise 'de re Metallica,' lays particular stress on the mysterious words pronounced by those persons who employed the divining rod during his time. But I make not a doubt that the divining rod is one of those secrets of natural magic, the mystery of which is to be explained by the sympathies existing between physical things operated upon by the planets, and rendered efficacious by the strong faith of the individual. Let the divining rod be properly gathered at the proper time of the moon, cut into the proper form, used with the necessary ceremonies, and with a perfect faith in its efficacy, and I can confidently recommend it to my fellow-citizens as an infallible means of discovering the various places on the island of the Manhattoes where treasure hath been buried in the olden time. D.K."]

Wolfert's heart leaped with joy at having met with so learned and able a coadjutor. Every thing went on secretly, but swimmingly. The doctor had many consultations with his patient, and the good women of the household lauded the comforting effect of his visits. In the meantime, the wonderful divining rod, that great key to nature's secrets, was duly prepared. The doctor had thumbed over all his books of knowledge for the occasion; and Mud Sam was engaged to take them in his skiff to the scene of enterprise; to work with spade and pick-axe in unearthing the treasure; and to freight his bark with the weighty spoils they were certain of finding.

At length the appointed night arrived for this perilous undertaking. Before Wolfert left his home he counselled his wife and daughter to go to bed, and feel no alarm if he should not return during the night. Like reasonable women, on being told not to feel alarm, they fell immediately into a panic. They saw at once by his manner that something unusual was in agitation; all their fears about the unsettled state of his mind were roused with tenfold force: they hung about him entreating him not to expose himself to the night air, but all in vain. When Wolfert was once mounted on his hobby, it was no easy matter to get him out of the saddle. It was a clear starlight night, when he issued out of the portal of the Webber palace. He wore a large napped hat tied under the chin with a handkerchief of his daughter's, to secure him from the night damp, while Dame Webber threw her long red cloak about his shoulders, and fastened it round his neck.

The doctor had been no less carefully armed and accoutred by his house-keeper, the vigilant Frau Ilsy, and sallied forth in his camblet robe by way of surtout; his black velvet cap under his cocked hat, a thick clasped book under his arm, a basket of drugs and dried herbs in one hand, and in the other the miraculous rod of divination.

The great church clock struck ten as Wolfert and the doctor passed by the church-yard, and the watchman bawled in hoarse voice a long and doleful "All's well!" A deep sleep had already fallen upon this primitive little burgh; nothing disturbed this awful silence, excepting now and then the bark of some profligate night-walking dog, or the serenade of some romantic cat. It is true, Wolfert fancied more than once that he heard the sound of a stealthy footfall at a distance behind them; but it might have been merely the echo of their own steps echoing along the quiet streets. He thought also at one time that he saw a tall figure skulking after them— stopping when they stopped, and moving on as they proceeded; but the dim and uncertain lamp light threw such vague gleams and shadows, that this might all have been mere fancy.

They found the negro fisherman waiting for them, smoking his pipe in the stern of his skiff, which was moored just in front of his little cabin. A pick-axe and spade were lying in the bottom of the boat, with a dark lanthorn, and a stone jug of good Dutch courage, in which honest Sam no doubt, put even more faith than Dr. Knipperhausen in his drugs.

Thus then did these three worthies embark in their cockleshell of a skiff upon this nocturnal expedition, with a wisdom and valor equalled only by the three wise men of Gotham, who went to sea in a bowl. The tide was rising and running rapidly up the Sound. The current bore them along, almost without the aid of an oar. The profile of the town lay all in shadow. Here and there a light feebly glimmered from some sick chamber, or from the cabin window of some vessel at anchor in the stream. Not a cloud obscured the deep starry firmament, the lights of which wavered on the surface of the placid river; and a shooting meteor, streaking its pale course in the very direction they were taking, was interpreted by the doctor into a most propitious omen.

In a little while they glided by the point of Corlears Hook with the rural inn which had been the scene of such night adventures. The family had retired to rest, and the house was dark and still. Wolfert felt a chill pass over him as they passed the point where the buccaneer had disappeared. He pointed it out to Dr. Knipperhausen. While regarding it, they thought they saw a boat actually lurking at the very place; but the shore cast such a shadow over the border of the water that they could discern nothing distinctly. They had not proceeded far when they heard the low sounds of distant oars, as if cautiously pulled. Sam plied his oars with redoubled vigor, and knowing all the eddies and currents of the stream, soon left their followers, if such they were, far astern. In a little while they stretched across Turtle bay and Kip's bay, then shrouded themselves in the deep shadows of the Manhattan shore, and glided swiftly along, secure from observation. At length Sam shot his skiff into a little cove, darkly embowered by trees, and made it fast to the well known iron ring. They now landed, and lighting the lanthorn, gathered their various implements and proceeded slowly through the bushes. Every sound startled them, even that of their footsteps among the dry leaves; and the hooting of a screech owl, from the shattered chimney of father red-cap's ruin, made their blood run cold.

In spite of all Wolfert's caution in taking note of the landmarks, it was some time before they could find the open place among the trees, where the treasure was supposed to be buried. At length they came to the ledge of rock; and on examining its surface by the aid of the lanthorn, Wolfert recognized the three mystic crosses. Their hearts beat quick, for the momentous trial was at hand that was to determine their hopes.

The lanthorn was now held by Wolfert Webber, while the doctor produced the divining rod. It was a forked twig, one end of which was grasped firmly in each hand, while the centre, forming the stem, pointed perpendicularly upwards. The doctor moved this wand about, within a certain distance of the earth, from place to place, but for some time without any effect, while Wolfert kept the light of the lanthorn turned full upon it, and watched it with the most breathless interest. At length the rod began slowly to turn. The doctor grasped it with greater earnestness, his hand trembling with the agitation of his mind. The wand continued slowly to turn, until at length the stem had reversed its position, and pointed perpendicularly downward; and remained pointing to one spot as fixedly as the needle to the pole.

"This is the spot!" said the doctor in an almost inaudible tone.

Wolfert's heart was in his throat.

"Shall I dig?" said Sam, grasping the spade.

"Pots tousends, no!" replied the little doctor, hastily. He now ordered his companions to keep close by him and to maintain the most inflexible silence. That certain precautions must be taken, and ceremonies used to prevent the evil spirits which keep about buried treasure from doing them any harm. The doctor then drew a circle round the place, enough to include the whole party. He next gathered dry twigs and leaves, and made a fire, upon which he threw certain drugs and dried herbs which he had brought in his basket. A thick smoke rose, diffusing a potent odor, savoring marvellously of brimstone and assafoetida, which, however grateful it might be to the olfactory nerves of spirits, nearly strangled poor Wolfert, and produced a fit of coughing and wheezing that made the whole grove resound. Doctor Knipperhausen then unclasped the volume which he had brought under his arm, which was printed in red and black characters in German text. While Wolfert held the lanthorn, the doctor, by the aid of his spectacles, read off several forms of conjuration in Latin and German. He then ordered Sam to seize the pick-axe and proceed to work. The close-bound soil gave obstinate signs of not having been disturbed for many a year. After having picked his way through the surface, Sam came to a bed of sand and gravel, which he threw briskly to right and left with the spade.

"Hark!" said Wolfert, who fancied he heard a trampling among the dry leaves, and a rustling through the bushes. Sam paused for a moment, and they listened. No footstep was near. The bat flitted about them in silence; a bird roused from its nest by the light which glared up among the trees, flew circling about the flame. In the profound stillness of the woodland they could distinguish the current rippling along the rocky shore, and the distant murmuring and roaring of Hell Gate.

Sam continued his labors, and had already digged a considerable hole. The doctor stood on the edge, reading formulae every now and then from the black letter volume, or throwing more drugs and herbs upon the fire; while Wolfert bent anxiously over the pit, watching every stroke of the spade. Any one witnessing the scene thus strangely lighted up by fire, lanthorn, and the reflection of Wolfert's red mantle, might have mistaken the little doctor for some foul magician, busied in his incantations, and the grizzled-headed Sam as some swart goblin, obedient to his commands.

At length the spade of the fisherman struck upon something that sounded hollow. The sound vibrated to Wolfert's heart. He struck his spade again.

"'Tis a chest," said Sam.

"Full of gold, I'll warrant it!" cried Wolfert, clasping his hands with rapture.

Scarcely had he uttered the words when a sound from overhead caught his ear. He cast up his eyes, and lo! by the expiring light of the fire he beheld, just over the disk of the rock, what appeared to be the grim visage of the drowned buccaneer, grinning hideously down upon him.

Wolfert gave a loud cry and let fall the lanthorn. His panic communicated itself to his companions. The negro leaped out of the hole, the doctor dropped his book and basket and began to pray in German. All was horror and confusion. The fire was scattered about, the lanthorn extinguished. In their hurry-skurry they ran against and confounded one another. They fancied a legion of hobgoblins let loose upon them, and that they saw by the fitful gleams of the scattered embers, strange figures in red caps gibbering and ramping around them. The doctor ran one way, Mud Sam another, and Wolfert made for the water side. As he plunged struggling onwards through bush and brake, he heard the tread of some one in pursuit.

He scrambled frantically forward. The footsteps gained upon him. He felt himself grasped by his cloak, when suddenly his pursuer was attacked in turn: a fierce fight and struggle ensued—a pistol was discharged that lit up rock and bush for a period, and showed two figures grappling together—all was then darker than ever. The contest continued—the combatants clenched each other, and panted and groaned, and rolled among the rocks. There was snarling and growling as of a cur, mingled with curses in which Wolfert fancied he could recognize the voice of the buccaneer. He would fain have fled, but he was on the brink of a precipice and could go no farther.

Again the parties were on their feet; again there was a tugging and struggling, as if strength alone could decide the combat, until one was precipitated from the brow of the cliff and sent headlong into the deep stream that whirled below. Wolfert heard the plunge, and a kind of strangling bubbling murmur, but the darkness of the night hid every thing from view, and the swiftness of the current swept every thing instantly out of hearing. One of the combatants was disposed of, but whether friend or foe Wolfert could not tell, nor whether they might not both be foes. He heard the survivor approach and his terror revived. He saw, where the profile of the rocks rose against the horizon, a human form advancing. He could not be mistaken: it must be the buccaneer. Whither should he fly! a precipice was on one side; a murderer on the other. The enemy approached: he was close at hand. Wolfert attempted to let himself down the face of the cliff. His cloak caught in a thorn that grew on the edge. He was jerked from off his feet and held dangling in the air, half choked by the string with which his careful wife had fastened the garment round his neck. Wolfert thought his last moment had arrived; already had he committed his soul to St. Nicholas, when the string broke and he tumbled down the bank, bumping from rock to rock and bush to bush, and leaving the red cloak fluttering like a bloody banner in the air.

It was a long while before Wolfert came to himself. When he opened his eyes the ruddy streaks of the morning were already shooting up the sky. He found himself lying in the bottom of a boat, grievously battered. He attempted to sit up but was too sore and stiff to move. A voice requested him in friendly accents to lie still. He turned his eyes toward the speaker: it was Dirk Waldron. He had dogged the party, at the earnest request of Dame Webber and her daughter, who, with the laudable curiosity of their sex, had pried into the secret consultations of Wolfert and the doctor. Dirk had been completely distanced in following the light skiff of the fisherman, and had just come in time to rescue the poor money-digger from his pursuer.

Thus ended this perilous enterprise. The doctor and Mud Sam severally found their way back to the Manhattoes, each having some dreadful tale of peril to relate. As to poor Wolfert, instead of returning in triumph, laden with bags of gold, he was borne home on a shutter, followed by a rabble route of curious urchins. His wife and daughter saw the dismal pageant from a distance, and alarmed the neighborhood with their cries: they thought the poor man had suddenly settled the great debt of nature in one of his wayward moods. Finding him, however, still living, they had him conveyed speedily to bed, and a jury of old matrons of the neighborhood assembled to determine how he should be doctored. The whole town was in a buzz with the story of the money-diggers. Many repaired to the scene of the previous night's adventures: but though they found the very place of the digging, they discovered nothing that compensated for their trouble. Some say they found the fragments of an oaken chest and an iron pot lid, which savored strongly of hidden money; and that in the old family vault there were traces of holes and boxes, but this is all very dubious.

In fact, the secret of all this story has never to this day been discovered: whether any treasure was ever actually buried at that place, whether, if so, it was carried off at night by those who had buried it; or whether it still remains there under the guardianship of gnomes and spirits until it shall be properly sought for, is all matter of conjecture. For my part I incline to the latter opinion; and make no doubt that great sums lie buried, both there and in many other parts of this island and its neighborhood, ever since the times of the buccaneers and the Dutch colonists; and I would earnestly recommend the search after them to such of my fellow citizens as are not engaged in any other speculations.

There were many conjectures formed, also, as to who and what was the strange man of the seas who had domineered over the little fraternity at Corlears Hook for a time; disappeared so strangely, and reappeared so fearfully. Some supposed him a smuggler stationed at that place to assist his comrades in landing their goods among the rocky coves of the island. Others that he was a buccaneer; one of the ancient comrades either of Kidd or Bradish, returned to convey away treasures formerly hidden in the vicinity. The only circumstance that throws any thing like a vague light over this mysterious matter is a report that prevailed of a strange foreign-built shallop, with the look of a piccaroon, having been seen hovering about the Sound for several days without landing or reporting herself, though boats were seen going to and from her at night: and that she was seen standing out of the mouth of the harbor, in the gray of the dawn after the catastrophe of the money-diggers.

I must not omit to mention another report, also, which I confess is rather apocryphal, of the buccaneer, who was supposed to have been drowned, being seen before daybreak, with a lanthorn in his hand, seated astride his great sea-chest and sailing through Hell Gate, which just then began to roar and bellow with redoubled fury.

While all the gossip world was thus filled with talk and rumor, poor Wolfert lay sick and sorrowful in his bed, bruised in body and sorely beaten down in mind. His wife and daughter did all they could to bind up his wounds both corporal and spiritual. The good old dame never stirred from his bedside, where she sat knitting from morning till night; while his daughter busied herself about him with the fondest care. Nor did they lack assistance from abroad. Whatever may be said of the desertions of friends in distress, they had no complaint of the kind to make. Not an old wife of the neighborhood but abandoned her work to crowd to the mansion of Wolfert Webber, inquire after his health and the particulars of his story. Not one came, moreover, without her little pipkin of pennyroyal, sage, balm, or other herb-tea, delighted at an opportunity of signalizing her kindness and her doctorship. What drenchings did not the poor Wolfert undergo, and all in vain. It was a moving sight to behold him wasting away day by day; growing thinner and thinner and ghastlier and ghastlier, and staring with rueful visage from under an old patchwork counterpane upon the jury of matrons kindly assembled to sigh and groan and look unhappy around him.

Dirk Waldron was the only being that seemed to shed a ray of sunshine into this house of mourning. He came in with cheery look and manly spirit, and tried to reanimate the expiring heart of the poor money-digger, but it was all in vain. Wolfert was completely done over. If any thing was wanting to complete his despair, it was a notice served upon him in the midst of his distress, that the corporation were about to run a new street through the very centre of his cabbage garden. He saw nothing before him but poverty and ruin; his last reliance, the garden of his forefathers, was to be laid waste, and what then was to become of his poor wife and child?

His eyes filled with tears as they followed the dutiful Amy out of the room one morning. Dirk Waldron was seated beside him; Wolfert grasped his hand, pointed after his daughter, and for the first time since his illness broke the silence he had maintained.

"I am going!" said he, shaking his head feebly, "and when I am gone—my poor daughter—"

"Leave her to me, father!" said Dirk, manfully—"I'll take care of her!"

Wolfert looked up in the face of the cheery, strapping youngster, and saw there was none better able to take care of a woman.

"Enough," said he, "she is yours!—and now fetch me a lawyer—let me make my will and die."

The lawyer was brought—a dapper, bustling, round-headed little man, Roorback (or Rollebuck, as it was pronounced) by name. At the sight of him the women broke into loud lamentations, for they looked upon the signing of a will as the signing of a death-warrant. Wolfert made a feeble motion for them to be silent. Poor Amy buried her face and her grief in the bed-curtain. Dame Webber resumed her knitting to hide her distress, which betrayed itself, however, in a pellucid tear, that trickled silently down and hung at the end of her peaked nose; while the cat, the only unconcerned member of the family, played with the good dame's ball of worsted, as it rolled about the floor.

Wolfert lay on his back, his nightcap drawn over his forehead; his eyes closed; his whole visage the picture of death. He begged the lawyer to be brief, for he felt his end approaching, and that he had no time to lose. The lawyer nibbed his pen, spread out his paper, and prepared to write.

"I give and bequeath," said Wolfert, faintly, "my small farm—"

"What—all!" exclaimed the lawyer.

Wolfert half opened his eyes and looked upon the lawyer.

"Yes—all" said he.

"What! all that great patch of land with cabbages and sunflowers, which the corporation is just going to run a main street through?"

"The same," said Wolfert, with a heavy sigh and sinking back upon his pillow.

"I wish him joy that inherits it!" said the little lawyer, chuckling and rubbing his hands involuntarily.

"What do you mean?" said Wolfert, again opening his eyes.

"That he'll be one of the richest men in the place!" cried little Rollebuck.

The expiring Wolfert seemed to step back from the threshold of existence: his eyes again lighted up; he raised himself in his bed, shoved back his red worsted nightcap, and stared broadly at the lawyer.

"You don't say so!" exclaimed he.

"Faith, but I do!" rejoined the other. "Why, when that great field and that piece of meadow come to be laid out in streets, and cut up into snug building lots—why, whoever owns them need not pull off his hat to the patroon!"

"Say you so?" cried Wolfert, half thrusting one leg out of bed, "why, then I think I'll not make my will yet!"

To the surprise of everybody the dying man actually recovered. The vital spark which had glimmered faintly in the socket, received fresh fuel from the oil of gladness, which the little lawyer poured into his soul. It once more burnt up into a flame.

Give physic to the heart, ye who would revive the body of a spirit-broken man! In a few days Wolfert left his room; in a few days more his table was covered with deeds, plans of streets and building lots. Little Rollebuck was constantly with him, his right-hand man and adviser, and instead of making his will, assisted in the more agreeable task of making his fortune. In fact, Wolfert Webber was one of those worthy Dutch burghers of the Manhattoes whose fortunes have been made, in a manner, in spite of themselves; who have tenaciously held on to their hereditary acres, raising turnips and cabbages about the skirts of the city, hardly able to make both ends meet, until the corporation has cruelly driven streets through their abodes, and they have suddenly awakened out of a lethargy, and, to their astonishment, found themselves rich men.

Before many months had elapsed a great bustling street passed through the very centre of the Webber garden, just where Wolfert had dreamed of finding a treasure. His golden dream was accomplished; he did indeed find an unlooked-for source of wealth; for, when his paternal lands were distributed into building lots, and rented out to safe tenants, instead of producing a paltry crop of cabbages, they returned him an abundant crop of rents; insomuch that on quarter day, it was a goodly sight to see his tenants rapping at his door, from morning to night, each with a little round-bellied bag of money, the golden produce of the soil.

The ancient mansion of his forefathers was still kept up, but instead of being a little yellow-fronted Dutch house in a garden, it now stood boldly in the midst of a street, the grand house of the neighborhood; for Wolfert enlarged it with a wing on each side, and a cupola or tea room on top, where he might climb up and smoke his pipe in hot weather; and in the course of time the whole mansion was overrun by the chubby-faced progeny of Amy Webber and Dirk Waldron.

As Wolfert waxed old and rich and corpulent, he also set up a great gingerbread-colored carriage drawn by a pair of black Flanders mares with tails that swept the ground; and to commemorate the origin of his greatness he had for a crest a fullblown cabbage painted on the pannels, with the pithy motto *Alles Kopf* that is to say, ALL HEAD; meaning thereby that he had risen by sheer head-work.

To fill the measure of his greatness, in the fullness of time the renowned Ramm Rapelye slept with his fathers, and Wolfert Webber succeeded to the leathern-bottomed arm-chair in the inn parlor at Corlears Hook; where he long reigned greatly honored and respected, insomuch that he was never known to tell a story without its being believed, nor to utter a joke without its being laughed at.

RACHEL DYER

John Neal

1828

A Quaker from Portland, Maine, John Neal was born in 1793. He entered law school in Baltimore, Maryland, in 1815, and began writing to support himself there. He founded a literary society called the Delphian Club and edited their monthly journal, The Portico.

Among his fellow Delphians, Neal was renowned for the speed with which he wrote. They dubbed him "Jehu O'Cataract" for his prolific output, and he wrote at this time that "I shall write, as others drink, for exhilaration." In 1823 he left for England, on a mission to win recognition there for American literature, writing articles for the influential Blackwood's *Magazine among others, and publishing a novel titled* Brother Jonathan, or the New Englanders.

Neal returned to Portland in 1827, establishing a law practice and founding a short-lived literary journal called The Yankee. *He was an accomplished boxer and architect, and was active in the fields of women's rights, temperance and prohibition, and health and fitness. He founded several gymnasiums, and is sometimes called "the father of Maine athletics." He remained healthy and vigorous into old age, throwing a stubborn cigar smoker off a nonsmoking streetcar at the age of seventy-nine.*

Subtitled A North American Story, *his novel* Rachel Dyer *deals with the bigotry and scapegoating that surrounded the Salem witch trials, and shows the dangers of religious hysteria. Chapter IV, reproduced here, gives a fictionalized account of the origins and early growth of the Salem witch hysteria, which is no less horrific for its lack of overt supernatural content.*

Neal shows the prejudices of his day against nonwhite races—and strangely, he makes the slave Tituba Native American instead of African—but perhaps the most difficult aspect of his writing to the modern reader will be the torrent of passionate dialogue at the end of the chapter, delivered entirely without quotation marks. As with earlier writers, his text has not been amended for this collection, but is presented here in its original form.

CHAPTER IV

Bridget Pope was of a thoughtful serious turn—the little Abby the veriest romp that ever breathed. Bridget was the elder, by about a year and a half, but she looked five years older than Abby, and was in every way a remarkable child. Her beauty was like her stature, and both were above her age; and her aptitude for learning was the talk of all that knew her. She was a favorite every where and with every body—she had such a sweet way with her, and was so unlike the other children of her age—so that when she appeared to merit reproof, as who will not in the heyday of innocent youth, it was quite impossible to reprove her, except with a mild voice, or a kind look, or a very affectionate word or two. She would keep away from her slate and book for whole days together, and sit for half an hour at a time without moving her eyes off the page, or turning away her head from the little window of their school-house (a log-hut plastered with blue clay in stripes and patches, and lighted with horn, oiled-paper and isinglass) which commanded a view of Naumkeag, or Salem village, with a part of the original woods of North America—huge trees that were found there on the first arrival of the white man; crowded together and covered with moss and dropping to pieces of old age; a meeting-house with a short wooden spire, and the figure of death on the top for a weathercock, a multitude of cottages that appeared to be lost in the landscape, and a broad beautiful approach from the sea.

Speak softly to Bridget Pope at such a time, or look at her with a look of love, and her quiet eyes would fill, and her childish heart would run over—it would be impossible to say why. But if you spoke sharply to her, when her head was at the little window, and her thoughts were away, nobody knew where, the poor little thing would grow pale and serious, and look at you with such a look of sorrow—and then go away and do what she was bid with a gravity that would go to your heart. And it would require a whole day after such a rebuke to restore the dye of her sweet lips, or to persuade her that you were not half so angry as you might have appeared. At every sound of your voice, at every step that came near, she would catch her breath, and start and look up, as if she expected something dreadful to happen.

But as for Abigail Paris, the pretty little blue-eyed cousin of Bridget Pope, there was no dealing with her in that way. If you shook your finger at her, she would laugh in your face; and if you did it with a grave air, ten to one but she made you laugh too. If you scolded her, she would scold you in return but always in such a way that you could not possibly be angry with her; she would mimic your step with her little naked feet, or the toss of your head, or the very curb of your mouth perhaps, while you were trying to terrify her. The little wretch!—everybody was tired to death of her in half an hour, and yet everybody was glad to see her again. Such was Abigail Paris, before Bridget Pope came to live in the house with her, but in the course of about half a year after that, she was so altered that her very play-fellows twitted her with being "afeard o' Bridgee Pope." She began to be tidy in her dress, to comb her bright hair, to speak low, to keep her shoes on her feet, and her stockings from about her heels, and before a twelve-month was over, she left off wading in the snow, and grew very fond of her book.

They were always together now, creeping about under the old beach-trees, or hunting for hazle nuts, or searching for sun-baked apples in the short thick grass, or feeding the fish in the smooth clear sea—Bridget poring over a story that she had picked up, nobody knows where, and Abigail, whatever the story might be, and although the water might stand in her eyes at the time, always ready for a roll in the wet grass, a dip in the salt wave, or a slide from the very top of the hay-mow. They rambled about in the great woods together on tip-toe, holding their breath and saying their prayers at every step; they lay down together and slept together on the very track of the wolf, or the she-bear; and if they heard a noise afar off, a howl or a war-whoop, they crept in among the flowers of the solitary spot and were safe, or hid themselves in the shadow of trees that were spread out over the whole sky, or of shrubbery that appeared to cover the whole earth—

Where the wild grape hangs dropping in the shade,
O'er unfledged minstrels that beneath are laid;

Where the scarlet barberry glittered among the sharp green leaves like threaded bunches of coral,—where at every step the more brilliant ivory-plumbs or clustered bunch-berries rattled among the withered herbage and rolled about their feet like a handful of beads,—where they delighted to go even while they were afraid to speak above a whisper, and kept fast hold of each other's hands, every step of the way. Such was their love, such their companionship, such their behaviour while •p pressed with fear. They were never apart for a day, till the time of our story; they were together all day and all night, going to sleep together and waking up together, feeding out of the same cup, and sleeping in the same bed, year after year.

But just when the preacher was ready to believe that his Father above had not altogether deserted him—for he was ready to cry out with joy whenever he looked upon these dear children; they were so good and so beautiful, and they loved each other so entirely; just when there appeared to be no evil in his path, no shadow in his way to the grave, a most alarming change took place in their behavior to each other. He tried to find out the cause, but they avoided all inquiry. He talked with them together, he talked with them apart, he tried every means in his power to know the truth, but all to no purpose. They were afraid of each other, and that was all that either would say. Both were full of mischief and appeared to be possessed with a new temper. They were noisy and spiteful toward each other, and toward every body else. They were continually hiding away from each other in holes and corners, and if they were pursued and plucked forth to the light, they were always found occupied with mischief above their age. Instead of playing together as they were wont, or sitting together in peace, they would creep away under the tables and chairs and beds, and behave as if they were hunted by something which nobody else could see; and they would lie there by the hour, snapping and snarling at each other, and at everybody that passed near. They had no longer the look of health, or of childhood, or of innocence. They were meagre and pale, and their eyes were fiery, and their fingers were skinny and sharp, and they delighted in devilish tricks and in outcries yet more devilish. They would play by themselves in the dead of the night, and shriek with a preternatural voice, and wake everybody with strange laughter—a sort of smothered giggle, which would appear to issue from the garret, or from the top of the house, while they were asleep, or pretending to be dead asleep in the great room below. They would break out all over in a fine sweat like the dew on a rose bush, and fall down as if they were struck to the heart with a knife, while they were on the way to meeting or school, or when the elders of the church were talking to them and every eye was fixed on their faces with pity or terror. They would grow pale as death in a moment, and seem to hear voices in the wind, and shake as with an ague while standing before a great fire, and look about on every side with such a piteous look for children, whenever it thundered or lightened, or whenever the sea roared, that the eyes of all who saw them would fill with tears. They would creep away backwards from each other on their hands and feet, or hide their faces in the lap of the female Indian Tituba, and if the preacher spoke to them, they would fall into a stupor, and awake with fearful cries and appear instantly covered all over with marks and spots like those which are left by pinching or bruising the flesh. They would be struck dumb while repeating the Lord's prayer, and all their features would be distorted with a savage and hateful expression.

The heads of the church were now called together, and a day of general fasting, humiliation and prayer was appointed, and after that, the best medical men of the whole country were consulted, the pious and the gifted, the interpreters of dreams, the soothsayers, and the prophets of the Lord, every man of power, and every woman of power,—but no relief was had, no cure, no hope of cure.

Matthew Paris now began to be afraid of his own child. She was no longer the hope of his heart, the joy of his old age, the live miniature of his buried wife. She was an evil thing—she was what he had no courage to think of, as he covered his old face and tore his white hair with a grief that would not be rebuked nor appeased. A new fear fell upon him, and his knees smote together, and the hair of his flesh rose, and he saw a spirit, and the spirit said to him look! And he looked, and lo! the truth appeared to him; for he saw neighbour after neighbour flying from his path, and all the heads of the church keeping aloof and whispering together in a low voice. Then knew he that Bridget Pope and Abigail Paris were bewitched.

A week passed over, a whole week, and every day and every hour they grew worse and worse, and the solitude in which he lived, more dreadful to him; but just when there appeared to be no hope left, no chance for escape, just when he and the few that were still courageous enough to speak with him, were beginning to despair, and to wish for the speedy death of the little sufferers, dear as they had been but a few weeks before to every body that knew them, a discovery was made which threw the whole country into a new paroxysm of terror. The savages who had been for a great while in the habit of going to the house of the preacher to eat and sleep "without money and without price," were now seen to keep aloof and to be more than usually grave; and yet when they were told of the children's behaviour, they showed no sort of surprise, but shook their heads with a smile, and went their way, very much as if they were prepared for it.

When the preacher heard this, he called up the two Indians before him, and spoke to Tituba and prayed to know why her people who for years had been in the habit of lying before his hearth, and eating at his table, and coming in and going out of his habitation at all hours of the day and night, were no longer seen to approach his door.

"Tituppa no say—Tituppa no know," she replied.

But as she replied, the preacher saw her make a sign to Peter Wawpee, her Sagamore, who began to show his teeth as if he knew something more than he chose to tell; but before the preacher could rebuke him as he deserved, or pursue the inquiry with Tituba, his daughter screamed out and fell upon her face and lay for a long while as if she were death-struck.

The preacher now bethought him of a new course, and after watching Tituba and Wawpee for several nights, became satisfied from what he saw, that she was a woman of diabolical power. A part of what he saw, he was afraid even to speak of; but he declared on oath before the judges, that he had seen sights, and heard noises that took away his bodily strength, his hearing and his breath for a time; that for nearly five weeks no one of her tribe, nor of Wawpee's tribe had slept upon his hearth, or eaten of his bread, or lifted the latch of his door either by night or by day; that notwithstanding this, the very night before, as he went by the grave-yard where his poor wife lay, he heard the whispering of a multitude; that having no fear in such a place, he made a search; and that after a long while he found his help Tituba concealed in the bushes, that he said nothing but went his way, satisfied in his own soul however that the voices he heard were the voices of her tribe; and that after the moon rose he saw her employed with a great black Shadow on the rock of death, where as every body knew, sacrifices had been offered up in other days by another people to the god of the Pagan—the deity of the savage—employed in a way that made him shiver with fright where he stood; for between her and the huge black shadow there lay what he knew to be the dead body of his own dear child stretched out under the awful trees—her image rather, for she was at home and abed and asleep at the time. He would have spoken to it if he could—for he saw what he believed to be the shape of his wife; he would have screamed for help if he could, but he could not get his breath, and that was the last he knew; for when he came to himself he was lying in his own bed, and Tituba was sitting by his side with a cup of broth in her hand which he took care to throw away the moment her back was turned; for she was a creature of extraordinary art, and would have persuaded him that he had never been out of his bed for the whole day.

The judges immediately issued a warrant for Tituba and Wawpee, both of whom were hurried off to jail, and after a few days of proper inquiry, by torture, she was put upon trial for witchcraft. Being sorely pressed by the word of the preacher and by the testimony of Bridget Pope and Abigail Paris, who with two more afflicted children (for the mischief had spread now in every quarter) charged her and Sarah Good with appearing to them at all hours, and in all places, by day and by night, when they were awake and when they were asleep, and with tormenting their flesh. Tituba pleaded guilty and confessed before the judges and the people that the poor children spoke true, that she was indeed a witch, and that, with several of her sister witches of great power—among whom was mother Good, a miserable woman who lived a great way off, nobody knew where—and passed the greater part of her time by the sea-side, nobody knew how, she had been persuaded by the black man to pursue and worry and vex them. But the words were hardly out of her mouth before she herself was taken with a fit, which lasted so long that the judges believed her to be dead. She was lifted up and carried out into the air; but though she recovered her speech and her strength in a little time, she was altered in her looks from that day to the day of her death.

But as to mother Good, when they brought her up for trial, she would neither confess to the charge nor pray the court for mercy; but she stood up and mocked the jury and the people, and reproved the judges for hearkening to a body of accusers who were collected from all parts of the country, were of all ages, and swore to facts, which if they ever occurred at all, had occurred years and years before—facts which it would have been impossible for her to contradict, even though they had all been, as a large part of them obviously were, the growth of mistake or of superstitious dread. Her behavior was full of courage during the trial; and after the trial was over, and up to the last hour and last breath of her life, it was the same.

You are a liar! said she to a man who called her a witch to her teeth, and would have persuaded her to confess and live. You are a liar, as God is my judge, Mike! I am no more a witch than you are a wizard, and you know it Mike, though you be so glib at prayer; and if you take away my life, I tell you now that you and yours, and the people here, and the judges and the elders who are now thirsting for my blood shall rue the work of this day, forever and ever, in sackcloth and ashes; and I tell you further as Elizabeth Hutchinson told you. Ah ha! . . . . how do you like the sound of that

name, Judges? You begin to be afraid I see; you are all quiet enough now!
. . . . But I say to you nevertheless, and I say to you here, even here, with
my last breath, as Mary Dyer said to you with her last breath, and as poor
Elizabeth Hutchinson said to you with hers, if you take away my life, the
wrath of God shall pursue you!—you and yours!—forever and ever! Ye are
wise men that I see, and mighty in faith, and ye should be able with such
faith to make the deep boil like a pot, as they swore to you I did, to remove
mountains, yea to shake the whole earth by a word—mighty in faith or how
could you have swallowed the story of that knife-blade, or the story of the
sheet? Very wise are you, and holy and fixed in your faith, or how could
you have borne with the speech of that bold man, who appeared to you
in court, and stood face to face before you when you believed him to be afar
off, or lying at the bottom of the sea, and would not suffer you to take
away the life even of such a poor unhappy old creature as I am, without
reproving you as if he had authority from the Judge of judges and the King
of kings to stay you in your faith!

Poor soul but I do pity thee! whispered a man who stood near with
a coiled rope in one hand and a drawn sword in the other. It was the
high-sheriff.

Her eyes filled and her voice faltered for the first time, when she
heard this, and she put forth her hand with a smile, and assisted him
in preparing the rope, saying as the cart stopped under the large beam.
Poor soul indeed!—You are too soft-hearted for your office, and of the
two, you are more to be pitied than the poor old woman you are a-going
to choke.

Mighty in faith she continued, as the high-sheriff drew forth a watch
and held it up for her to see that she had but a few moments to live.
I address myself to you, ye Judges of Israel! and to you ye teachers of
truth! Believe ye that a mortal woman of my age, with a tope about
her neck, hath power to prophesy? If ye do, give ear to my speech and
remember my words. For death, ye shall have death! For blood, ye shall
have blood—blood on the earth! Blood in the sky! blood in the waters!
Ye shall drink blood and breathe blood, you and yours, for the work of
this day!

Woman, woman! we pray thee to forbear! cried a voice from afar off.

I shall not forbear, Cotton Mather—it is your voice that I hear. But for you and such as you, miserable men that ye are, we should now be happy and at peace one with another. I shall not forbear—why should I? What have I done that I may not speak to the few that love me before we are parted by death?

Be prepared woman—if you will die, for the clock is about to strike said another voice.

Be prepared, sayest thou? William Phips, for I know the sound of thy voice top thou hard-hearted miserable man! Be prepared, sayest thou? Behold—stretching forth her arms to the sky, and lifting herself up and speaking so that she was heard of the people on the house-tops afar off, Lo! I am ready! Be ye also ready, for now!—now!—even while I speak to you, he is preparing to reward both my accusers and my judges—

He!—who!

Who, brother Joseph? said somebody in the crowd.

Why the Father of lies to be sure! what a question for you to ask, after having been of the jury!

Thou scoffer!—

Paul! Paul, beware!—

Hark—what's that! Lord have mercy upon us!

The Lord have mercy upon us! cried the people, giving way on every side, without knowing why, and looking toward the high-sea, and holding their breath.

Pho, pho, said the scoffer, a grey-haired man who stood leaning over his crutch with eyes full of pity and sorrow, pho, pho, the noise that you hear is only the noise of the tide.

Nay, nay. Elder Smith, nay, nay, said an associate of the speaker. If it is only the noise of the tide, why have we not heard it before? and why do we not hear it now? just now, when the witch is about to be—

True . . . true . . . it may not be the Evil one, after all.

The Evil one, Joe Libby! No, no! it is God himself, our Father above! cried the witch, with a loud voice, waving her arms upward, and fixing her eye upon a group of two or three individuals who stood aloof, decorated with the badges of authority. Our Father above, I say! The Governor of governors, and the Judge of judges! . . . The cart began to move here . . .

He will reward you for the work of this day! He will refresh you with blood for it! and you too Jerry Pope, and you too Micajah Noyes, and you too Job Smith, and you . . . and you . . . and you . . .

Yea of a truth! cried a woman who stood apart from the people with her hands locked and her eyes fixed upon the chief-judge. It was Rachel Dyer, the grandchild of Mary Dyer. Yea of a truth I for the Lord will not hold him guiltless that spilleth his brother's blood, or taketh his sister's life by the law—and her speech was followed by a shriek from every hill-top and every house-top, and from every tree and every rock within sight of the place, and the cart moved away, and the body of the poor old creature swung to and fro in the convulsions of death.

MOLL PITCHER

John Greenleaf Whittier

1832

Born in 1807, John Greenleaf Whittier was one of the "Fireside Poets," a group whose membership included Henry Wadsworth Longfellow and Oliver Wendell Holmes, Sr., the father of the famous American jurist. The first American poets to rival the popularity of British writers like Tennyson, the Fireside Poets received their name from the fact that their works were read and recited at firesides throughout the country. Their works were unashamedly American in character, often featuring reformist themes.

A Quaker from Massachusetts, Whittier campaigned against slavery and was the editor of a Boston temperance weekly. He was one of the founding contributors to Atlantic Monthly *magazine (now* The Atlantic *magazine). He is best known for his long narrative poem* Snow-Bound, *in which a New England family, snowbound for a week in their home, tell each other stories to while away the time. Several of his poems have been turned into hymns, including* "Dear Lord and Father of Mankind."

Whittier wrote the nine-hundred-line Moll Pitcher *early in his career. Moll (not to be confused with the Revolutionary War heroine Molly Pitcher, who was*

*probably fictional) was a real woman who lived near Lynn, Massachusetts. Prob-
ably born around 1736, she died in 1813. She was well-known as a clairvoyant and
fortune-teller, but Whittier, perhaps inspired by the image of New England witches
that developed after the Salem witch trials, paints her in an altogether darker light.*

*Moll Pitcher was not Whittier's only foray into the realm of the supernatural,
though it remains the longest. The previous year he had written "The Weird Gathering," inspired by Cotton Mather's account of the Salem witches, and in 1867 he
rendered a Rhode Island ghost story into verse as "The Palatine."*

PART I

Ha, ha—ha, ha—ha, ha!—
The old witch laughed outright
Ha, ha—ha, ha—ha, ha!—
That cold and dismal night.
The wind was blowing from the sea
as raw and chill as wind might be—
Driving the waves, as if their master
Towards the black shore, fast and faster,—
Tossing their foam against the rocks
Which scowl along yon island's verge,
And shake their gray and mossy locks
Secure above the warring surge.
Keen blew the wind, and cold,
The moon shone dim and faintly forth,
Between the gray cloud's parting fold,
As if it sickened of the earth,
So very pale and ghastly lay

Its broken light along the bay,
Silvering the fisher's stealing skiff—
Or whitening o'er the jagged cliff,
Or resting on the homes of men,
As if its awful sheen had been
A white funeral shroud outspread
By some kind spirit o'er the dead;
And, now and then, a wan star burned.
Where'er its cloudy veil was rended—
A moment's light, but seen and ended,
As if some angel from on high
Had fixed on earth his brilliant eye,
And back to Heaven his glances turned!
She stood upon a bare, tall crag,
Which overlooked her ragged cot—
A wasted, gray and meagre hag,
In features evil as her lot.
She had the crooked nose of a witch,
And a crooked back and chin,
And in her gait she had a hitch,
And in her hand she carried a switch,
To aid her work of sin,
A twig of wizard-hazle, which
Had grown beside a haunted ditch,
Where a mother her nameless child had thrown
To the running water and merciless stone.
Who's coming up the winding path,
Worn faintly in the mossy rock?—
Enveloped in its ample cloak
The form a woman's semblance hath.
Why laughs the witch to see her come
So stealthily towards her home?
Knows she that dim shape thus afar,
When scarce one shorn and shadowed star,
With its faint line of wizard light

Crosses the shadow of the night?
Long laughed the witch—and then she spoke,
And echo answered from the rock,
As if some wild and evil elf
Within its caverns dared to mock
Her strange communion with herself.
"And so," she cried, "she's come at last,—
The oak will kneel before the blast,
And wherefore should the sapling frail
Bend its light form against the gale?
The heart is strong—but passion stronger
And love than human pride is longer—
And ill may woman's weakness scorn
What manhood's strength hath hardly borne!
I know her tread—'tis haughty yet,
As if she could not all forget
Her early scorn of me and mine.
Ay. let her come!—the early spell,
Which binds her heart so sweetly well,
Shall serpent-like around it twine!
I know the charm—I know the word,
Which, powerless as the snake-charmed bird,
Shall bind her with its fearful tone—
Her cherished thoughts shall all be heard,
Her secret hopes shall all be known.
Again she laughed as down the crag
She swung her meagre skeleton—
No fears for thee, thou hateful hag—
The Devil keeps his own!
"Walk in, walk in my pretty maid
This night is fitting for my trade!"
"Ha, mother Moll—'tis well—I've come,
Like other fools to know my doom."
The twain passed in—a low dark room
With here and there a crazy chair,

A broken glass—a dusty loom—
A spinning-wheel—a birchen broom,
The witch's courier of the air—
As potent as that steed of wings
On which the Meccan prophet rode
Above the wreck of meaner things
Unto the Houri's bright abode.
A low dull fire by flashes shone
Across the gray and cold hearth-stone
Flinging at times a trembling glare
On the low roof and timbers bare.
How has New England's romance fled,
Even as a vision of the morning!
Its rites foregone—its guardians dead—
Its altar-fires extinguished—
Its priestesses, bereft of dread,
Waking the veriest urchin's scorning!
No more along the shadowy glen,
Glide the dim ghosts of murdered men,—
No more the unquiet church-yard dead,
Glimpse upward from their turfy bed,
Startling the traveller, late and lone;
As, on some night of cloudy weather,
They commune silently together.
Each sitting on his own head-stone!
The roofless house, decayed, deserted,
Its living tenants all departed,
No longer rings with midnight revel
Of witch, or ghost, or goblin evil;
No hellish flame sends out its flashes
Through creviced roof and shattered sashes!—
The witch-grass round the hazle spring,
May sharply to the night air sing,
But there no more shall withered hags
Refresh at ease, their broomstick nags;

Or taste those hazle-shadowed waters
As beverage meet for Satan's daughters;
No more their mimic tones be heard—
The mew of cat—the chirp of bird,
Shrill blending with the hoarser laughter
Of the fell demon following after!
The cautious good man nails no more
A horse shoe on his outer door,
Lest some unseemly hag should fit
To his own mouth her bridle bit—
The good wife's churn no more refuses
Its wonted culinary uses,
Until with heated needle burned
The witch has to her place returned!
Our witches are no longer old
And wrinkled beldames, Satan sold,
But young and gay and laughing creatures,
With the heart's sunshine on their features—
Their sorcery—the light which dances
Where the raised lid unveils its glances;
Or the low breathed and gentle tone
Faintly responding unto ours,
Soft, dream-like, as a fairy's moan
Above its nightly closing flowers!
Sweeter than that which sighed of yore,
Along the charmed Ausonian shore!
Even she, our own weired heroine,
Sole Pythoness of ancient Lynn—
Despite her fortune telling sin,
Sleeps calmly where the living laid her;
And the wide realm of sorcery,
Left, by its latest mistress, free,
Hath found no gray and skilled invader
So perished Albion's "glammarye,"
With him in Melrose Abbey sleeping,

His charmed torch beside his knee
That even the dead himself might see
The magic scroll within his keeping.
And hence our modern Yankee sees
Nor omens, spells nor mysteries;
And nought above, below, around,
Of life or death, of sight or sound,
Whate'er its nature, form or look.
Excites his terror or surprise—
All seeming to his knowing eyes
Familiar as his "catechize,"
Or, "Webster's Spelling Book."
But to our tale.—In contrast strange,
Within the fire-light's fading range
The stranger stands in maiden pride,
By that mysterious woman's side.
The cloak hath fallen from her shoulder
Revealing such a form as steals
Away the heart of the beholder
As, all unconsciously it kneels
Before the beauty which had shone
Ere this upon its dreams alone.
If you have seen a summer star,
Liquidly soft and faintly far,
Beaming a smiling glance on earth
As if it watched the flowret's birth,
Then have you seen a light less fair
Than that young maiden's glances were.
Dark fell her tresses—you have seen
A rent cloud tossing in the air,
And, showing the pure sky between
Its floating fragments here and there—
Then may you fancy faintly, how
The falling tress—the ring-like curl
Disclosed or shadowed o'er the brow

And neck of that fair girl.
Her cheek was delicately thin,
And through its pure, transparent white
The rose-hue wandered out and in,
As you have seen th' inconstant light
Flush o'er the Northern sky of night—
Her playful lip was gently full,
Soft curving to the graceful chin,
And colored like the fruit which glows
Upon the sunned pomegranite boughs;—
And oh, her soft, low voice might lull
The spirit to a dream of bliss,
As if the voices sweet and bland
Which murmur in the seraph land
Were warbling in a world like this!
Out spoke the witch—"I know full well,
Why thou has sought my humble cot—
Come sit thee down—the tale I tell
May not be soon forgot."
She threw her pale blue cloak aside,
And stirred the whitening embers up,
And long and curiously she eyed
The figures of her mystic cup—
And low she muttered, while the light
Gave to her lips a ghastlier white,
And her sunk eye's unearthly glaring
Seemed like the taper's latest flaring:
"Dark hair—eyes black—a goodly form—
A maiden weeping—wild dark sea—
A tall ship tossing in the storm—
A black wreck floating—where is he?
Give me the hand—how soft and warm
And fair its tapering fingers seem—
And who that sees it now would dream
That winter's snow would seem less chill

Ere long than these soft fingers will?
A lovely palm!—how delicate
Its veined and wandering lines are drawn!
Yet each are prophets of thy fate—
Ha—this is sure a fearful one!
That sudden cross—that blank beneath—
What may these evil signs betoken?
Passion and sorrow, fear and death—
A human spirit crushed and broken!
Oh, thine hath been a pleasant dream.
But darker shall its waking seem!"
Something between a sigh and groan
Burst from the list'ner's panting heart
How was her cherished secret known
To that dark woman's art?
She strove to smile—and one might mark
A sudden dimple trembling, where
A moment after cold despair
Rested beneath her tresses dark,
As if the hue of death were there.
A human smile!—how beautiful
Sometimes its blissful presence seems,
Sweet as the gentle airs which lull
To sleep the holy flowers of Gul
Which blossoms in the Persian's dreams
A lovely light whene'er it beams
On beauty's brow—on beauty's eye
And not one token lingers nigh
On lip, or eye, or cheek unbidden
To tell of anguish vainly hidden!
But oh there is a smile which steals
Sometimes upon the brow of care
And like the North's cold light reveals
But gathering darkness there.
You've seen the lightning flash at night

Play briefly o'er its cloudy pile—
The moonshine trembling on the height
Where winter glistens cold and white,
And like that flash, and like that light,
Is sorrow's vain and heartless smile.
Like a cold hand upon her heart
The dark words of the sorceress lay,
Something to scare her spirit's rest
Forevermore away.
Each word had seemed so strangely true,
Calling her inmost thoughts in view.
And pointing to the form which came
Before her in her dreary sleep,
Whose answered love—whose very name,
Though naught of breathing life was near,
She scarce had given the winds to keep,
Or murmured in a sister's ear.
Her secret love!—oh, she had kept
Its fire within her heart unseen,
And tears, in silent musing wept,
Its sacrifice had been.
In public gaze—in loneliness—
In fashion's gay and wild excess—
In every change of scene or lot
Its cherished name was uttered not.
For early had she learned to keep
Her gift of love enshrined and deep—
Pure as the vestal's altar-stone
Known and familiar but to one—
A harp whose chords might only move
In answer to its idol love,
Like Memnon's music heard alone
When sunlight on its statue shone!
Like the mimosa shrinking from
The blight of some familiar finger—

Like flowers which but in secret bloom,
Where age the sheltering shadows linger.
And which, beneath the hot noon ray
Would fold their leaves and fade away—
The flowers of Love, in secret cherished,
In loneliness and silence nourished,
Shrink backward from the searching eye,
Until the stem whereon they flourished,
Their shrine, the human heart, has perished,
Although themselves may never die.
Of woe—of deep and nameless grief.
That wild and evil hag had spoken—
Of agony which mocks relief—
Of human spirits broken.
And in her mutterings vague and dim
How strangely had she pictured HIM!
The dark eye and the darker hair—
The manly form and features fair—
A weeping girl—a wild dark sea—
A storm—a wreck—and "WHERE IS HE?"
Ay, where WAS he!—long months before,
His boat was rocking on the shore
His ship was tossing in the bay:
And she was folded to his heart—
Her fair cheek on her lover's lay.
While Love forgot the veil of art;
And softly blushed through falling tears,
The natural glow of virgin shame,
That feelings held apart for years,
And cherished hopes she scarce might name
To her own pillow's loneliness,
Had burned upon her answering kiss.
And thrilled upon her lip of flame!
And she had found herself alone,
Beneath the twilight cold and gray.

When heavily pealed the signal gun
And the proud vessel swept away—
Watching her lover's broad sail fade,
Like a white wing in upper air.
And leaving neither track nor shade
On the blue waste of waters there!
Smile not that on the maiden's heart.
The sybil's dark and cunning art
Had power to picture future ill,
And tinge the present darker still.
Life's sunniest hours are not without
The shadow of some lingering doubt—
Amidst its brightest joys will steal
Spectres of evil yet to feel;
Its warmest love is blent with fears,
Its confidence—a trembling one—
Its smile—the harbinger of tears—
Its hope—the change of April's sun
A weary lot,—in mercy given,
To fit the chastened soul for Heaven,
Prompting with change and weariness,
Its yearning for that better sky,
Which, as the shadows close on this,
Grows brighter to the longing eye.

PART II

Nahant, thy beach is beautiful!—
A dim line through the tossing waves,
Along whose verge the spectre gull
Her thin and snowy plumage laves—
What time the Summer's greenness lingers
Within thy sunned and sheltered nooks,
And the green vine with twining fingers

184

Creeps up and down thy hanging rocks!
Around—the blue and level main—
Above—a sunshine rich, as fell,
Bright'ning of old, with golden rain,
The isle Apollo loved so well!—
And far off, dim and beautiful
The snow-white sail and graceful hull,
Slow, dipping to the billow's swell.
Bright spot!—the Isles of Greece may share
A flowery earth—a gentle air;
The orange-bough may blossom well
In warm Bermuda's sunniest dell;—
But fairer shores and brighter waters,
Gazed on by purer, lovelier daughters,
Beneath the light of kindlier skies,
The wanderer to the farthest bound
Of peopled Earth hath never found
Than thine—New England's Paradise!
Land of the forest and the rock—
Of dark blue lake, and mighty river—
Of mountains reared aloft to mock
The storm's career—the lightning's shock—
My own, green land, forever!
Land of the beautiful and brave—
The freeman's home—the martyr's grave—
The nursery of giant men,
Whose deeds have linked with every glen,
And every hill and every stream,
The romance of some warrior-dream!
Oh—never may a son of thine,
Where'er his wandering steps incline,
Forget the sky which bent above
His childhood like a dream of love—
The stream beneath the green hill flowing—
The broad-armed trees above it growing—

The clear breeze through the foliage blowing
Or, hear unmoved, the taunt of scorn
Breathed o'er the brave New-England born;—
Or mark the stranger's Jaguar hand
Disturb the ashes of thy dead—
The buried glory of a land
Whose soil with noble blood is red,
And sanctified in every part,
Nor feel resentment, like a brand,
Unsheathing from his fiery heart!
Oh—greener hills may catch the sun
Beneath the glorious heaven of France;
And streams, rejoicing as they run
Like life beneath the day-beam's glance,
May wander where the orange-bough
With golden fruit is bending low;—
And there may bend a brighter sky
O'er green and classic Italy—
And pillared fane and ancient grave
Bear record of another time,
And over shaft and architrave
The green luxuriant ivy climb;—
And far towards the rising sun
The palm may shake its leaves on high,
Where flowers are opening, one by one,
Like stars upon the twilight sky,
And breezes soft as sighs of love
Above the broad banana stray.
And through the Brahmin's sacred grove
A thousand bright-hued pinions play!
Yet, unto thee, New-England, still
Thy wondering sons shall stretch their arms,
And thy rude chart of rock and hill
Seem dearer than the land of palms!
Thy massy oak and mountain pine

More welcome than the banyan's shade,
And every free, blue stream of thine
Seem richer than the golden bed
Of Oriental waves, which glow
And sparkle with the wealth below!

A frail, fair form is stealing out
Upon the long and sandy bar,
With wild glance, wandering all about
Uncertain and irregular.
The sea-gull screams aloud above her—
The thin waves circle at her feet,
Beyond, the white and timid plover
Is stooping its embrace to meet.
What doth she there?—her head is bare—
And backward streams her wild, dark hair;
Damp with the moist sea-atmosphere
It shades a neck as white and clear,
As pearls which shed their pure, pale glow,
Where in their crimson beauty sleep
The coral blossoms of the deep
A thousand fathoms down below.
Beautiful one!—her cheek is pale,
Even as the foam the wave hath lent
To rocks whereon its wrath is spent,
Like that which lingers on the rein
Which some fierce steed hath spurned in vain;
And ever and anon a wail
Soft as some grieving spectre's moan.
Plaintively low—a dreamer's tone.
Blends faintly with the rising gale.
She stands upon a rock that lifts
Its bleak brow to the chilling waters—
The thin gray mist above it drifts,
And dim within its fold, she seems

Like something of our early dreams—
A messenger from Ocean's daughters!
Her thin hand pointing to the sea
As eager—as imploringly—
As if across that blue expanse,
Her eye had caught some answering glance
And sadly now she turns aside,
With slow and weary step returning
Drooping her head as if to hide
The tearful traces of her mourning.
The morn will find her there again
—GOD'S PITY ON THE STRICKEN BRAIN!—
It is a fearful thing to turn
The heart's warm current icy chill
To bid the brain with madness burn,
And freeze the torpid bosom still,
Fearful to cloud the spiritual light
Which shines upon our mortal night—
To jar apart those chords of mind
Which God's mysterious hand hath twined
And for the music once their own
Call out a harsh and maniac tone.
We talk of death—we shudder o'er
The cold, pale form—the rayless eye,
As if that fearful change were more,
Than the mind's hour of liberty—
The opening of its prison-door.
Yet look upon the maniac's form
Whence reason's holy light hath fled;
Where being lingers wild and warm,
Even when its very soul is dead.
Look on the snaky eye of madness—
And hear that laugh—but not of gladness—
That shriek at midnight, shrilly blending
With the dull clanking of the chain—

And pluck away those fingers rending
From the hot cheek its bursting vein!—
Alas—the quiet sepulchre
Than such a state were welcomer.
Yet hers is not that fiercer mood—
Gentle and lovely even in madness,
She only asks for solitude
To nurse her most unearthly sadness.
Oh! it is painful to behold
Her pale face on her hand reclining,
Or buried in her 'kerchief's fold,
With hot tears through her fingers shining.
And then to mark her 'wildered start,
Her quick glance in the vacant air,
Her thin hand pressing on her heart,
As if a sudden pang were there:
And then to list her murmured words
Sad as a mate-forsaken bird's,
Telling a wild and moving tale
Of wrecked ships driving in the gale—
Of voices shrieking in the blast—
Of wreathing arms on spar and mast—
Of one dark eye above the billow
Up glancing to the storm-fire's gleam;—
And that long sleep which hath no dream—
With ocean's weedy rock its pillow,
Down where the sea-plant's green arms cover
The cold, unwaking sleeper over.
She seeks the spot where she has strayed
Upon HIS arm in fondness leaning—
When by the trembling light which played,
Amidst the leafy summer shade,
The kindling eye of either lover
In silent fondness told each rover,
The hidden heart's unwhispered meaning.

Beneath the old, familiar oak,
A carpet of the living green
Is round her; and from out a rock
Like that which felt the Prophet's stroke
Its mossed and yawning clefts between,

PART III

A tall ship tossing in the bay!—
How glorious the stranger seems—
With tapering masts and streamers gay,
Rejoicing in the glad sunbeams!
Beautiful voyager!—she has been,
Unshrinking upon God's high sea—
Bearing right onward bravely when
The storm-wind followed free!
There's one upon her seamy deck,
With keen eye fastened on the shore,
As if some faithful loved one's beck
Were welcoming once more
From toil and fear to love and her
The worn and weary mariner.
Oh! he hath been a wanderer
Beneath Magellan's moveless cloud,
And where in murmurs hoarse and loud
The Demon of the Cape was heard;
And where the tropic sunset came
O'er the rich bowers of Indostan,
And many a strange and brilliant bird
Shone brighter in the western flame:
And through the bending jungle ran
The boa for his nightly food,
The tiger slumbering in the wood.
He sought for gold—for yellow gold—

His dreams were full of wealth untold;
Of stately barks that hailed to him;
Of gorgeous halls and grottos dim,
Of streams rejoicing in the shade,
By bower and trelliced arbor made,
Of smiling servants gathered near
In grateful love, but not in fear;
And more than these—his own loved one—
With her white brow and soft dark eyes,
Fair as the new-born flower, whereon
Never hath looked the noon-day sun,
The Houri of his Paradise!

Yet his was not a sordid heart.
He did not love the merchant's mart,
His finer soul revolted when
He mingled thus with selfish men—
Yet long and wearily he bore
The burthen of incessant care,
Unfriended, on a stranger shore,
While Hope still hovered dimly o'er
One object which he valued more
Than all the wealth he gathered there;
The loved one in his native land,
More dear than gems of Sarmacand.
Welcome as the voice of kindness,
To him, who in some dungeon dim
Moves slow with pain his fettered limb,
Or light to those who sit in blindness,
Is home's green shore to him.
He stands upon his native earth—
Voices of greeting and of mirth
Are round him,—but his anxious eye
Turns from the throng impatiently—
One hurried word—one clasp of hand

And he has bounded from the strand!
On, swiftly on—even now he sees
Her white-walled dwelling through the trees!
Quick, from behind a leafy screen—
The gateway wreathed in creeping green,
With wild flowers twined in every curl—
And flashing from her brilliant eye
The wildness of insanity.
Darted the maniac girl.
"MY OWN ADELA! "—At his tone
She started—and as memory went
Back to the joys her youth had known,
Over each vacant lineament,
One gleam of banished reason shone!
Briefly it shone—a smile as chill
As moonshine on a wintry hill
Met the fixed, ardent gaze of love—
"Oh! Henry, it is kind to leave
That glad and happy home above,
Where spirits never learn to grieve
To whisper comfort to the ear
That loved thy living words to hear."
And then she smiled again so sadly,
So soft, so sweet—alas—so MADLY!
Oh—God!—was this a human greeting?
Was this an ardent lover's meeting?
The wanderer pressed his burning brain,
With marble lip, and eye unweeping
While to its lid the tears were creeping
Hot, slow, like drops of fiery rain!
The tears of manhood!—they are such,
As may not speak of selfish woe,
Beneath some Heaven-directed touch
Like Horeb's rock alone they flow!
And oh! if man could always wear

That strength of pride which loves—to bear
With a firm lip and blenchless eye
The keenest human agony:—
If the strong spirit might not falter
Beneath the chastening of Heaven,
If ever on affliction's altar
A tearless sacrifice were given,—
Then might that spirit scorn to seek
Contrition's narrow path and lonely,
Or kneel in penitence, where—meek
And humble faith availeth only.
Chained down to low material things,
The soul forgetful of its birth—
Forgetful of its upward wings
Would half become a thing of earth—
And hence each blow misfortune gives
But breaks some chain which binds us here
And every shade the heart receives,
But makes the eye of faith more clear!

The twain are wandering on the beach
Beneath the pleasant morning sun,
Now stealing from the billow's reach,
Now following where its circles run.
It is a strange, yet lovely sight—
That dark eyed wanderer of the sea
Leading beneath the golden light,
The victim of insanity!
She thinks—how strange the thoughts will be
Of those whose mental light is dim!—
That one of that bright company
Who bend in Heaven the seraph's knee
Is near her in the form of him,
Who bending o'er her lovingly
Would half confirm her childish whim.

And hence her bearing is like one
Who would not seek, who would not shun
the kindness strangely proffered her
By some angelic messenger:
And yet an awe is on her face,
With trusting confidence contending
Either alternate, yielding place,
Like human love with reverence blending.
He chides her not; but soothingly,
And kindly, checks her wayward mood:
And to his gentle guidance, she
Attends with simple gratitude.
The thousand fancies which were nursed
In madness, vanish one by one,
And even as though its clouds will burst
the veiled but triumphant sun,
The brightness of her soul again
Shines through the murky veil of madness,
And once again her spirit's gladness,
Revives, like sere grass after rain.
Gentle as angels' ministry
The guiding hand of love should be
Which seeks again those chords to hind
Which human woe hath rent apart—
To heal again the wounded mind,
And bind anew the broken heart.
The hand which tunes to harmony,
The cunning harp whose strings are riven
Must move as light and quietly
As that meek breath of Summer heaven,
Which woke of old its melody
And kindness to the dim of soul,
Whilst aught of rude and stern control,
The clouded heart can deeply feel,
Is welcome as the odors fanned

From some unseen and flowery land,
Around the weary seaman's keel!
The mist hath vanished from her brain,
Like clouds the sun of noon has met;
And reason lights her eye again;
Again its glance is one of those,
Which, flashing from their calm repose,
Like star-beams at the daylight's close,
The gazer may not soon forget;—
A glance to haunt him in his sleep,
Wild, beautiful, and like the quiver,
Of moonlight, mirrored in the deep
Dark current of some shadowy river,—
A changeful, but unfading light—
A lustre from the spirit caught,
Varying indeed, but ever bright
With the unshadowed hues of thought!
Again the roses of her heart,
Are in their brightest blossoming:
And, as the frosted root will start,
With fresh, young—lip and brow of pearl,
Shadowed by many a natural curl,
Of unconfined and flowing hair—
With the moist eye of pitying care,
Is bending like a seraph there:
A seeming child in every thing
Save in her ripening maiden charms,
As nature wears the smile of spring,
When sinking into summer's arms.
From that long trance of torpid sleep,
Which sometimes on the eve of death,
Binds down the pulses, still and deep,
Unbroken by the passing breath,
The Witch hath roused her, at the tone,
To her old ear so seldom known,

Of pity, murmured faintly o'er her,
By the fair child, who, half in fear,
And half in sorrow, stealing near,
Stands in the dim twilight before her.
Upstarting from her wretched bed,
And pushing back her grizzly hair;
With that dull eye whose rayless glare,
Seems like the vision of the dead,
She peers into that young girl's face,
Most earnestly, as if to trace
Something which thrills the broken chain
Of memory over, once again.
"Ha—who art thou?—her daughter?"—
She murmurs in those tones of fear,
Which mingle with the gasping breath
Like voices from the tongue of death,—
"She, whom my hate hath cursed so long—
Hath she forgot her deadly wrong?—
And, maiden, hath she bidden thee,
Bend kindly o'er a wretch, like me?—
Nay, then, Heaven bless her! "—with some word
Unuttered is that white lip stirred—
Alas—Heaven rest the spirit gone!
Maiden!—thou'rt with the dead alone.

THE BIRTH-MARK

Nathaniel Hawthorne

1843

Nathaniel Hawthorne needs no introduction to American readers. His Puritan morality tale The Scarlet Letter *(1850) assured his place in the American literary canon, and much of his other work is colored by his favorite themes of sin and morality.*

Born Nathaniel Hathorne, he added the "w" to his name to hide his descent from the Salem judge John Hathorne. He graduated from Bowdoin College in 1825 and published his first novel, Fanshawe, *in 1828. Based on Hawthorne's experiences as a college student, the book was well-reviewed but sold poorly. He published short stories in various periodicals, publishing the collection* Twice-Told Tales *in 1837. These stories include several moral allegories that foreshadowed the tone of* The Scarlet Letter, *but some showed a lightness of touch that was more like the work of Washington Irving. "Doctor Heidegger's Experiment," for example, is a satire on human vanity featuring the legendary Elixir of Youth.*

Several of Hawthorne's tales of the uncanny are worth reading, even by those who do not have fond high-school memories of The Scarlet Letter. *Hawthorne's 1846 collection* Mosses from an Old Manse *includes the gloomy, atmospheric "Roger*

Malvin's Burial," the allegorical "Young Goodman Brown" (which owes something to John Bunyan's The Pilgrim's Progress *and something to the common American folk-tale motif of a meeting with the Devil at a crossroads), and "Drowne's Wooden Image," a Pygmalion-like tale set in the port of Boston.*

Mosses from an Old Manse *also contains "The Birth-Mark," which was first published in the March, 1843 edition of* The Pioneer. *While not as heavy-handed as his schoolroom standard* The Scarlet Letter, *the relentless pursuit of perfection has tragic consequences in this tale of eighteenth-century science and romance. An almost perfect blend of romanticism, allegory, and scientific horror, "The Birth-Mark" can stand alongside the work of Mary Shelley and Edgar Allan Poe with its head held high.*

I n the latter part of the last century there lived a man of science, an eminent proficient in every branch of natural philosophy, who not long before our story opens had made experience of a spiritual affinity more attractive than any chemical one. He had left his laboratory to the care of an assistant, cleared his fine countenance from the furnace smoke, washed the stain of acids from his fingers, and persuaded a beautiful woman to become his wife. In those days when the comparatively recent discovery of electricity and other kindred mysteries of Nature seemed to open paths into the region of miracle, it was not unusual for the love of science to rival the love of woman in its depth and absorbing energy. The higher intellect, the imagination, the spirit, and even the heart might all find their congenial aliment in pursuits which, as some of their ardent votaries believed, would ascend from one step of powerful intelligence to another, until the philosopher should lay his hand on the secret of creative force and perhaps make new worlds for himself. We know not whether Aylmer possessed this degree of faith in man's ultimate control over Nature. He had devoted himself, however, too unreservedly to scientific studies ever to be weaned from them by any second passion. His love for his young wife might prove the stronger of the two; but it could only be by intertwining itself with his love of science, and uniting the strength of the latter to his own.

Such a union accordingly took place, and was attended with truly remarkable consequences and a deeply impressive moral. One day, very soon after their marriage, Aylmer sat gazing at his wife with a trouble in his countenance that grew stronger until he spoke.

"Georgiana," said he, "has it never occurred to you that the mark upon your cheek might be removed?"

"No, indeed," said she, smiling; but perceiving the seriousness of his manner, she blushed deeply. "To tell you the truth it has been so often called a charm that I was simple enough to imagine it might be so."

"Ah, upon another face perhaps it might," replied her husband; "but never on yours. No, dearest Georgiana, you came so nearly perfect from the hand of Nature that this slightest possible defect, which we hesitate whether to term a defect or a beauty, shocks me, as being the visible mark of earthly imperfection."

"Shocks you, my husband!" cried Georgiana, deeply hurt; at first reddening with momentary anger, but then bursting into tears. "Then why did you take me from my mother's side? You cannot love what shocks you!"

To explain this conversation it must be mentioned that in the centre of Georgiana's left cheek there was a singular mark, deeply interwoven, as it were, with the texture and substance of her face. In the usual state of her complexion—a healthy though delicate bloom—the mark wore a tint of deeper crimson, which imperfectly defined its shape amid the surrounding rosiness. When she blushed it gradually became more indistinct, and finally vanished amid the triumphant rush of blood that bathed the whole cheek with its brilliant glow. But if any shifting motion caused her to turn pale there was the mark again, a crimson stain upon the snow, in what Aylmer sometimes deemed an almost fearful distinctness. Its shape bore not a little similarity to the human hand, though of the smallest pygmy size. Georgiana's lovers were wont to say that some fairy at her birth hour had laid her tiny hand upon the infant's cheek, and left this impress there in token of the magic endowments that were to give her such sway over all hearts. Many a desperate swain would have risked life for the privilege of pressing his lips to the mysterious hand. It must not be concealed, however, that the impression wrought by this fairy sign manual varied exceedingly, according to the difference of temperament in the beholders. Some fastidious persons—but they were exclusively of her own sex—affirmed that the bloody hand, as they chose to call it, quite destroyed the effect of Georgiana's beauty, and rendered her countenance even hideous. But it would be as reasonable to say that one of those small blue stains which sometimes occur in the purest statuary marble would convert the Eve of Powers to a monster. Masculine observers, if the birthmark did not heighten their admiration, contented themselves with wishing it away, that the world might possess one living specimen of ideal loveliness without the semblance of a flaw. After his marriage,—for he thought little or nothing of the matter before,—Aylmer discovered that this was the case with himself.

Had she been less beautiful,—if Envy's self could have found aught else to sneer at,—he might have felt his affection heightened by the prettiness of this mimic hand, now vaguely portrayed, now lost, now stealing forth again and glimmering to and fro with every pulse of emotion that throbbed within her heart; but seeing her otherwise so perfect, he found this one defect grow more and more intolerable with every moment of their united lives. It was the fatal flaw of humanity which Nature, in one shape or another, stamps ineffaceably on all her productions, either to imply that they are temporary and finite, or that their perfection must be wrought by toil and pain. The crimson hand expressed the ineludible gripe in which mortality clutches the highest and purest of earthly mould, degrading them into kindred with the lowest, and even with the very brutes, like whom their visible frames return to dust. In this manner, selecting it as the symbol of his wife's liability to sin, sorrow, decay, and death, Aylmer's sombre imagination was not long in rendering the birthmark a frightful object, causing him more trouble and horror than ever Georgiana's beauty, whether of soul or sense, had given him delight.

At all the seasons which should have been their happiest, he invariably and without intending it, nay, in spite of a purpose to the contrary, reverted to this one disastrous topic. Trifling as it at first appeared, it so connected itself with innumerable trains of thought and modes of feeling that it became the central point of all. With the morning twilight Aylmer opened his eyes upon his wife's face and recognized the symbol of imperfection; and when they sat together at the evening hearth his eyes wandered stealthily to her cheek, and beheld, flickering with the blaze of the wood fire, the spectral hand that wrote mortality where he would fain have worshipped. Georgiana soon learned to shudder at his gaze. It needed but a glance with the peculiar expression that his face often wore to change the roses of her cheek into a deathlike paleness, amid which the crimson hand was brought strongly out, like a bass-relief of ruby on the whitest marble.

Late one night when the lights were growing dim, so as hardly to betray the stain on the poor wife's cheek, she herself, for the first time, voluntarily took up the subject.

"Do you remember, my dear Aylmer," said she, with a feeble attempt at a smile, "have you any recollection of a dream last night about this odious hand?"

"None! none whatever!" replied Aylmer, starting; but then he added, in a dry, cold tone, affected for the sake of concealing the real depth of his emotion, "I might well dream of it; for before I fell asleep it had taken a pretty firm hold of my fancy."

"And you did dream of it?" continued Georgiana, hastily; for she dreaded lest a gush of tears should interrupt what she had to say. "A terrible dream! I wonder that you can forget it. Is it possible to forget this one expression?— 'It is in her heart now; we must have it out!' Reflect, my husband; for by all means I would have you recall that dream."

The mind is in a sad state when Sleep, the all-involving, cannot confine her spectres within the dim region of her sway, but suffers them to break forth, affrighting this actual life with secrets that perchance belong to a deeper one. Aylmer now remembered his dream. He had fancied himself with his servant Aminadab, attempting an operation for the removal of the birthmark; but the deeper went the knife, the deeper sank the hand, until at length its tiny grasp appeared to have caught hold of Georgiana's heart; whence, however, her husband was inexorably resolved to cut or wrench it away.

When the dream had shaped itself perfectly in his memory, Aylmer sat in his wife's presence with a guilty feeling. Truth often finds its way to the mind close muffled in robes of sleep, and then speaks with uncompromising directness of matters in regard to which we practise an unconscious self-deception during our waking moments. Until now he had not been aware of the tyrannizing influence acquired by one idea over his mind, and of the lengths which he might find in his heart to go for the sake of giving himself peace.

"Aylmer," resumed Georgiana, solemnly, "I know not what may be the cost to both of us to rid me of this fatal birthmark. Perhaps its removal may cause cureless deformity; or it may be the stain goes as deep as life itself. Again: do we know that there is a possibility, on any terms, of unclasping the firm gripe of this little hand which was laid upon me before I came into the world?"

"Dearest Georgiana, I have spent much thought upon the subject," hastily interrupted Aylmer. "I am convinced of the perfect practicability of its removal."

"If there be the remotest possibility of it," continued Georgiana, "let the attempt be made at whatever risk. Danger is nothing to me; for life, while this hateful mark makes me the object of your horror and disgust,—life is a burden which I would fling down with joy. Either remove this dreadful hand, or take my wretched life! You have deep science. All the world bears witness of it. You have achieved great wonders. Cannot you remove this little, little mark, which I cover with the tips of two small fingers? Is this beyond your power, for the sake of your own peace, and to save your poor wife from madness?"

"Noblest, dearest, tenderest wife," cried Aylmer, rapturously, "doubt not my power. I have already given this matter the deepest thought—thought which might almost have enlightened me to create a being less perfect than yourself. Georgiana, you have led me deeper than ever into the heart of science. I feel myself fully competent to render this dear cheek as faultless as its fellow; and then, most beloved, what will be my triumph when I shall have corrected what Nature left imperfect in her fairest work! Even Pygmalion, when his sculptured woman assumed life, felt not greater ecstasy than mine will be."

"It is resolved, then," said Georgiana, faintly smiling. "And, Aylmer, spare me not, though you should find the birthmark take refuge in my heart at last."

Her husband tenderly kissed her cheek—her right cheek—not that which bore the impress of the crimson hand.

The next day Aylmer apprised his wife of a plan that he had formed whereby he might have opportunity for the intense thought and constant watchfulness which the proposed operation would require; while Georgiana, likewise, would enjoy the perfect repose essential to its success. They were to seclude themselves in the extensive apartments occupied by Aylmer as a laboratory, and where, during his toilsome youth, he had made discoveries in the elemental powers of Nature that had roused the admiration of all the learned societies in Europe. Seated calmly in this laboratory, the pale philosopher had investigated the secrets of the highest cloud region and of the profoundest mines; he had satisfied himself of the causes that kindled and kept alive the fires of the volcano; and had explained the mystery of fountains, and how it is that they gush forth, some so bright and pure, and others with such rich medicinal virtues, from the dark bosom of the earth. Here, too, at an earlier period, he had studied the wonders of the human frame, and attempted to fathom the very process by which Nature assimilates all her precious influences from earth and air, and from the spiritual world, to create and foster man, her masterpiece. The latter pursuit, however, Aylmer had long laid aside in unwilling recognition of the truth—against which all seekers sooner or later stumble—that our great creative Mother, while she amuses us with apparently working in the broadest sunshine, is yet severely careful to keep her own secrets, and, in spite of her pretended openness, shows us nothing but results. She permits us, indeed, to mar, but seldom to mend, and, like a jealous patentee, on no account to make. Now, however, Aylmer resumed these half-forgotten investigations; not, of course, with such hopes or wishes as first suggested them; but because they involved much physiological truth and lay in the path of his proposed scheme for the treatment of Georgiana.

As he led her over the threshold of the laboratory, Georgiana was cold and tremulous. Aylmer looked cheerfully into her face, with intent to reassure her, but was so startled with the intense glow of the birthmark upon the whiteness of her cheek that he could not restrain a strong convulsive shudder. His wife fainted.

"Aminadab! Aminadab!" shouted Aylmer, stamping violently on the floor.

Forthwith there issued from an inner apartment a man of low stature, but bulky frame, with shaggy hair hanging about his visage, which was grimed with the vapors of the furnace. This personage had been Aylmer's underworker during his whole scientific career, and was admirably fitted for that office by his great mechanical readiness, and the skill with which, while incapable of comprehending a single principle, he executed all the details of his master's experiments. With his vast strength, his shaggy hair, his smoky aspect, and the indescribable earthiness that incrusted him, he seemed to represent man's physical nature; while Aylmer's slender figure, and pale, intellectual face, were no less apt a type of the spiritual element.

"Throw open the door of the boudoir, Aminadab," said Aylmer, "and burn a pastil."

"Yes, master," answered Aminadab, looking intently at the lifeless form of Georgiana; and then he muttered to himself, "If she were my wife, I'd never part with that birthmark."

When Georgiana recovered consciousness she found herself breathing an atmosphere of penetrating fragrance, the gentle potency of which had recalled her from her deathlike faintness. The scene around her looked like enchantment. Aylmer had converted those smoky, dingy, sombre rooms, where he had spent his brightest years in recondite pursuits, into a series of beautiful apartments not unfit to be the secluded abode of a lovely woman. The walls were hung with gorgeous curtains, which imparted the combination of grandeur and grace that no other species of adornment can achieve; and as they fell from the ceiling to the floor, their rich and ponderous folds, concealing all angles and straight lines, appeared to shut in the scene from infinite space. For aught Georgiana knew, it might be a pavilion among the clouds. And Aylmer, excluding the sunshine, which would have interfered with his chemical processes, had supplied its place with perfumed lamps, emitting flames of various hue, but all uniting in a soft, impurpled radiance. He now knelt by his wife's side, watching her earnestly, but without alarm; for he was confident in his science, and felt that he could draw a magic circle round her within which no evil might intrude.

"Where am I? Ah, I remember," said Georgiana, faintly; and she placed her hand over her cheek to hide the terrible mark from her husband's eyes.

"Fear not, dearest!" exclaimed he. "Do not shrink from me! Believe me, Georgiana, I even rejoice in this single imperfection, since it will be such a rapture to remove it."

"Oh, spare me!" sadly replied his wife. "Pray do not look at it again. I never can forget that convulsive shudder."

In order to soothe Georgiana, and, as it were, to release her mind from the burden of actual things, Aylmer now put in practice some of the light and playful secrets which science had taught him among its profounder lore. Airy figures, absolutely bodiless ideas, and forms of unsubstantial beauty came and danced before her, imprinting their momentary footsteps on beams of light. Though she had some indistinct idea of the method of these optical phenomena, still the illusion was almost perfect enough to warrant the belief that her husband possessed sway over the spiritual world. Then again, when she felt a wish to look forth from her seclusion, immediately, as if her thoughts were answered, the procession of external existence flitted across a screen. The scenery and the figures of actual life were perfectly represented, but with that bewitching, yet indescribable difference which always makes a picture, an image, or a shadow so much more attractive than the original. When wearied of this, Aylmer bade her cast her eyes upon a vessel containing a quantity of earth. She did so, with little interest at first; but was soon startled to perceive the germ of a plant shooting upward from the soil. Then came the slender stalk; the leaves gradually unfolded themselves; and amid them was a perfect and lovely flower.

"It is magical!" cried Georgiana. "I dare not touch it."

"Nay, pluck it," answered Aylmer,—"pluck it, and inhale its brief perfume while you may. The flower will wither in a few moments and leave nothing save its brown seed vessels; but thence may be perpetuated a race as ephemeral as itself."

But Georgiana had no sooner touched the flower than the whole plant suffered a blight, its leaves turning coal-black as if by the agency of fire.

"There was too powerful a stimulus," said Aylmer, thoughtfully.

To make up for this abortive experiment, he proposed to take her portrait by a scientific process of his own invention. It was to be effected by rays of light striking upon a polished plate of metal. Georgiana assented; but, on looking at the result, was affrighted to find the features of the portrait blurred and indefinable; while the minute figure of a hand appeared where the cheek should have been. Aylmer snatched the metallic plate and threw it into a jar of corrosive acid.

Soon, however, he forgot these mortifying failures. In the intervals of study and chemical experiment he came to her flushed and exhausted, but seemed invigorated by her presence, and spoke in glowing language of the resources of his art. He gave a history of the long dynasty of the alchemists, who spent so many ages in quest of the universal solvent by which the golden principle might be elicited from all things vile and base. Aylmer appeared to believe that, by the plainest scientific logic, it was altogether within the limits of possibility to discover this long-sought medium; "but," he added, "a philosopher who should go deep enough to acquire the power would attain too lofty a wisdom to stoop to the exercise of it." Not less singular were his opinions in regard to the elixir vitae. He more than intimated that it was at his option to concoct a liquid that should prolong life for years, perhaps interminably; but that it would produce a discord in Nature which all the world, and chiefly the quaffer of the immortal nostrum, would find cause to curse.

"Aylmer, are you in earnest?" asked Georgiana, looking at him with amazement and fear. "It is terrible to possess such power, or even to dream of possessing it."

"Oh, do not tremble, my love," said her husband. "I would not wrong either you or myself by working such inharmonious effects upon our lives; but I would have you consider how trifling, in comparison, is the skill requisite to remove this little hand."

At the mention of the birthmark, Georgiana, as usual, shrank as if a red-hot iron had touched her cheek.

Again Aylmer applied himself to his labors. She could hear his voice in the distant furnace room giving directions to Aminadab, whose harsh, uncouth, misshapen tones were audible in response, more like the grunt or growl of a brute than human speech. After hours of absence, Aylmer reappeared and proposed that she should now examine his cabinet of chemical products and natural treasures of the earth. Among the former he showed her a small vial, in which, he remarked, was contained a gentle yet most powerful fragrance, capable of impregnating all the breezes that blow across a kingdom. They were of inestimable value, the contents of that little vial; and, as he said so, he threw some of the perfume into the air and filled the room with piercing and invigorating delight.

"And what is this?" asked Georgiana, pointing to a small crystal globe containing a gold-colored liquid. "It is so beautiful to the eye that I could imagine it the elixir of life."

"In one sense it is," replied Aylmer; "or, rather, the elixir of immortality. It is the most precious poison that ever was concocted in this world. By its aid I could apportion the lifetime of any mortal at whom you might point your finger. The strength of the dose would determine whether he were to linger out years, or drop dead in the midst of a breath. No king on his guarded throne could keep his life if I, in my private station, should deem that the welfare of millions justified me in depriving him of it."

"Why do you keep such a terrific drug?" inquired Georgiana in horror.

"Do not mistrust me, dearest," said her husband, smiling; "its virtuous potency is yet greater than its harmful one. But see! here is a powerful cosmetic. With a few drops of this in a vase of water, freckles may be washed away as easily as the hands are cleansed. A stronger infusion would take the blood out of the cheek, and leave the rosiest beauty a pale ghost."

"Is it with this lotion that you intend to bathe my cheek?" asked Georgiana, anxiously.

"Oh, no," hastily replied her husband; "this is merely superficial. Your case demands a remedy that shall go deeper."

In his interviews with Georgiana, Aylmer generally made minute inquiries as to her sensations and whether the confinement of the rooms and the temperature of the atmosphere agreed with her. These questions had such a particular drift that Georgiana began to conjecture that she was already subjected to certain physical influences, either breathed in with the fragrant air or taken with her food. She fancied likewise, but it might be altogether fancy, that there was a stirring up of her system—a strange, indefinite sensation creeping through her veins, and tingling, half painfully, half pleasurably, at her heart. Still, whenever she dared to look into the mirror, there she beheld herself pale as a white rose and with the crimson birthmark stamped upon her cheek. Not even Aylmer now hated it so much as she.

To dispel the tedium of the hours which her husband found it necessary to devote to the processes of combination and analysis, Georgiana turned over the volumes of his scientific library. In many dark old tomes she met with chapters full of romance and poetry. They were the works of philosophers of the middle ages, such as Albertus Magnus, Cornelius Agrippa, Paracelsus, and the famous friar who created the prophetic Brazen Head. All these antique naturalists stood in advance of their centuries, yet were imbued with some of their credulity, and therefore were believed, and perhaps imagined themselves to have acquired from the investigation of Nature a power above Nature, and from physics a sway over the spiritual world. Hardly less curious and imaginative were the early volumes of the Transactions of the Royal Society, in which the members, knowing little of the limits of natural possibility, were continually recording wonders or proposing methods whereby wonders might be wrought.

But to Georgiana the most engrossing volume was a large folio from her husband's own hand, in which he had recorded every experiment of his scientific career, its original aim, the methods adopted for its development, and its final success or failure, with the circumstances to which either event was attributable. The book, in truth, was both the history and emblem of his ardent, ambitious, imaginative, yet practical and laborious life. He handled physical details as if there were nothing beyond them; yet spiritualized them all, and redeemed himself from materialism by his strong and eager aspiration towards the infinite. In his grasp the veriest clod of earth assumed a soul. Georgiana, as she read, reverenced Aylmer and loved him more profoundly than ever, but with a less entire dependence on his judgment than heretofore. Much as he had accomplished, she could not but observe that his most splendid successes were almost invariably failures, if compared with the ideal at which he aimed. His brightest diamonds were the merest pebbles, and felt to be so by himself, in comparison with the inestimable gems which lay hidden beyond his reach. The volume, rich with achievements that had won renown for its author, was yet as melancholy a record as ever mortal hand had penned. It was the sad confession and continual exemplification of the shortcomings of the composite man, the spirit burdened with clay and working in matter, and of the despair that assails the higher nature at finding itself so miserably thwarted by the earthly part. Perhaps every man of genius in whatever sphere might recognize the image of his own experience in Aylmer's journal.

So deeply did these reflections affect Georgiana that she laid her face upon the open volume and burst into tears. In this situation she was found by her husband.

"It is dangerous to read in a sorcerer's books," said he with a smile, though his countenance was uneasy and displeased. "Georgiana, there are pages in that volume which I can scarcely glance over and keep my senses. Take heed lest it prove as detrimental to you."

"It has made me worship you more than ever," said she.

"Ah, wait for this one success," rejoined he, "then worship me if you will. I shall deem myself hardly unworthy of it. But come, I have sought you for the luxury of your voice. Sing to me, dearest."

So she poured out the liquid music of her voice to quench the thirst of his spirit. He then took his leave with a boyish exuberance of gayety, assuring her that her seclusion would endure but a little longer, and that the result was already certain. Scarcely had he departed when Georgiana felt irresistibly impelled to follow him. She had forgotten to inform Aylmer of a symptom which for two or three hours past had begun to excite her attention. It was a sensation in the fatal birthmark, not painful, but which induced a restlessness throughout her system. Hastening after her husband, she intruded for the first time into the laboratory.

The first thing that struck her eye was the furnace, that hot and feverish worker, with the intense glow of its fire, which by the quantities of soot clustered above it seemed to have been burning for ages. There was a distilling apparatus in full operation. Around the room were retorts, tubes, cylinders, crucibles, and other apparatus of chemical research. An electrical machine stood ready for immediate use. The atmosphere felt oppressively close, and was tainted with gaseous odors which had been tormented forth by the processes of science. The severe and homely simplicity of the apartment, with its naked walls and brick pavement, looked strange, accustomed as Georgiana had become to the fantastic elegance of her boudoir. But what chiefly, indeed almost solely, drew her attention, was the aspect of Aylmer himself.

He was pale as death, anxious and absorbed, and hung over the furnace as if it depended upon his utmost watchfulness whether the liquid which it was distilling should be the draught of immortal happiness or misery. How different from the sanguine and joyous mien that he had assumed for Georgiana's encouragement!

"Carefully now, Aminadab; carefully, thou human machine; carefully, thou man of clay!" muttered Aylmer, more to himself than his assistant. "Now, if there be a thought too much or too little, it is all over."

"Ho! ho!" mumbled Aminadab. "Look, master! look!"

Aylmer raised his eyes hastily, and at first reddened, then grew paler than ever, on beholding Georgiana. He rushed towards her and seized her arm with a gripe that left the print of his fingers upon it.

"Why do you come hither? Have you no trust in your husband?" cried he, impetuously. "Would you throw the blight of that fatal birthmark over my labors? It is not well done. Go, prying woman, go!"

"Nay, Aylmer," said Georgiana with the firmness of which she possessed no stinted endowment, "it is not you that have a right to complain. You mistrust your wife; you have concealed the anxiety with which you watch the development of this experiment. Think not so unworthily of me, my husband. Tell me all the risk we run, and fear not that I shall shrink; for my share in it is far less than your own."

"No, no, Georgiana!" said Aylmer, impatiently; "it must not be."

"I submit," replied she calmly. "And, Aylmer, I shall quaff whatever draught you bring me; but it will be on the same principle that would induce me to take a dose of poison if offered by your hand."

"My noble wife," said Aylmer, deeply moved, "I knew not the height and depth of your nature until now. Nothing shall be concealed. Know, then, that this crimson hand, superficial as it seems, has clutched its grasp into your being with a strength of which I had no previous conception. I have already administered agents powerful enough to do aught except to change your entire physical system. Only one thing remains to be tried. If that fail us we are ruined."

"Why did you hesitate to tell me this?" asked she.

"Because, Georgiana," said Aylmer, in a low

"Danger? There is but one danger—that thi
left upon my cheek!" cried Georgiana. "Remove
the cost, or we shall both go mad!"

"Heaven knows your words are too true," said
dearest, return to your boudoir. In a little whil

He conducted her back and took leave of he
which spoke far more than his words how much
departure Georgiana became rapt in musings. S
of Aylmer, and did it completer justice than at
heart exulted, while it trembled, at his honora
that it would accept nothing less than perfecti
contented with an earthlier nature than he ha
much more precious was such a sentiment th
would have borne with the imperfection for h
of treason to holy love by degrading its per
actual; and with her whole spirit she prayed t
might satisfy his highest and deepest concepti
she well knew it could not be; for his spirit
ascending, and each instant required somethi
of the instant before.

The sound of her husband's footsteps ar
goblet containing a liquor colorless as water
draught of immortality. Aylmer was pale; b
quence of a highly-wrought state of mind an
or doubt.

"The concoction of the draught has been
Georgiana's look. "Unless all my science ha

"Save on your account, my dearest Aylm
wish to put off this birthmark of mortality
in preference to any other mode. Life is bu
have attained precisely the degree of moral
Were I weaker and blinder it might be hap
be endured hopefully. But, being what I fi
mortals the most fit to die."

"Y
"But
upon
On
blotch
tity of
roots
to be
"Th
I joyfu
"Dr
ration.
too, sh
She
"It i
from a
fragrar
for ma
over m
She
almost
lingerir
lost in s
tions pr
the proc
philoso
minutes
irregula
through
he wrote
every pi
concentr
Whil
not with
he presse

u are fit for heaven without tasting death!" replied her husband.
hy do we speak of dying? The draught cannot fail. Behold its effect
his plant."

the window seat there stood a geranium diseased with yellow
s, which had overspread all its leaves. Aylmer poured a small quan-
the liquid upon the soil in which it grew. In a little time, when the
f the plant had taken up the moisture, the unsightly blotches began
tinguished in a living verdure.

ere needed no proof," said Georgiana, quietly. "Give me the goblet
ly stake all upon your word."

nk, then, thou lofty creature!" exclaimed Aylmer, with fervid admi-
'There is no taint of imperfection on thy spirit. Thy sensible frame,
ll soon be all perfect."

quaffed the liquid and returned the goblet to his hand.

grateful," said she with a placid smile. "Methinks it is like water
heavenly fountain; for it contains I know not what of unobtrusive
e and deliciousness. It allays a feverish thirst that had parched me
y days. Now, dearest, let me sleep. My earthly senses are closing
spirit like the leaves around the heart of a rose at sunset."

poke the last words with a gentle reluctance, as if it required
nore energy than she could command to pronounce the faint and
syllables. Scarcely had they loitered through her lips ere she was
umber. Aylmer sat by her side, watching her aspect with the emo-
per to a man the whole value of whose existence was involved in
ss now to be tested. Mingled with this mood, however, was the
hic investigation characteristic of the man of science. Not the
symptom escaped him. A heightened flush of the cheek, a slight
ity of breath, a quiver of the eyelid, a hardly perceptible tremor
the frame,—such were the details which, as the moments passed,
down in his folio volume. Intense thought had set its stamp upon
vious page of that volume, but the thoughts of years were all
ted upon the last.

thus employed, he failed not to gaze often at the fatal hand, and
ut a shudder. Yet once, by a strange and unaccountable impulse
l it with his lips. His spirit recoiled, however, in the very act, and

Georgiana, out of the midst of her deep sleep, moved uneasily and murmured as if in remonstrance. Again Aylmer resumed his watch. Nor was it without avail. The crimson hand, which at first had been strongly visible upon the marble paleness of Georgiana's cheek, now grew more faintly outlined. She remained not less pale than ever; but the birthmark with every breath that came and went, lost somewhat of its former distinctness. Its presence had been awful; its departure was more awful still. Watch the stain of the rainbow fading out the sky, and you will know how that mysterious symbol passed away.

"By Heaven! it is well-nigh gone!" said Aylmer to himself, in almost irrepressible ecstasy. "I can scarcely trace it now. Success! success! And now it is like the faintest rose color. The lightest flush of blood across her cheek would overcome it. But she is so pale!"

He drew aside the window curtain and suffered the light of natural day to fall into the room and rest upon her cheek. At the same time he heard a gross, hoarse chuckle, which he had long known as his servant Aminadab's expression of delight.

"Ah, clod! ah, earthly mass!" cried Aylmer, laughing in a sort of frenzy, "you have served me well! Matter and spirit—earth and heaven—have both done their part in this! Laugh, thing of the senses! You have earned the right to laugh."

These exclamations broke Georgiana's sleep. She slowly unclosed her eyes and gazed into the mirror which her husband had arranged for that purpose. A faint smile flitted over her lips when she recognized how barely perceptible was now that crimson hand which had once blazed forth with such disastrous brilliancy as to scare away all their happiness. But then her eyes sought Aylmer's face with a trouble and anxiety that he could by no means account for.

"My poor Aylmer!" murmured she.

"Poor? Nay, richest, happiest, most favored!" exclaimed he. "My peerless bride, it is successful! You are perfect!"

"My poor Aylmer," she repeated, with a more than human tenderness, "you have aimed loftily; you have done nobly. Do not repent that with so high and pure a feeling, you have rejected the best the earth could offer. Aylmer, dearest Aylmer, I am dying!"

Alas! it was too true! The fatal hand had grappled with the mystery of life, and was the bond by which an angelic spirit kept itself in union with a mortal frame. As the last crimson tint of the birthmark—that sole token of human imperfection—faded from her cheek, the parting breath of the now perfect woman passed into the atmosphere, and her soul, lingering a moment near her husband, took its heavenward flight. Then a hoarse, chuckling laugh was heard again! Thus ever does the gross fatality of earth exult in its invariable triumph over the immortal essence which, in this dim sphere of half development, demands the completeness of a higher state. Yet, had Aylmer reached a profounder wisdom, he need not thus have flung away the happiness which would have woven his mortal life of the selfsame texture with the celestial. The momentary circumstance was too strong for him; he failed to look beyond the shadowy scope of time, and, living once for all in eternity, to find the perfect future in the present.

A TALE OF THE RAGGED MOUNTAINS

Edgar Allan Poe

1844

Although he is frequently hailed as the father of American horror fiction, Edgar Allan Poe wrote very few tales that were actually set in America. Much of his work, like "The Masque of the Red Death" and "The Pit and the Pendulum," is set in the Europe of Gothic convention; other stories, such as "The Fall of the House of Usher," are without any indication of time or place.

A heady blend of science and occultism, "A Tale of the Ragged Mountains" was first published in Godey's Lady's Book *in April 1844. It appeared the following year in the collection* Tales. *Poe seems to have been particularly interested in Meserism at this time: his metaphysical tale "Mesmeric Revelation" appeared in* Columbian Magazine *a few months after "A Tale of the Ragged Mountains" was published, and the more well-known story "The Facts in the Case of M. Valdemar" first appeared in* The American Review *in December of the following year.*

On one level, this tale can be seen as an account of an extended hallucination induced by drugs and hypnotism, possibly influenced by Thomas de Quincey's Confessions of an English Opium-Eater; *on another, it reads like one of Lovecraft's Dreamlands tales, which it may very well have influenced in its turn. Some of Poe's favorite themes—disease, fringe science, and exoticism—serve to haunting effect in a tale that, in the hands of a lesser author, might have become a straightforward pulp adventure, and in the final lines one can almost see Poe winking at the reader, unable at the last to take his own work too seriously.*

During the fall of the year 1827, while residing near Charlottesville, Virginia, I casually made the acquaintance of Mr. Augustus Bedloe. This young gentleman was remarkable in every respect, and excited in me a profound interest and curiosity. I found it impossible to comprehend him either in his moral or his physical relations. Of his family I could obtain no satisfactory account. Whence he came, I never ascertained. Even about his age—although I call him a young gentleman—there was something which perplexed me in no little degree. He certainly seemed young—and he made a point of speaking about his youth—yet there were moments when I should have had little trouble in imagining him a hundred years of age. But in no regard was he more peculiar than in his personal appearance. He was singularly tall and thin. He stooped much. His limbs were exceedingly long and emaciated. His forehead was broad and low. His complexion was absolutely bloodless. His mouth was large and flexible, and his teeth were more wildly uneven, although sound, than I had ever before seen teeth in a human head. The expression of his smile, however, was by no means unpleasing, as might be supposed; but it had no variation whatever. It was one of profound melancholy—of a phaseless and unceasing gloom. His eyes were abnormally large, and round like those of a cat. The pupils, too, upon any accession or diminution of light, underwent contraction or dilation, just such as is observed in the feline tribe. In moments of excitement the orbs grew bright to a degree almost inconceivable; seeming to emit luminous rays, not of a reflected but of an intrinsic lustre, as does a candle or the sun; yet their ordinary condition was so totally vapid, filmy, and dull as to convey the idea of the eyes of a long-interred corpse.

These peculiarities of person appeared to cause him much annoyance, and he was continually alluding to them in a sort of half explanatory, half apologetic strain, which, when I first heard it, impressed me very painfully. I soon, however, grew accustomed to it, and my uneasiness wore off. It seemed to be his design rather to insinuate than directly to assert that, physically, he had not always been what he was—that a long series of neuralgic attacks had reduced him from a condition of more than usual personal beauty, to that which I saw. For many years past he had been attended by a physician, named Templeton—an old gentleman, perhaps seventy years of age—whom he had first encountered at Saratoga, and from whose attention, while there, he either received, or fancied that he received, great benefit. The result was that Bedloe, who was wealthy, had made an arrangement with Dr. Templeton, by which the latter, in consideration of a liberal annual allowance, had consented to devote his time and medical experience exclusively to the care of the invalid.

Doctor Templeton had been a traveller in his younger days, and at Paris had become a convert, in great measure, to the doctrines of Mesmer. It was altogether by means of magnetic remedies that he had succeeded in alleviating the acute pains of his patient; and this success had very naturally inspired the latter with a certain degree of confidence in the opinions from which the remedies had been educed. The Doctor, however, like all enthusiasts, had struggled hard to make a thorough convert of his pupil, and finally so far gained his point as to induce the sufferer to submit to numerous experiments. By a frequent repetition of these, a result had arisen, which of late days has become so common as to attract little or no attention, but which, at the period of which I write, had very rarely been known in America. I mean to say, that between Doctor Templeton and Bedloe there had grown up, little by little, a very distinct and strongly marked rapport, or magnetic relation. I am not prepared to assert, however, that this rapport extended beyond the limits of the simple sleep-producing power, but this power itself had attained great intensity. At the first attempt to induce the magnetic somnolency, the mesmerist entirely failed. In the fifth or sixth he succeeded very partially, and after long continued effort. Only at the twelfth was the triumph complete. After this the will of the patient succumbed rapidly to that of the physician, so that, when I first became acquainted with the two, sleep was brought about almost instantaneously by the mere volition of the operator, even when the invalid was unaware of his presence. It is only now, in the year 1845, when similar miracles are witnessed daily by thousands, that I dare venture to record this apparent impossibility as a matter of serious fact.

The temperature of Bedloe was, in the highest degree sensitive, excitable, enthusiastic. His imagination was singularly vigorous and creative; and no doubt it derived additional force from the habitual use of morphine, which he swallowed in great quantity, and without which he would have found it impossible to exist. It was his practice to take a very large dose of it immediately after breakfast each morning—or, rather, immediately after a cup of strong coffee, for he ate nothing in the forenoon—and then set forth alone, or attended only by a dog, upon a long ramble among the chain of wild and dreary hills that lie westward and southward of Charlottesville, and are there dignified by the title of the Ragged Mountains.

Upon a dim, warm, misty day, toward the close of November, and during the strange interregnum of the seasons which in America is termed the Indian Summer, Mr. Bedloe departed as usual for the hills. The day passed, and still he did not return.

About eight o'clock at night, having become seriously alarmed at his protracted absence, we were about setting out in search of him, when he unexpectedly made his appearance, in health no worse than usual, and in rather more than ordinary spirits. The account which he gave of his expedition, and of the events which had detained him, was a singular one indeed.

"You will remember," said he, "that it was about nine in the morning when I left Charlottesville. I bent my steps immediately to the mountains, and, about ten, entered a gorge which was entirely new to me. I followed the windings of this pass with much interest. The scenery which presented itself on all sides, although scarcely entitled to be called grand, had about it an indescribable and to me a delicious aspect of dreary desolation. The solitude seemed absolutely virgin. I could not help believing that the green sods and the gray rocks upon which I trod had been trodden never before by the foot of a human being. So entirely secluded, and in fact inaccessible, except through a series of accidents, is the entrance of the ravine, that it is by no means impossible that I was indeed the first adventurer—the very first and sole adventurer who had ever penetrated its recesses.

"The thick and peculiar mist, or smoke, which distinguishes the Indian Summer, and which now hung heavily over all objects, served, no doubt, to deepen the vague impressions which these objects created. So dense was this pleasant fog that I could at no time see more than a dozen yards of the path before me. This path was excessively sinuous, and as the sun could not be seen, I soon lost all idea of the direction in which I journeyed. In the meantime the morphine had its customary effect—that of enduing all the external world with an intensity of interest. In the quivering of a leaf—in the hue of a blade of grass—in the shape of a trefoil—in the humming of a bee—in the gleaming of a dew-drop—in the breathing of the wind—in the faint odors that came from the forest—there came a whole universe of suggestion—a gay and motley train of rhapsodical and immethodical thought.

"Busied in this, I walked on for several hours, during which the mist deepened around me to so great an extent that at length I was reduced to an absolute groping of the way. And now an indescribable uneasiness possessed me—a species of nervous hesitation and tremor. I feared to tread, lest I should be precipitated into some abyss. I remembered, too, strange stories told about these Ragged Hills, and of the uncouth and fierce races of men who tenanted their groves and caverns. A thousand vague fancies oppressed and disconcerted me—fancies the more distressing because vague. Very suddenly my attention was arrested by the loud beating of a drum.

"My amazement was, of course, extreme. A drum in these hills was a thing unknown. I could not have been more surprised at the sound of the trump of the Archangel. But a new and still more astounding source of interest and perplexity arose. There came a wild rattling or jingling sound, as if of a bunch of large keys, and upon the instant a dusky-visaged and half-naked man rushed past me with a shriek. He came so close to my person that I felt his hot breath upon my face. He bore in one hand an instrument composed of an assemblage of steel rings, and shook them vigorously as he ran. Scarcely had he disappeared in the mist before, panting after him, with open mouth and glaring eyes, there darted a huge beast. I could not be mistaken in its character. It was a hyena.

"The sight of this monster rather relieved than heightened my terrors—for I now made sure that I dreamed, and endeavored to arouse myself to waking consciousness. I stepped boldly and briskly forward. I rubbed my eyes. I called aloud. I pinched my limbs. A small spring of water presented itself to my view, and here, stooping, I bathed my hands and my head and neck. This seemed to dissipate the equivocal sensations which had hitherto annoyed me. I arose, as I thought, a new man, and proceeded steadily and complacently on my unknown way.

"At length, quite overcome by exertion, and by a certain oppressive close-ness of the atmosphere, I seated myself beneath a tree. Presently there came a feeble gleam of sunshine, and the shadow of the leaves of the tree fell faintly but definitely upon the grass. At this shadow I gazed wonderingly for many minutes. Its character stupefied me with astonishment. I looked upward. The tree was a palm.

"I now arose hurriedly, and in a state of fearful agitation—for the fancy that I dreamed would serve me no longer. I saw—I felt that I had perfect command of my senses—and these senses now brought to my soul a world of novel and singular sensation. The heat became all at once intolerable. A strange odor loaded the breeze. A low, continuous murmur, like that arising from a full, but gently flowing river, came to my ears, intermingled with the peculiar hum of multitudinous human voices.

"While I listened in an extremity of astonishment which I need not attempt to describe, a strong and brief gust of wind bore off the incumbent fog as if by the wand of an enchanter.

"I found myself at the foot of a high mountain, and looking down into a vast plain, through which wound a majestic river. On the margin of this river stood an Eastern-looking city, such as we read of in the Arabian Tales, but of a character even more singular than any there described. From my position, which was far above the level of the town, I could perceive its every nook and corner, as if delineated on a map. The streets seemed innumerable, and crossed each other irregularly in all directions, but were rather long winding alleys than streets, and absolutely swarmed with inhabitants. The houses were wildly picturesque. On every hand was a wilderness of balconies, of verandas, of minarets, of shrines, and fantastically carved oriels. Bazaars abounded; and in these were displayed rich wares in infinite variety and profusion—silks, muslins, the most dazzling cutlery, the most magnificent jewels and gems. Besides these things, were seen, on all sides, banners and palanquins, litters with stately dames close veiled, elephants gorgeously caparisoned, idols grotesquely hewn, drums, banners, and gongs, spears, silver and gilded maces. And amid the crowd, and the clamor, and the general intricacy and confusion—amid the million of black and yellow men, turbaned and robed, and of flowing beard, there roamed a countless multitude of holy filleted bulls, while vast legions of the filthy but sacred ape clambered, chattering and shrieking, about the cornices of the mosques, or clung to the minarets and oriels. From the swarming streets to the banks of the river, there descended innumerable flights of steps leading to bathing places, while the river itself seemed to force a passage with difficulty through the vast fleets of deeply-burthened ships that far and wide encountered its surface. Beyond the limits of the city arose, in frequent majestic groups, the palm and the cocoa, with other gigantic and weird trees of vast age, and here and there might be seen a field of rice, the thatched hut of a peasant, a tank, a stray temple, a gypsy camp, or a solitary graceful maiden taking her way, with a pitcher upon her head, to the banks of the magnificent river.

"You will say now, of course, that I dreamed; but not so. What I saw— what I heard—what I felt—what I thought—had about it nothing of the unmistakable idiosyncrasy of the dream. All was rigorously self-consistent. At first, doubting that I was really awake, I entered into a series of tests, which soon convinced me that I really was. Now, when one dreams, and, in the dream, suspects that he dreams, the suspicion never fails to confirm itself, and the sleeper is almost immediately aroused. Thus Novalis errs not in saying that 'we are near waking when we dream that we dream.' Had the vision occurred to me as I describe it, without my suspecting it as a dream, then a dream it might absolutely have been, but, occurring as it did, and suspected and tested as it was, I am forced to class it among other phenomena."

"In this I am not sure that you are wrong," observed Dr. Templeton, "but proceed. You arose and descended into the city."

"I arose," continued Bedloe, regarding the Doctor with an air of profound astonishment, "I arose, as you say, and descended into the city. On my way I fell in with an immense populace, crowding through every avenue, all in the same direction, and exhibiting in every action the wildest excitement. Very suddenly, and by some inconceivable impulse, I became intensely imbued with personal interest in what was going on. I seemed to feel that I had an important part to play, without exactly understanding what it was. Against the crowd which environed me, however, I experienced a deep sentiment of animosity. I shrank from amid them, and, swiftly, by a circuitous path, reached and entered the city. Here all was the wildest tumult and contention. A small party of men, clad in garments half-Indian, half-European, and officered by gentlemen in a uniform partly British, were engaged, at great odds, with the swarming rabble of the alleys. I joined the weaker party, arming myself with the weapons of a fallen officer, and fighting I knew not whom with the nervous ferocity of despair. We were soon overpowered by numbers, and driven to seek refuge in a species of kiosk. Here we barricaded ourselves, and, for the present were secure. From a loop-hole near the summit of the kiosk, I perceived a vast crowd, in furious agitation, surrounding and assaulting a gay palace that overhung the river. Presently, from an upper window of this place, there descended an effeminate-looking person, by means of a string made of the turbans of his attendants. A boat was at hand, in which he escaped to the opposite bank of the river.

"And now a new object took possession of my soul. I spoke a few hurried but energetic words to my companions, and, having succeeded in gaining over a few of them to my purpose made a frantic sally from the kiosk. We rushed amid the crowd that surrounded it. They retreated, at first, before us. They rallied, fought madly, and retreated again. In the mean time we were borne far from the kiosk, and became bewildered and entangled among the narrow streets of tall, overhanging houses, into the recesses of which the sun had never been able to shine. The rabble pressed impetuously upon us, harrassing us with their spears, and overwhelming us with flights of arrows. These latter were very remarkable, and resembled in some respects the writhing creese of the Malay. They were made to imitate the body of a creeping serpent, and were long and black, with a poisoned barb. One of them struck me upon the right temple. I reeled and fell. An instantaneous and dreadful sickness seized me. I struggled—I gasped—I died."

"You will hardly persist now," said I smiling, "that the whole of your adventure was not a dream. You are not prepared to maintain that you are dead?"

When I said these words, I of course expected some lively sally from Bedloe in reply, but, to my astonishment, he hesitated, trembled, became fearfully pallid, and remained silent. I looked toward Templeton. He sat erect and rigid in his chair—his teeth chattered, and his eyes were starting from their sockets. "Proceed!" he at length said hoarsely to Bedloe.

"For many minutes," continued the latter, "my sole sentiment—my sole feeling—was that of darkness and nonentity, with the consciousness of death. At length there seemed to pass a violent and sudden shock through my soul, as if of electricity. With it came the sense of elasticity and of light. This latter I felt—not saw. In an instant I seemed to rise from the ground. But I had no bodily, no visible, audible, or palpable presence. The crowd had departed. The tumult had ceased. The city was in comparative repose. Beneath me lay my corpse, with the arrow in my temple, the whole head greatly swollen and disfigured. But all these things I felt—not saw. I took interest in nothing. Even the corpse seemed a matter in which I had no concern. Volition I had none, but appeared to be impelled into motion, and flitted buoyantly out of the city, retracing the circuitous path by which I had entered it. When I had attained that point of the ravine in the mountains at which I had encountered the hyena, I again experienced a shock as of a galvanic battery, the sense of weight, of volition, of substance, returned. I became my original self, and bent my steps eagerly homeward—but the past had not lost the vividness of the real—and not now, even for an instant, can I compel my understanding to regard it as a dream."

"Nor was it," said Templeton, with an air of deep solemnity, "yet it would be difficult to say how otherwise it should be termed. Let us suppose only, that the soul of the man of to-day is upon the verge of some stupendous psychal discoveries. Let us content ourselves with this supposition. For the rest I have some explanation to make. Here is a watercolor drawing, which I should have shown you before, but which an unaccountable sentiment of horror has hitherto prevented me from showing."

We looked at the picture which he presented. I saw nothing in it of an extraordinary character, but its effect upon Bedloe was prodigious. He nearly fainted as he gazed. And yet it was but a miniature portrait—a miraculously accurate one, to be sure—of his own very remarkable features. At least this was my thought as I regarded it.

"You will perceive," said Templeton, "the date of this picture—it is here, scarcely visible, in this corner—1780. In this year was the portrait taken. It is the likeness of a dead friend—a Mr. Oldeb—to whom I became much attached at Calcutta, during the administration of Warren Hastings. I was then only twenty years old. When I first saw you, Mr. Bedloe, at Saratoga, it was the miraculous similarity which existed between yourself and the painting which induced me to accost you, to seek your friendship, and to bring about those arrangements which resulted in my becoming your constant companion. In accomplishing this point, I was urged partly, and perhaps principally, by a regretful memory of the deceased, but also, in part, by an uneasy, and not altogether horrorless curiosity respecting yourself.

"In your detail of the vision which presented itself to you amid the hills, you have described, with the minutest accuracy, the Indian city of Benares, upon the Holy River. The riots, the combat, the massacre, were the actual events of the insurrection of Cheyte Sing, which took place in 1780, when Hastings was put in imminent peril of his life. The man escaping by the string of turbans was Cheyte Sing himself. The party in the kiosk were sepoys and British officers, headed by Hastings. Of this party I was one, and did all I could to prevent the rash and fatal sally of the officer who fell, in the crowded alleys, by the poisoned arrow of a Bengalee. That officer was my dearest friend. It was Oldeb. You will perceive by these manuscripts," (here the speaker produced a note-book in which several pages appeared to have been freshly written,) "that at the very period in which you fancied these things amid the hills, I was engaged in detailing them upon paper here at home."

In about a week after this conversation, the following paragraphs appeared in a Charlottesville paper:

"We have the painful duty of announcing the death of Mr. Augustus Bedlo, a gentleman whose amiable manners and many virtues have long endeared him to the citizens of Charlottesville.

"Mr. B., for some years past, has been subject to neuralgia, which has often threatened to terminate fatally; but this can be regarded only as the mediate cause of his decease. The proximate cause was one of especial singularity. In an excursion to the Ragged Mountains, a few days since, a slight cold and fever were contracted, attended with great determination of blood to the head. To relieve this, Dr. Templeton resorted to topical bleeding. Leeches were applied to the temples. In a fearfully brief period the patient died, when it appeared that in the jar containing the leeches, had been introduced, by accident, one of the venomous vermicular sangsues which are now and then found in the neighboring ponds. This creature fastened itself upon a small artery in the right temple. Its close resemblance to the medicinal leech caused the mistake to be overlooked until too late.

"N. B. The poisonous sangsue of Charlottesville may always be distinguished from the medicinal leech by its blackness, and especially by its writhing or vermicular motions, which very nearly resemble those of a snake."

I was speaking with the editor of the paper in question, upon the topic of this remarkable accident, when it occurred to me to ask how it happened that the name of the deceased had been given as Bedlo.

"I presume," I said, "you have authority for this spelling, but I have always supposed the name to be written with an e at the end."

"Authority?—no," he replied. "It is a mere typographical error. The name is Bedlo with an e, all the world over, and I never knew it to be spelt otherwise in my life."

"Then," said I mutteringly, as I turned upon my heel, "then indeed has it come to pass that one truth is stranger than any fiction—for Bedloe, without the e, what is it but Oldeb conversed! And this man tells me that it is a typographical error."

THE LAKE GUN

James Fenimore Cooper

1850

James Fenimore Cooper was expelled from Yale in his third year after blowing up the door to a classmate's room; he had previously locked a donkey in a recitation room. He spent eleven months at sea as a common seaman before joining the United States Navy in January, 1808. After a tour aboard the bomb ketch USS Vesuvius he was posted to Oswego, New York, to help build the brig USS Oneida on Lake Ontario in preparation for the War of 1812. He also served aboard a gunboat on Lake Champlain.

Cooper's familiarity with the former Iroquois territory of upstate New York, between Lake Ontario and his home at Cooperstown, informed his best-known works. The Last of the Mohicans was published in 1826, the second of his five Leatherstocking Tales adventure novels featuring the resourceful scout Natty Bumppo, better known as "Hawkeye."

In addition to the Leatherstocking Tales, Cooper wrote a number of novels exploring themes of conflict and justice in the relationship between native and white Americans, as well as tales of the sea and a so-called European trilogy exploring Old

World sociopolitical attitudes. He also wrote a history of the U.S. Navy among other nonfiction.

Cooper wrote comparatively few short stories. First published in 1850—the last year of Cooper's life—in a miscellany titled The Parthenon, *"The Lake Gun" concerns a mysterious sonic phenomenon that continues to be reported from Seneca Lake in upstate New York.*

Beneath the surface, it has been claimed, this story is a satire on American political demagogues in general, and in particular on William Henry Seward (1801–1872), whose name and renowned nose appear clearly in the tale. By 1850 Cooper feared that unscrupulous political extremists, mobilizing public opinion behind causes such as abolitionism, were leading America toward civil war. Cooper probably heard the folklore about Seneca Lake while visiting his son Paul, who attended Geneva College (now Hobart College) from 1840 to 1844.

The Seneca is remarkable for its "Wandering Jew," and the "Lake Gun." The first is a tree so balanced that when its roots are clear of the bottom it floats with its broken and pointed trunk a few feet above the surface of the water, driving before the winds, or following in the course of the currents. At times, the "Wandering Jew" is seen off Jefferson, near the head of this beautiful sheet; and next it will appear anchored, as it might be, in the shallow water near the outlet.

For more than half a century has this remnant of the forest floated about, from point to point, its bald head whitening with time, until its features have become familiar to all the older inhabitants of that region of country. The great depth of the Seneca prevents it from freezing; and summer and winter, springtime and autumn, is this wanderer to be observed; occasionally battling with the ice that makes a short distance from the shore, now pursuing its quiet way before a mild southern air in June, or, again, anchored, by its roots touching the bottom, as it passes a point, or comes in contact with the flats. It has been known to remain a year or two at a time in view of the village of Geneva, until, accustomed to its sight, the people began to think that it was never to move from its berth any more; but a fresh northerly breeze changes all this; the "Jew" swings to the gale, and, like a ship unmooring, drags clear of the bottom, and goes off to the southward, with its head just high enough above water to be visible. It would seem really that his wanderings are not to cease as long as wood will float.

No white man can give the history of this "Jew." He was found laving his sides in the pure waters of the Seneca by the earliest settlers, and it may have been ages since his wanderings commenced. When they are to cease is a secret in the womb of time.

The "Lake Gun" is a mystery. It is a sound resembling the explosion of a heavy piece of artillery, that can be accounted for by none of the known laws of nature. The report is deep, hollow, distant, and imposing. The lake seems to be speaking to the surrounding hills, which send back the echoes of its voice in accurate reply. No satisfactory theory has ever been broached to explain these noises. Conjectures have been hazarded about chasms, and the escape of compressed air by the sudden admission of water; but all this is talking at random, and has probably no foundation in truth. The most that can be said is, that such sounds are heard, though at long intervals, and that no one as yet has succeeded in ascertaining their cause.

It is not many lustrums since curiosity induced an idler, a traveler, and one possessed of much attainment derived from journeys in distant lands, first to inquire closely into all the traditions connected with these two peculiarities of the Seneca, and, having thus obtained all he could, to lead him to make the tour of the entire lake, in the hope of learning more by actual personal observation. He went up and down in the steamboat; was much gratified with his trip, but could see or hear nothing to help him in his investigation. The "Gun" had not been heard in a long time, and no one could tell him what had become of the "Wandering Jew." In vain did his eyes roam over the broad expanse of water; they could discover nothing to reward their search. There was an old man in the boat, of the name of Peter, who had passed his life on the Seneca, and to him was our traveler referred, as the person most likely to gratify his curiosity. Fuller (for so we shall call the stranger for the sake of convenience) was not slow to profit by this hint, and was soon in amicable relations with the tough, old, fresh-water mariner. A half-eagle opportunely bestowed opened all the stores of Peter's lore; and he professed himself ready to undertake a cruise, even, for the especial purpose of hunting up the "Jew."

"I haven't seen that ere crittur now"—Peter always spoke of the tree as if it had animal life—"these three years. We think he doesn't like the steamboats. The very last time I seed the old chap he was a-goin' up afore a smart norwester, and we was a-comin' down with the wind in our teeth, when I made out the 'Jew,' about a mile, or, at most, a mile and a half ahead of us, and right in our track. I remember that I said to myself, says I, 'Old fellow, we'll get a sight of your countenance this time.' I suppose you know, sir, that the 'Jew' has a face just like a human?"

"I did not know that; but what became of the tree?"

"Tree," answered Peter, shaking his head, "why, can't we cut a tree down in the woods, saw it and carve it as we will, and make it last a hundred years? What become of the tree, sir;—why, as soon as the 'Jew' saw we was a-comin' so straight upon him, what does the old chap do but shift his helm, and make for the west shore. You never seed a steamer leave sich a wake, or make sich time. If he went half a knot, he went twenty!"

This little episode rather shook Fuller's faith in Peter's accuracy; but it did not prevent his making an arrangement by which he and the old man were to take a cruise in quest of the tree, after having fruitlessly endeavored to discover in what part of the lake it was just then to be seen.

"Some folks pretend he's gone down," said Peter, in continuation of a discourse on the subject, as he flattened in the sheets of a very comfortable and rather spacious sailboat, on quitting the wharf of Geneva, "and will never come up ag'in. But they may just as well tell me that the sky is coming down, and that we may set about picking up the larks. That 'Jew' will no more sink than a well-corked bottle will sink."

This was the opinion of Peter. Fuller cared but little for it, though he still fancied he might make his companion useful in hunting up the object of his search. These two strangely-assorted companions cruised up and down the Seneca for a week, vainly endeavoring to find the "Wandering Jew." Various were the accounts they gleaned from the different boatmen.

One had heard he was to be met with off this point; another, in that bay: all believed he might be found, though no one had seen him lately—some said, in many years.

"He'll turn up," said Peter, positively, "or the Seneca would go down bows foremost. We shall light on the old chap when we least expect it."

It must be confessed that Peter had many sufficient reasons for entertaining these encouraging hopes. He was capitally fed, had very little more to do than to ease off, or flatten in a sheet, the boat being too large to be rowed; and cigars, and liquors of various sorts were pretty much at his command, for the obvious reason that they were under his care. In delivering his sentiments, however, Peter was reasonably honest, for he had the most implicit faith, not only in the existence of this "Jew," but in the beneficent influence of his visits. His presence was universally deemed a sign of good luck.

Fuller passed most of the nights in a comfortable bed, leaving Peter in the boat; sometimes asking for lodgings in a farm-house, and, at others, obtaining them in an inn. Wherever he might be, he inquired about the "Wandering Jew" and the "Lake Gun," bent on solving these two difficult problems, if possible, and always with the same success. Most persons had seen the former, but not lately; while about one in ten had heard the latter. It occurred to our traveler that more of the last were to be found nearer to the northern than to the southern end of the lake.

The cruise continued a fortnight in this desultory manner, with the same want of success. One morning, as Fuller was returning to the boat, after passing the night in a farm-house, he was struck by the statue-like appearance of a figure which stood on the extreme point of a low, rocky promontory, that was considerably aside from any dwelling or building. The place was just at the commencement of the hill country, and where the shores of the Seneca cease to offer those smiling pictures of successful husbandry that so much abound farther north. A somber, or it might be better to say a sober, aspect gave dignity to the landscape, which, if not actually grand, had, at least, most of the elements that characterize the noble in nature.

But Fuller, at the moment, was less struck with the scenery, charming as that certainly was, than with the statue-like and immovable form on the little promontory. A single tree shaded the spot where the stranger stood, but it cast its shadows toward the west, at that early hour, leaving the erect and chiseled form in clear sun-light. Stimulated by curiosity, and hoping to learn something that might aid him in his search from one as curious as himself, Fuller turned aside, and, instead of descending to the spot where Peter had the boat ready for his reception, he crossed a pleasant meadow, in the direction of the tree.

Several times did our traveler stop to gaze on that immovable form. A feeling of superstition came over him when he saw that not the smallest motion, nor relief of limb or attitude, was made for the ten minutes that his eye had rested on the singular and strange object. At he drew nearer, however, the outlines became more and more distinct, and he fancied that the form was actually naked. Then the truth became apparent: it was a native of the forest, in his summer garb, who had thrown aside his blanket, and stood in his leggings, naked. Phidias could not have cut in stone a more faultless form; for active, healthful youth had given to it the free and noble air of manly but modest independence.

"Sago," said Fuller, drawing near to the young Indian, who did not betray surprise or emotion of any sort, as the stranger's foot-fall came unexpectedly on his ear, using the salutation of convention, as it is so generally practiced between the two races. The Indian threw forward an arm with dignity, but maintained his erect and otherwise immovable attitude.

"Oneida?" demanded Fuller, while he doubted if any young warrior of that half-subdued tribe could retain so completely the air and mien of the great forests and distant prairies.

"Seneca," was the simple answer. The word was uttered in a tone so low and melancholy that it sounded like saddened music. Nothing that Fuller had ever before heard conveyed so much meaning so simply, and in so few syllables. It illuminated the long vista of the past, and cast a gloomy shadow into that of the future, alluding to a people driven from their haunts, never to find another resting-place on earth. That this young warrior so meant to express himself—not in an abject attempt to extort sympathy, but in the noble simplicity of a heart depressed by the fall of his race—Fuller could not doubt; and every generous feeling of his soul was enlisted in behalf of this young Indian.

"Seneca," he repeated slowly, dropping his voice to something like the soft, deep tones of the other; "then you are in your own country, here?"

"My country," answered the red man, coldly, "no; my *father's* country, yes."

His English was good, denoting more than a common education, though it had a slightly foreign or peculiar accent. The intonations of his voice were decidedly those of the Indian.

"You have come to visit the land of your fathers?"

A slight wave of the hand was the reply. All this time the young Seneca kept his eye fastened in one direction, apparently regarding some object in the lake. Fuller could see nothing to attract this nearly riveted gaze, though curiosity induced him to make the effort.

"You admire this sheet of water, by the earnest manner in which you look upon it?" observed Fuller.

"See!" exclaimed the Indian, motioning toward a point near a mile distant. "He moves! may be he will come here."

"Moves! I see nothing but land, water, and sky. What moves?"

"The Swimming Seneca. For a thousand winters he is to swim in the waters of this lake. Such is the tradition of my people. Five hundred winters are gone by since he was thrown into the lake; five hundred more must come before he will sink. The curse of the Manitou is on him. Fire will not burn him; water will not swallow him up; the fish will not go near him; even the accursed axe of the settler can not cut him into chips! There he floats, and must float, until his time is finished!"

"You must mean the 'Wandering Jew?'"

"So the pale-faces call him; but he was never a Jew. 'Tis a chief of the Senecas, thrown into the lake by the Great Spirit, for his bad conduct. Whenever he tries to get upon the land, the Spirit speaks to him from the caves below, and he obeys."

"THAT must mean the 'Lake Gun?'"

"So the pale-faces call it. It is not strange that the names of the red man and of the pale-faces should differ."

"The races are not the same, and each has its own traditions. I wish to hear what the Senecas say about this floating tree; but first have the goodness to point it out to me."

The young Indian did as Fuller requested. Aided by the keener vision of the red man, our traveler at length got a glimpse of a distant speck on the water, which his companion assured him was the object of their mutual search. He himself had been looking for the "Jew" a week, but had asked no assistance from others, relying on the keenness of his sight and the accuracy of his traditions. That very morning he had first discovered the speck on the water, which he now pointed out to his companion.

"You think, then, that yonder object is the 'Wandering Jew?'" asked Fuller.

"It is the Swimming Seneca. Five hundred winters has he been obliged to keep in the chilled waters of the lake; in five hundred more the Manitou will let him rest on its bottom."

"What was the offense that has drawn down upon this chief so severe a punishment?"

"Listen to our traditions, and you shall know. When the Great Spirit created man, He gave him laws to obey, and duties to perform—"

"Excuse me, Seneca, but your language is so good that I hardly know what to make of you."

An almost imperceptible smile played about the compressed lip of the young Indian, who, at first, seemed disposed to evade an explanation; but, on reflection, he changed his purpose, and communicated to Fuller the outlines of a very simple, and, by no means, unusual history. He was a chief of the highest race in his tribe, and had been selected to receive the education of a pale-face at one of the colleges of that people. He had received a degree, and, yielding to the irrepressible longings of what might almost be termed his nature, he no sooner left the college in which he had been educated, than he resumed the blanket and leggings, under the influence of early recollections, and a mistaken appreciation of the comparative advantages between the civilized condition, and those of a life passed in the forest and on the prairies. In this respect our young Seneca resembles the white American, who, after a run of six months in Europe, returns home with the patriotic declaration in his mouth, that his native land is preferable to all other lands. Fuller soon understood the case, when both reverted to their common object in coming thither. The young Seneca thereupon resumed his explanation.

"These laws of the Great Spirit," continued the Seneca, "were not difficult to obey so long as the warrior was of a humble mind, and believed himself inferior to the Manitou, who had fashioned him with His hands, and placed him between the Seneca and the Cayuga, to hunt the deer and trap the beaver. But See-wise was one of those who practiced arts that you pale-faces condemn, while you submit to them. He was a demagogue among the red men, and set up the tribe in opposition to the Manitou."

"How," exclaimed Fuller, "did the dwellers in the forest suffer by such practices?"

"Men are every where the same, let the color, or the tribe, or the country be what it may. It was a law of our people, one which tradition tells us came direct from the Great Spirit, that the fish should be taken only in certain seasons, and for so many moons. Some thought this law was for the health of the people; others, that it was to enable the fish to multiply for the future. All believed it wise, because it came from the Manitou, and had descended to the tribe through so many generations: all but See-wise. He said that an Indian ought to fish when and where he pleased; that a warrior was not a woman; that the spear and the hook had been given to him to be used, like the bow and arrow, and that none but cowardly Indians would scruple to take the fish when they wished. Such opinions pleased the common Indians, who love to believe themselves greater than they are. See-wise grew bolder by success, until he dared to say in council, that the red men made the world themselves, and for themselves, and that they could do with it what they pleased. He saw no use in any night; it was inconvenient; an Indian could sleep in the light as well as in the darkness; there was to be eternal day; then the hunt could go on until the deer was killed, or the bear treed. The young Indians liked such talk. They loved to be told they were the equals of the Great Spirit. They declared that See-wise should be their principal chief. See-wise opened his ears wide to this talk, and the young men listened to his words as they listened to the song of the mocking-bird. They liked each other, because they praised each other. It is sweet to be told that we are better and wiser than all around us. It is sweet to the red man; the pale-faces may have more sober minds—"

The Seneca paused an instant, and Fuller fancied that a smile of irony again struggled about his compressed lip. As the traveler made no remark, however, the youthful warrior resumed his tale.

"I hear a great deal of what demagogues are doing among your people, and of the evil they produce. They begin by flattering, and end by ruling.

He carries a strong hand, who makes all near him help to uphold it. In the crowd few perceive its weight until it crushes them.

"Thus was it with See-wise. Half the young men listened to him, and followed in his trail. The aged chiefs took counsel together. They saw that all the ancient traditions were despised, and that new conduct was likely to come in with new opinions. They were too old to change. What was done has never been said, but See-wise disappeared. It was whispered that he had gone down among the fish he loved to take out of season. There is one tradition, that he speared an enormous salmon, and the fish, in its struggles, drew him out of his canoe, and that his hands could not let go of the handle of his spear. Let this be as it may, no one ever saw See-wise any more, in the form in which he had been known to his people. At length the trunk of a tree was seen floating about the Seneca, and one of the oldest of the chiefs, pointing to it, pronounced the name of 'See-wise.' He would fish out of season, and his spirit is condemned, they say, to float among the salmon, and trout, and eels, for a thousand winters. It was not long after this that the lake began to speak, in a voice loud as the thunder from the clouds. The Seneca traditions say this is the Manitou calling to See-wise, when he goes down after the fish, out of season."

"And do you, an educated man, believe in this tale?" asked Fuller.

"I can not say. The things learned in childhood remain the longest on the memory. They make the deepest marks. I have seen the evil that a demagogue can do among the pale-faces; why should I not believe the same among my own people?"

"This is well enough, as respects the curse on the demagogue; but lakes do not usually—"

Fuller had got thus far, when the Seneca, as if in mockery, emitted the sound that has obtained the name of the "Lake Gun" among those who have lived on its banks in these later times. Perhaps it was, in part, the influence of the Seneca's legend, united to the opinions and statements of the inhabitants of that region, which conspired to make our traveler start, in awe and surprise; for, certainly, the deep-mouthed cannon never gave forth a more impressive and sudden concussion on the ear.

"It does, indeed, sound very like a gun!" said Fuller, after a long pause had enabled him to speak.

"It is the voice of the Great Spirit, forbidding See-wise to fish," answered the Seneca. "For a time the demagogue has all the talking to himself, but, sooner or later, the voice of truth is heard, which is the voice of the Manitou. But I must go nearer to the tree—ha! What has become of it?"

Fuller looked, and, sure enough, the speck on the water had vanished. This might have been by an unobserved movement in a current; or it might have been owing to a sudden variation in the light; certain it was, no tree could now be seen. Fuller then proposed to use his boat, in endeavoring to get nearer to the "Jew." The Seneca gave a very cheerful assent, and, throwing his light summer blanket, with an air of manly grace, over a shoulder, he followed to the water-side.

"Most red men," resumed the young warrior, as he took his place in the boat, "would see something marvelous in this appearance and disappearance of the swimming Seneca, and would hesitate about going any nearer to him; but this is not my feeling—error is strengthened by neglecting to look into truth. I hope yet to go near See-wise."

Fuller hardly knew what to think of his companion's credulity. At times he appeared to defer to the marvelous and the traditions of his tribe; then, again, the lights of education would seem to gleam upon the darkness of his superstition, and leave him a man of inductive reason. As for himself, he was probably not altogether as much of the last as his pride of race would have led him to hope.

Peter had seen nothing, but he had heard the "Gun."

"'Twas a mere flash in the pan to what I have heard, when the lake is in 'arnest," said the old fellow, with the love of exaggeration so common with the vulgar. "Still, it was a gun."

"A signal that the 'Wandering Jew' is near by; so, haul aft the sheets, and let us depart."

In a quarter of an hour the boat was lying with her foresheet hauled over, and her helm down, within a hundred yards of the object of the long search of the whole party. It was deep water, and a slight ripple under what might be termed the cutwater of the tree indicated a movement. Perhaps a lower current forced forward the roots, which, in their turn, urged the trunk ahead. As often happens in such cases, the accidental formation of the original fracture, aided by the action of the weather, had given to the end of the trunk a certain resemblance to a human countenance. Peter was the first to point out the peculiarity, which he looked upon uneasily. Fuller soon observed it, and said the aspect was, in sooth, that of a demagogue. The forehead retreated, the face was hatchet-shaped, while the entire expression was selfish, yet undecided. As for the Seneca, he gazed on these signs with wonder, mingled with awe.

"We see here the wicked See-wise. The Great Spirit—call him Manitou, or call him God—does not forget what is wrong, or what is right. The wicked may flourish for a while, but there is a law that is certain to bring him within the power of punishment. Evil spirits go up and down among us, but there is a limit they can not pass. But Indians like this Swimming Seneca do much harm. They mislead the ignorant, arouse evil passions, and raise themselves into authority by their dupes. The man who tells the people their faults is a truer friend than he who harps only on their good qualities. Be that only a tree, or be it a man bound in this form, for a thousand winters, by the hand of the Great Spirit, it tells the same story. See-wise did once live. His career comes to us in traditions, and we believe all that our fathers told us. Accursed be the man who deceives, and who opens his mouth only to lie! Accursed, too, is the land that neglects the counsels of the fathers to follow those of the sons!"

"There is a remarkable resemblance between this little incident in the history of the Senecas and events that are passing among our pale-faced race of the present age. Men who, in their hearts, really care no more for mankind than See-wise cared for the fish, lift their voices in shouts of a spurious humanity, in order to raise themselves to power, on the shoulders of an excited populace. Bloodshed, domestic violence, impracticable efforts to attain an impossible perfection, and all the evils of a civil conflict are forgotten or blindly attempted, in order to raise themselves in the arms of those they call the people."

"I know your present condition," answered the young Seneca, openly smiling. "The Manitou may have ordered it for your good. Trust to *him*. There are days in which the sun is not seen—when a lurid darkness brings a second night over the earth. It matters not. The great luminary is always there. There may be clouds before his face, but the winds will blow them away. The man or the people that trust in God will find a lake for every See-wise."

IN THE PINES

W. F. Mayer

1859

New Jersey's dismal Pine Barrens are best known as the home of the Jersey Devil, one of America's first homegrown legends.

On a stormy night in 1735, the story goes, Mother Leeds gave birth to a child which turned into a hoofed, winged monster before the midwife's eyes: for Mother Leeds was a witch and the baby's father was the Devil. Another version of the story says that when Mrs. Leeds found out she was pregnant with her thirteenth child, she said that if she were to have one more child, "may it be a devil." In either case, the newborn monster killed the midwife and escaped up the chimney. Sightings have been reported in the area ever since.

Tracking down the origin of this tale is a difficult task. Almost nothing was written about it until 1909, when hundreds of alleged sightings were reported from South Jersey through Delaware and into Maryland. These seem to have been the work of a hoaxer who fitted a tame kangaroo with claws and bat-like wings in an attempt to publicize a Philadelphia museum, but they propelled the Jersey Devil into the mainstream of public consciousness and ever since it has rivaled Bigfoot as America's favorite monster.

Recent research suggests that the monster tale may have arisen as a kind of political satire or allegory in the early eighteenth century. The Leeds family published anti-Quaker pamphlets after the Quakers suppressed Daniel Leeds's almanac for its "pagan" use of astrology, starting a feud that lasted for two generations and saw Daniel's son Titan Leeds accused of being "Satan's Harbinger." The conflict is scarcely remembered today, but it is perhaps significant that the Leeds family crest, which appeared on all Leeds publications under Titan's editorship, was three wyverns—two-legged, bat-winged dragons that in the Leeds version looked very much like devils.

The following extract is from the May 1859 Atlantic Monthly. *It is one of the earliest extant accounts of the Jersey Devil myth, and includes several other pieces of Pine Barrens folklore.*

I f I were a crow, or, at least, had the faculty of flying with that swift directness which is proverbially attributed to the corvine tribe, and were to wing a southwesterly course from the truck of the flag-staff which rises from the Battery at New York, I should find myself, within a very short time, about fifty miles from the turbulent city, and hovering over a region of country as little like the civilized emporium just quitted as it is well possible to conceive. Not being a crow, however, nor fitted up with an apparatus for flying,—destitute even of a balloon,—I am compelled to adopt the means of locomotion which the bounty of God or the ingenuity of man affords me, and to spend a somewhat longer time in transit to my destination.

Over the New Jersey Railroad, then, I rattled, one fine, sunshiny autumn morning, in the year that has recently taken leave of us, as far as

Bordentown, a distance of some fifty-seven miles, on my way to a locality the very existence of which is scarcely dreamed of by thousands in the metropolis, who can tell you how many square miles of malaria there are in the Roman Campagna, and who have got the topography of Caffre Land at their fingers' ends. It is a region aboriginal in savagery, grand in the aspects of untrammelled Nature; where forests extend in uninterrupted lines over scores of miles; where we may wander a good day's journey without meeting half-a-dozen human faces; where stately deer will bound across our path, and bears dispute our passage through the cedar-brakes; where, in a word, we may enjoy the undiluted essence, the perfect wildness, of woodland life. Deep and far "under the shade of melancholy boughs" we shall be taken, if together we visit the ancient Pines of New Jersey.

In order to do so, we must make at Bordentown the acquaintance of Mr. Cox, and take our seats in his stage for a jolt, twelve miles long, to the village of New Egypt, on the frontier of the Pines. Although the forest is accessible from many points, and may be entered by a number of distinct approaches, I, the writer hereof, selected that *via* New Egypt as the most convenient to a comer from New York, and as, perhaps, the least fatiguing to accomplish.

But, oh! the horrors of those New Jersey roads! Mud? 'Tis as if all the rains of heaven had been concentrated upon all the marls and clays of earth, and all the sticky stratum plastered down in a wiggling line of unascertainable length and breadth! Holes? As if a legion of sharpshooters had been detailed for the defence of Sandy Hook, and had excavated for themselves innumerable rifle-pits or caverns for the discomfiture of unhappy passengers! Up hill and down dale,—with merciless ruts and savage ridges,—now, a slough, to all appearance destitute of bottom, and, next, a treacherous stretch of sand, into which the wheels sink deeper and deeper at every revolution, as if the vehicle were France, and the road disorder,—such is a faint adumbration of the state of affairs in the benighted interior of our petulant little whiskey-drinking sister State!

But all earthly things come to an end, and so, accordingly, did our three-hours' drive. The stage pompously rolled into the huddled street of its terminus, and deposited me, in the neighborhood of noon, on the stoop of the only tavern supported in the deadly-lively place. No long sojourn, however, was in store for me. Presently—ere I had grown tired of watching the couple of clodhoppers, well-bespattered as to boots and undergarments with Jersey mud, who, leaning against a fence in true agricultural laziness, deliberately eyed, or rather, gloated over the inoffensive traveller, as though he were that "daily stranger," for whom, as is well known, every Jerseyman offers up matutinal supplications—a buggy appeared in the distance, and I was shortly asked for. It was the vehicle in which I was to seek my destination in the Pines; and my back was speedily turned upon the queer little village with the curiously chosen name. My driver, an intelligent, sharp-featured old man, soon informs me that he was born and has lived for fifty years in the forest. A curious, old-world mortal,—our father's "serving-man," to the very life! The Pines are to him what Banks and City Halls and Cooper Institutes and Astor Houses are to a poor *cittadini*; every tree is individualized; and I doubt not he could find his way by night from one end to the other of the forest.

We had driven no great distance, when my companion lifted his whip, and, pointing to a long, dark, indistinct line which crossed the road in the distance, blocking the prospect ahead and on either side, as far as the eye could reach, exclaimed: "Them's the Pines!" As we approached the forest, a change, theatrical in its suddenness, took place in the scenery through which our course was taken. The rich and smiling pasture-lands, interspersed with fields of luxuriant corn, were left behind, the red clay of the road was exchanged for a gritty sand, and the road itself dwindled to a mere pathway through a clearing. The locality looked like a plagiarism from the Ohio backwoods. On both sides of our path spread the graceful undergrowth, waving in an ocean of green, and hiding the stumps with which the plain was covered, while far away, to right and left, the prospect was bounded by forest walls, and gloomy bulwarks and parapets of pines arose in front, as if designed, in their perfect denseness, to exclude the world from some bosky Garden of Paradise beyond. Not so, however; for our pathway squeezes itself between two melancholy sentinel-pines, tracing its white scroll into the forest farther than the eye can follow, and in a few moments we leave the clearing behind, and pass into the shadow of the endless avenue, and bow beneath the trailing branches of the silent, stern, immovable warders at the gate.

We were fairly in the Pines; and a drive of somewhat more than three miles lay before us still.

The immense forest region I had thus entered covers an extensive portion of Burlington County, and nearly the whole of Ocean, beside parts of Monmouth, Camden, Atlantic, Gloucester, and other counties. The prevailing soils of this great area—some sixty miles in length by ten in breadth, and reaching from the river Delaware to the very shore of the Atlantic—are marls and sands of different qualities, of which the most common is a fine, white, angular sand, of the kind so much in request for building-purposes and the manufacture of glass. In such an arid soil the *coniferae* alone could flourish, and accordingly we find that the wide-spreading region is overgrown almost entirely with white and yellow pine, hemlock, and cedar. Hence its distinctive appellation.

It was a most lovely afternoon, warm and serene as only an American autumn afternoon knows how to be; and while we hurried past the mute, monotonous, yet ever-shifting array of pines and cedars, the very rays of the sun seemed to be perfumed with the aroma of the fragrant twigs, about which humming-birds now and then whirred and fluttered as we startled them, scarcely more brilliant in color than the gorgeous maples which grew in one or two dry and open spots. For three-quarters of an hour our drive continued, until at length a slight undulation broke the level of the sand, and a fence, inclosing a patch of Indian corn, from which the forest had been driven back, betokened for the first time the proximity of some habitation. In fact, having reached the summit of the slope, I found myself in the centre of an irregular range of dwellings, scattered here and there in picturesque disregard of order, and next moment my hand was grasped by my friend B. I had reached my destination,—Hanover Iron-Works,—and was soon walking up, past the white gateway, to the Big House.

Somewhat less than eighty years ago, Mr. Benjamin Jones, a merchant of Philadelphia, invested a portion of his fortune in the purchase of one hundred thousand acres of land in the then unbroken forest of the Pines. The site of the present hamlet of Hanover struck him as admirably adapted for the establishment of a smelting-furnace, and he accordingly projected a settlement on this spot. The Rancocus River forms here a broad embayment, the damming of which was easily accomplished, and one of the best of water-privileges was thus obtained. On the north of this bay or pond, moreover, there rises a sloping bluff, which was covered, at the period of its purchase, with ancient trees, but upon which a large and commodious mansion was soon erected. Here Mr. Jones planted himself, and quickly drew around him a settlement which rose in number to some four hundred souls; and here he commenced the manufacture of iron. At frequent intervals in the Pines were found surface-deposits of ore, the precipitate from waters holding iron in solution, which frequently covered an area of many acres, and reached a depth of from two or three inches to as many feet. The ore thus existing in surface-deposits was smelted in the iron-works, and the metal thence obtained was at once molten and moulded in the adjoining foundry. Here, in the midst of these spreading forests, many a ponderous casting, many a fiery rush of tons of molten metal, has been seen. Here, five-and-forty years ago, the celebrated Decatur superintended, during many weeks, the casting of twenty-four pounders, to be used in the famous contest with the Algerine pirates whom he humbled; and the echoes of the forest were awakened with strange thunders then. As the great guns were raised from the pits in which they had been cast, and were declared ready for proof, Decatur ordered each one to be loaded with repeated charges of powder and ball, and pointed into the woods. Then, for miles between the grazed and quivering boles, crashed the missiles of destruction, startling bear and deer and squirrel and raccoon, and leaving traces of their passage which are even still occasionally discovered. The cannon-balls themselves are now and then found imbedded in the sand of the forest. In this manner the guns were tried which were to thunder the challenge of America against the dens of Mediterranean pirates.

Hanover, too, in its day of pride, furnished many a city with its iron tubes for water and for gas, many a factory and workshop with its castings, many a farmer with his tools, but the glow of the furnace is quenched forever now. The slowly gathering ferruginous deposits have been exhausted, and three years have elapsed since the furnace-fires were lighted. The blackened shell of the building stands in cold decrepitude, a melancholy vestige of usefulness outlived. In consequence of the stoppage of the works, Hanover has lost seven-eighths of its population, and only about fifty inhabitants remain in the white cottages grouped about the Big House, who are employed in agricultural labors and occupations connected with the forest. Yet in this solitary nook the elegances and the tastes of the most cultivated society are to be found. The Big House, surrounded by its well-trimmed gardens sloping down to the broad Rancocus, with its comfortable apartments, and the diversified prospect which it commands, offers a resting-place which, although deep in the genuine forest, combines urban refinement with the quiet and seclusion of country-life.

Bright and early on the morning after my arrival, Friend B. was at my door; and after a savory, if hasty breakfast, we sounded *boute-selle*. Outside the gate a couple of forest-ponies were waiting,—stout, lively, five-year-olds, equal, if not to a two-forty heat, yet to twenty miles of steady trot without distress,—brown and sleek as you please, with the knowingest eyes, and intelligence expressed in the impatient stamp of the fore-foot, and good-humor in the twitching of the ear. Into the saddle and off, with the cheery breeze to bathe us in exhilaration, as it went humming around us laden with aromatic odors and mysterious whisperings of the pine-trees to the sea,—through the dew-diamonded grass of the little lawn at the top of the hill,—past the great elm with its glistening foliage, and its carolling crew of just-awakened birds,—then a canter down the sandy slope to the edge of the forest, and again the pines are around us.

Before us lay a four-mile ride over a devious track among trees which my companion knows by heart. Paths diverge into the forest on either side, running north and south, east and west, straight and crooked, narrow and broad; but B. follows unerringly the right, though undistinguished trail. This knowledge of woodcraft,—how it appalls and wonder-strikes the unlearned metropolitan, accustomed as he is to numbered houses and name-boarded streets! No omnibus-driver threading the confusion of a great thoroughfare could shape his course with greater assurance and lack of hesitation than does B. through these endless avenues of heavy-foliaged pines, broken only now and then by some tangled, impenetrable brake of cedars, or by a charred and blackened clearing, where the coaler has been at work. I gradually grew to believe that he could call every tree by its name, as generals have been said to know every soldier in their armies.

At length we reached a clearing of one or two acres in extent, the site of Cranberry Lodge, and the terminus of our ride. In the centre of the lone expanse two unusually tall pines were left standing, at the base of which a curious structure nestled, which had been for several weeks the occasional hermitage of my companion. It was built entirely with his own hands, of cedar rails and white-pine planks, which he had cut and sawed from trees that his own hands had felled. A queer little cabin, some nine feet in length by five or six in breadth, standing all alone in the forest, with not a neighbor within a distance of at least four miles!

Dismounting, we fastened our horses to a couple of saplings, and I was introduced to the interior of Cranberry Lodge, which was tenanted only by the "hired man," who, in the absence of Mr. B., reigned supreme in the clearing. The dwelling I found no less primitive in internal than in its external appearance. Three persons, moderately doubled up and squeezed, could find room in the interior, which was furnished with a bench for the safe-keeping of sundry pots, pans, and other culinary necessaries, and with a shelf on which some blankets were laid, constituting my companion's bedstead and bed, when he slept in Cranberry Lodge. Beneath the "bunk" a small hole scooped in the sand stood in lieu of a cellar, and contained a stock of provisions of Mr. B.'s own cooking.

Such a backwoodish dwelling as Cranberry Lodge, existing in the year 1858, within seventy miles of New York, requires some explanation. Its foundation is—pies! Cape Cod, the great emporium of the cranberry-trade, has been running short for the last few years; in other words, its supply is unequal to the demand. The heavy Britishers have awakened to the fact, since 1851, that, of all condiments and delicacies, cranberry-sauce and cranberry-pie are best in their way; and John Bull takes many a barrel clean out of our market now. It so happened that in the Pines of New Jersey cranberries superior to those of Cape Cod have grown unheeded for centuries,—grew red and purple and white and pink when Columbus was unthought of, as well as when Washington passed through the Pines,—and for sixty or seventy years have furnished a certain class of gypsies—of whom more anon—with merchandise which sold well in the neighboring villages and cities. No one thought of cultivating cranberries; no one, but the gypsies aforesaid, of gathering them for sale. But it came to pass that a certain farmer of Hanover was, like many another, unsuccessful during several years. As a last resource, he purchased of the owner of the Big House a cranberry-bog,—that is to say, one of the many marshy spots which are interspersed in the forest,—for which he paid five dollars the acre. There were a little more than one hundred acres in the bog. At a cost of some six hundred dollars Mr. F. fenced in his bog, and spent three months in watching the cranberries as they ripened, to protect them from depredation. To his intense astonishment, he found, in October, that the yield was between two and three hundred bushels to the acre, and that his land and fencing were paid for, with a balance left over for next year. In consequence of this success, a little mania for cranberry-farming seized upon the denizens of the Pines, and bogs acquired a value they had never borne before. This was in 1857. Early in 1858, one of these plots of land, with an adjoining piece of forest, was rented by Mr. B., who, like a right-down Yankee, determined to cultivate it himself. So, with the aid of one hired man, a clearing was made in his forest-patch, a hut built, four miles from the nearest habitation, and the trees cut down were converted into rails, wherewith to fence in the cranberry-land. At the time of my visit, the crop was just beginning to think of getting ripe, and the great lazy vines, each one creeping for several feet along the ground, were severally loaded with dozens of delicately-tinted berries, plump and fair as British beauties, which silently drew to themselves and absorbed the rays of the sun, turning them to color and succulent subacidulousness. A most glorious sight that same hundred-acre bog must have been a couple of weeks later, when the berries had ripened, and a carpet of rosy redness blushed upwards to the waning sun! Yet 1858 (the even year) was a bad season for cranberries,—the yield was *only* sufficient to pay for the land and fencing, with a modicum over to begin 1859 with!

So cranberries grew to be institutions in the Pines, and all the bogs for miles around the site of the first experiment were hired by sanguine farmers. But the cranberry-cultivator has one enemy, which is neither bird, nor worm, nor blight, but biped,—a Rat, two-legged, erect, or moderately so, talking, even, in audible and intelligible speech,—the Pine Rat, namely. Few but New Jerseymen, and of them chiefly those who dwell about the forest, have heard of this human species; it has not yet had its Agassiz nor its Wyman,—yet there it flourishes and repeats itself!

My friend, Mr. B., considerately undertook to initiate me into some of the mysteries of this race, which has proved minatory, though not destructive, to his blushing crop,—and accordingly led me through brake and brier, past wild and gloomy cedar-swamps, over brooks insecurely bridged with fallen logs, or, perchance, with stepping-blocks of pine-stumps, far into the silent forest, and to a little dell or dingle,—a natural clearing,—where a couple of tents were pitched, and the smoke of a struggling fire told infallibly of human neighborhood. The barking of a splenetic little terrier brought from one of the tents a man of some fifty years, lank and gaunt of visage, with matted hair, and wild, uncivilized eyes, dressed in a ragged jacket and what had once been a pair of trousers. His face wore no expression of intelligence; but a look of intense, though animal cunning lurked in his eyes. While I was gazing on this individual, who stood in silence by his tent, there emerged from the other an ancient female, who might have been eighty years of age, but who hobbled towards us with much briskness.

"Good evening, Hannah Butler," said Mr. B.; "I've brought you some tomatoes from the Big House. This is my friend, Mr. Smith of York."

Mr. Smith of York (grimly repressing a smile, as his mischievous memory whispered something about Brooks of Sheffield) bowed gravely to Mrs. Butler. Mr. B. whispers,—"That's the Queen of the Pine Rats!" Hannah meanwhile mumbles over one of the fleshy tomatoes.

The man whom we had first seen held in his hand a tattered shawl, with which he now began patching a portion of his tent, saying at the same time that there was a storm a-brewing.

"Ay, is there!" said Mrs. Butler; "and a storm like the one when I seed Leeds's devil"—

"Hush!" interrupted her ragged companion, with a look of terror. "What's the good o' namin' him, and allus talkin' about him, when yer don't never know as he ar'n't byside ye?"

"I'll devil yer!" shrieked the crone, through a half-eaten tomato. "Finish mendin' up yer cover, yer mean cranberry-thief!"

The spiteful terrier, which had meanwhile evinced an unpleasant interest in the thickness of my pantaloons, added his yelping to the clamor, and Mr. B., pointing to the clouds, thought we had better hasten homewards. So we bade farewell to Hannah and her nephew, as I learned that the unfortunate vessel of her wrath in reality was, and dived into the gloomy recesses of the Pines again.

Long ere we got back to Cranberry Lodge, all doubts of an impending tempest had disappeared. The eastern sky, cloudless an hour before, was now overhung with a livid bank of ash-gray clouds, which were incessantly riven by broad and terrible flashes of silent lightning. A slight westerly breeze was blowing, and evidently impeded the progress of the storm, which was beating up from seaward against the wind. Plunging through prickly thickets and dashing through the turbid brooks, we hastened toward the clearing, committed Cranberry Lodge to the custody of the "hired man," and untied our horses from the saplings to which they were made fast. In another moment we were on the back trail. Scarcely, however, was the clearing shut out of view when a little hesitating puff of wind from the east blew chill upon us; the breeze had veered, and the tempest was at hand. In the twinkling of an eye, the western horizon was overhung with the same ghastly storm-bank that threatened in the east, while a monitory gust rustled through the sighing pines, wildly twisting and tossing the undergrowth,—overspread with a quivering pallor as it bent before the breeze,—and bade us be prepared. Next moment, a clap of thunder, rattling like the artillery of ten thousand sieges, or like millions of bars of iron dashed furiously together, broke upon the forest. It was the most awful sound, terrible even in its expected suddenness, that I ever heard. Simultaneously a flash of purple lightning fell from the zenith to the horizon, splitting the clouds asunder, and with it there descended rain in a cataract rather than in torrents, so that in the twinkling of an eye the thirsty sand was saturated, and bubbling pools of water pattered in the deluged path. Crash after crash, each clap more terrific than the one preceding, came the awful thunder; blinding flashes of lightning darted around us;—but still our phlegmatic ponies galloped on, and only once started violently, when a peal which really seemed as if its shock must burst the heavens asunder dazed us momentarily with its almost unendurable sound. The gloomy canopy above us, meanwhile, was overrun by incessant streams of purple lightning, and the deluge of rain still fell. At length we reached the Big House, (somewhat ostentatiously reducing the speed of our horses to a walk as we came within sight of its embowered windows,) and were soon dripping in the kitchen. A change of apparel, calling into requisition Mexican *ponchos* and other picturesque garments, with a smoke beside a roaring fire, completely obviated all dangerous consequences; nor was it without feelings of great satisfaction that B. and myself watched tranquilly from our comfortable ensconcement the beatings of the storm on the encircling forest.

The Big House, I found, was full of legends of the Pine Rats. This extraordinary race of beings are lineal descendants of the New Jersey Tories, who, during the Revolution, made the Pines their refuge, whence they sallied in perpetual forays against the farms and dwellings of the partisans of the opposite cause. Several hundreds of these fanatical desperadoes made the forest their home, and laid waste the surrounding townships by their sudden raids. Most barbarous cruelties were practised on both sides, in the contests which continually took place between Whigs and Tories, and the unnatural seven-years' war possessed nowhere darker features than in the neighborhood of the New Jersey Pines. Remains of these forest-freebooters are still discovered from time to time, in the process of clearing the woods, and unmistakable relics are occasionally met with in the denser portions of the forest, which must have been comparatively open eighty years ago.

The degraded descendants of these Tories constitute the principal difficulty with which a proprietor in this region has to contend. Completely besotted and brutish in their ignorance, they are incapable of obtaining an honest living, and have supported themselves, from a time which may be called immemorial, by practising petty larceny on an organized plan. The Pine Rat steals wood, steals game, steals cranberries, steals anything, in fact, that his hand can be laid upon; and woe to the property of the man who dares attempt to restrain him! A few weeks may, perhaps, elapse, after the tattered savage has received a warning or a reprimand, and then a column of smoke will be seen stealing up from some quarter in the forest;— he has set the woods on fire! Conflagrations of this kind will sometimes sweep away many hundreds of acres of the most valuable timber; while accidental fires are also of frequent occurrence. When indications of a fire are noticed, every available hand—men, women, and children alike—is hurried to the spot for the purpose of "fighting" it. Getting to leeward of the flames, the "fighters" kindle a counter-conflagration, which is drawn or sucked against the wind to the part already burning, and in this manner a vacant space is secured, which proves a barrier to the flames. Dexterity in fighting fires is a prime requisite in a forest overseer or workman.

"And now, something about Leeds's devil!" I said to my friend, after satisfactory definition of the Pine Rat; "what fiend may he be, if you please?"

"I will answer,—I will tell you," replies Mr. B. "There lived, in the year 1735, in the township of Burlington, a woman. Her name was Leeds, and she was shrewdly suspected of a little amateur witchcraft. Be that as it may, it is well established, that, one stormy, gusty night, when the wind was howling in turret and tree, Mother Leeds gave birth to a son, whose father could have been no other than the Prince of Darkness. No sooner did he see the light than he assumed the form of a fiend, with a horse's head, wings of bat, and a serpent's tail. The first thought of the newborn Caliban was to fall foul of his mother, whom he scratched and bepommelled soundly, and then flew through the window out into the village, where he played the mischief generally. Little children he devoured, maidens he abused, young men he mauled and battered; and it was many days before a holy man succeeded in repeating the enchantment of Prospero. At length, however, Leeds's devil was laid,—but only for one hundred years.

"During an entire century, the memory of that awful monster was preserved, and, as 1835 drew nigh, the denizens of Burlington and the Pines looked tremblingly for his rising. Strange to say, however, no one but Hannah Butler has had a personal interview with the fiend; though, since 1835, he has frequently been heard howling and screaming in the forest at night, to the terror of the Rats in their lonely encampments. Hannah Butler saw the devil, one stormy night, long ago; though some skeptical individuals affirm, that very possibly she may have been led, under the influence of liquid Jersey lightning, to invest a pine-stump, or, possibly, a belated bear, with diabolical attributes and a Satanic voice. However that may be, you cannot induce a Rat to leave his hut after dark,—nor, indeed, will you find many Jerseymen, though of a higher order of intelligence, who will brave the supernatural terrors of the gloomy forest at night, unless secure in the strength of numbers."

The Pine Rat, in his vocation as a picker-up of every unconsidered trifle, is an adept at charcoal-burning, on the sly. The business of legitimate charcoal-manufacture is also largely practised in the Pines, although the growing value of wood interferes sadly with the coalers. Here and there, however, a few acres are marked out every year for charring, and the coal-pits are established in the clearing made by felling the trees. The "coaling," as it is technically termed, is an assemblage of "pits," or piles of wood, conical in form, and about ten feet in height by twenty in diameter. The wood is cut in equal lengths, and is piled three or four tiers high, each log resting on the end of that below it, and inclining slightly inwards. An opening is left in the centre of the pile, serving as a chimney; and the exterior is overlaid with strips of turf, called "floats," which form an almost air-tight covering. When the pile is overlaid, fire is set at various small apertures in the sides, and when the whole "pit" is fairly burning, the chimney is closed, in order to prevent too rapid combustion, and the whole pile is slowly converted into charcoal. The application of the term "pit" to these piles is worthy of remark. It is due, of course, to the fact, that for centuries it was customary to burn charcoal in excavated pits, until it was discovered that gradual combustion could be as well secured by another and less tedious method.

The Pine Rat glories in his surreptitious coal-pits. In secluded portions of the forest, he may continually be discovered pottering over a "coaling," for which he has stolen the wood. This, indeed, is his only handicraft,—the single labor to which he condescends or is equal. Two or three men sometimes band together and build themselves huts after the curious fashion peculiar to the Rat, namely, by piling sticks or branches in a slope on each side of some tall pine, so that a wigwam, with the trunk of the tree in the centre, is constructed. Inside this triangular shelter—the idea of which was probably borrowed from the Indians—the Pine Rat ensconces himself with his whiskey-bottle at night, crouching in dread of the darkness, or of Leeds's devil, aforesaid. In this respect he singularly resembles the Bohemian charcoal-burner, who trembles at the thought of Rübezahl, that malicious goblin, who has an army of mountain-dwarfs and gnomes at his command. So long as the sunlight inspires our Rat with confidence, however, he will work at his coal-pit, while one comrade is away in the forest, snaring game, and another has, perhaps, been dispatched to the precincts of civilization with his wagon-load of coal. Yes! the Pine Rat sometimes treads the streets of cities,—nay, even extends his wanderings to the banks of the Delaware and the Hudson, to Philadelphia and Trenton, to Jersey City and New York. Then, who so sharp as the grimy tatterdemalion, who passes from street to street and from house to house, with his swart and rickety wagon, and his jangling bell, the discordant clangor of which, when we hear it, calls up horrible recollections of the bells that froze our hearts in plague-stricken cities of other lands, when doomed galley-slaves and *forçats* wheeled awful vehicles of putrefaction through the streets, clashing and clinking their clamorous bells for more and still more corpses, and foully jesting over the Death which they knew was already upon them! But the long-drawn, monotonous, nasal cry of the charcoal-vender—who has not heard it?—"Cha-r-coa'! Cha-r-coa'!"—is more cheerful than the demoniac laughter of the desperate galley-slaves, and his bell sounds musically when we hear it and think of theirs. Sometimes a couple of these peregrinants may be seen to encounter each other in the streets, and straightway there is an adjournment to the nearest bar-room, where the most scientific method of "springing the arch" is discussed over a glass of whiskey, at three cents the quart. Springing the arch, though few may be able to interpret the phrase, is a trick by which every housewife has suffered. It is the secret of piling the coal into the measure in such a manner as to make the smaller quantity pass for the larger, or, in other words, to make three pecks go for a bushel. So the Pine Rat vindicates his claim to a common humanity with all the rest of us men and women; for have not we all our secret and most approved method of springing the arch,—of palming off our three short pecks for a full and bounteous imperial bushel? Ah, yes! brothers and sisters, whisper it, if you will, below your breath, but we all can do the Pine Rat's trick!

We shall not suffer his company much longer in this world,—poor, neglected, pitiable, darkened soul that he is, this fellow-citizen of ours. He must move on; for civilization, like a stern, prosaic policeman, will have no idlers in the path. There must be no vagrants, not even in the forest, the once free and merry greenwood, our policeman-civilization says; nay, the forest, even, must keep a-moving! We must have farms here, and happy homesteads, and orchards heavy with promise of cider, and wheat golden as hope, instead of silent aisles and avenues of mournful pine-trees, sheltering such forlorn miscreations as our poor cranberry-stealing friends! Railways are piercing the Pines; surveyors are marking them out in imaginary squares; market-gardeners are engaging land; and farmers are clearing it. The Rat is driven from point to point, from one means of subsistence to another; and shortly, he will have to make the bitter choice between regulated labor and starvation clean off from the face of the earth. There is no room for a gypsy in all our wide America! The Rat must follow the Indian,—must fade like breath from a window-pane in winter!

In fact, the forest, left so long in its aboriginal savagery, is about to be regenerated. A railroad is to be constructed, this year, which will place Hanover and the centre of the forest within one hour's travel of Philadelphia; and it is scarcely too much to anticipate, that, within five years, thousands of acres, now dense with pines and cedars of a hundred rings, will be laid out in blooming market-gardens and in fields of generous corn. Such little cultivation as has hitherto been attempted has been attended by the most astonishing results; and persons have actually returned from the West and South, in order to occupy farms in the neighborhood of Hanover.

In one respect *c'est dommage*; one is grieved to part with the game that is now so plentiful in the Pines. Owing to the beneficent provision of the laws of New Jersey, which stringently forbid every description of hunting in the State during alternate periods of five years, game of all kinds has an opportunity to multiply; and at the termination of the season of rest, in October, 1858, there was some noble hunting in the neighborhood of Hanover. Five years hence, bears and deer will be a tradition, panthers and raccoons a myth, partridges and quails a vain and melancholy recollection, in what shall then be known as what was once the Pines.

THE ROMANCE OF CERTAIN OLD CLOTHES

Henry James

1868

James's novel The Turn of the Screw *(1898) is regarded as a classic ghost story, and has been reprinted and filmed many times. Thirty years earlier, James wrote "The Romance of Certain Old Clothes," one of his few stories to be set in the past.*

James's fiction often showed Americans encountering Europe, and in the last year of his life he became a British subject. In addition to fiction he wrote a great deal of literary criticism as well as travel writing, biography, autobiography, and plays. He was nominated three times for the Nobel Prize in Literature.

Born in New York to a family of independently wealthy dilettantes, James went to Harvard Law School in 1862, but quickly found that the law did not interest him. His first published work, a review of a stage play, saw print the following year, followed a year later by his first published fiction: a short story titled "A Tragedy of Error."

"The Romance of Certain Old Clothes" belongs to this period of James's life, when he was making a name for himself as a writer of fiction. The year after it was first

published he set off on the first of his European travels, making this tale, argu-
ably, among the last of his early stories. On his European journey of 1869-1870,
James was to meet Charles Dickens, Mary Ann Evans (known to her readers as
George Eliot), John Ruskin, William Morris, and other luminaries of the contem-
porary arts world, which could not fail to have a profound effect on his subsequent
thinking and writing.

James spent much of his adult life in Europe. His 1878 novella Daisy Miller
established his reputation on both sides of the Atlantic, and was followed in 1880-
1881 by Portrait of a Lady, *his first successful novel and one that is still regarded*
as among his finest. He wrote a handful of stories that might be considered ghost
stories, but very few of them were overtly supernatural. "The Romance of Certain
Old Clothes" is perhaps the most traditional of all his ghost stories, and the only one
to be set in the eighteenth century.

1

Towards the middle of the eighteenth century there lived in the Province of Massachusetts a widowed gentlewoman, the mother of three children, by name Mrs. Veronica Wingrave. She had lost her husband early in life, and had devoted herself to the care of her progeny. These young persons grew up in a manner to reward her tenderness and to gratify her highest hopes. The first-born was a son, whom she had called Bernard, in remembrance of his father. The others were daughters—born at an interval of three years apart. Good looks were traditional in the family, and this youthful trio were not likely to allow the tradition to perish. The boy was of that fair and ruddy complexion and that athletic structure which in those days (as in these) were the sign of good English descent—a frank, affectionate young fellow, a deferential son, a patronising brother, a steadfast friend. Clever, however, he was not; the wit of the family had been apportioned chiefly to his sisters. The late Mr. William Wingrave had been a great reader of Shakespeare, at a time when this pursuit implied more freedom of thought than at the present day, and in a community where it required much courage to patronise the drama even in the closet; and he had wished to call attention to his admiration of the great poet by calling his daughters out of his favourite plays. Upon the elder he had bestowed the romantic name of Rosalind, and the younger he had called Perdita, in memory of a little girl born between them, who had lived but a few weeks.

When Bernard Wingrave came to his sixteenth year his mother put a brave face upon it and prepared to execute her husband's last injunction. This had been a formal command that, at the proper age, his son should be sent out to England, to complete his education at the University of Oxford, where he himself had acquired his taste for elegant literature. It was Mrs. Wingrave's belief that the lad's equal was not to be found in the two hemispheres, but she had the old traditions of literal obedience. She swallowed her sobs, and made up her boy's trunk and his simple provincial outfit, and sent him on his way across the seas. Bernard presented himself at his father's college, and spent five years in England, without great honour, indeed, but with a vast deal of pleasure and no discredit. On leaving the university he made the journey to France. In his twenty-fourth year he took ship for home, prepared to find poor little New England (New England was very small in those days) a very dull, unfashionable residence. But there had been changes at home, as well as in Mr. Bernard's opinions. He found his mother's house quite habitable, and his sisters grown into two very charming young ladies, with all the accomplishments and graces of the young women of Britain, and a certain native-grown originality and wildness, which, if it was not an accomplishment, was certainly a grace the more. Bernard privately assured his mother that his sisters were fully a match for the most genteel young women in the old country; whereupon poor Mrs. Wingrave, you may be sure, bade them hold up their heads. Such was Bernard's opinion, and such, in a tenfold higher degree, was the opinion of Mr. Arthur Lloyd. This gentleman was a college-mate of Mr. Bernard, a young man of reputable family, of a good person and a handsome inheritance; which latter appurtenance he proposed to invest in trade in the flourishing colony. He and Bernard were sworn friends; they had crossed the ocean together, and the young American had lost no time in presenting him at his mother's house, where he had made quite as good an impression as that which he had received and of which I have just given a hint.

The two sisters were at this time in all the freshness of their youthful bloom; each wearing, of course, this natural brilliancy in the manner that became her best. They were equally dissimilar in appearance and character. Rosalind, the elder—now in her twenty-second year—was tall and white, with calm gray eyes and auburn tresses; a very faint likeness to the Rosalind of Shakespeare's comedy, whom I imagine a brunette (if you will), but a slender, airy creature, full of the softest, quickest impulses. Miss Wingrave, with her slightly lymphatic fairness, her fine arms, her majestic height, her slow utterance, was not cut out for adventures. She would never have put on a man's jacket and hose; and, indeed, being a very plump beauty, she may have had reasons apart from her natural dignity. Perdita, too, might very well have exchanged the sweet melancholy of her name against something more in consonance with her aspect and disposition. She had the cheek of a gipsy and the eye of an eager child, as well as the smallest waist and lightest foot in all the country of the Puritans. When you spoke to her she never made you wait, as her handsome sister was wont to do (while she looked at you with a cold fine eye), but gave you your choice of a dozen answers before you had uttered half your thought.

The young girls were very glad to see their brother once more; but they found themselves quite able to spare part of their attention for their brother's friend. Among the young men their friends and neighbours, the *belle jeunesse* of the Colony, there were many excellent fellows, several devoted swains, and some two or three who enjoyed the reputation of universal charmers and conquerors. But the homebred arts and somewhat boisterous gallantry of these honest colonists were completely eclipsed by the good looks, the fine clothes, the punctilious courtesy, the perfect elegance, the immense information, of Mr. Arthur Lloyd. He was in reality no paragon; he was a capable, honourable, civil youth, rich in pounds sterling, in his health and complacency and his little capital of uninvested affections. But he was a gentleman; he had a handsome person; he had studied and travelled; he spoke French, he played on the flute, and he read verses aloud with very great taste. There were a dozen reasons why Miss Wingrave and her sister should have thought their other male acquaintance made but a poor figure before such a perfect man of the world. Mr. Lloyd's anecdotes told our little New England maidens a great deal more of the ways and means of people of fashion in European capitals than he had any idea of doing. It was delightful to sit by and hear him and Bernard talk about the fine people and fine things they had seen. They would all gather round the fire after tea, in the little wainscoted parlour, and the two young men would remind each other, across the rug, of this, that and the other adventure. Rosalind and Perdita would often have given their ears to know exactly what adventure it was, and where it happened, and who was there, and what the ladies had on; but in those days a well-bred young woman was not expected to break into the conversation of her elders, or to ask too many questions; and the poor girls used therefore to sit fluttering behind the more languid—or more discreet—curiosity of their mother.

2

That they were both very fine girls Arthur Lloyd was not slow to discover; but it took him some time to make up his mind whether he liked the big sister or the little sister best. He had a strong presentiment—an emotion of a nature entirely too cheerful to be called a foreboding—that he was destined to stand up before the parson with one of them; yet he was unable to arrive at a preference, and for such a consummation a preference was certainly necessary, for Lloyd had too much young blood in his veins to make a choice by lot and be cheated of the satisfaction of falling in love. He resolved to take things as they came—to let his heart speak. Meanwhile he was on a very pleasant footing. Mrs. Wingrave showed a dignified indifference to his 'intentions', equally remote from a carelessness of her daughter's honour and from that sharp alacrity to make him come to the point, which, in his quality of a young man of property, he had too often encountered in the worldly matrons of his native islands. As for Bernard,

all that he asked was that his friend should treat his sisters as his own; and
as for the poor girls themselves, however each may have secretly longed that
their visitor should do or say something 'marked', they kept a very modest
and contented demeanour.

Towards each other, however, they were somewhat more on the offensive
They were good friends enough, and accommodating bedfellows (the
shared the same four-poster), betwixt whom it would take more than a
day for the seeds of jealousy to sprout and bear fruit; but they felt that the
seeds had been sown on the day that Mr. Lloyd came into the house. Each
made up her mind that, if she should be slighted, she would bear her grief
in silence, and that no one should be any the wiser; for if they had a great
deal of ambition, they had also a large share of pride. But each prayed in
secret, nevertheless, that upon *her* the selection, the distinction, might fall.
They had need of a vast deal of patience, of self-control, of dissimulation.
In those days a young girl of decent breeding could make no advances
whatever, and barely respond, indeed, to those that were made. She was
expected to sit still in her chair, with her eyes on the carpet, watching the
spot where the mystic handkerchief should fall. Poor Arthur Lloyd was
obliged to carry on his wooing in the little wainscoted parlour, before the
eyes of Mrs. Wingrave, her son, and his prospective sister-in-law. But youth
and love are so cunning that a hundred signs and tokens might travel to and
fro, and not one of these three pairs of eyes detect them in their passage.
The two maidens were almost always together, and had plenty of chances
to betray themselves. That each knew she was being watched, however,
made not a grain of difference in the little offices they mutually rendered,
or in the various household tasks they performed in common. Neither
flinched nor fluttered beneath the silent battery of her sister's eyes. The
only apparent change in their habits was that they had less to say to each
other. It was impossible to talk about Mr. Lloyd, and it was ridiculous to
talk about anything else. By tacit agreement they began to wear all their
choice finery, and to devise such little implements of conquest, in the way
of ribbons and top-knots and kerchiefs, as were sanctioned by indubitable
modesty. They executed in the same inarticulate fashion a contract of fair
play in this exciting game. "Is it better so?" Rosalind would ask, tying a
bunch of ribbons on her bosom, and turning about from her glass to her

sister. Perdita would look up gravely from her work and examine the decoration. "I think you had better give it another loop," she would say, with great solemnity, looking hard at her sister with eyes that added, 'upon my honour!' So they were for ever stitching and trimming their petticoats, and pressing out their muslins, and contriving washes and ointments and cosmetics, like the ladies in the household of the vicar of Wakefield. Some three or four months went by; it grew to be midwinter, and as yet Rosalind knew that if Perdita had nothing more to boast of than she, there was not much to be feared from her rivalry. But Perdita by this time—the charming Perdita— felt that her secret had grown to be tenfold more precious than her sister's.

One afternoon Miss Wingrave sat alone—that was a rare accident— before her toilet-glass, combing out her long hair. It was getting too dark to see; she lit the two candles in their sockets, on the frame of her mirror, and then went to the window to draw her curtains. It was a gray December evening; the landscape was bare and bleak, and the sky heavy with snow-clouds. At the end of the large garden into which her window looked was a wall with a little postern door, opening into a lane. The door stood ajar, as she could vaguely see in the gathering darkness, and moved slowly to and fro, as if some one were swaying it from the lane without. It was doubtless a servant-maid who had been having a tryst with her sweetheart. But as she was about to drop her curtain Rosalind saw her sister step into the garden and hurry along the path which led to the house. She dropped the curtain, all save a little crevice for her eyes. As Perdita came up the path she seemed to be examining something in her hand, holding it close to her eyes. When she reached the house she stopped a moment, looked intently at the object, and pressed it to her lips.

Poor Rosalind slowly came back to her chair and sat down before her glass, where, if she had looked at it less abstractedly, she would have seen her handsome features sadly disfigured by jealousy. A moment afterwards the door opened behind her and her sister came into the room, out of breath, and her cheeks aglow with the chilly air.

Perdita started. "Ah," said she, "I thought you were with our mother." The ladies were to go to a tea-party, and on such occasions it was the habit of one of the young girls to help their mother to dress. Instead of coming in, Perdita lingered at the door.

"Come in, come in," said Rosalind. "We have more than an hour yet. I should like you very much to give a few strokes to my hair." She knew that her sister wished to retreat, and that she could see in the glass all her movements in the room. "Nay, just help me with my hair," she said, "and I will go to mamma."

Perdita came reluctantly, and took the brush. She saw her sister's eyes, in the glass, fastened hard upon her hands. She had not made three passes when Rosalind clapped her own right hand upon her sister's left, and started out of her chair. "Whose ring is that?" she cried, passionately, drawing her towards the light.

On the young girl's third finger glistened a little gold ring, adorned with a very small sapphire. Perdita felt that she need no longer keep her secret, yet that she must put a bold face on her avowal. "It's mine," she said proudly.

"Who gave it to you?" cried the other.

Perdita hesitated a moment. "Mr. Lloyd."

"Mr. Lloyd is generous, all of a sudden."

"Ah no," cried Perdita, with spirit, "not all of a sudden! He offered it to me a month ago."

"And you needed a month's begging to take it?" said Rosalind, looking at the little trinket, which indeed was not especially elegant, although it was the best that the jeweller of the Province could furnish. "I wouldn't have taken it in less than two."

"It isn't the ring," Perdita answered, "it's what it means!"

"It means that you are not a modest girl!" cried Rosalind. "Pray, does your mother know of your intrigue? does Bernard?"

"My mother has approved my 'intrigue', as you call it. Mr. Lloyd has asked for my hand, and mamma has given it. Would you have had him apply to you, dearest sister?"

Rosalind gave her companion a long look, full of passionate envy and sorrow. Then she dropped her lashes on her pale cheeks and turned away. Perdita felt that it had not been a pretty scene; but it was her sister's fault. However, the elder girl rapidly called back her pride, and turned herself about again. "You have my very best wishes," she said, with a low curtsey. "I wish you every happiness, and a very long life."

Perdita gave a bitter laugh. "Don't speak in that tone!" she cried. "I would rather you should curse me outright. Come, Rosy," she added, "he couldn't marry both of us."

"I wish you very great joy," Rosalind repeated, mechanically, sitting down to her glass again, "and a very long life, and plenty of children."

There was something in the sound of these words not at all to Perdita's taste. "Will you give me a year to live at least?" she said. "In a year I can have one little boy—or one little girl at least. If you will give me your brush again I will do your hair."

"Thank you," said Rosalind. "You had better go to mamma. It isn't becoming that a young lady with a promised husband should wait on a girl with none."

"Nay," said Perdita, good-humouredly, "I have Arthur to wait upon me. You need my service more than I need yours."

But her sister motioned her away, and she left the room. When she had gone poor Rosalind fell on her knees before her dressing-table, buried her head in her arms, and poured out a flood of tears and sobs. She felt very much the better for this effusion of sorrow. When her sister came back she insisted upon helping her to dress—on her wearing her prettiest things. She forced upon her acceptance a bit of lace of her own, and declared that now that she was to be married she should do her best to appear worthy of her lover's choice. She discharged these offices in stern silence; but, such as they were, they had to do duty as an apology and an atonement; she never made any other.

Now that Lloyd was received by the family as an accepted suitor nothing remained but to fix the wedding-day. It was appointed for the following April, and in the interval preparations were diligently made for the marriage. Lloyd, on his side, was busy with his commercial arrangements, and with establishing a correspondence with the great mercantile house to which he had attached himself in England. He was therefore not so frequent a visitor at Mrs. Wingrave's as during the months of his diffidence and irresolution, and poor Rosalind had less to suffer than she had feared from the sight of the mutual endearments of the young lovers. Touching his future sister-in-law Lloyd had a perfectly clear conscience. There had not been a particle of love-making between them, and he had not the slightest suspicion that he had dealt her a terrible blow. He was quite at his ease; life promised so well, both domestically and financially. The great revolt of the Colonies was not yet in the air, and that his connubial felicity should take a tragic turn it was absurd, it was blasphemous, to apprehend. Meanwhile, at Mrs. Wingrave's, there was a greater rustling of silks, a more rapid clicking of scissors and flying of needles, than ever. The good lady had determined that her daughter should carry from home the genteelest outfit that her money could buy or that the country could furnish. All the sage women in the Province were convened, and their united taste was brought to bear on Perdita's wardrobe. Rosalind's situation, at this moment, was assuredly not to be envied. The poor girl had an inordinate love of dress, and the very best taste in the world, as her sister perfectly well knew. Rosalind was tall, she was stately and sweeping, she was made to carry stiff brocade and masses of heavy lace, such as belong to the toilet of a rich man's wife. But Rosalind sat aloof, with her beautiful arms folded and her head averted, while her mother and sister and the venerable women aforesaid worried and wondered over their materials, oppressed by the multitude of their resources. One day there came in a beautiful piece of white silk, brocaded with heavenly blue and silver, sent by the bridegroom himself—it not being thought amiss in those days that the husband-elect should contribute to the bride's trousseau. Perdita could think of no form or fashion which would do sufficient honour to the splendour of the material.

"Blue's your colour, sister, more than mine," she said, with appealing eyes. "It's a pity it's not for you. You would know what to do with it."

Rosalind got up from her place and looked at the great shining fabric, as it lay spread over the back of a chair. Then she took it up in her hands and felt it—lovingly, as Perdita could see—and turned about toward the mirror with it. She let it roll down to her feet, and flung the other end over her shoulder, gathering it in about her waist with her white arm, which was bare to the elbow. She threw back her head, and looked at her image, and a hanging tress of her auburn hair fell upon the gorgeous surface of the silk. It made a dazzling picture. The women standing about uttered a little "Look, look!" of admiration. "Yes, indeed," said Rosalind, quietly, "blue is my colour." But Perdita could see that her fancy had been stirred, and that she would now fall to work and solve all their silken riddles. And indeed she behaved very well, as Perdita, knowing her insatiable love of millinery, was quite ready to declare. Innumerable yards of lustrous silk and satin, of muslin, velvet and lace, passed through her cunning hands, without a jealous word coming from her lips. Thanks to her industry, when the wedding-day came Perdita was prepared to espouse more of the vanities of life than any fluttering young bride who had yet received the sacramental blessing of a New England divine.

It had been arranged that the young couple should go out and spend the first days of their wedded life at the country-house of an English gentleman—a man of rank and a very kind friend to Arthur Lloyd. He was a bachelor; he declared he should be delighted to give up the place to the influence of Hymen. After the ceremony at church—it had been performed by an English clergyman—young Mrs. Lloyd hastened back to her mother's house to change her nuptial robes for a riding-dress. Rosalind helped her to effect the change, in the little homely room in which they had spent their undivided younger years. Perdita then hurried off to bid farewell to her mother, leaving Rosalind to follow. The parting was short; the horses were at the door, and Arthur was impatient to start. But Rosalind had not followed, and Perdita hastened back to her room, opening the door abruptly. Rosalind, as usual, was before the glass, but in a position which caused the other to stand still, amazed. She had dressed herself in Perdita's cast-off wedding veil and wreath, and on her neck she had hung the full string of pearls which the young girl had received from her husband as a wedding-gift. These things had been hastily laid aside, to await their possessor's disposal on her return from the country. Bedizened in this unnatural garb Rosalind stood before the mirror, plunging a long look into its depths and reading heaven knows what audacious visions. Perdita was horrified. It was a hideous image of their old rivalry come to life again. She made a step toward her sister, as if to pull off the veil and the flowers. But catching her eyes in the glass, she stopped.

"Farewell, sweetheart," she said. "You might at least have waited till I had got out of the house!" And she hurried away from the room.

Mr. Lloyd had purchased in Boston a house which to the taste of those days appeared as elegant as it was commodious; and here he very soon established himself with his young wife. He was thus separated by a distance of twenty miles from the residence of his mother-in-law. Twenty miles, in that primitive era of roads and conveyances, were as serious a matter as a hundred at the present day, and Mrs. Wingrave saw but little of her daughter during the first twelvemonth of her marriage. She suffered in no small degree from Perdita's absence; and her affliction was not diminished by the fact that Rosalind had fallen into terribly low spirits and was not to be roused or cheered but by change of air and company. The real cause of the young lady's dejection the reader will not be slow to suspect. Mrs. Wingrave and her gossips, however, deemed her complaint a mere bodily ill, and doubted not that she would obtain relief from the remedy just mentioned. Her mother accordingly proposed, on her behalf, a visit to certain relatives on the paternal side, established in New York, who had long complained that they were able to see so little of their New England cousins. Rosalind was despatched to these good people, under a suitable escort, and remained with them for several months. In the interval her brother Bernard, who had begun the practice of the law, made up his mind to take a wife. Rosalind came home to the wedding, apparently cured of her heartache, with bright roses and lilies in her face and a proud smile on her lips. Arthur Lloyd came over from Boston to see his brother-in-law married, but without his wife, who was expecting very soon to present him with an heir. It was nearly a year since Rosalind had seen him. She was glad—she hardly knew why—that Perdita had stayed at home. Arthur looked happy, but he was more grave and important than before his marriage. She thought he looked 'interesting'—for although the word, in its modern sense, was not then invented, we may be sure that the idea was. The truth is, he was simply anxious about his wife and her coming ordeal. Nevertheless, he by no means failed to observe Rosalind's beauty and splendour, and to note how she effaced the poor little bride. The allowance that Perdita had enjoyed for her dress had now been transferred to her sister, who turned it to wonderful account. On the morning after the wedding he had a lady's saddle put on the horse of the servant who had come with him from town, and went out with the young girl for a ride. It was a keen, clear morning in January; the ground was bare and hard, and the horses in good condition—to say nothing of Rosalind, who was charming in her hat and plume, and her dark blue riding coat, trimmed with fur. They rode all the morning, they lost their way, and were obliged to stop for dinner at a farm-house. The early winter dusk had fallen when they got home. Mrs. Wingrave met them with a long face. A messenger had arrived at noon from Mrs. Lloyd; she was beginning to be ill, she desired her husband's immediate return. The young man, at the thought that he had lost several hours, and that by hard riding he might already have been with his wife, uttered a passionate oath. He barely consented to stop for a mouthful of supper, but mounted the messenger's horse and started off at a gallop.

He reached home at midnight. His wife had been delivered of a little girl. "Ah, why weren't you with me?" she said, as he came to her bedside.

"I was out of the house when the man came. I was with Rosalind," said Lloyd, innocently.

Mrs. Lloyd made a little moan, and turned away. But she continued to do very well, and for a week her improvement was uninterrupted. Finally, however, through some indiscretion in the way of diet or exposure, it was checked, and the poor lady grew rapidly worse. Lloyd was in despair. It very soon became evident that she was breathing her last. Mrs. Lloyd came to a sense of her approaching end, and declared that she was reconciled with death. On the third evening after the change took place she told her husband that she felt she should not get through the night. She dismissed her servants, and also requested her mother to withdraw—Mrs. Wingrave having arrived on the preceding day. She had had her infant placed on the bed beside her, and she lay on her side, with the child against her breast, holding her husband's hands. The night-lamp was hidden behind the heavy curtains of the bed, but the room was illumined with a red glow from the immense fire of logs on the hearth.

"It seems strange not to be warmed into life by such a fire as that," the young woman said, feebly trying to smile. "If I had but a little of it in my veins! But I have given all *my* fire to this little spark of mortality." And she dropped her eyes on her child. Then raising them she looked at her husband with a long, penetrating gaze. The last feeling which lingered in her heart was one of suspicion. She had not recovered from the shock which Arthur had given her by telling her that in the hour of her agony he had been with Rosalind. She trusted her husband very nearly as well as she loved him; but now that she was called away for ever she felt a cold horror of her sister. She felt in her soul that Rosalind had never ceased to be jealous of her good fortune; and a year of happy security had not effaced the young girl's image, dressed in her wedding-garments, and smiling with simulated triumph. Now that Arthur was to be alone, what might not Rosalind attempt? She was beautiful, she was engaging; what arts might she not use, what impression might she not make upon the young man's saddened heart? Mrs. Lloyd looked at her husband in silence. It seemed hard, after all, to doubt of his constancy. His fine eyes were filled with tears; his face was convulsed with weeping; the clasp of his hands was warm and passionate. How noble he looked, how tender, how faithful and devoted! 'Nay,' thought Perdita, 'he's not for such a one as Rosalind. He'll never forget me. Nor does Rosalind truly care for him; she cares only for vanities and finery and jewels.' And she lowered her eyes on her white hands, which her husband's liberality had covered with rings, and on the lace ruffles which trimmed the edge of her night-dress. 'She covets my rings and my laces more than she covets my husband.'

At this moment the thought of her sister's rapacity seemed to cast a dark shadow between her and the helpless figure of her little girl. "Arthur," she said, "you must take off my rings. I shall not be buried in them. One of these days my daughter shall wear them—my rings and my laces and silks. I had them all brought out and shown me to-day. It's a great wardrobe—there's not such another in the Province; I can say it without vanity, now that I have done with it. It will be a great inheritance for my daughter when she grows into a young woman. There are things there that a man never buys twice, and if they are lost you will never again see the like. So you will watch them well. Some dozen things I have left to Rosalind; I have named them to my mother. I have given her that blue and silver; it was meant for her; I wore it only once, I looked ill in it. But the rest are to be sacredly kept for this little innocent. It's such a providence that she should be my colour; she can wear my gowns; she has her mother's eyes. You know the same fashions come back every twenty years. She can wear my gowns as they are. They will lie there quietly waiting till she grows into them—wrapped in camphor and rose-leaves, and keeping their colours in the sweet-scented darkness. She shall have black hair, she shall wear my carnation satin. Do you promise me, Arthur?"

"Promise you what, dearest?"

"Promise me to keep your poor little wife's old gowns."

"Are you afraid I shall sell them?"

"No, but that they may get scattered. My mother will have them properly wrapped up, and you shall lay them away under a double-lock. Do you know the great chest in the attic, with the iron bands? There is no end to what it will hold. You can put them all there. My mother and the housekeeper will do it, and give you the key. And you will keep the key in your secretary, and never give it to any one but your child. Do you promise me?"

"Ah, yes, I promise you," said Lloyd, puzzled at the intensity with which his wife appeared to cling to this idea.

"Will you swear?" repeated Perdita.

"Yes, I swear."

"Well—I trust you—I trust you," said the poor lady, looking into his eyes with eyes in which, if he had suspected her vague apprehensions, he might have read an appeal quite as much as an assurance.

Lloyd bore his bereavement rationally and manfully. A month after his wife's death, in the course of business, circumstances arose which offered him an opportunity of going to England. He took advantage of it, to change the current of his thoughts. He was absent nearly a year, during which his little girl was tenderly nursed and guarded by her grandmother. On his return he had his house again thrown open, and announced his intention of keeping the same state as during his wife's lifetime. It very soon came to be predicted that he would marry again, and there were at least a dozen young women of whom one may say that it was by no fault of theirs that, for six months after his return, the prediction did not come true. During this interval he still left his little daughter in Mrs. Wingrave's hands, the latter assuring him that a change of residence at so tender an age would be full of danger for her health. Finally, however, he declared that his heart longed for his daughter's presence and that she must be brought up to town. He sent his coach and his housekeeper to fetch her home. Mrs. Wingrave was in terror lest something should befall her on the road; and, in accordance with this feeling, Rosalind offered to accompany her. She could return the next day. So she went up to town with her little niece, and Mr. Lloyd met her on the threshold of his house, overcome with her kindness

269

and with paternal joy. Instead of returning the next day Rosalind stayed out the week; and when at last she reappeared, she had only come for her clothes. Arthur would not hear of her coming home, nor would the baby. That little person cried and choked if Rosalind left her; and at the sight of her grief Arthur lost his wits, and swore that she was going to die. In fine, nothing would suit them but that the aunt should remain until the little niece had grown used to strange faces.

It took two months to bring this consummation about; for it was not until this period had elapsed that Rosalind took leave of her brother-in-law. Mrs. Wingrave had shaken her head over her daughter's absence; she had declared that it was not becoming, that it was the talk of the whole country. She had reconciled herself to it only because, during the girl's visit, the household enjoyed an unwonted term of peace. Bernard Wingrave had brought his wife home to live, between whom and her sister-in-law there was as little love as you please. Rosalind was perhaps no angel; but in the daily practice of life she was a sufficiently good-natured girl, and if she quarrelled with Mrs. Bernard, it was not without provocation. Quarrel, however, she did, to the great annoyance not only of her antagonist, but of the two spectators of these constant altercations. Her stay in the household of her brother-in-law, therefore, would have been delightful, if only because it removed her from contact with the object of her antipathy at home. It was doubly—it was ten times—delightful, in that it kept her near the object of her early passion. Mrs. Lloyd's sharp suspicions had fallen very far short of the truth. Rosalind's sentiment had been a passion at first, and a passion it remained—a passion of whose radiant heat, tempered to the delicate state of his feelings, Mr. Lloyd very soon felt the influence. Lloyd, as I have hinted, was not a modern Petrarch; it was not in his nature to practise an ideal constancy. He had not been many days in the house with his sister-in-law before he began to assure himself that she was, in the language of that day, a devilish fine woman. Whether Rosalind really practised those insidious arts that her sister had been tempted to impute to her it is needless to inquire. It is enough to say that she found means to appear to the very best advantage. She used to seat herself every morning before the big fireplace in the dining-room, at work upon a piece of tapestry, with her little niece disporting herself on the carpet at her feet, or on the train of her dress, and playing with her woollen balls. Lloyd would have been a very stupid fellow if he had remained insensible to the rich suggestions of this charming picture. He was exceedingly fond of his little girl, and was never weary of taking her in his arms and tossing her up and down, and making her crow with delight. Very often, however, he would venture upon greater liberties than the young lady was yet prepared to allow, and then she would suddenly vociferate her displeasure. Rosalind, at this, would drop her tapestry, and put out her handsome hands with the serious smile of the young girl whose virgin fancy has revealed to her all a mother's healing arts. Lloyd would give up the child, their eyes would meet, their hands would touch, and Rosalind would extinguish the little girl's sobs upon the snowy folds of the kerchief that crossed her bosom. Her dignity was perfect, and nothing could be more discreet than the manner in which she accepted her brother-in-law's hospitality. It may almost be said, perhaps, that there was something harsh in her reserve. Lloyd had a provoking feeling that she was in the house and yet was unapproachable. Half-an-hour after supper, at the very outset of the long winter evenings, she would light her candle, make the young man a most respectful curtsey, and march off to bed. If these were arts, Rosalind was a great artist. But their effect was so gentle, so gradual, they were calculated to work upon the young widower's fancy with a crescendo so finely shaded, that, as the reader has seen, several weeks elapsed before Rosalind began to feel sure that her returns would cover her outlay. When this became morally certain she packed up her trunk and returned to her mother's house. For three days she waited; on the fourth Mr. Lloyd made his appearance—a respectful but pressing suitor. Rosalind heard him to the end, with great humility, and accepted him with infinite modesty. It is hard to imagine that Mrs. Lloyd would have forgiven her husband; but if anything might have disarmed her resentment it would have been the ceremonious continence of this interview. Rosalind imposed upon her lover but a short probation. They were married, as was becoming, with great privacy—almost with secrecy—in the hope perhaps, as was waggishly remarked at the time, that the late Mrs. Lloyd wouldn't hear of it.

The marriage was to all appearance a happy one, and each party obtained what each had desired—Lloyd 'a devilish fine woman', and Rosalind—but Rosalind's desires, as the reader will have observed, had remained a good deal of a mystery. There were, indeed, two blots upon their felicity, but time would perhaps efface them. During the first three years of her marriage Mrs. Lloyd failed to become a mother, and her husband on his side suffered heavy losses of money. This latter circumstance compelled a material retrenchment in his expenditure, and Rosalind was perforce less of a fine lady than her sister had been. She contrived, however, to carry it like a woman of considerable fashion. She had long since ascertained that her sister's copious wardrobe had been sequestrated for the benefit of her daughter, and that it lay languishing in thankless gloom in the dusty attic. It was a revolting thought that these exquisite fabrics should await the good pleasure of a little girl who sat in a high chair and ate bread-and-milk with a wooden spoon. Rosalind had the good taste, however, to say nothing about the matter until several months had expired. Then, at last, she timidly broached it to her husband. Was it not a pity that so much finery should be lost?—for lost it would be, what with colours fading, and moths eating it up, and the change of fashions. But Lloyd gave her so abrupt and peremptory a refusal, that she saw, for the present, her attempt was vain. Six months went by, however, and brought with them new needs and new visions. Rosalind's thoughts hovered lovingly about her sister's relics. She went up and looked at the chest in which they lay imprisoned. There was a sullen defiance in its three great padlocks and its iron bands which only quickened her cupidity. There was something exasperating in its incorruptible immobility. It was like a grim and grizzled old household servant, who locks his jaws over a family secret. And then there was a look of capacity in its vast extent, and a sound as of dense fullness, when Rosalind knocked its side with the toe of her little shoe, which caused her to flush with baffled longing. "It's absurd," she cried; "it's improper, it's wicked"; and she forthwith resolved upon another attack upon her husband. On the following day, after dinner, when he had had his wine, she boldly began it. But he cut her short with great sternness.

"Once for all, Rosalind," said he, "it's out of the question. I shall be gravely displeased if you return to the matter."

"Very good," said Rosalind. "I am glad to learn the esteem in which I am held. Gracious heaven," she cried, "I am a very happy woman! It's an agreeable thing to feel one's self sacrificed to a caprice!" And her eyes filled with tears of anger and disappointment.

Lloyd had a good-natured man's horror of a woman's sobs, and he attempted—I may say he condescended—to explain. "It's not a caprice, dear, it's a promise," he said—"an oath."

"An oath? It's a pretty matter for oaths! and to whom, pray?"

"To Perdita," said the young man, raising his eyes for an instant, but immediately dropping them.

"Perdita—ah, Perdita!" and Rosalind's tears broke forth. Her bosom heaved with stormy sobs—sobs which were the long-deferred sequel of the violent fit of weeping in which she had indulged herself on the night when she discovered her sister's betrothal. She had hoped, in her better moments, that she had done with her jealousy; but her temper, on that occasion, had taken an ineffaceable fold. "And pray, what right had Perdita to dispose of my future?" she cried. "What right had she to bind you to meanness and cruelty? Ah, I occupy a dignified place, and I make a very fine figure! I am welcome to what Perdita has left! And what has she left? I never knew till now how little! Nothing, nothing, nothing."

This was very poor logic, but it was very good as a 'scene'. Lloyd put his arm around his wife's waist and tried to kiss her, but she shook him off with magnificent scorn. Poor fellow! he had coveted a 'devilish fine woman', and he had got one. Her scorn was intolerable. He walked away with his ears tingling—irresolute, distracted. Before him was his secretary, and in it the sacred key which with his own hand he had turned in the triple lock. He marched up and opened it, and took the key from a secret drawer, wrapped in a little packet which he had sealed with his own honest bit of blazonry. *Je garde*, said the motto—'I keep'. But he was ashamed to put it back. He flung it upon the table beside his wife.

"Put it back!" she cried. "I want it not. I hate it!"

"I wash my hands of it," cried her husband. "God forgive me!"

Mrs. Lloyd gave an indignant shrug of her shoulders, and swept out of the room, while the young man retreated by another door. Ten minutes later Mrs. Lloyd returned, and found the room occupied by her little step-daughter and the nursery-maid. The key was not on the table. She glanced at the child. Her little niece was perched on a chair, with the packet in her hands. She had broken the seal with her own small fingers. Mrs. Lloyd hastily took possession of the key.

At the habitual supper-hour Arthur Lloyd came back from his counting-room. It was the month of June, and supper was served by daylight. The meal was placed on the table, but Mrs. Lloyd failed to make her appearance. The servant whom his master sent to call her came back with the assurance that her room was empty, and that the women informed him that she had not been seen since dinner. They had, in truth, observed her to have been in tears, and, supposing her to be shut up in her chamber, had not disturbed her. Her husband called her name in various parts of the house, but without response. At last it occurred to him that he might find her by taking the way to the attic. The thought gave him a strange feeling of discomfort, and he bade his servants remain behind, wishing no witness in his quest. He reached the foot of the staircase leading to the topmost flat, and stood with his hand on the banisters, pronouncing his wife's name. His voice trembled. He called again louder and more firmly. The only sound which disturbed the absolute silence was a faint echo of his own tones, repeating his question under the great eaves. He nevertheless felt irresistibly moved to ascend the staircase. It opened upon a wide hall, lined with wooden closets, and terminating in a window which looked westward, and admitted the last rays of the sun. Before the window stood the great chest. Before the chest, on her knees, the young man saw with amazement and horror the figure of his wife. In an instant he crossed the interval between them, bereft of utterance. The lid of the chest stood open, exposing, amid their perfumed napkins, its treasure of stuffs and jewels. Rosalind had fallen backward from a kneeling posture, with one hand supporting her on the floor and the other pressed to her heart. On her limbs was the stiffness of death, and on her face, in the fading light of the sun, the terror of something more than death. Her lips were parted in entreaty, in dismay, in agony; and on her blanched brow and cheeks there glowed the marks of ten hideous wounds from two vengeful ghostly hands.

AN AUTHENTICATED HISTORY OF THE BELL WITCH

Martin van Buren Ingram

1894

When millions of moviegoers flocked to see The Blair Witch Project *in 1999, very few of them knew that the story of this smash hit was based on a tale from American folklore. Since then, the story of the Bell Witch has been retold multiple times on screen, although without the success of the ground-breaking 1999 movie.*

The story of the Bell Witch originated in Tennessee in 1817, when the farm belonging to the Bell family came under supernatural attack, apparently as the result of a witch's curse. As with most local folklore, the details of the story varied from teller to teller: in some versions the witch was someone Bell had cheated; in others, the curse came from the spirit of a male slave whom Bell had killed. Some accounts had Bell being poisoned. Some claim that Andrew Jackson himself, moved to come and investigate the reports, was put to flight by the haunting, although there is no corroborating evidence. In its broad outlines, the story of the Bell Witch resembles many accounts of poltergeist hauntings from other times and places, but clearly this tale was beginning to grow in the telling.

This piece of local lore merited no more than a paragraph in Goodspeed's 1886–1887 History of Tennessee, *but seven years later newspaper publisher Martin van Buren Ingram published* An Authenticated History of the Bell Witch, *which he claimed was based on the diary of Richard Bell, who would have between six and ten years old at the time of the hauntings. The main target of the attacks, according to this version, was Richard's sister Betsy, and the trouble increased after she became engaged to one Joshua Gardner.*

The heart of Ingram's book is Chapter 8, which quotes extensively from Bell's diary. One section, concerning the troublesome spirit's relationship with the Bells' slaves, is not reproduced below because its racist language and attitudes are offensive to the modern reader. Those who wish to search it out will be able to find copies if they wish.

Chapter 8

OUR FAMILY TROUBLE: THE STORY OF THE BELL WITCH
AS DETAILED BY RICHARD WILLIAMS BELL

The reader is already familiar with the motives that inspired Richard Williams Bell to write this sketch of "Our Family Trouble," a phenomenal mystery that continued to be a living sensation long after John Bell's death, the mention of which in any Robertson County family, even to this good day, leads to a recital of events as they have been handed down through tradition.

After a brief biography of his parents and the family, which is more fully recorded elsewhere, Mr. Bell goes on writing:

After settling on Red River in Robertson County, Tenn., my father prospered beyond his own expectations. He was a good manager, and hard worker himself, making a regular hand on the farm. He indulged no idleness around him, and brought up his children to work, endeavoring to make their employment pleasurable. Mother was equally frugal and careful in her domestic affairs, and was greatly devoted to the proper moral training of children, keeping a restless watch over every one, making sacrifices for their pleasure and well being, and both were steadfast in their religious faith, being members of the Baptist church, and set Christian examples before their children. Father was always forehanded, paid as he went, was never in his life served with a warrant or any legal process, and never had occasion to fear the sheriff or any officer of the law, and was equally faithful in bearing his share of whatever burden was necessary to advance morality and good society.

In the meanwhile he gave all of his children the best education the schools of the country could afford, Zadok being educated for a lawyer, while the other boys chose to follow agriculture. Jesse and Esther had both married, settled, and everything seemed to be going smoothly, when our trouble commenced. I was a boy when the incidents, which I am about to record, known as the Bell Witch took place. In fact, strange appearances and uncommon sounds had been seen and heard by different members of the family at times, some year or two before I knew anything about it, because they indicated nothing of a serious character, gave no one any concern, and would have passed unnoticed but for after developments. Even the knocking on the door, and the outer walls of the house, had been going on for some time before I knew of it, generally being asleep, and father, believing that it was some mischievous person trying to frighten the family, never discussed the matter in the presence of the younger children, hoping to catch the prankster. Then, after the demonstrations became known to all of us, father enjoined secrecy upon every member of the family, and it was kept a profound secret until it became intolerable. Therefore no notes were made of these demonstrations or the exact dates.

The importance of a diary at that time did not occur to any one, for we were all subjected to the most intense and painful excitement from day to day, and week to week, to the end, not knowing from whence came the disturber, the object of the visitation, what would follow next, how long it would continue, nor the probable result. Therefore I write from memory, such things as came under my own observations, impressing my mind, and incidents known by other members of the family and near neighbors to have taken place, and are absolutely true. However, I do not pretend to record the half that did take place, for that would be impossible without daily notes, but will note a sufficient number of incidents to give the reader a general idea of the phenomena and the afflictions endured by our family.

As before stated, the knocking at the door, and scratching noise on the outer wall, which continued so long, never disturbed me, nor was I the least frightened until the demonstrations within became unendurable. This I think was in May, 1818. Father and mother occupied a room on the first floor, Elizabeth had the room above, and the boys occupied another room on the second floor; John and Drewry had a bed together, and Joel and myself slept in another bed. As I remember it was on Sunday night, just after the family had retired, a noise commenced in our room like a rat gnawing vigorously on the bed post. John and Drew got up to kill the rat. But the moment they were out of bed the noise ceased. They examined the bedstead, but discovered no marks made by a rat. As soon as they returned to bed the noise commenced again, and thus it continued until a late hour or some time after midnight, and we were all up a half dozen times or more searching the room all over, every nook and corner, for the rat, turning over everything, and could find nothing, not even a crevice by which a rat could possibly enter. This kind of noise continued from night to night, and week after week, and all of our investigations were in vain.

The room was overhauled several times, everything moved and carefully examined, with the same result. Finally when we would search for the rat in our room, the same noise would appear in sister Elizabeth's chamber, disturbing her, and arousing all the family. And so it continued going from room to room, stopping when we were all up, and commencing again as soon as we returned to bed, and was so exceedingly annoying that no one could sleep. The noise was, after a while, accompanied by a scratching sound, like a dog clawing on the floor, and increased in force until it became evidently too strong for a rat. Then every room in the house was torn up, the furniture, beds and clothing carefully examined, and still nothing irregular could be found, nor was there a hole or crevice by which a rat could enter, and nothing was accomplished beyond the increase of our confusion and evil forebodings. The demonstrations continued to increase, and finally the bed covering commenced slipping off at the foot of the beds as if gradually drawn by some one, and occasionally a noise like the smacking of lips, then a gulping sound, like some one choking or strangling, while the vicious gnawing at the bed post continued, and there was no such thing as sleep to be thought of until the noise ceased, which was generally between one and three o'clock in the morning.

Some new performance was added nearly every night, and it troubled Elizabeth more than anyone else. Occasionally the sound was like heavy stones falling on the floor, then like trace chains dragging, and chairs falling over. I call to mind my first lively experience, something a boy is not likely to forget. We had become somewhat used to the mysterious noise, and tried to dismiss it from mind, taking every opportunity for a nap. The family had all retired early, and I had just fallen into a sweet doze, when I felt my hair beginning to twist, and then a sudden jerk, which raised me. It felt like the top of my head had been taken off. Immediately Joel yelled out in great fright, and next Elizabeth was screaming in her room, and ever after that something was continually pulling at her hair after she retired to bed. This transaction frightened us so badly that father and mother remained up nearly all night. After this, the main feature in the phenomenon was that of pulling the cover off the beds as fast as we could replace it, also continuing other demonstrations. Failing in all efforts to discover the source of the annoyance, and becoming convinced that it was something out of the natural course of events, continually on the increase in force, father finally determined to solicit the cooperation of Mr. James Johnson, who was his nearest neighbor and most intimate friend, in trying to detect the mystery, which had been kept a secret within the family up to this time. So Mr. Johnson and wife, at father's request, came over to spend a night in the investigation.

At the usual hour for retiring, Mr. Johnson, who was a very devout Christian, led in family worship, as was his custom, reading a chapter in the Bible, singing and praying. He prayed fervently, and very earnestly for our deliverance from the frightful disturbance, or that its origin, cause and purpose might be revealed. Soon after we had all retired, the disturbance commenced as usual; gnawing, scratching, knocking on the wall, over-turning chairs, pulling the cover off of beds, etc., every act being exhibited as if on purpose to show Mr. Johnson what could be done, appearing in his room, as in other rooms, and so soon as a light would appear, the noise would cease, and the trouble begin in another room. Mr. Johnson listened attentively to all of the sounds and capers, and that which appeared like some one sucking air through the teeth, and smacking of lips, indicated to him that some intelligent agency gave force to the movements, and he determined to try speaking to it, which he did, inquiring, "In the name of the Lord, what or who are you? What do you want and why are you here?" This appeared to silence the noise for considerable time, but it finally com-menced again with increased vigor, pulling the cover from the beds in spite of all resistance, repeating other demonstrations, going from one room to another, becoming fearful. The persecutions of Elizabeth were increased to an extent that excited serious apprehensions. Her cheeks were frequently crimsoned as by a hard blow from an open hand, and her hair pulled until she would scream with pain. Mr. Johnson said the phenomenon was beyond his comprehension; it was evidently preternatural or supernatural, of an intelligent character. He arrived at this conclusion from the fact that it ceased action when spoken to, and certainly understood language. He advised father to invite other friends into the investigation, and try all means for detecting the mystery, to which he consented, and from this time on, it became public.

All of our neighbors were invited and committees formed, experiments tried, and a close watch kept, in and out, every night, but all of their wits were stifled, the demonstrations all the while increasing in force, and sister was so severely punished that father and mother became alarmed for her safety when alone and the neighboring girls came almost every night to keep her company. Especially were Theny Thorn and Rebecca Porter very courageous and kind to her in this trying ordeal. It was suggested that sister should spend the nights with some one of the neighbors to get rid of the trouble, and all were very kind to invite her. In fact our neighbors were all touched with generous sympathy and were unremitting in their efforts to alleviate our distress, for it had become a calamity, and they came every night to sit and watch with us. The suggestion of sending Elizabeth from home was acted upon. She went to different places, James Johnson's, John Johnson's, Jesse Bell's, and Bennett Porter's, but it made no difference, the trouble followed her with the same severity, disturbing the family where she went as it did at home, nor were we in anywise relieved. This gave rise to a suspicion in the minds of some persons that the mystery was some device or stratagem originated by sister, from the fact that it appeared wherever she went, and this clue was followed to a logical demonstration of the phenomena was gradually developed, proving to be an intelligent character.

When asked a question in a way, that it could be answered by numbers, for instance, "How many persons present? How many horses in the barn? How many miles to a certain place?" The answers would come in raps, like a man knocking on the wall, the bureau or the bedpost with his fist, or by so many scratches on the wall like the noise of a nail or claws, and the answers were invariably correct. During the time, it was not uncommon to see lights like a candle or lamp flitting across the yard and through the field, and frequently when father, the boys and hands were coming in late from work, chunks of wood and stones would fall along the way as if tossed by some one, but we could never discover from whence, or what direction they came. In addition to the demonstrations already described, it took to slapping people on the face, especially those who resisted the action of pulling the cover from the bed, and those who came as detectives to expose the trick. The blows were heard distinctly, like the open palm of a heavy hand, while the sting was keenly felt, and it did not neglect to pull my hair, and make Joel squall as often.

THE WITCH COMMENCED WHISPERING

The phenomena continued to develop force, and visitors persisted in urging the witch to talk, and tell what was wanted, and finally it commenced whistling when spoken to, in a low broken sound, as if trying to speak in a whistling voice, and in this way it progressed, developing until the whistling sound was changed to a weak faltering whisper uttering indistinct words. The voice, however, gradually gained strength in articulating, and soon the utterances became distinct in a low whisper, so as to be understood in the absence of any other noise. I do not remember the first intelligent utterance, which, however, was of no significance, but the voice soon developed sufficient strength to be distinctly heard by every one in the room.

A DISTURBED SPIRIT

This new development added to the sensation already created. The news spread, and people came in larger numbers, and the great anxiety concerning the mystery prompted many questions in the effort to induce the witch to disclose its own identity and purpose. Finally, in answer to the question, "Who are you and what do you want?" the reply came, "I am a spirit; I was once very happy but have been disturbed." This was uttered in a very feeble voice, but sufficiently distinct to be understood by all present, and this was all the information that could be elicited for the time.

THE SEER'S PROPHECY

The next utterance of any note that I remember, occurred on a Sunday night, when the voice appeared stronger, and the witch talking more freely, in fact speaking voluntarily, and appeared to be exercised over a matter that was being discussed by the family. Brother John Bell had for some time contemplated a trip to North Carolina to look after father's share of an estate that was being wound up, and was to start next morning (Monday) on horseback, and this was the matter that interested the family and was being discussed, the long tiresome journey, his probable long absence, the situation of affairs, concerning which father was giving him instructions. Several neighbors were present, taking an interest, volunteering some good natured advice to John, when the witch put in, remonstrating against the trip, dissuading John from going, predicting bad luck, telling him that he would have a hard trip for nothing, that the estate had not been wound up and could not be for some time, and he would get no money, but return empty handed. As a further argument to dissuade John, the witch told him that an elegant young lady from Virginia was then on her way to visit friends in Robertson county, who would please him, and he could win her if he would stay; that she was wealthy, possessing forty Negroes and considerable money. John laughed at the revelation as supremely ridiculous, and left on the following morning as contemplated, and was absent six months or more, returning empty handed as predicted. Very soon after his departure, the young lady in question arrived, and left before his return, and John never met her.

A SPIRIT HUNTING A LOST TOOTH

The witch continued to develop the power of articulation, talking freely, and those who engaged in conversation with the invisible persevered in plying questions to draw out an explanation of the mystery, and again the question was pressed, inquiring, "Who are you and what do you want?" and the witch replied, stating the second time, "I am a spirit who was once very happy, but have been disturbed and made unhappy." Then followed the question, "How were you disturbed, and what makes you unhappy?" The reply to this question was, "I am the spirit of a person who was buried in the woods near by, and the grave has been disturbed, my bones disinterred and scattered, and one of my teeth was lost under this house, and I am here looking for that tooth."

This statement revived the memory of a circumstance that occurred some three or four years previously, and had been entirely forgotten. The farm hands while engaged in clearing a plot of land, discovered a small mound of graves, which father supposed to be an Indian burying ground, and worked around it without obliterating the marks. Several days later Corban Hall, a young man of the neighborhood, came to our place, and was told by Drew the circumstance of finding the Indian graves. Hall thought the graves probably contained some relics which Indians commonly buried with their dead, and proposed to open one and see, to which Drew agreed, and they proceeded to disinter the bones. Finding nothing else, Hall brought a jawbone to the house, and while sitting in the passage he threw it against the opposite wall, and the jarring knocked out a loose tooth, which dropped through a crack in the floor.

Father passed through the hall in the mean while, and reprimanded the boys severely for their action, and made one of the Negro men take the jawbone back, replacing all the disinterred bones, and filling in the grave. This was evidently the circumstance referred to by the "spirit," so long forgotten, and to be reminded of the fact so mysteriously was very perplexing, and troubled father no little. He examined the floor just where the bone dropped when it struck the wall, as the boys had left it, and there was the crack referred to, and he was pestered, and decided to take up a portion of the floor and see if the tooth could be found. The dirt underneath was raked up, sifted and thoroughly examined, but the tooth was not found. The witch then laughed at father, declaring that it was all a joke to fool "Old Jack."

THE BURIED TREASURE

The excitement in the country increased as the phenomena developed. The fame of the witch had become widely spread, and people came from all quarters to hear the strange and unaccountable voice. Some were detectives, confident of exposing the mystery. Various opinions were formed and expressed; some credited its own story, and believed it an Indian spirit; some thought it was an evil spirit, others declared it was witchcraft, and a few unkindly charged that it was magic art and trickery gotten up by the Bell family to draw crowds and make money. These same people had stayed as long as they wished, enjoyed father's hospitality, and paid not a cent for it, nor did it ever cost any one a half shilling. The house was open to every one that came; father and mother gave them the best they had, their horses were fed, and no one allowed to go away hungry; many offered pay and urged father to receive it, insisting that he could not keep up entertaining so many without pay, but he persistently declined remuneration, and not one of the family ever received a cent for entertaining.

Father regarded the phenomena as an affliction, a calamity, and such accusations were very galling, but were endured. Inquisitive people continued to exercise all of their wits in plying the witch with questions concerning its personality or character, but elicited no further information until the question was put by James Gunn, then came the reply: "I am the spirit of an early emigrant, who brought a large sum of money and buried my treasure for safe keeping until needed. In the meanwhile I died without divulging the secret, and I have returned in the spirit for the purpose of making known the hiding place, and I want Betsy Bell to have the money." The spirit was then urged to tell where the money was concealed. This was refused and the secret withheld until certain pledges were made that the conditions would be complied with. The conditions were that Drew Bell and Bennett Porter would agree to exhume the money and give every dollar to Betsy, and that "Old Sugar Mouth" (Mr. James Johnson) would go with them and see that the injunction was fairly discharged, and that he should count the money and take charge of it for Betsy.

The story was questioned and laughed at, and then discussed. The witch had made some remarkable revelations, and it was thought possible there might be something in it, and the proposition was acceded to. Drew and Bennett agreed to do the work, and Mr. Johnson consented to become the guardian and see that the right thing was done. The spirit then went on to state that the money was under a large flat rock at the mouth of the spring on the southwest corner of the farm, on Red River, describing the surroundings so minutely that there could be no mistake. Every one was acquainted with the spring, having frequented the place, but no one could have described it so minutely, and this all tended to strengthen faith in the revelation. The spirit insisted that the committee selected should start very early the next morning at the dawn of day, lest the secret should get out, and some fiend should beat them to the place and get the money. This was also agreed to, and by the break of day next morning all hands met and proceeded to the spring.

They found everything as described, the huge stone intact, and were sure they were on time. They observed that it was an excellent place for hiding money where no human being would ever dream of looking for a treasure, or care to move the great stone for any purpose, and yet susceptible of such a minute description that no one could be mistaken in the revelation. They carried along an axe and mattock, and were pretty soon at work, devising ways and means for moving the big rock, which was so firmly imbedded in the ground. It was no light job, but they cut poles, made levers and fixed prizes, after first removing much dirt from around the stone, so as to get under it. Then Drew and Porter prized and tugged, Mr. Johnson occasionally lending a helping hand, and after a half day's very hard work, the stone was raised and moved from its bedding, but no money appeared. Then followed a consultation and discussion of the situation. They reasoned that the glittering treasure was possibly sunk in the earth, and the stone imbedded over it to elude suspicion, and they decided to dig for it, and went to work in earnest, Porter digging, and Drew scratching the loosened dirt out with his hands, and so on they progressed until they had opened a hole about six feet square and nearly as many feet deep, and still no money was found. Exhausted and very hungry, they gave up the job, returning to the house late in the afternoon much disgusted and chagrined.

That night the "spirit" appeared in great glee laughing and tantalizing the men for being so easily duped, describing everything that occurred at the spring in the most ludicrous way, telling how they tugged at the big stone, and repeating what was said by each one. Bennett Porter staved the mattock in up to the eye every pop, and oh how it made him sweat. It told how "Old Sugar Mouth" looked on prayerfully, encouraging the boys. The dirt taken out was mixed with small stones, gravel, sand, etc., leaves and sticks, all of which indicated that the earth had been removed and put back. Drew, the witch said, could handle a sight of dirt, his hands were made for that purpose, and were better than a shovel; no gold could slip through his fingers. The witch's description of the affair kept the house in an uproar of laughter, and it was repeated with equal zest to all new comers for a month.

PRIEST CRAFT AND SCRIPTURAL KNOWLEDGE

There were but very few churches in the country at this period of the century, nevertheless, ours was a very religious community. Most of those coming from the older States brought their religion with them, and inculcated the principle in their families. The influence of Revs. James and Thomas Gunn, Rev. Sugg Fort, Mr. James Johnson, and other good men, swayed mightily. Every man erected an altar in his own home, and it was common for neighbors to meet during the week at one or another's house for prayer and exhortation, and Bible study. In the absence of the preachers, Mr. James Johnson was the principal leader in these exercises, and the meetings were held alternately at his house and father's, and occasionally at one or the other of the Gunn's. There was no spirit of denominational jealousy existing, and all Christians mingled in these meetings like brethren of the same faith. The witch, as it accumulated force, dissembled this spirit, giving wonderful exhibitions of a thorough knowledge of the Bible and Christian faith. The voice was not confined to darkness, as were the physical demonstrations. The talking was heard in lighted rooms, as in the dark; and finally in the day at any hour.

The first exhibition of a religious nature was the assimilation of Mr. James Johnson's character and worship, repeating the song and prayer, uttering precisely the same petition made by the old gentleman the night himself and wife came for the purpose of investigation, and the impersonation of Mr. Johnson was so perfect that it appeared like himself present. It was not uncommon after this for the witch to introduce worship, by lining a hymn, as was the custom, singing it through, and then repeat Mr. Johnson's prayer, or the petitions of some one of the ministers. It could sing any song in the hymn books of that time, and quote any passage of Scripture in the Bible from Genesis to Revelations.

The propensity for religious discussion was strongly manifested, and in quoting Scripture the text was invariably correctly cited, and if any one misquoted a verse, they would be promptly corrected. It could quote Scripture as fast as it could talk, one text after another, citing the book, chapter, and number of the verse. It was a common test to open the Bible at any chapter, and call on the spirit to repeat a certain verse, and this was done accurately, as fast as the leaves were turned from one chapter of the book to another. It delighted in taking issue on religious subjects, with those well versed in Scripture, and was sure to get the best of the argument, being always quick with a passage to sustain its point. This manifest knowledge of Scripture on the part of the witch was unmistakable, and was the most mystifying of all the developments, and strangers who came from a long distance were eager to engage the seer in religious discussions, and were as often confounded; and they were no less astounded when the witch would remind them of events and circumstances in their history in a way that was marvelous.

Just here one circumstance I call to mind. The discussion had turned on the command against covetousness and theft. A man, whose name I will call John, put in remarking that he did not believe there was any sin in stealing something to eat when one was reduced to hunger, and could not obtain food for his labor. Instantly the witch perniciously inquired of John "if he ate that sheepskin." This settled John. He was dumb as an oyster, and as soon as the subject was changed he left the company, and was conspicuously absent after that. The result was the revival of an old scandal, so long past that it had been forgotten, in which John was accused of stealing a sheepskin. This warlock was indeed a great tattler, and made mischief in the community. Some people very much feared the garrulity of its loquacious meddling and were extremely cautious, and it was this class who the invisible delighted in torturing most. Nothing of moment occurred in the country or in any family, which was not reported by the witch at night. The development of this characteristic led the people to inquire after the news and converse with the witch as they would with a person, very often inquiring what was then transpiring at a certain place or house in the neighborhood. Sometimes the answer would be, "I don't know, wait a minute and I will go and see," and in less than five minutes it would report, and the report was generally verified. This feature of the phenomena was discovered in this way: Brother Jesse Bell lived within one mile of the homestead. He had been absent several days on a trip, and was expected home on a certain evening.

After supper mother entered the room, inquiring if any of us knew whether Jesse had returned or not. No one had heard, or could inform her. The witch manifested much regard for mother on all occasions, and never afflicted her in any way. On this occasion it spoke promptly, saying: "Wait a minute Luce, I will go and see for you." Scarcely a minute had elapsed when the voice reported that Jesse was at home, describing

his position, sitting at table reading by the light of a candle. The next morning Jesse came to see us, and when told the circumstance, he said it was true, and just at that time there was a distinct rap on his door, and before he could move the door opened and closed immediately. His wife, he said, noticed it also, and asked me what caused it, and I replied that I reckoned it was the witch. Every Sabbath service that occurred within the bounds was reported at night, the text, hymn, etc., and the preacher also criticized, and everything of peculiar note was described. The company was treated one night to a repetition of one of Rev. James Gunn's best sermons, preached in the vicinity, the witch personating Mr. Gunn, lining the hymn, quoting his text and prayer, and preaching so much like Mr. Gunn, that it appeared the minister himself was present.

A number of persons were present who attended the meeting that day, and recognized the declamation as the same sermon. Shortly after this, Rev. James Gunn preached on Sunday at Bethel Methodist Church, six miles southeast, and Rev. Sugg Fort filled his appointment at Drake's Pond Baptist Church, seven miles northwest, thirteen miles apart, both preaching at the same hour, eleven o'clock. It so happened that both ministers came to visit our family that evening, finding quite a crowd of people gathered in, as was the case every day during the excitement. Directly after supper the witch commenced talking as usual, directing the conversation to Brother Gunn, discussing some points in his sermon that day. Mr. Gunn asked the witch how it knew what he had preached about?

The answer was, "I was present and heard you." This statement being questioned, the "vociferator" began, quoted the text and repeated the sermon verbatim, and the closing prayer, all of which the preacher said was correct. Some one suggested that Brother Fort had the advantage of the witch this time, that having attended Brother Gunn's service, it could tell nothing about Brother Fort's discourse at Drake's Pond. "Yes I can," was the prompt reply. How do you know? was the inquiry. "I was there and heard him." Then assimilating Rev. Fort's style, it proceeded to quote his text and repeated his sermon, greatly delighting the company. There was no one present who had heard either sermon, but both ministers admitted that their sermons had been accurately reproduced, and no one could doubt the fact, or were more greatly surprised than themselves.

THE AFFLICTIONS OF BETSY AND FATHER

The reader will understand that no feature of the exhibitions already introduced was ever abandoned, but continued developing virulence, or beneficence and felicity. The practice of pulling the cover off the beds was a favorite pastime, and frequently the sheets would be pulled from under the sleepers, or the pillows jerked from under their heads, and other new performances added to the exhibitions. The most serious consequence, however, was the afflictions of Elizabeth and father. Notwithstanding the invisible agency feigned a tender regard at times for Betsy, as it affectionately called her, it did not cease tormenting in many ways, increasing her punishment. The feint pretext for this was a manifest opposition to the attention paid her by a certain young gentleman, who was much esteemed by the family, often interposing impertinent objections, urging that these mutual relations be severed. At least there was no other cause manifested, or this would not be mentioned. Sister was now subjected to fainting spells, followed by prostration, characterized by shortness of breath and smothering sensations, panting as it were for life, and becoming entirely exhausted and lifeless, losing her breath for nearly a minute between gasps, and was rendered unconscious. She would revive and then relapse, and it appeared that her suffering was prolonged by the greater exertions used for her restoration. These spells lasted from thirty to forty minutes, and passed off suddenly, leaving her perfectly restored after a few minutes in which she recovered from the exhaustion.

There is no positive evidence that these spells were produced by the witch. However, that was the conclusion, from the fact that there was no other apparent cause. She was a very stout girl, and with this exception, the personification of robust health, and was never subject to hysteria or anything of the kind. Moreover, the spells came on at regular hours in the evening, just at the time the witch usually appeared, and immediately after the spells passed off the mysterious voice commenced talking, but never uttered a word during the time of her prostration. In the meanwhile father was strangely afflicted, which should have been mentioned in the outset, but he had never regarded his trouble as of any consequence until after sister recovered from the attacks just described. In fact his ailment commenced with the incipiency of the witch demonstration, or before he recognized the phenomenal disturbance. He complained of a curious sensational feeling in his mouth, a stiffness of the tongue, and something like a stick crosswise, punching each side of his jaws.

This sensation did not last long, did not recur very often, or cause pain, and therefore gave him but little concern. But as the phenomena developed, this affliction increased, his tongue swelling from the sides and pressing against his jaws, so that he could neither talk nor eat for ten or fifteen hours. In the meanwhile the witch manifested a pernicious dislike for father, using the most vile and malignant epithets toward him, declaring that it would torment "Old Jack Bell" to the end of his life. As father's trouble increased, Elizabeth was gradually relieved from her severe spells, and soon recovered entirely from the affliction, and never had another symptom of the kind. But father was seized with another malady that caused him much trouble and suffering. This was contortions of the face, a twitching and dancing of his flesh, which laid him up for the time. These spells gradually increased, and undoubtedly carried him to his grave, of which I will have more to say further on.

THE WITCH NAMED "KATE"

People continued to ply our loquacious visitor with shrewd eager questions, trying to elicit some information concerning the mystery, which were with equal dexterity evaded, or a misleading answer given. First, it was a disturbed spirit hunting a lost tooth; next, a spirit that had returned to reveal the hiding place of a buried treasure. Then it told Calvin Johnson that it was the spirit of a child buried in North Carolina, and told John Johnson that it was his step mother's witch. At last Rev. James Gunn manifested a very inquisitive desire to penetrate the greatest of all secrets, and put the question very earnestly. The witch replied, saying that Brother Gunn had put the question in a way that it could no longer be evaded, and it would not do to tell the preacher a flat lie, and if the plain truth must be known, it was nobody else and nothing but "Old Kate Batts' witch," determined to torment "Old Jack Bell" out of his life. This was a startling announcement and most unfortunate under the circumstances, because too many were willing to believe it, and it created a profound sensation.

Mrs. Kate Batts was the wife of Frederick Batts, who was terribly afflicted, and she had become the head of the family, taking charge of her husband's affairs. She was very eccentric and sensitive. Some people were disposed to shun her, which was still more irritating to her sensitive nature. No harm could be said of Mrs. Batts. She was kind hearted, and a good neighbor toward those she liked. Mr. Gunn, of course, did not believe the witch's statement, but many did, or professed to, and the matter made Mrs. Batts very mad, causing a lively sensation in the community. Ever after this the goblin was called "Kate," and answered readily when addressed by that name, and for convenience sake I shall hereafter call the witch Kate, though not out of any disregard for the memory of Mrs. Batts, for after all she was a clever lady, and did not deserve the cruel appellation of "witch."

THE WITCH FAMILY—BLACKDOG, MATHEMATICS, CYPOCRYPHY, AND JERUSALEM

The next development was the introduction of four characters, assuming the above names, purporting to be a witch family, each one acting a part making night hideous in their high carnivals, using the most offensive language and uttering vile threats. Up to this time the strange visitor had spoken in the same soft delicate voice, except when personating some individual. Now there were four distinct voices. Blackdog assumed to be the head of the family, and spoke in a harsh feminine tone. The voices of Mathematics and Cypocryphy were different, but both of a more delicate feminine tone. Jerusalem spoke like a boy. These exhibitions were opened like a drunken carousal, and became perfect pandemoniums, frightful to the extreme, from which there was no escape.

Father would most gladly have abandoned home and everything and fled with his family to some far away scene to have escaped this intolerable persecution, but there was no hope, no escape. The awful thing had sworn vengeance, and for what cause it never named, nor could any one ever surmise. Nevertheless, when the question of moving was discussed, it declared it would follow "Old Jack" to the remotest part of the earth, and father believed it. The family was frightened into consternation, apprehending that a terrible crisis was rapidly approaching. Many of our neighbors were frightened away, fearing they would become involved in a tragic termination. Others, however, drew nearer, and never forsook us in this most trying ordeal. James Johnson and his two sons, John and Calvin, the Gunn families, the Fort's, Gooch, William Porter, Frank Miles, Jerry Batts, Major Bartlett, Squire Byrns and Major Picketing were faithful and unremitting in their sympathy, and attentions, and consolations, making many sacrifices for our comfort, and not a night passed that four or more were not present to engage the witch in conversation, and relieve father of the necessary attention to strangers, giving him much rest.

These demoniac councils were introduced by singing songs of every character, followed by quarreling with each other, employing obscene language and blasphemous oaths, making a noise like a lot of drunken men fighting. At this stage of the proceedings Blackdog would appear as peacemaker, denouncing the others with vehemence and scurrility, uttering bitter curses and threats of murder unless the belligerents should desist and behave themselves, and sometimes would apparently thrash Jerusalem unmercifully for disobeying orders. These carousals were ended only by the command of Blackdog, professedly sending the family away on different errands of deviltry, one or two remaining to keep up the usual disturbance in different rooms at the same time. On one occasion all four appeared almost beastly drunk, talking in a maudlin sentimental strain, fuming the house with the scent of whiskey. Blackdog said they got the whiskey at John Gardner's still house, which was some four miles distant. At other times the unity appeared more civil, and would treat our company to some delightful singing, a regular concert of rich feminine voices, modulated to the sweetest cadence and intonation, singing any hymn called for with solemnity and wonderful effect.

The carousals did not continue long, much to the gratification of the family and friends, and our serious apprehensions were relieved. These concerts were agreeable closing exercises of this series of meetings, and after they were suspended the four demons or unity never, apparently, met again. It was plain old Kate from that time on who assumed all characters, good or bad, sometimes very pious and then extremely wicked.

THE MYSTERIOUS HAND SHAKING

The Johnson brothers, John and Calvin, perhaps had more intercourse with the witch than any other two men who visited our place during the excitement. That is they talked more with the invisible, entered more earnestly into the investigation by cultivating friendly and intimate relations. They were both very honorable men, of high standing in the community, but were very dissimilar in character. Calvin was a plain unassuming man of strict integrity, free from deception, faithful in everything he pretended, and would not swerve from the truth or break a promise knowingly and willfully under any circumstances. John was more dexterous, of a shrewd investigating turn of mind, guided by policy, and would make use of all legitimate means at hand to gain a point or accomplish a purpose, and he cultivated the witch more than any one else for the purpose of facilitating his investigations.

Kate was very fond of gab, and John Johnson made use of every opportunity to engage the mage in conversation, hoping to draw out something that would give a clue to the mystery, but it appears that all of his wits were baffled, and that the seer was all the while aware of his purpose. The question arose as to the character of the blows received by so many persons on the cheek after retiring. The sound was like a slap of an open hand, and every one testified that it left a sting like that of a hand, even to the prints of the fingers being felt. Calvin Johnson conceived the idea of asking the witch to shake hands with him. After much persuasion Kate agreed to comply with the request, on one condition, that Calvin would first promise not to try to grasp or hold the hand that would be laid in his.

This he agreed to, and then holding out his hand, in an instant he felt the pressure of the invisible. Mr. Johnson testified that he felt it very sensibly, and that the touch was soft and delicate like the hand of a lady, and no one ever doubted his statement. John Johnson begged Kate to shake hands with him, persisting that he was as good a friend as his brother, but the witch refused, telling John "No, you only want a chance to catch me." John vowed that he would not attempt anything of the kind. Kate still refused, replying, "I know you, Jack Johnson; you are a grand rascal, trying to find me out, and I won't trust you." Two or three other persons claimed to have shaken hands with the witch, which I don't know about, though many testified to the force of the hand as felt on the cheek.

HE STOLE HIS WIFE

It was not uncommon for Kate to recognize strangers the moment they entered the house, speaking to them on familiar terms. Here is one instance I will note. Four strangers who had traveled a long distance (whose names I cannot now remember, there were so many unknown callers), arrived late—on a dark night, and knocking at the door, and were admitted.

They were unknown to any one in the house or on the place, but the moment they entered the door, and before they could speak to introduce themselves, Kate announced one by name, exclaiming, "He is the grand rascal who stole his wife. He pulled her out of her father's house through a window, and hurt her arm, making her cry; then he whispered to her, 'Hush honey don't cry, it will soon get well.'" The strangers were greatly confused. They stood dumbfounded, pausing some time before they could speak. The gentleman was asked before leaving if the witch had stated the facts in regard to his matrimonial escapade. He said yes, the circumstance occurred just as stated.

DETECTIVE WILLIAMS

A good looking stranger arrived who introduced himself as Mr. Williams, a professional detective, stating that he had heard much of the witch mystery, which no one could explain, and having considerable experience in unraveling tangled affairs and mysteries, he had traveled a long distance for the purpose of investigating this matter, if he should be permitted to do so; further stating that he did not believe in either preternatural or supernatural things, and professed to be an expert in detecting jugglery, sleight-of-hand performances, illusions, etc., and would certainly expose these manifestations, so much talked of if given a fair chance. Father bid the gentleman a hearty welcome, telling him that he was just the man that was wanted. "Make my house your home, and make free with everything here as if your own, as long as you think proper to stay," said father, and Mr. Williams politely accepted the invitation and hung up his hat. Mr. Williams was rather a portly, strong-muscled, well dressed, handsome gentleman. He was no less self-possessed, and wise in his own conceit, full of gab, letting his tongue run continually, detailing to the company his wonderful exploits in the detective business, and was very sure he would bring Kate to grief before leaving.

A day and night passed and Kate, for some cause best known to the witch, kept silent, making no show except a little scratching on the walls and thumping about the room, just enough to let the company know that the spirit was present. Mr. Williams became very impatient, appearing disgruntled, and spoke his mind more freely. He said to a coterie of gentlemen who were discussing the witch, that he was convinced that the whole thing was a family affair, an invention gotten up for a sensation to draw people and make money, and the actors were afraid to make any demonstrations while he was present, knowing his profession and business, and that he would most assuredly expose the trick. One of the gentlemen told father what Williams had said, and it made him very indignant. He felt outraged that such a charge should be made without the evidence, by a man professing to be a gentleman, to whom he had extended every courtesy and hospitality, and had proffered any assistance he might call for, and in a rage he threatened to order Williams from the place immediately. Just at this juncture Kate spoke, "No you don't, old Jack, let him stay; I will attend to the gentleman and satisfy him that he is not so smart as he thinks." Father said no more, nor did he take any action in the matter, but treated Mr. Williams gentlemanly as he did the others, nor was anything more heard from Kate. The house was crowded with visitors that night, all expectantly and anxious to hear the witch talk, and sat till late bed time awaiting the sound of the mystifying voice, but not a word or single demonstration of any kind was heard from Kate. This confirmed the detective in his conjectures,

and he repeated to several visitors his conclusions, declaring that the witch would not appear again as long as he remained.

After they were all tired out, mother had straw mattresses spread over the floor to accommodate the company. Mr. Williams, being the largest gentleman present, selected one of these pallets to himself. All retired and the light was extinguished, and a night of quiet rest was promising. As soon as perfect quiet prevailed, and every one appeared to be in a dose of sleep, Mr. Williams found himself pinioned, as it were, to the floor by some irresistible force from which he was utterly powerless to extricate himself, stout as he was, and the witch scratching and pounding him with vengeance. He yelled out to the top of his voice calling for help and mercy. Kate held up long enough to inquire of the detective, which one of the family he thought had him, and then let in again, giving him an unmerciful beating, while the man plead for life. All of this occurred in less than two minutes, and before a candle could be lighted, and as soon as the light appeared the pounding ceased, but Kate did a good deal of talking, more than Mr. Williams cared to hear.

The detective was badly used up and the worst scared man that ever came to our house. He sat up on a chair the balance of the night, with a burning candle by his side, subjected to the witch's tantalizing sarcasm, ridicule and derision, questioning him as to which of the family was carrying on the devilment, how he liked the result of his investigations, how long he intended to stay, etc. As soon as day dawned, Mr. Williams ordered his horse, and could not be prevailed upon to remain until after breakfast.

KATE GETS IN BED WITH WILLIAM PORTER

William Porter was a very prominent citizen of the community, a gentleman of high integrity, regarded for his strict veracity. He was also a good friend to our family, and spent many nights with us during the trouble, taking his turn with others in entertaining Kate, which was necessary to have any peace at all, and also agreeable to those of an investigating turn of mind who were not afraid, and this was Mr. Porter's character; like John Johnson, he rather cultivated the spirit, and said he was fond of gabbing with Kate.

This seemed to please the witch, and they got along on good terms. William Porter was at this time a bachelor, occupying his house alone. The building was a large hewn log house, with a partition dividing it into two rooms. There was one chimney having a very large fireplace, and the other end was used for a bedroom—entered by a door in the partition. I give this as related by Mr. Porter himself, to a large company at Father's, and as he has often repeated the same to many persons, and no one doubted his truthfulness. Said he:

"It was a cold night and I made a big log fire before retiring to keep the house warm. As soon as I got in bed I heard scratching and thumping about the bed, just like Kate's tricks, as I thought, but was not long in doubt as to the fact. Presently I felt the cover drawling to the backside, and immediately the witch spoke, when I recognized the unmistakable voice of Kate. 'Billy, I have come to sleep with you and keep you warm.' I replied, 'Well, Kate, if you are going to sleep with me, you must behave yourself.' I clung to the cover, feeling that it was drawing from me, as it appeared to be raised from the bed on the other side, and something snake-like crawling under. I was never afraid of the witch, or apprehended that it would do me any harm but somehow this produced a kind of chilly sensation that was simply awful. The cover continued to slip in spite of my tenacious grasp, and was twisted into a roll on the back side of the bed, just like a boy would roll himself in a quilt, and not a strip was left on me.

I jumped out of bed in a second, and observing that Kate had rolled up in the cover, the thought struck me, 'I have got you now, you rascal, and will burn you up.' In an instant I grabbed the roll of cover in my arms and started to the fire, intending to throw the cover, witch and all in the blaze. I discovered that it was very weighty, and smelt awful. I had not gone half way across the room before the luggage got so heavy and became so offensive that I was compelled to drop it on the floor and rush out of doors for a breath of fresh air. The odor emitted from the roll was the most offensive stench I ever smelt. It was absolutely stifling and I could not have endured it another second. After being refreshed I returned to the room, and gathered up the roll of bed clothing shook them out, but Kate had departed, and there was no unusual weight or offensive odor remaining, and this is just how near I came catching the witch."

OUR SCHOOL DAY EXPERIENCE

Major Garaldus Pickering, who was a distinguished man of that day, kept a large school near by, which Joel and myself attended, and had many little experiences with Kate along the way. The custom was to take in school as soon as the teacher could get there, a little after sunrise, and dismiss about thirty minutes before sunset. Our route was through the woods, and some briar patches and hazel thickets by the wayside. Passing these thickets, returning home, sticks of wood and rocks were often tossed at us, but never with much force, and we soon learned not to fear any harm from this pastime, and frequently cut notches on the sticks, casting them back into the thicket from whence they came, and invariably the same sticks would be hurled back at us. After night Kate would recount everything that occurred along the way. Even if one of us stumped a toe, falling over, the witch claimed to have caused it, and would describe how it appeared in the form of a rabbit or something else at certain places. Our most serious trouble, however, was experienced at home, the witch continually pulling the cover off, and twisting our hair, and it was hard for a tired boy to get any sleep.

JOEL SEVERELY WHIPPED

It happened that Joel and myself were left to occupy a room alone one night, and were troubled less than usual in the early part of the night, but Kate put in good time just before day. It was quite a cold morning, and rather too early to get up, but Kate continued pulling the cover off and jerking my hair, and I got out of bed and dressed myself. Joel, however, was much vexed, and said some ugly things about "Old Kate," and gathering up the cover from the floor, he rolled himself up in it for another nap. Directly the witch snatched it from him again. Joel became enraged, pulling at the cover while Kate seemed to be hawking and spitting in his face, and he had to turn loose the cover. This made Joel raving mad, and he laid flat on his back, kicking with all his might, calling old Kate the meanest kind of names. "Go away from here, you nasty old thing," he exclaimed. Kate became furious also, exclaiming, "You little rascal, I'll let you know who you are talking to."

That moment Joel felt the blows falling fast and heavy, and no boy ever received such a spanking as he got that morning, and he never forgot it. It was absolutely frightful. I could do nothing for his relief. He yelled frantically with all of his might, arousing the whole house, nor did his punisher cease spanking until father entered the door with a light, finding him almost lifeless. The blows sounded like the spanking of an open heavy hand, and certainly there was no one in the room but Joel and myself, and if there had been, there was no way of escaping except by the door which father entered, and that would have been impossible unobserved.

CHASING THE SHAKERS

The Shakertown People at that time kept their trading men on the road continually, traveling through the country, dealing with the people. They went in two's, generally on horseback, and could be distinguished from other people at a distance by their broad brim hats and peculiarity in dress. The two who traveled through our section always made it convenient to call at our house for dinner or a night's lodging. It was about the regular time for these gentlemen to come around, and near the dinner hour one of the servants came in announcing to mother that the Shakers were coming down the lane. This was a notice to increase the contents of the dinner pot.

Kate spoke up immediately, exclaiming, "Them damn Shakers shan't stop this time." Father was troubled a good deal by breachy stock on the outside pushing the fences down, and generally sent Harry, a Negro boy, around every day to drive away stock and see that the fences were up. There were three large dogs on the place that the boy always carried along, and he had them well trained and always eager for a chase, and would start at his call, yelping furiously. Harry was nowhere about. He was out on the farm with the other hands. But instantly after Kate spoke Harry's voice was heard in the front yard calling the dogs, "Here Caesar, here Tiger, here Bulger, here, here, sic, sic," slapping his hands. Not a soul but the Shakers coming down the lane could be seen.

The dogs, however, responded with savage yelping, going in a fury, following the voice that left the way egging them on, and just as the Shakers were nearing the turning in gate, the dogs leaped the fence at their horses' heels, and Harry's voice was there too, hollering, "Sic, sic, take 'em." The Shakers put whip to their horses and the dogs after them, and Kate vehemently aging the dogs on and hilariously enjoying the sport. It was a lively chase, and broke the Shakers from coming that way again. The witch enjoyed the sport greatly, laughing and repeating the affair to visitors, injecting many funny expressions in describing the chase, and how the Shakers held on to their big hats.

MOTHER BELL'S ILLNESS—THE WITCH SINGS SWEET SONGS AND BRINGS HER HAZELNUTS AND GRAPES

The story of the hazelnuts and grapes brought to mother during her illness was hard for many to believe, and it may prove a severe strain on the credulity of the reader, but it is nevertheless true, and will be verified by several worthy persons who witnessed the facts and have stated the same to many people. Kate had all along manifested a high regard for mother, often remarking, "Old Luce is a good woman." This was very gratifying to the family; we were all much devoted to her, and this earnest expression of tender respect for her; so often repeated, was to a great extent an assurance that whatever might befall other members of the family, mother would be spared personal affliction. She was fearful of the thing, and could not see any good sense or policy in antagonizing what was now evidently a powerful, intelligent and incomprehensible agency, and therefore she conceived it to be the best policy to cultivate the kind manifestations of the witch, and she exercised all the gentleness of her nature toward Kate, as she did her tender affections for her children.

This proved to be the best policy, for it is evident that she appeased the seer's malice in many instances, except in father's case, toward whom the malignity was unrelenting and beyond control. About the middle of September, 1820, mother was taken down with a spell of pleurisy, and then it was that Kate manifested a sorrowful nature, growing more plaintive every day as the disease progressed, giving utterance to woeful expressions that were full of touching sympathy. "Luce, poor Luce, I am so sorry you are sick. Don't you feel better, Luce? What can I do for you, Luce?"

These and many other expressions of sympathy and anxious inquiries were given vent by the saddened voice, that now appeared to remain constantly in mother's room prattling all through the day, changing to a more joyful tone when she indicated any temporary relief. The persistent jabbering and disquietude was enough to craze a well person, but mother bore it all patiently, frequently replying to questions. Sometimes she would reply, "Oh Kate, I am too sick to talk to you." Then the voice would hush for some time, as if choking expression. When anything was wanted or called for that was needed for mother's comfort, the witch would speak promptly, telling precisely, where the article could be found. And so the strange voice continued from day to day, mystifying everyone who came to visit and minister to mother's wants, and it was utterly impossible to distinguish from whence it came, and yet so pathetic as to affect the sympathy of everyone who came within hearing.

It was noticeable also that Kate kept quiet when mother was apparently at rest or sleeping. She rested better in the latter part of the night, and was somewhat refreshed for the morning, and as soon as she was aroused Kate was heard inquiring, "How do you feel this morning, Luce? Did you rest well through the night? Don't you want to hear a song, Luce?" Mother was very fond of vocal music, in which Kate excelled, and it was her pleasure to reply, "Yes Kate, sing something sweet." While the witch sung a number of beautiful stanzas, the following was the favorite, which was sung every day:

> Come my heart and let us try
> For a little season
> Every burden to lay by
> Come and let us reason.
> What is this that casts you down?
> Who are those that grieve you?
> Speak and let the worst be known,

Speaking may relieve you.
Christ by faith I sometimes see
And He doth relieve me,
But my fears return again,
These are they that grieve me.
Troubled like the restless Sea,
Feeble, faint and fearful,
Plagued with every sore disease,
How can I be cheerful?

No rhythmical sound or melody ever fell upon the ear with sweeter pathos, coming as it did like a volume of symphony from a bursting heart. I have seen the tears trickle down mother's fevered cheeks, while friends would turn away to hide repressed weeping. Sick as she was, mother never neglected to compliment the song. "Thank you Kate, that was so sweet and beautiful, it makes me feel better," which the witch seemed to appreciate. Mother gradually grew worse, the disease reaching a serious stage. The doctor was still very hopeful, but the family and our good neighbors were feeling the deepest concern. Father became very restless and apprehensive of the worst.

Her appetite failed entirely, and this distressed Kate woefully. The neighbors brought all sorts of tempting good things to induce her to eat, and this example the observing witch imitated, conceiving the idea, no doubt, that the most important thing was the discovery of something agreeable to her appetite, and this was the circumstance that seemed to have inspired the action of the witch in bringing the nuts and grapes. Wild fruits were plentiful in the bottoms and woods around the place, and were then ripening. The first instance was the appearance of the hazelnuts. The same plaintive voice was heard exclaiming, "Luce, poor Luce, how do you feel now? Hold out your hands, Luce, and I will give you something." Mother stretched her arms, holding her hands together open, and the hazelnuts were dropped from above into her hands. This was witnessed by several ladies who had called in to see mother, and it was so incredible that the floor above was examined to see if there was not a loose plank or some kind of opening through which they were dropped, but it was found to be perfectly secure, and not even a crevice through which a pin could pass.

After some time the amazement was increased by the same voice inquiring, "Say Luce, why don't you eat the hazelnuts?" Mother replied that she could not crack them. Then the exclamation, "Well I will crack some for you," and instantly the sound of the cracking was heard, and the cracked nuts dropped on her bed within hand's reach, and the same passionate voice continued insisting on mother's eating the nuts, that they would do her good. Next came the grapes in the same way, the voice importuning her to eat them, that they would do her good. Mother was thoughtful in expressing her thanks, remarking, "You are so kind, Kate, but I am too sick to eat them."

From this time on mother steadily improved, coming out of a severe spell that held her down some twenty days, and no one could express more joy and gladness than Kate, who also praised Dr. Hopson, the good physician who brought her through safely. As soon as mother was convalescent, Kate devoted more attention to the entertainment of the large number of visitors who were constantly coming to hear the mysterious voice. One evening the room was full of company, all deeply interested in discussing the phenomena of the grapes, etc., when the presence of the witch was announced by the voice exclaiming, "Who wants some grapes?" and before any one could answer, a large bunch of luscious wild grapes fell out on Elizabeth's lap. The bunch was passed around and all tasted of the fruit, and were satisfied that it was no illusion. Kate evinced remarkable knowledge of the forest, and would tell us where to find plenty of grapes, hazelnuts, herbs of every kind, good hickory for axe handles, or tough sticks for a maul.

MRS. MARTHA BELL'S STOCKINGS

Kate, as before intimated, visited the family of Brother Jesse Bell quite often, making demonstrations, but never to the extent of the manifestations at home. Jesse's wife, whom the witch called "Pots," observed mother's policy in humoring the warlock, paying kindly attention to its gabble, incurring favor or kindly relations, and she too was treated with such consideration as to relieve her fears of any immediate harm. Jesse Bell and Bennett Porter had determined to move with their families to Panola county, Mississippi, and were shaping their affairs to that end, as soon as circumstances would admit.

This phenomena I give as related by Martha herself, there being no other witnesses to the circumstance, but I can not doubt her statement, which is borne out by other facts. Late in the afternoon she was sitting out some ten steps on the east side in the shade of the house, engaged in peeling apples for drying. She heard a kind of buzzing or indistinct whispering in her ear, and recognized at once that it was the voice of the witch, and spoke to it, inquiring, "What do you want, Kate? Speak out so I can understand you." Then the witch spoke plainly, saying, "Pots, I have brought you a present to keep in remembrance of me when you go to your far away new home. Will you accept it?" She replied, "Certainly Kate, I will gladly accept any present you may bring. What is it?"

Just then a small roll, neatly wrapped in paper, fell on her lap. She looked up and around in every direction, but no one was near, nor could she discover from whence it came. In her confusion the witch spoke again, saying, "I brought it, Pots; see what a nice pair of stockings. I want you to keep them for your burial, to remember me, and never wear them." She then stripped off the paper and found a pair of elegant black silk hose, for which she thanked Kate, promising to keep them as requested. Martha said she discovered an ugly splotch on one of the hose, which she was eyeing with much curiosity, when the witch spoke very promptly, remarking, "That is blood. They killed a beef at Kate Batts' this morning, and the blood spattered on the stocking." Martha said she was so disconcerted and perplexed that she could not speak, and Kate departed, or said nothing more.

Jesse Bell came in from the field very soon, and when made acquainted with all the facts as above stated, determined to go at once to the Batts home and ascertain the facts regarding the witch's story of the butchering that morning. He did not mention the circumstance, but very soon Mrs. Batts expressed herself as very glad that he had called, stating that they had killed a fine young beef that morning, and intended sending Patsy (his wife) a piece, but had had no opportunity, and wished him to take it, which he did. So this part of the witch's story was confirmed, and Jesse further ascertained from Mrs. Batts that it had been a very busy day, and not one of the family had left the place during the day, or but for the pressing engagement she would have sent the beef to his house. Moreover, Martha Bell had not left the premises, nor had any visitor been on the place.

DR. MIZE, THE WIZARD

During the period of these exciting demonstrations, ever so many detectives, wise men, witch doctors, or conjurers, came to exercise their skill on Kate, and were permitted to practice schemes and magic arts to their heart's content, and all were brought to grief in some way, confessing that the phenomena was something beyond comprehension. One notable instance was that of Dr. Mize, of Simpson County, Ky., some thirty-five miles away, whose fame as a magician had been widely spread, and many brought word to father of his genius, urging him to send for the noted conjurer. The truth is, father had become alarmed about his own condition. His spells of contortions of the face, twitching of the flesh and stiffness of the tongue, were gradually growing more frequent and severe.

His friends observed this, and also that the animosity of the witch toward him was increasing in vehemence, every word spoken to him being a blast of calumnious aspersions, and threatenings of some dire evil which was horrifying. He had also become convinced from his observations, that this terrible thing had the power, as it claimed, to so afflict him, and that the purpose was to torture his life out, as it also declared; and under these circumstances he yielded to the many persuasions to exhaust all means and efforts to free himself and family from the pestilence. He consulted with Mr. James Johnson about the matter, who thought it would be well to give Dr. Mize a trial, and farther proposed to go with Drew after the famous wizard. So it was agreed that Mr. Johnson and Drew were to start on the hunt for Dr. Mize after three o'clock in the morning, while Kate was not about, and clear the neighborhood before the morning hour for the witch's appearance.

The whole matter was to be kept a profound secret, and no one was let into the understanding. Drew made ready to accompany Mr. Johnson on a business trip, to be absent two or three days, and that was all that was known about it. They got off according to the arrangement in good time, and had perhaps passed Springfield before day. Kate came as usual that morning, observing first Drew's absence, setting up an anxious inquiry for him. Not one of the family could give any information concerning him, and the witch seemed baffled and disappeared, and was not heard again during the day, but returned that night in great glee, having discovered the whole secret, telling all about Drew and Mr. Johnson's trip. Kate went on to say, "I got on their track and overtook them twenty miles on the way, and followed along some distance, and when I hopped in the road before them, looking like a poor old sick rabbit, 'Old Sugar Mouth' said, 'There is your witch, Drew; take her up in your lap. Don't you see how tired she is?'" Kate continued to gossip about the trip in a hilarious way, manifesting much satisfaction in discovering the deep laid scheme, but no one knew how true the story was until Mr. Johnson and Drew returned the following evening, when they confirmed everything that Kate had stated.

Mr. Johnson said that he did not really believe at the time of calling Drew's attention to the rabbit, that it was the witch, but spoke of its peculiar action in a jocular way, as a mere matter of pastime, nor did Drew think otherwise of it. They found Dr. Mize at his home east of Franklin, Ky., told him the story of our trouble, and the information received concerning his power to dispel witchery, etc. The Doctor said it was out of the ordinary line of phenomena, but he had no doubt of his ability to remove the spell and expose the craft that had brought it on, and he set the time, some ten days ahead, when he would be ready to begin the experiment. Accordingly, the wise man put in his appearance, having studied the question, and was prepared for business, making boasts of his knowledge of spirits and skill in casting out devils, much to the disgust of father, who had about sized him up on sight. However, like others, Mize was treated courteously and allowed to pursue his own plans. The wizard stayed three or four days, hearing not a breath from Kate.

In the meanwhile he found an old shotgun that had been out of repair some time, and he at once discovered that the witch had put a spell on it. He soon cleaned the old gun, readjusted the lock and trigger, performed some conjurations, making the gun shoot as well as ever. This much, taken in consideration with the fact that the witch had kept perfectly quiet since his arrival, he considered as remarkable progress, and he doubted the return of Kate. Certain he was that the witch would hardly show up as long as he remained; witches, he said, were always shy of him. So Mize continued, working sorcery, making curious mixtures, performing incantations, etc., to the amusement of those who observed his actions. Finally Kate put in, questioning the conjurer impertinently as to what he was doing, and the object of his sorcery. Mize was nonplussed by the mysterious voice, which he had not before heard, recognizing that the witch had come to keep company with him. He tried to be reticent and evasive, intimating that a witch had no business prying into his affairs.

Kate, however, continued to ply him with hard questions, and finally suggested to Dr. Mize that he had omitted some very important ingredients for his charm mixture. "What is that?" inquired Mize with astonishment. "If you were a witch doctor you would know how to aerify that mess, so as to pass into the aeriform state, and see the spirit that talks to you, without asking silly questions," replied Kate. "What do you know about this business, anyhow?" again inquired the bewildered conjurer. Kate then told him that he was an old fool and didn't know what he was doing, and then started in to cursing Mize like blue blazes. Such a string of blasting oaths was never heard, and Dr. Mize was frightened out of his wits, and was anxious to get away. "That thing," he said, knew so much more about witchcraft than he did, that he could do nothing with it.

Mize arranged for an early start home the next morning. Somehow his horse refused to go off kindly, rearing and kicking up. Finally Kate came to the rescue, proposing to make the horse go, and accompany the Doctor home. Immediately the horse started with a rush, kicking and snorting, and went off at full speed with the Doctor hanging on to the mane. The witch came that night in great glee, describing the trip home with the "old fraud," and the tricks played on him along the way, just as Mize described the affair to his neighbors.

THE DOUBLES OR APPARITIONS

Much has been talked about Bennett Porter shooting at the witch. Porter, according to his own statement, did shoot at an object that appeared to his wife and Elizabeth, as described by them, but saw nothing himself, except the bent saplings in motion. This circumstance occurred during the time the witch family appeared on scene. Elizabeth was there on a visit to her sister. Bennett Porter was absent during the day, filling an engagement at Fort's mill, which was in course of construction, and returned home late in the afternoon. The hens were laying about the stables, which were located on the opposite side of the lane from the house.

Esther started across the lane that afternoon to gather up the eggs. Just as she passed from the yard into road, she observed a woman walking slowly up the lane toward the house, and she hurried on her mission and returned just in time to meet the lady at the front entrance. She recognized the person as one of her neighbors, and spoke to her pleasantly, to which the woman made no reply. She repeated the salutation, which again failed to elicit any response. The woman appeared to have taken off her bonnet and let her hair down, and was engaged in combing out her hair as she walked, and stopped just opposite the house, where Esther met her, continuing the combing, and appeared deeply absorbed or troubled. Esther said she invited the lady in the house, repeating the solicitation several times, to which the woman paid no attention.

She felt much chagrined by the strange conduct of her neighbor, and concluded that something was wrong with the lady or that she had become offended towards her, and she passed in, leaving the woman standing in the lane, combing her hair. She called Elizabeth's attention to the woman and her conduct, and they both observed her still in the same attitude. Presently she climbed on the yard fence, sitting there some five minutes, still combing her hair, and then she tucked it up in the usual way and left the fence, crossing over into the stable lot, where she could not have possibly had any business. The lot enclosed some three or four acres, a grove mostly of young saplings on the further side, in the midst of which was a large knotty log.

The woman walked across the lot, passing around the log, when there appeared three other persons, two younger women or girls, and a boy. Each one bent down a sapling, sitting upon them and riding up and down, giving motion to the spring afforded by the bush. While this exercise still continued, Bennett Porter returned home, finding Esther and Elisabeth excited over the strange demonstrations that they tried to point out to him. He said he could see the bushes in motion, but could not see the persons described. He suggested that they were the witch apparitions, and got his gun, insisting that Esther should shoot at one of the objects. While he was getting his rifle, the appearances let the saplings up and took positions behind the log, first one and then another showing a head above the log. Esther refused to shoot, but directed Porter to shoot near a large knot on the log, where one of the heads appeared. He fired and his bullet cut the bark on the log just where he aimed, but nothing more was seen of the four persons, nor could they, as Porter thought, have escaped from the lot without detection. They all three went to the log, and searched the lot over, and could discover no signs except the bent saplings, and the mark of the bullet on the log.

Now whether these were doubles, apparitions, witches, or real persons, the witch family in their carousal that night made much ado about it, declaring to the company present that Bennett Porter had shot at Jerusalem and had broken his arm with the bullet.

THE POISONOUS VIAL—THE LAST ILLNESS
AND DEATH OF JOHN BELL, SR.

I have already written more about this abomination than contemplated in the outset, and still have not told the half; but have presented enough, to which others can testify, to enable the reader to form some idea of the heinous thing, and the horrors that our family had to endure during the early settlement of Robertson county, from an unknown enemy, and for an unknown cause. Whether it was witchery, such as afflicted people in past centuries and the darker ages, whether some gifted fiend of hellish nature, practicing sorcery for selfish enjoyment, or some more modern science akin to that of mesmerism, or some hobgoblin native to the wilds of the country, or a disembodied soul shut out from heaven, or an evil spirit like those Paul drove out of the man into the swine, setting them mad; or a demon let loose from hell, I am unable to decide; nor has any one yet divined its nature or cause for appearing, and I trust this description of the monster in all forms and shapes, and of many tongues, will lead experts who may come with a wiser generation, to a correct conclusion and satisfactory explanation.

However, no part of what I have written would be complete without the finale; the climax which I now approach with a shudder that fills my frame with horror, bringing fresh to memory scenes and events that chilled the blood in my young veins, cheating me out of twenty years of life. It hangs over me like the pall of death, and sends weary thoughts like fleeting shadows through my brain, reviving in memory those demoniac shrieks that came so oft from an invisible and mysterious source, rending the air with vile and hideous curses that drove me frantic with fear.

It is no ghastly dream of a fevered brain that comes to haunt one's thoughts, but a sad, fearful reality, a tremendous truth, that thrills the heart with an unspeakable fear that no word painting can portray on paper. Courageous men in battle line may rush upon bristling bayonets and blazing musketry, and face the roaring cannon's month, because they can see the enemy and know who and what they are fighting; but when it comes to meeting an unknown enemy of demonstrative power, with gall upon its tongue and venom in its bosom, heaving bitter curses and breathing threats of dire consequences, which one knows not of, nor can judge in what shape or form the calamity is to come, the stoutest heart will prove a coward, faltering and quivering with painful fear.

Why should my father, John Bell, be inflicted with such a terrible curse? Why should such a fate befall a man striving to live uprightly? I would be untrue to myself and my parentage, should I fail to state boldly that John Bell was a man every inch of him and in every sense of the term. No man was ever more faithful and swift in the discharge of every duty, to his family, to the church, to his neighbor's, to his fellow man, and to his God, in the fullness of his capacity and that faith which led him to love and accept Christ as a Savior. No mortal man ever brought a charge of delinquency or dishonor to his door. Not even the ghastly fiend that haunted him to his death, in all of its vile curses and evil threats, ever brought an accusation against him, or uttered a solitary word that reflected upon his honor, his character, his courage, or his integrity.

He lived in peace, and in the enjoyment of the full confidence of his neighbors, and lacked not for scores of friends in his severest trials. Then why this affliction? Where the cause? Which no man, saint, angel from heaven, or demon from hell, has ever assigned. If there was any hidden or unknown cause why he should have thus suffered, or if it was in the providence of God a natural consequence, then why should the torments of a demon have been visited upon Elizabeth, who was a girl of tender years, brought up under the careful training of a Christian mother, and was free from guile and the wiles of the wicked world, and innocent of all offense? Yet this vile, heinous, unknown devil, torturer of human flesh, that preyed upon the fears of people like a ravenous vulture, spared not her, but rather chose her as a shining mark for an exhibition of its wicked stratagems and devilish tortures. And never did it cease to practice upon her fears, insult her modesty, stick pins in her body, pinching and bruising her flesh, slapping her cheeks, disheveling and tangling her hair, tormenting her in many ways, until she surrendered that most cherished hope which animates every young heart.

Was this the stratagem of a human genius skilled in the black art; was it an enchantment, a freak in destiny, or the natural consequence of disobedience to some law in nature? Let a wiser head than mine answer and explain the mystery. Another problem in the development of these mysterious manifestations, that has always puzzled my understanding: Why should the husband and father, the head of the family, and the daughter, the pet and pride of the household, the centre of all family affections, be selected to bear the invectives of this terrible visitation, while demonstrations of the tenderest love from the same source was bestowed upon the wife and mother? If it was a living, intelligent creature, what could have been the dominating faculty of its nature, which made this discrimination? Could it have been an intelligent human devotion springing from an emotional nature that could so love the wife and mother, and cherish such bitter enmity for her husband and offspring, both of whom she loved most devotedly? I think not; only a fiend of a hellish nature, with poisoned blood and seared conscience, if a conscience at all, could have possessed such attributes.

Yet we, who experienced or witnessed the demonstration, know that there was a wonderful power of intelligence, possessing knowledge of men and things, a spirit of divination, that could read minds, tell men's secrets, quote the Scriptures, repeat sermons, sing hymns and songs, assume bodily forms, and with all, an immense physical force behind the manifestations.

Father continued to suffer with spells as I have already described, the jerking and twitching of his face, and the swelling of his tongue, fearfully distorting his whole physiognomy. These spells would last from one to two days, and after passing off, he would be up and about his business, apparently in strong robust health. As time advanced the spells grew more frequent and severe, and there was no periodical time for their return, and along toward the last I stayed with him all the time, especially when he left the house, going with him wherever he went. The witch also grew more angry and virulent in disposition. Every word uttered to "Old Jack" was a blast of curses and heinous threats, while to mother, "Old Luce," it continued most tender, loving and kind. About the middle of October father had a very severe attack, which kept him confined to the house six or eight days.

The witch cursed and raved like a maniac for several days, and ceased not from troubling him. However, he temporarily overcame this attack, and was soon able to be out, though he would not venture far from the house. But it was not destined that he should enjoy a long respite. After a week's recuperation he felt much stronger, and called me very early one morning to go with him to the hog pen, some three hundred yards from the house, for the purpose of giving directions in separating the porkers intended for fattening from the stock hogs. We had not gone far before one of his shoes was jerked off. I replaced it on his foot, drawing the strings tight, tying a double hard knot. After going a few steps farther, the other shoe flew off in the same manner, which was replaced and tied as in the case of the first.

In no way that I could tie them would they hold, notwithstanding his shoes fitted close and were a little hard to put on, and we were walking over a smooth, dry road. This worried him prodigiously; nevertheless, he bore up strongly, and after much delay and worry we reached the place, and he gave directions, seeing the hogs properly separated as he desired, and the hands left for other work, and we started back for the house. We had not gone many steps before his shoes commenced jerking off as before, and presently he complained of a blow on his face, which felt like an open hand, that almost stunned him, and he sat down on a log that lay by the road side. Then his face commenced jerking with fearful contortions, soon his whole body, and then his shoes would fly off as fast as I could put them on. The situation was trying and made me shudder. I was terrified by the spectacle of the contortions that seized father, as if to convert him into a very demon to swallow me up. Having finished tying father's shoes, I raised myself up to hear the reviling sound of derisive songs piercing the air with terrorizing force. As the demoniac shrieks died away in triumphant rejoicing, the spell passed off, and I saw the tears chasing down father's yet quivering cheeks.

The trace of faltering courage marked every lineament of his face with a wearied expression of fading hope. He turned to me with an expression of tender, compassionate fatherly devotion, exclaiming in a woeful passionate tone, "Oh my son, my son, not long will you have a father to wait on so patiently. I cannot much longer survive the persecutions of this terrible thing. It is killing me by slow tortures, and I feel that the end is nigh." This expression sent a pang to my bosom which I had never felt before. Mingled sorrow and terror took possession of me and sent a tremor through my frame that I can never forget. If the earth could have opened and swallowed us up, it would have been a joyful deliverance. My heart bleeds now at every pore as I pen these lines, refreshing my memory with thoughts of the terror that possessed me then in anticipation of a fearful tragedy that might be enacted before father could move from his position. That moment he turned his eyes upward and lifted his soul to heaven in a burst of fervent passionate prayer, such as I had never heard him utter before. He prayed the Lord that if it were possible, to let this terrible affliction pass.

He beseeched God to forsake him not in the trying ordeal, but to give him courage to meet this unknown devastating enemy in the trying emergency, and faith to lift him to the confidence and love of a blessed Savior, and with all to relieve his family and loved ones from the terrible afflictions of this wicked, unknown, terrifying, blasphemous agency. It was in this strain that father prayed, pouring out his soul in a passionate force that seemed to take hold of Christ by a powerful faith that afforded fresh courage and renewed strength. After he had finished his prayer, a feeling of calmness and reconciliation seemed to possess him, and he appeared to have recovered from the severe shock. The reviling songster had disappeared, and he rose up remarking that he felt better and believed he could walk to the house, and he did, meeting with no more annoyance as we proceeded on the way. However, he took to his bed immediately on arriving at the house, and though able to be up and down for several weeks, he never left the house again, and seemed all the while perfectly reconciled to the terrible fate that awaited him. He gradually declined; nothing that friends could do brought any relief. Mother was almost constantly at his bedside with all the devotion of her nature.

Brother John attended closely in the room, ministering to him, and good neighbors were in constant attendance. The witch was carrying on its deviltry more or less all the while.

The crisis, however, came on the morning of December 19th. Father, sick as he was, had not up to this time failed to awake at his regular hour, according to his long custom, and arouse the family. That morning he appeared to be sleeping so soundly, mother quietly slipped, out of the room to superintend breakfast, while brothers John and Drew looked after the farm hands and feeding the stock, and would not allow him to be disturbed until after breakfast. Noticing then that he was sleeping unnaturally, it was thought best to awaken him, when it was discovered that he was in a deep stupor, and could not be aroused to any sensibility. Brother John attended to giving him medicine, and went immediately to the cupboard where he had carefully put away the medicines prescribed for him, but instead he found a smoky looking vial, which was about one-third full of dark colored liquid.

He set up an inquiry at once to know who had moved the medicine, and no one had touched it, and neither could any one on the place give any account of the vial. Dr. George Hopson, of Port Royal, was sent for in great haste and soon arrived; also neighbors John Johnson, Alex. Gunn and Frank Miles arrived early, and were there when the vial was found. Kate, the witch, in the meantime broke out with joyous exultation, exclaiming, "It's useless for you to try to relieve Old Jack, I have got him this time; he will never get up from that bed again." Kate was then asked about the vial of medicine found in the cupboard, and replied, "I put it there, and gave Old Jack a big dose out of it last night while he was asleep, which fixed him." This was all the information that could be drawn from the witch or any other source concerning the vial of medicine. Certain it was that no member of the family ever saw it before, or could tell anything about it. In fact no vial and no medicine of any kind had been brought to the house by any one else except by Dr. Hopson, and then it was handled carefully. Dr. Hopson, on arrival, examined the vial and said he did not leave it, and could not tell what it contained. It was then suggested that the contents be tested on something. Alex. Gunn caught a cat, and Brother John ran a straw into the vial and drew it through the cat's mouth, wiping the straw on its tongue. The cat jumped and whirled over a few times, stretched out, kicked, and died very quick.

DEATHBED OF JOHN BELL

Father lay all day and night in a deep stupor, as if under the influence of some opiate, and could not be aroused to take any medicine. The Doctor said he could detect something on his breath that smelt very much like the contents of the vial that he had examined. How father could have gotten it was a mystery that could not be explained in any other way except that testified by the witch. The vial and contents was thrown into the fire, and instantly a blue blaze shot up the chimney like a flash of powder. Father never revived or returned to consciousness for a single moment. He lingered along through the day and night, gradually wearing away, and on the morning of December 20th, 1820, breathed his last. Kate was around during the time, indulging in wild exultations and derisive songs.

After father breathed his last nothing more was heard from Kate until after the burial was completed. It was a bright December day and a great crowd of people came to attend the funeral. Rev. Sugg Fort and Revs. James and Thomas Gunn conducted the services. After the grave was filled, and the friends turned to leave the sad scene, the witch broke out in a loud voice singing, "Row me up some brandy O," and continued singing this until the family and friends had all entered the house. And thus ended one chapter in the series of exciting and frightful events that kept the whole neighborhood so long in a frenzy, and worked upon our fears from day to day.

KATE'S DEPARTURE AND RETURN AFTER SEVEN YEARS

After the death of John Bell, Sr., the fury of the witch was greatly abated. There were but two purposes, seemingly, developed in the visitation. One was the persecution of father to the end of his life. The other the vile purpose of destroying the anticipated happiness that thrilled the heart of Betsy. This latter purpose, however, was not so openly manifested as the first, and was of such a delicate nature that it was kept a secret as much as possible in the family and ignored when talked about. But it never ceased its tormenting until her young dream was destroyed.

The witch remained with us after father's death, through the Winter and Spring of 1821, all the while diminishing or becoming less demonstrative. Finally it took leave of the family, bidding mother, "Luce," an affectionate farewell, saying that it would be absent seven years, but would surely return to see us and would then visit every house in the neighborhood. This promise was fulfilled as regards the old homestead, but I do not know that it visited other homes in the vicinity.

It returned during February, 1828. The family was then nearly broken up. Mother, Joel and myself were the only occupants left at the old home-stead, the other members of the family having settled off to themselves. The demonstrations announcing its return were precisely the same that characterized its first appearance. Joel occupied a bed in mother's room, and I slept in another apartment alone. After considerable scratching on the weatherboarding on the outside, it appeared in the same way on the inside, scratching on the bed post and pulling the cover from my bed as fast as I could replace it, keeping me up nearly all night. It went on in this way for several nights, and I spoke not a word about it, lest I should frighten mother.

However, one night later, after worrying me for some time, I heard a noise in mother's room, and knew at once what was to pay. Very soon mother and Joel came rushing into my room, much frightened, telling me about the disturbance and something pulling the cover off. We sat up till a late hour discussing the matter, satisfied that it was the same old Kate, and agreed not to talk to the witch, and that we would keep the matter a profound secret to ourselves, worrying with it the best we could, hoping that it would soon leave, as it did, after disturbing us in this way for some two weeks. This was my last experience with Kate. The witch came and went, hundreds of people witnessed its wonderful demonstrations, and many of the best people of Robertson and adjoining counties have testified to these facts, telling the story over and over to the younger generation, and for this and other reasons as before stated I have written this much of the details as correctly as it is possible to state the exciting events. So far no one has ever given any intelligent or comprehensive explanation of the great mystery. Those who came as experts were worse confounded than all others.

As I before stated, a few mendacious calumniators were mean enough to charge that it was tricks and inventions of the Bell family to make money, and I write for the purpose of branding this version as an infamous false-hood. It was well known in the vicinity and all over the county that every investigation confirmed the fact that the Bell family were the greatest, if not the only sufferers from the visitation, and that no one, or a dozen persons in collusion, could have so long, regularly and persistently practiced such a fraud without detection, nor could they have known the minds and secrets of strangers visiting the place, and detailed events that were then occurring or had just transpired in different localities. Moreover the visitation entailed great sacrifice. As to how long this palavering phenomenon continued in the vicinity, I am unable to state. It did not disturb the remaining members of the family at the old place anymore. Mother died shortly after this and the house was entirely deserted, the land and other property being divided among the heirs.

The old house stood for some years and was used for storing grain and other farm products, and was finally torn down and moved away. Many persons professed to have seen sights and heard strange sounds about the old house and in the vicinity all along up to this day. Several have described to me flitting lights along the old lane and through the farm, while others profess to have heard sounds of wonderfully sweet music and strange voices uttering indistinct word. And it is said that such things have been seen and heard at various places in the neighborhood, but I have no personal knowledge of the facts.

MYTHS AND LEGENDS OF OUR OWN LAND

Charles M. Skinner

1896

Charles Montgomery Skinner (1852-1907) was born in Victor, a town in upstate New York not far from Rochester. He was a journalist and edited the Brooklyn Daily Eagle *for a time. He wrote plays and also published several articles on gardening in America's rapidly expanding cities.*

He is best known, though, for his collections of America's folklore, which was growing almost as rapidly as the nation itself during the last decades of the nineteenth century. Myths and Legends of Our Own Land *was published in nine volumes: each of the first eight books covered a specific geographical area, from the Hudson Valley to the Pacific coast, while the ninth collected stories of buried treasure. In 1900, Skinner added a companion volume,* Myths and Legends of Our New Possessions and Protectorate, *which collected stories from American-controlled lands in the Caribbean and the Pacific.*

Most of the stories in Skinner's books are fairly short, so the following pages offer a selection of eight tales from various parts of the country. "The Last Revel in Printz Hall" is a rather traditional supernatural tale set in Pennsylvania, and would not have been out of place among the works of Washington Irving. "Jack Welch's Death Light" is a typically grim New England ghost story, while "Mogg Megone" is set against the background of a bloody incident during the Fourth Anglo–Abenaki War of 1722–1725. "The Owl Tree" is a tale of guilt and retribution that evokes something of the spirit of Nathaniel Hawthorne. "Howe's Masquerade," set during a pivotal time in the course of the Revolutionary War, is one of those tales in which one can see history being fashioned into mythology. "The Salem Alchemist" is the kind of tale one can imagine delighting a young H. P. Lovecraft, while "The Red Dwarf of Detroit" is a pleasant retelling of a local legend going back to the earliest days of European settlement, and possibly beyond. "The Skull in the Wall" tells of a grisly relic from Revolutionary times, and "The Green Picture" is an example of the homegrown American vampire tradition, which is distinct from that of Europe.

THE LAST REVEL IN PRINTZ HALL

Young man, I'll give thee five dollars a week to be care-taker in Printz Hall," said Quaker Quidd to fiddler Matthews, on an autumn evening.

Young Matthews had just been taunting the old gentleman with being afraid to sleep on his own domain, and as the eyes of all the tavern loungers were on him he could hardly decline so flattering a proposition, so, after some hemming and hawing, he said he would take the Quaker at his word. He played but two or three more tunes that evening, did Peter Matthews, and played them rather sadly; then, as Quidd had finished his mulled cider and departed, he took his homeward way in thoughtful mood. Printz Hall stood in a lonely, weed-grown garden near Chester, Pennsylvania, and thither repaired Peter, as next day's twilight shut down, with a mattress, blanket, comestibles, his beloved fiddle, and a flask of whiskey. Ensconcing himself in the room that was least depressing in appearance he stuffed rags into the vacant panes, lighted a candle, started a blaze in the fireplace, and ate his supper.

"Not so bad a place, after all," mumbled Peter, as he warmed himself at the fire and the flask; then, taking out his violin, he began to play. The echo of his music emphasized the emptiness of the house, the damp got into the strings so that they sounded tubby, and there were unintentional quavers in the melody whenever the trees swung against the windows and splashed them with rain, or when a distant shutter fell a-creaking. Finally, he stirred the fire, bolted the door, snuffed his candle, took a courageous pull at the liquor, flung off his coat and shoes, rolled his blanket around him, stretched himself on the mattress, and fell asleep. He was awakened by—well, he could not say what, exactly, only he became suddenly as wide awake as ever he had been in his life, and listened for some sound that he knew was going to come out of the roar of the wind and the slamming, grating, and whistling about the house. Yes, there it was: a tread and a clank on the stair. The door, so tightly bolted, flew open, and there entered a dark figure with steeple-crowned hat, cloak, jack-boots, sword, and corselet. The terrified fiddler wanted to howl, but his voice was gone. "I am Peter Printz, governor-general of his Swedish Majesty's American colonies, and builder of this house," said the figure. "'Tis the night of the autumnal equinox, when my friends meet here for revel. Take thy fiddle and come. Play, but speak not."

And whether he wished or no, Peter was drawn to follow the figure, which he could make out by the phosphor gleam of it. Down-stairs they went, doors swinging open before them, and along corridors that clanged to the stroke of the spectre's boot heels. Now they came to the ancient reception-room, and as they entered it Peter was dazzled. The floor was smooth with wax, logs snapped in the fireplace, though the flame was somewhat blue, the old hangings and portraits looked fresh, and in the light of wax candles a hundred people, in the brave array of old times, walked, courtesied, and seemed to laugh and talk together. As the fiddler appeared, every eye was turned on him in a disquieting way, and when he addressed himself to his bottle, from every throat came a hollow laugh. Finding his way to a chair he sank into it and put his instrument in position. At the first note the couples took hands, and as he struck into a jig they began to circle swiftly, leaping wondrous high.

Faster went the music, for the whiskey was at work in Peter's noddle, and wilder grew the dance. It was as if the storm had come in through the windows and was blowing these people hither and yon, around and around. The fiddler vaguely wondered at himself, for he had never played so well, though he had never heard the tune before. Now loomed Governor Printz in the middle of the room, and extending his hand he ordered the dance to cease. "Thou hast played well, fiddler," he said, "and shalt be paid." Then, at his signal, came two negro men tugging at a strong box that Printz unlocked. It was filled with gold pieces. "Hold thy fiddle bag," commanded the governor, and Peter did so, watching, open mouthed, the transfer of a double handful of treasure from box to sack. Another such handful followed, and another. At the fourth Peter could no longer contain himself. He forgot the injunction not to speak, and shouted gleefully, "Lord Harry! Here's luck!"

There was a shriek of demon laughter, the scene was lost in darkness, and Peter fell insensible. In the morning a tavern-haunting friend, anxious to know if Peter had met with any adventure, entered the house and went cautiously from room to room, calling on the watcher to show himself. There was no response. At last he stumbled on the whiskey bottle, empty, and knew that Peter must be near. Sure enough, there he lay in the great room, with dust and mould thick on everything, and his fiddle smashed into a thousand pieces. Peter on being awakened looked ruefully about him, then sprang up and eagerly demanded his money. "What money?" asked his friend. The fiddler clutched at his green bag, opened it, shook it; there was nothing. Nor was there any delay in Peter's exit from that mansion, and when, twenty-four hours after, the house went up in flames, he averred that the ghosts had set it afire, and that he knew where they brought their coals from.

JACK WELCH'S DEATH LIGHT

Pond Cove, Maine, is haunted by a light that on a certain evening, every summer, rises a mile out at sea, drifts to a spot on shore, then whirls with a buzz and a glare to an old house, where it vanishes. Its first appearance was simultaneous with the departure of Jack Welch, a fisherman. He was seen one evening at work on his boat, but in the morning he was gone, nor has he since shown himself in the flesh.

On the tenth anniversary of this event three fishermen were hurrying up the bay, hoping to reach home before dark, for they dreaded that uncanny light, but a fog came in and it was late before they reached the wharf. As they were tying their boat a channel seemed to open through the mist, and along that path from the deep came a ball of pallid flame with the rush of a meteor. There was one of the men who cowered at the bottom of the boat with ashen face and shaking limbs, and did not watch the light, even though it shot above his head, played through the rigging, and after a wide sweep went shoreward and settled on his house. Next day one of his comrades called for him, but Tom Wright was gone, gone, his wife said, before the day broke. Like Jack Welch's disappearance, this departure was unexplained, and in time he was given up for dead.

Twenty years had passed, when Wright's presumptive widow was startled by the receipt of a letter in a weak, trembling hand, signed with her husband's name. It was written on his death-bed, in a distant place, and held a confession. Before their marriage, Jack Welch had been a suitor for her hand, and had been the favored of the two. To remove his rival and prosper in his place, Wright stole upon the other at his work, killed him, took his body to sea, and threw it overboard. Since that time the dead man had pursued him, and he was glad that the end of his days was come. But, though Tom Wright is no more, his victim's light comes yearly from the sea, above the spot where his body sank, floats to the scene of the murder on the shore, then flits to the house where the assassin lived and for years simulated the content that comes of wedded life.

MOGG MEGONE

Hapless daughter of a renegade is Ruth Bonython. Her father is as unfair to his friends as to his enemies, but to neither of them so merciless as to Ruth. Although he knows that she loves Master Scammon in spite of his desertion and would rather die than wed another, he has promised her to Mogg Megone, the chief who rules the Indians at the Saco mouth. He, blundering savage, fancies that he sees to the bottom of her grief, and one day, while urging his suit, he opens his blanket and shows the scalp of Scammon, to prove that he has avenged her. She looks in horror, but when he flings the bloody trophy at her feet she baptizes it with a forgiving tear. What villainy may this lead to? Ah, none for him, for Bonython now steps in and plies him with flattery and drink, gaining from the chief, at last, his signature—the bow totem—to a transfer of the land for which he is willing to sell his daughter. Ruth, maddened at her father's meanness and the Indian's brutality, rushes on the imbruted savage, grasps from his belt the knife that has slain her lover, cleaves his heart in twain, and flies into the wood, leaving Bonython stupid with amazement.

Father Rasles, in his chapel at Norridgewock, is affecting his Indian converts against the Puritans, who settled to the southward of him fifty years before. To him comes a woman with torn garments and frightened face. Her dead mother stood before her last night, she says, and looked at her reprovingly, for she had killed Mogg Megone. The priest starts back in wrath, for Mogg was a hopeful agent of the faith, and bids her go, for she can ask no pardon. Brooding within his chapel, then, he is startled by the sound of shot and hum of arrows. Harmon and Moulton are advancing with their men and crying, "Down with the beast of Rome! Death to the Babylonish dog!" Ruth, knowing not what this new misfortune may mean, runs from the church and disappears.

Some days later, old Baron Castine, going to Norridgewock to bury and revenge the dead, finds a woman seated on the earth and gazing over a field strewn with ashes and with human bones. He touches her. She is cold. There has been no life for days. It is Ruth.

THE OWL TREE

One day in October, 1827, Rev. Charles Sharply rode into Alfred, Maine, and held service in the meeting-house. After the sermon he announced that he was going to Waterborough to preach, and that on his circuit he had collected two hundred and seventy dollars to help build a church in that village. Would not his hearers add to that sum? They would and did, and that evening the parson rode away with over three hundred dollars in his saddlebags. He never appeared in Waterborough. Some of the country people gave tongue to their fear that the possession of the money had made him forget his sacred calling and that he had fled the State.

On the morning after his disappearance, however, Deacon Dickerman appeared in Alfred riding on a horse that was declared to be the minister's, until the tavern hostler affirmed that the minister's horse had a white star on forehead and breast, whereas this horse was all black. The deacon said that he found the horse grazing in his yard at daybreak, and that he would give it to whoever could prove it to be his property. Nobody appeared to demand it, and people soon forgot that it was not his. He extended his business at about that time and prospered; he became a rich man for a little place; though, as his wealth increased, he became morose and averse to company.

One day a rumor went around that a belated traveller had seen a misty thing under "the owl tree" at a turn of a road where owls were hooting, and that it took on a strange likeness to the missing clergyman. Dickerman paled when he heard this story, but he shook his head and muttered of the folly of listening to boy nonsense. Ten years had gone by—during that time the boys had avoided the owl tree after dark—when a clergyman of the neighborhood was hastily summoned to see Mr. Dickerman, who was said to be suffering from overwork. He found the deacon in his house alone, pacing the floor, his dress disordered, his cheek hectic.

"I have not long to live," said he, "nor would I live longer if I could. I am haunted day and night, and there is no peace, no rest for me on earth. They say that Sharply's spirit has appeared at the owl tree. Well, his body lies there. They accused me of taking his horse. It is true. A little black dye on his head and breast was all that was needed to deceive them. Pray for me, for I fear my soul is lost. I killed Sharply." The clergyman recoiled. "I killed him," the wretched man went on, "for the money that he had. The devil prospered me with it. In my will I leave two thousand dollars to his widow and five thousand dollars to the church he was collecting for. Will there be mercy for me there? I dare not think it. Go and pray for me." The clergyman hastened away, but was hardly outside the door when the report of a pistol brought him back. Dickerman lay dead on the floor. Sharply's body was exhumed from the shade of the owl tree, and the spot was never haunted after.

HOWE'S MASQUERADE

During the siege of Boston Sir William Howe undertook to show his contempt for the raw fellows who were disrespectfully tossing cannon-balls at him from the batteries in Cambridge and South Boston, by giving a masquerade. It was a brilliant affair, the belles and blades of the loyalist set being present, some in the garb of their ancestors, for the past is ever more picturesque than the present, and a few roisterers caricaturing the American generals in ragged clothes, false noses, and absurd wigs. At the height of the merriment a sound of a dirge echoing through the streets caused the dance to stop. The funeral music paused before the doors of Province House, where the dance was going on, and they were flung open. Muffled drums marked time for a company that began to file down the great stair from the floor above the ball-room: dark men in steeple-hats and pointed beards, with Bibles, swords, and scrolls, who looked sternly at the guests and descended to the street.

Colonel Joliffe, a Whig, whose age and infirmity had prevented him from joining Washington, and whose courtesy and intelligence had made him respected by his foes, acted as chorus: "These I take to be the Puritan governors of Massachusetts: Endicott, Winthrop, Vane, Dudley, Haynes, Bellingham, Leverett, Bradstreet." Then came a rude soldier, mailed, begirt with arms: the tyrant Andros; a brown-faced man with a sailor's gait: Sir William Phipps; a courtier wigged and jewelled: Earl Bellomont; the crafty, well-mannered Dudley; the twinkling, red-nosed Shute; the ponderous Burnet; the gouty Belcher; Shirley, Pownall, Bernard, Hutchinson; then a soldier, whose cocked hat he held before his face. "'Tis the shape of Gage!" cried an officer, turning pale. The lights were dull and an uncomfortable silence had fallen on the company. Last, came a tall man muffled in a military cloak, and as he paused on the landing the guests looked from him to their host in amazement, for it was the figure of Howe himself. The governor's patience was at an end, for this was a part of the masquerade that had not been looked for. He fiercely cried to Joliffe, "There is a plot in this. Your head has stood too long on a traitor's shoulders."

"Make haste to cut it off, then," was the reply, "for the power of Sir William Howe and of the king, his master, is at an end. These shadows are mourners at his funeral. Look! The last of the governors."

Howe rushed with drawn sword on the figure of himself, when it turned and looked at him. The blade clanged to the floor and Howe fell back with a gasp of horror, for the face was his own. Hand nor voice was raised to stay the double-goer as it mournfully passed on. At the threshold it stamped its foot and shook its fists in air; then the door closed. Mingled with the strains of the funeral march, as it died along the empty streets, came the tolling of the bell on South Church steeple, striking the hour of midnight. The festivities were at an end and, oppressed by a nameless fear, the spectators of this strange pageant made ready for departure; but before they left the booming of cannon at the southward announced that Washington had advanced. The glories of Province House were over. When the last of the royal governors left it he paused on the threshold, beat his foot on the stone, and flung up his hands in an attitude of grief and rage.

THE SALEM ALCHEMIST

In 1720 there lived in a turreted house at North and Essex Streets, in Salem, a silent, dark-visaged man,—a reputed chemist. He gathered simples in the fields, and parcels and bottles came and went between him and learned doctors in Boston; but report went around that it was not drugs alone that he worked with, nor medicines for passing ailments that he distilled. The watchman, drowsily pacing the streets in the small hours, saw his shadow move athwart the furnace glare in his tower, and other shadows seemed at the moment to flit about it—shadows that could be thrown by no tangible form, yet that had a grotesque likeness to the human kind. A clink of hammers and a hiss of steam were sometimes heard, and his neighbors devoutly hoped that if he secured the secret of the philosopher's stone or the universal solvent, it would be honestly come by.

But it was neither gold nor the perilous strong water that he wanted. It was life: the elixir that would dispel the chill and decrepitude of age, that would bring back the youthful sparkle to the eye and set the pulses bounding. He explored the surrounding wilderness day after day; the juices of its trees and plants he compounded, night after night, long without avail. Not until after a thousand failures did he conceive that he had secured the ingredients but they were many, they were perishable, they must be distilled within five days, for fermentation and decay would set in if he delayed longer. Gathering the herbs and piling his floor with fuel, he began his work, alone; the furnace glowed, the retorts bubbled, and through their long throats trickled drops—golden, ruddy, brown, and crystal—that would be combined into that precious draught.

And none too soon, for under the strain of anxiety he seemed to be aging fast. He took no sleep, except while sitting upright in his chair, for, should he yield entirely to nature's appeal, his fire would die and his work be spoiled. With heavy eyes and aching head he watched his furnace and listened to the constant drip, drip of the precious liquor. It was the fourth day. He had knelt to stir his fire to more active burning. Its brightness made him blink, its warmth was grateful, and he reclined before it, with elbow on the floor and head resting on his hand. How cheerily the logs hummed and crackled, yet how drowsily—how slow the hours were—how dull the watch! Lower, lower sank the head, and heavier grew the eyes. At last he lay full length on the floor, and the long sleep of exhaustion had begun.

He was awakened by the sound of a bell. "The church bell!" he cried, starting up. "And people going through the streets to meeting. How is this? The sun is in the east! My God! I have been asleep! The furnace is cold. The elixir!" He hastily blended the essences that he had made, though one or two ingredients were still lacking, and drank them off. "Faugh!" he exclaimed. "Still unfinished—perhaps spoiled. I must begin again." Taking his hat and coat he uttered a weary sigh and was about to open the door when his cheek blenched with pain, sight seemed to leave him, the cry for help that rose to his lips was stifled in a groan of anguish, a groping gesture brought a shelf of retorts and bottles to the floor, and he fell writhing among their fragments. The elixir of life, unfinished, was an elixir of death.

THE RED DWARF OF DETROIT

Among all the impish offspring of the Stone God, wizards and witches, that made Detroit feared by the early settlers, none were more dreaded than the *Nain Rouge* (Red Dwarf), or Demon of the Strait, for it appeared only when there was to be trouble. In that it delighted. It was a shambling, red-faced creature, with a cold, glittering eye and teeth protruding from a grinning mouth. Cadillac, founder of Detroit, having struck at it, presently lost his seigniory and his fortunes. It was seen scampering along the shore on the night before the attack on Bloody Run, when the brook that afterward bore this name turned red with the blood of soldiers. People saw it in the smoky streets when the city was burned in 1805, and on the morning of Hull's surrender it was found grinning in the fog. It rubbed its bony knuckles expectantly when David Fisher paddled across the strait to see his love, Soulange Gaudet, in the only boat he could find—a wheelbarrow, namely—but was sobered when David made a safe landing.

It chuckled when the youthful bloods set off on Christmas day to race the frozen strait for the hand of buffer Beauvais's daughter Claire, but when her lover's horse, a wiry Indian nag, came pacing in it fled before their happiness. It was twice seen on the roof of the stable where that sour-faced, evil-eyed old mumbler, Jean Beaugrand, kept his horse, Sans Souci—a beast that, spite of its hundred years or more, could and did leap every wall in Detroit, even the twelve-foot stockade of the fort, to steal corn and watermelons, and that had been seen in the same barn, sitting at a table, playing seven-up with his master, and drinking a liquor that looked like melted brass. The dwarf whispered at the sleeping ear of the old chief who slew Friar Constantine, chaplain of the fort, in anger at the teachings that had parted a white lover from his daughter and led her to drown herself—a killing that the red man afterward confessed, because he could no longer endure the tolling of a mass bell in his ears and the friar's voice in the wind.

The Nain Rouge it was who claimed half of the old mill, on Presque Isle, that the sick and irritable Josette swore that she would leave to the devil when her brother Jean pestered her to make her will in his favor, giving him complete ownership. On the night of her death the mill was wrecked by a thunder-bolt, and a red-faced imp was often seen among the ruins, trying to patch the machinery so as to grind the devil's grist. It directed the dance of black cats in the mill at Pont Rouge, after the widow's curse had fallen on Louis Robert, her brother-in-law. This man, succeeding her husband as director of the property, had developed such miserly traits that she and her children were literally starved to death, but her dying curse threw such ill luck on the place and set afloat such evil report about it that he took himself away. The Nain Rouge may have been the *lutin* that took Jacques L'Esperance's ponies from the stable at Grosse Pointe, and, leaving no tracks in sand or snow, rode them through the air all night, restoring them at dawn quivering with fatigue, covered with foam, bloody with the lash of a thorn-bush. It stopped that exercise on the night that Jacques hurled a font of holy water at it, but to keep it away the people of Grosse Pointe still mark their houses with the sign of a cross.

It was lurking in the wood on the day that Captain Dalzell went against Pontiac, only to perish in an ambush, to the secret relief of his superior, Major Gladwyn, for the major hoped to win the betrothed of Dalzell; but when the girl heard that her lover had been killed at Bloody Run, and his head had been carried on a pike, she sank to the ground never to rise again in health, and in a few days she had followed the victims of the massacre. There was a suspicion that the Nain Rouge had power to change his shape for one not less offensive. The brothers Tremblay had no luck in fishing through the straits and lakes until one of them agreed to share his catch with St. Patrick, the saint's half to be sold at the church-door for the benefit of the poor and for buying masses to relieve souls in purgatory. His brother doubted if this benefit would last, and feared that they might be lured into the water and turned into fish, for had not St. Patrick eaten pork chops on a Friday, after dipping them into holy water and turning them into trout? But his good brother kept on and prospered and the bad one kept on grumbling. Now, at Grosse Isle was a strange thing called the rolling muff, that all were afraid of, since to meet it was a warning of trouble;

but, like the *feu follet*, it could be driven off by holding a cross toward it or by asking it on what day of the month came Christmas. The worse of the Tremblays encountered this creature and it filled him with dismay. When he returned his neighbors observed an odor—not of sanctity—on his garments, and their view of the matter was that he had met a skunk. The graceless man felt convinced, however, that he had received a devil's baptism from the Nain Rouge, and St. Patrick had no stancher allies than both the Tremblays, after that.

THE SKULL IN THE WALL

A skull is built into the wall above the door of the court-house at Goshen, New York. It was taken from a coffin unearthed in 1842, when the foundation of the building was laid. People said there was no doubt about it: only Claudius Smith could have worn that skull, and he deserved to be publicly pilloried in that manner. Before the Revolutionary War, Smith was a farmer in Monroe, New York, and being prosperous enough to feel the king's taxes no burden, to say nothing of his jealousy of the advantage that an independent government would be to the hopes of his poorer neighbors, he declared for the King. After the declaration of independence had been published, his sympathies were illustrated in an unpleasantly practical manner by gathering a troop of other Tories about him, and, emboldened by the absence of most of the men of his vicinage in the Colonial Army, he began to harass the country as grievously in foray as the Red-Coats were doing in open field.

He pillaged houses and barns, then burned them; he insulted women, he drove away cattle and horses, he killed several persons who had undertaken to defend their property. His "campaigns" were managed with such secrecy that nobody knew when or whence to look for him. His murder of Major Nathaniel Strong, of Blooming Grove, roused indignation to such a point that a united effort was made to catch him, a money reward for success acting as a stimulus to the vigilance of the hunters, and at last he was captured on Long Island. He was sent back to Goshen, tried, convicted, and on January 22, 1779, was hanged, with five of his band. The bodies of the culprits were buried in the jail-yard, on the spot where the court-house stands, and old residents identified Smith's skeleton, when it was accidentally exhumed, by its uncommon size. A farmer from an adjacent town made off with a thigh bone, and a mason clapped mortar into the empty skull and cemented it into the wall, where it long remained.

THE GREEN PICTURE

In a cellar in Green Street, Schenectady, there appeared, some years ago, the silhouette of a human form, painted on the floor in mold. It was swept and scrubbed away, but presently it was there again, and month by month, after each removal, it returned: a mass of fluffy mold, always in the shape of a recumbent man. When it was found that the house stood on the site of the old Dutch burial ground, the gossips fitted this and that together and concluded that the mold was planted by a spirit whose mortal part was put to rest a century and more ago, on the spot covered by the house, and that the spirit took this way of apprising people that they were trespassing on its grave. Others held that foul play had been done, and that a corpse, hastily and shallowly buried, was yielding itself back to the damp cellar in vegetable form, before its resolution into simpler elements. But a darker meaning was that it was the outline of a vampire that vainly strove to leave its grave and could not, because a virtuous spell had been worked about the place.

A vampire is a dead man who walks about seeking for those whose blood he can suck, for only by supplying new life to its cold limbs can he keep the privilege of moving about the earth. He fights his way from his coffin, and those who meet his gray and stiffened shape, with fishy eyes and blackened mouth, lurking by open windows, biding his time to steal in and drink up a human life, fly from him in terror and disgust. In northern Rhode Island those who die of consumption are believed to be victims of vampires who work by charm, draining the blood by slow draughts as they lie in their graves. To lay this monster he must be taken up and burned; at least, his heart must be; and he must be disinterred in the daytime when he is asleep and unaware. If he died with blood in his heart he has this power of nightly resurrection. As late as 1892 the ceremony of heart-burning was performed at Exeter, Rhode Island, to save the family of a dead woman that was threatened with the same disease that removed her, namely, consumption. But the Schenectady vampire has yielded up all his substance, and the green picture is no more.

THE SALEM WOLF

Howard Pyle

1909

Howard Pyle is best known today for his colorful illustrations of pirates and knights, and for his collection The Merry Adventures of Robin Hood, *which is still in print almost 140 years after its first publication. More than any other artist, he is responsible for the popular image of the pirate that lives on in film and illustration.*

Starting as an illustrator for New York magazines such as Harper's Weekly, *he went on to teach illustration, eventually founding his own school in Wilmington, Delaware, which is now on the National Register of Historic Places. His students there included N. C. Wyeth—arguably the second-most influential illustrator of pirate tales in the world—and many other artists whose work created the so-called golden age of American illustration in the late nineteenth and early twentieth centuries.*

In 1909, Pyle took up mural painting, which was a popular form of public art at the time. He painted The Battle of Nashville *for the Minnesota State Capitol and other murals for courthouses in New Jersey. The following year, he went with his family to Italy, intending to study the old masters, but suffered from poor health for a year before dying of a kidney infection at the age of fifty-eight.*

First published in Harper's Monthly *in December 1909, "The Salem Wolf" is a tale of a werewolf and a witch's curse, as powerful as any European werewolf tale from the Middle Ages but perfectly translated to its Colonial American setting.*

I

These things happened in the year when the witches were so malignant at Salem, and the trouble began over a crock of cider.

Deacon Graves and Jerusha and little Ichabod and old Patrick Duncan were in the cider-shed at the time. Granny Whitlow came to the cider-press, bringing with her a great stoneware crock, and she begged for a crockful of cider.

That was in October before she was hanged for a witch, and she was already in ill odor with all God-fearing men and women. It was known by many that she had an evil eye, and that her malignant soul was as black as a coal and fit for nothing but hell-fire.

Deacon Graves was a stanch professor, and an upright believer in the gospel. "You'll get no cider here," says he. "Begone!" says he, "for I am a friend of God, and you are a friend of the devil."

Then up spoke old Patrick Duncan. He was born in Scotland and had fought in Poland with Douglas under King Karl Gustav of Sweden. It is known that the Scotch and Polish witches and warlocks are the worst in the world, and Patrick Duncan knew more about them and their ways than you could find in a book. "Master," says he, "you had best give her the cider, or else she'll maybe cast the evil eye on the whole pressing."

Then Granny Whitlow laughed very wickedly. "Do you speak of the evil eye?" says she. "Well, then, he may keep his cider, and he may take my black curse along with it," and with that she went out of the shed and left them. But she did not go far—only to the cow-house, and there sat down by the wall with her crock beside her.

By and by Patrick Duncan looked out from the door of the cider-shed and espied her where she sat. "Look, look, Master Graves!" says he. "Yonder sits the witch by the cow-house. Best drive her away, or else she will cast the evil eye upon the cattle."

So Deacon Graves went out to where Granny Whitlow sat and caught her by the arm, and lifted her to her feet, and says he: "Get you gone, witch! What mischief are you brewing here? Get you gone, I say!" Therewith, still holding her tight by the arm, he haled her down to the gate and thrust her out into the road. As he thrust her out she stumbled and fell, and her crock rolled into the ditch beside the road.

But she scrambled, very quickly up from the dusty road, and so got to her feet. She spat upon the ground, and shook her fist at Deacon Graves (all skin and bone it was, and withered like a dead leaf). "Ah!" cries she, "would you treat me so! Well, then, you'll be sorry for this; for I curse you once!—I curse you twice!—I curse you thrice! And if I'm sorry to-day, may you be sorry to-morrow!"

Thus she said, and then she went away down the road, leaving her crock in the ditch where it had fallen.

That was how the trouble began, and that was how Granny Whitlow came to set the evil eye upon Deacon Graves—upon him and his. In less than a fort-night afterward the best cow was taken with hollow-horn, and though they bored holes in both horns with a gimlet, yet the poor beast died inside of four hours.

That was the first curse come true.

A week afterward the Deacon's fine gray mare was bogged in the ditch in the lower pasture, and sprung her shoulder so that she was never good for anything afterward.

That was the second curse come true.

But the third curse was bitter and black to the very bottom.

II

Deacon Graves had a daughter named Miriam. When she fell sick no one knew what ailed her. She grew very strange and wild, and if anybody asked her what ailed her she would maybe scream out, or fall to weeping, or else she would fall into a furious rage, as though seized with a phrensy.

She was a likely girl, with eyes as black as sloes, and black hair, and black eyebrows, and red cheeks, and red lips, and teeth as white as those of a dog. She was promised to Abijah Butler, the son of Aaron Butler the cordwainer. and he came up from town twice or thrice a week to court her.

He saw, as everybody else saw, that she was not as she had been, but was grown very strange and wild. For a while he kept his thoughts to himself, but at last things grew so dark that he spoke very plainly to the girl's father and mother about the matter. "'Tis my belief," says he, "that Granny Whitlow has bewitched her." And neither Deacon Graves nor Dame Graves could find any word to deny what he said.

One Sabbath day Abijah came out from town in the afternoon, and Miriam was in bed. Nothing seemed to ail her, but she would not get up out of bed, but lay there all day, staring at the ceiling and saying nothing. Then Abijah stood up, and he said: "It is high time to do something about this business. If I am to marry Miriam, I must first know what it is ails her."

Dame Graves says: "We none of us know what ails her. We've given her mustard, and sulphur, and boneset, and nothing does her any good."

"Well," says Abijah Butler, "what I said stays where I stuck it. Unless I know what is the matter with Miriam, all is off between us, and I am away."

So Abijah Butler, and Deacon Graves, and Dame Graves, and Patrick Duncan, all four, went to the room where Miriam lay. There she was lying in bed and still as a log; but the moment they set foot in the room she cried out very loud and shrill, and snatched the coverlet over her head. Then she fell to shrieking and screaming as though she had gone mad, bidding them go away and let her lie in peace.

Deacon Graves went to the bedside and caught her very tight by the arm. "Be still!" says he. "Be still, or I will whip you!" and therewith she immediately fell silent, and lay trembling like any leaf.

Then Deacon Graves, still holding her tight by the arm, says to her, "What ails you?" And she said, speaking very weak and faint from under the bed coverlet, "Nothing ails me." Says he, "Tell me, are you bewitched?" and to that, she said nothing. Then he says, "Tell me who has bewitched you?" but still she would say nothing. He says, "Tell me who has bewitched you, or I will whip you."

At that she began crying under the coverlet, but still she would not say anything. Then Deacon Graves says, "Tell me, was it Granny Whitlow who bewitched you?" and at that she said "Yes."

After that they got the whole story from her by piecemeal. This was what she told them:

One day she was turning the bread in the oven. The kitchen door was open, and a great black cat came running in.

She struck at the cat with the bread-peel, but the creature paid no heed to her, but ran around and around the room. Then she grew frightened of the cat and climbed up on the dough-trough. The cat ran around and around the kitchen so fast that her head spun. Then the cat was gone, and Granny Whitlow stood there in the kitchen looking at her. Granny Whitlow's eyes burned like live coals, and she said, "Move your arm!" and Miriam tried to move her arm and could not do so. Then Granny Whitlow said, "Move your other arm!" and Miriam could not move that either. She could not move a single hair, but was like one in a dream, who tries to move and cannot. Then Granny Whitlow plucked three hairs out of her own head and came to Miriam where she sat on the dough-trough; and she tied the three hairs about the girl's little finger. "Now you are one of us," says she, and after that she went out of the kitchen, and Miriam came down from the dough-trough. Ever since that she had been bewitched.

This was the story she told, and after she had ended, her father tried to say something to her. At first he could not say anything, but could only swallow and swallow as though a nut stuck in his throat. Then at last he says—speaking in a voice as dry as a husk, "Tell me, have you ever been to the Devil's Meeting House?"

At that Miriam began to cry out very loud from under the coverlet. Deacon Graves says, "Tell me the truth, or I will whip you!" Thereupon Miriam from under the coverlet said, "Yes—once or twice." He says, "Who took you?" and she says, "It was Granny Whitlow took me."

Then Deacon Graves says, "Let me see your hand." And the girl reached her hand out from under the coverlet. They all looked, and, lo! there was a ring of hair tied about her little finger.

Dame Graves took a pair of scissors and cut the hairs, and after that they all went out of the room and left her. They sat for a while together in the kitchen, and were more happy than they had been for a long time, for they all thought that now that the hair ring was cut from her finger Miriam would be herself again.

By and by, Abijah Butler went home, and after he had gone, Dame Graves says to the Deacon: "You should not have asked Miriam about going to the Devil's Meeting House, and that before Abijah Butler. Who knows what he thinks! He might never come back again, and then where would we find another husband for the girl?" But Abijah Butler was wonderfully in love with Miriam, and even this, and worse than this, did not drive him away from her.

After that time, Miriam Graves was better for two or three days; then she became once more as wild as ever. By this they all knew either that the witchcraft had struck into her bones so that she could not rid herself of it, or else that she had been bewitched again. So a week or so after that (it was then about the middle of November) Deacon Graves went to town and saw Dominie Mather and told him the whole story from beginning to end, just as it was and without hiding anything.

When Granny Whitlow was tried for witchcraft, a great many things were testified against her that had never been known before.

A little girl named Ann Greenfield testified that she had one time been down in Bedloe's Swamp, and that she had there seen Granny Whitlow sitting at the root of a tree, stark and stiff as though she were dead. Little Ann said that she was very much afraid, but she did not run away. She said that, she stood and looked at Granny Whitlow, and by and by she saw something that came running very fast. It looked like a mouse running very fast among the leaves. She said it ran to Granny Whitlow, and ran up her breast and into her mouth, and then Granny Whitlow came to life again and opened her eyes. The little girl said that Granny Whitlow did not see her, but rose and went somewhere into the swamp.

Another girl, named Mercy Nailor, testified that she had once seen Granny Whitlow riding across Fielding's Clearing in the dusk seated astride of a goat as black as coal. Mercy Nailor afterward withdrew her testimony, and confessed that it was not true. But Ann Greenfield's testimony was true, and several other things that were testified were true, for they were never withdrawn.

Deacon Graves was in the crowd when Granny Whitlow rode to the gallows in the hangman's cart. She saw him where he stood, and called out to him from the cart. "Ah, Deacon!" says she, "is that you? And so you have come to see me hanged, have you? Well, then, look to yourself: the third curse is still on you, and something worse than hanging will happen to you before the year is out."

Shortly after that she was hanged.

They all thought that, now Granny Whitlow was hanged, Miriam would be released from the witchcraft that tormented her, but she was not. Things went from bad to worse with her, for, by and by, they found that she would run away at night, no one knew whither. They set a watch upon her, but if they did but wink two or three times, lo! she would be gone.

God knows whither she went, but every time she ran away she would come back betwixt midnight and morning, all wild of face, but weak and wan as though she had ridden long and far. And always after such a time she would go straight to bed and sleep, maybe, for a day and a night. Then she would wake and crave for something to eat, and when food was set before her she would eat, and eat, and eat like a wild creature that was starving.

III

Early in the winter the Salem wolf appeared at that place. Such a thing as a wolf had not been seen at Salem for thirty years and more, and folks were slow to believe that it really was a wolf that killed the sheep or the young cattle or the swine that every now and then were found dead and part eaten in the morning.

But afterward everybody knew that it was a wolf; for one bright moonlight night Eli Hackett saw it as he was coming home from town meeting. A thin snow had fallen, and the night was wonderfully cold and clear and bright. Eli Hackett saw the wolf as plain as though it had been daylight. It ran across the corner of an open lot, and so back of the rope-walk. It appeared to be chasing something, and paid no heed to him, but ran straight on. And then he saw it again when it came out from behind the rope-walk—it ran across Widow Calder's garden-patch, and so into the clearing beyond.

After that several others saw the wolf at different times, and once it chased Doctor Wilkinson on a dark night for above a half-mile, and into the very town itself. Then so many people saw the wolf that women and children were afraid to go out after nightfall, and even men would not go out without an axe or a club, or maybe a pistol in the belt. The wolf haunted the town for above a month, and a great many pigs and sheep and several calves were killed in that time.

Old Patrick Duncan and little Ichabod Graves slept together in the same bed in the attic. One night Patrick Duncan awoke, and found that little Ichabod was shaking his shoulder, and shaking it and shaking it.

Says Patrick Duncan: "What is it, child? What ails you?"

"Oh! Patrick Duncan," says the little boy. "Wake up! There is a great beast running about in the yard!'"

"What is it you say?" says Patrick Duncan. "A great beast? Pooh! pooh! child; you have been dreaming. Go to sleep again."

"Oh, Patrick Duncan!" says the little boy. "Wake up, for I am not dreaming! There is indeed a great beast out in the yard. For first I heard it, and then I looked out of the window and saw it with my very eyes, and it is there running about in the moonlight."

Then Patrick Duncan got up and went to the window of the attic and looked out, and there he saw that what little Ichabod had said was true. For there was the wolf, and it was running around and around the yard in the snow, and he could see it in the moonlight as plainly as though it were upon a sheet of white paper.

The wolf ran around and around in a circle as though it were at play, and every now and then it would snap up a mouthful of snow and cast it into the air. And every now and then it would run its muzzle into the snow and plough through the crust as though in playful sport.

Patrick Duncan said, "Is the musket in the kitchen loaded?" And little Ichabod said: "Yes; for I saw father load it and prime it fresh a week ago come Sabbath evening. For there was fresh talk of the wolf just then." "Then bide you here," says Patrick Duncan, "and I'll go fetch it." So by and by he came, bringing the musket from the kitchen.

There was a broken pane in the attic window and an old stocking in the broken place. Patrick Duncan drew out the stocking very softly, and all the while the great beast played around and around in the snow in the yard below. Patrick Duncan put the musket out through the broken place in the window pane. He took long aim and then he fired. The musket bellowed like thunder, and the air was all full of gunpowder smoke. Patrick Duncan felt sure that he had killed the wolf, but when the gunpowder smoke cleared away, there lay the yard as bare and as empty as the palm of the hand.

The whole house was awakened by the sound of the musket. They all came into the kitchen, except Miriam, who did not come out of her room. They stood about the hearth listening to what Patrick Duncan and little Ichabod had to tell them about the wolf. Patrick Duncan said: "I took a sure and certain aim, and I don't see how I could have missed my shot. I could see the sight of the gun as plain as daylight, and it was pointed straight at the heart of the beast."

As they stood there talking about it all, the kitchen door opened of a sudden very softly and quietly. For a moment it stood ajar, and then some one came into the house as still as a ghost. It was Miriam, and she was clad only in her shift and petticoat. They all looked at her as though they had been turned to stone, but she did not appear to see them. She went straight across the kitchen and to her room, and they could hear the bedstead squeak as she got into bed.

Then Dame Graves began crying. "Alas!" says she, "Miriam walks in her sleep and we can't keep her abed. Suppose the wolf had caught her and killed her!"

The next day, Miriam was churning in the kitchen. Patrick Duncan came in and found her there alone.

"I missed my aim last night, mistress," says he.

"So I hear tell," says she.

"I'll not miss it again," says he.

"Why not?" says she.

"Because," says he, "I am going to melt down this rix-dollar and cast it into a slug. I know this much," says he, "that sometimes a silver slug will go through a hide that will turn a lump of lead. So if ever you see the Salem wolf," says he, "just tell it that the next bullet I shoot at it will be made of silver."

Then the girl stopped churning, and said, "What concern is all this to me?"

"Well," says Patrick Duncan, "you know better than I do whether it concerns you or not."

After that, and for a while, no more was heard of the Salem wolf. It was said that Patrick Duncan's musket-shot had frightened the beast away, but Patrick knew better than that. He knew that it was the threat of the silver bullet that had driven it off.

Then after a while the wolf came back again, and more people saw it, and more sheep and pigs and some calves were found dead in the morning. Then came the worst of all, for one morning Ezra Doolittle was found dead in his own back yard, and his neck was all torn and rent by the savage wild beast.

That was the first that any one suspected that this was no ordinary wolf, but a man-wolf that was running loose among them.

IV

Late one afternoon Abijah Butler came out from town. Deacon Graves was not at home, and so he went down to the barn where Patrick Duncan was milking. "Patrick Duncan," says he. " tell me, what do you think ails Miriam Graves?"

Patrick Duncan's cheek was lying close against the belly of the cow as he milked, and he did not lift his head. "Why do you ask me?" says he. "Go ask her father and her mother what ails her."

Abijah Butler says, "Her father is not at home."

"Well," says Patrick Duncan, "go ask her mother."

"So I will," says Abijah Butler, "but I want you to come with me."

"Well," says Patrick Duncan. "I will go with you when I finish milking the cow."

So after Patrick Duncan had finished his milking they went together to the house, and Dame Graves sat alone in the kitchen at her spinning. Abijah Butler went to her and began speaking, but Patrick Duncan stood by the bench at the window, where he had set the milk pail.

"Tell me," says Abijah Butler, "what is it ails Miriam?"

Dame Graves put her hand to the wheel and stopped it. "You know what ails her as well as I do," says she, "for you heard what the girl said to her father."

"I heard what she said," says he, "but I fear me that worse even than witchcraft ails her. There are things said about her," says he, "that I can't bear to hear; so if I am to be her husband," says he, "I must know what ails her, or else I must break with her."

Then Dame Graves began crying, and says she, "Don't you be hard with us, Abijah Butler; nothing ails the girl, only that she walks in her sleep, and dreams she is awake."

Abijah Butler says, "Where is Miriam, now?"

At that Dame Graves flung her apron over her head, and cried out: "God knows where she is! She ran away half an hour ago!"

After that nobody spoke for a little while; then Abijah Butler says, "Where is Deacon Graves?" And Dame Graves said, "He went to town with a load of potatoes; he'll be back by now, or in a little while."

Abijah Butler says, "Well, I'll wait for him."

Then up spoke old Patrick Duncan. "Best not wait till the night comes down," said he, "for the wolf will be out to-night."

Abijah Butler laughed, and he turned back his overcoat and showed that he had his axe hanging at his belt. He clapped his hand to the shining head of his axe, and, says he: "How now! Need I be afraid?"

Just then Patrick Duncan said of a sudden: "Yonder comes the sledge! Now you can talk to Deacon Graves himself." Then in a moment he cries out: "How is this! The sledge is empty and the horse is running away!"

Thereafter, in a moment or two, the horse came running through the gate with the sledge behind it, and the sledge was empty and swung from this side to that. Thus the horse ran past the house with the empty sledge behind it, and so down to the barn. Abijah Butler and Patrick Duncan ran out of the house and down to the barnyard, and there they found the horse and the empty sledge. And the horse was all of a lather of sweat, and its eyes were starting, and it was trembling in every hair.

"God save us! The wolf!" cries Patrick Duncan. "Here is a bad business! Jump in quick, or we may be too late!"

So they both jumped into the sledge, and Patrick Duncan turned the horse about and drove away in a fury. And so they drove furiously down the road and toward the town.

Well, they had gone a little more than half a mile, when, all of a sudden, the horse stopped stock-still with a jerk that near threw them both out of the sledge. The poor creature stood with all four feet planted, and it snorted and snorted. The evening was then falling pretty fast, and Abijah Butler stood up in the sledge and looked. Then he cried out: "God of Mercy! What is that!" Then he cried out again: "God of Mercy! 'Tis Deacon Graves, and the wolf is at him!" With that he leaped out of the sledge into the snow, and even as he jumped he plucked away the axe from his belt.

By now the horse was leaping and plunging as though it had gone mad and would dash both the sledge and itself to pieces, so that Patrick Duncan had all that he could do to hold it in check.

Abijah Butler ran through the snow as fast as he could to where the wolf was worrying the man in the middle of the road, and he yelled with all his might at the wolf as he ran.

The man lay in the snow and the wolf was worrying him this way and that. The man lay still and did not move, and the wolf worried at him as a wicked dog worries at a sheep. And it was so busy at what it was about, that it paid no heed to Abijah Butler or to the plunging horse or to anything else.

It did not appear to be afraid and did not flee away, so that Abijah ran to it and caught it by the hair of its back and tried to drag it away from the man. And he yelled out: "Hell-hound! Let go!" and therewith he struck the beast a fearful blow upon the neck with his axe just where the neck joins the shoulder.

With that the wolf instantly let go the man, and whirled about several times in the road, howling and yelling.

Then it leaped, yelling, over the wall, and ran away in a great circle across the field beyond. And as it ran, Abijah Butler saw it shake its head now and then, and whenever it shook its head he saw that the blood would sprinkle over the snow. Then in a moment or two it stopped yelling and ran very silently—only every now and then it would shake its head and sprinkle more blood upon the snow. So it ran into the woods, and they could not see it any longer.

They lifted up the Deacon and looked at his hurts, for there was still some light, and by it they could see how much harm he had suffered. He was cut and torn in shoulder and neck, and about the ears and head, but he was in a swoon and not dead, for he wore a fur coat, and the collar of the coat had saved him when the wolf worried at him. Old Patrick Duncan stayed by the wounded man, and Abijah Butler ran across the fields to the Buckners' farmhouse. In a little while he came running back with old Simeon Buckner and his two sons. Deacon Graves had not yet come fully out of his swoon, so they lifted him and laid him in the sledge, covering him over with the sheep pelts that were there.

Simeon Buckner and his two sons drove the sledge home very slowly, and Abijah Butler and old Patrick Duncan went on ahead to tell what had happened. Neither said a word to the other, but each looked down at his feet and walked through the snow in silence.

v

As they came near the house they saw that there were lights moving about within. As they kicked the snow off of their feet against the door-step, the door was flung open, and there was Dame Graves standing on the door-sill. "Oh, Abijah Butler!" cries she. "Oh, Patrick Duncan! Come in quick, for Miriam has come back home and is sore hurt!"

Abijah Butler and Patrick Duncan looked at each other. They came into the house. Patrick Duncan took the candle from Dame Graves, and they all went into the room where Miriam lay. She lay in bed with a sheet drawn up to her chin, and the sheet was all stained red with blood.

Patrick Duncan came to the bedside, and catched the sheet, and pulled at it. Miriam tried to hold it, but he pulled it out of her hands and down over her shoulders. There was a great, terrible, deep wound in the girl's neck where the neck joins the shoulder, and the bed beneath her was all soaked red with blood.

Patrick Duncan cried out in a loud voice, "Where got you that hurt?"

Miriam said nothing, but only covered her face with both hands.

Patrick Duncan cries out in a still louder and more terrible voice, "Where got you that hurt?"

Upon that she began whimpering and whining just as a great dog would do, and she said, "Alas! I know not how I was hurt!"

Then Patrick Duncan cries out, "In God's name, I bid you tell me how you got that hurt!"

Upon that Miriam screamed out of a sudden very loud, and she cried: "Torment me not and I will tell you all! I walked in my sleep, I walked out into the barn, and I walked on the haymow, and all the while I was asleep. I slipped from the haymow, and I fell on the scythe blade and cut my neck."

That was what she said, and she had evidence for it; for the next day they found that there was blood in the barn where the scythe hung in the corner under the haymow. But the blood was there because she had put on her shift and petticoat at that place before she went into the house.

They have not hanged any more witches since they pressed old Giles Corey to death. But God knows how such things as this are to be prevented unless the world is rid of such devil's crew.

As for Miriam Graves, her wound festered and she catched a burning fever and died of it on the sixth day after she had been hurt, at three o'clock in the afternoon. But Deacon Graves got well of his hurts.

Abijah Butler went to Providence in Rhode Island, where he joined business with his uncle, Justification Butler; and old Patrick Duncan went to Deerfield to drill a militia company, and was shot by an Indian who had hid in a clearing.

THE CASE OF CHARLES DEXTER WARD

H. P. Lovecraft

1927

Howard Philips Lovecraft (1890–1937) needs no introduction to the modern reader. His Cthulhu Mythos has gone from being an obscure corner of American outré fiction to a ubiquitous pop culture meme that daily threatens to swallow the Internet.

The shadow of the Colonial era is one of Lovecraft's major themes. His fictional towns of Arkham and Kingsport are notable for their old-fashioned architecture, and stories such as "The Dreams in the Witch-House" and "He" face Lovecraft's protagonists with disturbing echoes of Colonial times that continue to be felt in the present day.

None of Lovecraft's stories is set entirely in Colonial times, but his short novel The Case of Charles Dexter Ward *contains an extended passage in which the story's protagonist learns some disturbing facts about one of his ancestors. Arguably, this section works better on its own than as a part of the original novel, where it interrupts the action to present a great deal of exposition. It presents one of Lovecraft's favorite themes: the hunger for knowledge leading an arrogant and reckless intellectual into madness and death at the hands of unknowable forces.*

AN EXTRACT

J oseph Curwen, as revealed by the rambling legends embodied in what Ward heard and unearthed, was a very astonishing, enigmatic, and obscurely horrible individual. He had fled from Salem to Providence— that universal haven of the odd, the free, and the dissenting—at the beginning of the great witchcraft panic; being in fear of accusation because of his solitary ways and queer chemical or alchemical experiments. He was a colourless-looking man of about thirty, and was soon found qualified to become a freeman of Providence; thereafter buying a home lot just north of Gregory Dexter's at about the foot of Olney Street. His house was built on Stampers' Hill west of the Town Street, in what later became Olney Court; and in 1761 he replaced this with a larger one, on the same site, which is still standing.

Now the first odd thing about Joseph Curwen was that he did not seem to grow much older than he had been on his arrival. He engaged in shipping enterprises, purchased wharfage near Mile-End Cove, helped rebuild the Great Bridge in 1713, and in 1723 was one of the founders of the Congregational Church on the hill; but always did he retain the nondescript aspect of a man not greatly over thirty or thirty-five. As decades mounted up, this singular quality began to excite wide notice; but Curwen always explained it by saying that he came of hardy forefathers, and practised a simplicity of living which did not wear him out. How such simplicity could be reconciled with the inexplicable comings and goings of the secretive merchant, and with the queer gleaming of his windows at all hours of night, was not very clear to the townsfolk; and they were prone to assign other reasons for his continued youth and longevity. It was held, for the most part, that Curwen's incessant mixings and boilings of chemicals had much to do with his condition. Gossip spoke of the strange substances he brought from London and the Indies on his ships or purchased in Newport, Boston, and New York; and when old Dr. Jabez Bowen came from Rehoboth and opened his apothecary shop across the Great Bridge at the Sign of the Unicorn and Mortar, there was ceaseless talk of the drugs, acids, and metals that the taciturn recluse incessantly bought or ordered from him. Acting on the assumption that Curwen possessed a wondrous and secret medical skill, many sufferers of various sorts applied to him for aid; but though he appeared to encourage their belief in a non-committal way, and always gave them odd-coloured potions in response to their requests, it was observed that his ministrations to others seldom proved of benefit. At length, when over fifty years had passed since the stranger's advent, and without producing more than five years' apparent change in his face and physique, the people began to whisper more darkly; and to meet more than half way that desire for isolation which he had always shewn.

Private letters and diaries of the period reveal, too, a multitude of other reasons why Joseph Curwen was marvelled at, feared, and finally shunned like a plague. His passion for graveyards, in which he was glimpsed at all hours, and under all conditions, was notorious; though no one had witnessed any deed on his part which could actually be termed ghoulish. On the Pawtuxet Road he had a farm, at which he generally lived during the summer, and to which he would frequently be seen riding at various odd times of the day or night. Here his only visible servants, farmers, and caretakers were a sullen pair of aged Narragansett Indians; the husband dumb and curiously scarred, and the wife of a very repulsive cast of countenance, probably due to a mixture of negro blood. In the lean-to of this house was the laboratory where most of the chemical experiments were conducted. Curious porters and teamers who delivered bottles, bags, or boxes at the small rear door would exchange accounts of the fantastic flasks, crucibles, alembics, and furnaces they saw in the low shelved room; and prophesied in whispers that the close-mouthed "chymist"—by which they meant *alchemist*—would not be long in finding the Philosopher's

Stone. The nearest neighbours to this farm—the Fenners, a quarter of a mile away—had still queerer things to tell of certain sounds which they insisted came from the Curwen place in the night. There were cries, they said, and sustained howlings; and they did not like the large number of livestock which thronged the pastures, for no such amount was needed to keep a lone old man and a very few servants in meat, milk, and wool. The identity of the stock seemed to change from week to week as new droves were purchased from the Kingstown farmers. Then, too, there was something very obnoxious about a certain great stone outbuilding with only high narrow slits for windows.

Great Bridge idlers likewise had much to say of Curwen's town house in Olney Court; not so much the fine new one built in 1761, when the man must have been nearly a century old, but the first low gambrel-roofed one with the windowless attic and shingled sides, whose timbers he took the peculiar precaution of burning after its demolition. Here there was less mystery, it is true; but the hours at which lights were seen, the secretiveness of the two swarthy foreigners who comprised the only menservants, the hideous indistinct mumbling of the incredibly aged French housekeeper, the large amounts of food seen to enter a door within which only four persons lived, and the *quality* of certain voices often heard in muffled conversation at highly unseasonable times, all combined with what was known of the Pawtuxet farm to give the place a bad name.

In choicer circles, too, the Curwen home was by no means undiscussed; for as the newcomer had gradually worked into the church and trading life of the town, he had naturally made acquaintances of the better sort, whose company and conversation he was well fitted by education to enjoy. His birth was known to be good, since the Curwens or Corwins of Salem needed no introduction in New England. It developed that Joseph Curwen had travelled much in very early life, living for a time in England and making at least two voyages to the Orient; and his speech, when he deigned to use it, was that of a learned and cultivated Englishman. But for some reason or other Curwen did not care for society. Whilst never actually rebuffing a visitor, he always reared such a wall of reserve that few could think of anything to say to him which would not sound inane.

There seemed to lurk in his bearing some cryptic, sardonic arrogance, as if he had come to find all human beings dull through having moved among stranger and more potent entities. When Dr. Checkley the famous wit came from Boston in 1738 to be rector of King's Church, he did not neglect calling on one of whom he soon heard so much; but left in a very short while because of some sinister undercurrent he detected in his host's discourse. Charles Ward told his father, when they discussed Curwen one winter evening, that he would give much to learn what the mysterious old man had said to the sprightly cleric, but that all diarists agree concerning Dr. Checkley's reluctance to repeat anything he had heard. The good man had been hideously shocked, and could never recall Joseph Curwen without a visible loss of the gay urbanity for which he was famed.

More definite, however, was the reason why another man of taste and breeding avoided the haughty hermit. In 1746 Mr. John Merritt, an elderly English gentleman of literary and scientific leanings, came from Newport to the town which was so rapidly overtaking it in standing, and built a fine country seat on the Neck in what is now the heart of the best residence section. He lived in considerable style and comfort, keeping the first coach and liveried servants in town, and taking great pride in his telescope, his microscope, and his well-chosen library of English and Latin books. Hearing of Curwen as the owner of the best library in Providence, Mr. Merritt early paid him a call, and was more cordially received than most other callers at the house had been. His admiration for his host's ample shelves, which besides the Greek, Latin, and English classics were equipped with a remarkable battery of philosophical, mathematical, and scientific works including Paracelsus, Agricola, Van Helmont, Sylvius, Glauber, Boyle, Boerhaave, Becher, and Stahl, led Curwen to suggest a visit to the farmhouse and laboratory whither he had never invited anyone before; and the two drove out at once in Mr. Merritt's coach.

Mr. Merritt always confessed to seeing nothing really horrible at the farmhouse, but maintained that the titles of the books in the special library of thaumaturgical, alchemical, and theological subjects which Curwen kept in a front room were alone sufficient to inspire him with a lasting loathing. Perhaps, however, the facial expression of the owner in exhibiting them contributed much of the prejudice. This bizarre collection, besides a host of standard works which Mr. Merritt was not too alarmed to envy, embraced nearly all the cabbalists, daemonologists, and magicians known to man; and was a treasure-house of lore in the doubtful realms of alchemy and astrology. Hermes Trismegistus in Mesnard's edition, the *Turba Philosophorum*, Geber's *Liber Investigationis*, and Artephius's *Key of Wisdom* all were there; with the cabbalistic *Zohar*, Peter Jammy's set of Albertus Magnus, Raymond Lully's *Ars Magna et Ultima* in Zetzner's edition, Roger Bacon's *Thesaurus Chemicus*, Fludd's *Clavis Alchimiae*, and Trithemius' *De Lapide Philosophico* crowding them close. Mediaeval Jews and Arabs were represented in profusion, and Mr. Merritt turned pale when, upon taking down a fine volume conspicuously labelled as the *Qanoon-e-Islam*, he found it was in truth the forbidden *Necronomicon* of the mad Arab Abdul Alhazred, of which he had heard such monstrous things whispered some years previously after the exposure of nameless rites at the strange little fishing village of Kingsport, in the Province of the Massachusetts-Bay.

But oddly enough, the worthy gentleman owned himself most impalpably disquieted by a mere minor detail. On the huge mahogany table there lay face downwards a badly worn copy of Borellus, bearing many cryptical marginalia and interlineations in Curwen's hand. The book was open at about its middle, and one paragraph displayed such thick and tremulous pen-strokes beneath the lines of mystic black-letter that the visitor could not resist scanning it through. Whether it was the nature of the passage underscored, or the feverish heaviness of the strokes which formed the underscoring, he could not tell; but something in that combination affected him very badly and very peculiarly. He recalled it to the end of his days, writing it down from memory in his diary and once trying to recite it to his close friend Dr. Checkley till he saw how greatly it disturbed the urbane rector. It read:

"The essential Saltes of Animals may be so prepared and preserved, that an ingenious Man may have the whole Ark of Noah in his own Studie, and raise the fine Shape of an Animal out of its Ashes at his Pleasure; and by the lyke Method from the essential Saltes of humane Dust, a Philosopher may, without any criminal Necromancy, call up the Shape of any dead Ancestour from the Dust whereinto his Bodie has been incinerated."

It was near the docks along the southerly part of the Town Street, however, that the worst things were muttered about Joseph Curwen. Sailors are superstitious folk; and the seasoned salts who manned the infinite rum, slave, and molasses sloops, the rakish privateers, and the great brigs of the Browns, Crawfords, and Tillinghasts, all made strange furtive signs of protection when they saw the slim, deceptively young-looking figure with its yellow hair and slight stoop entering the Curwen warehouse in Doubloon Street or talking with captains and supercargoes on the long quay where the Curwen ships rode restlessly. Curwen's own clerks and captains hated and feared him, and all his sailors were mongrel riff-raff from Martinique, St. Eustatius, Havana, or Port Royal. It was, in a way, the frequency with which these sailors were replaced which inspired the acutest and most tangible part of the fear in which the old man was held. A crew would be turned loose in the town on shore leave, some of its members perhaps charged with this errand or that; and when reassembled it would be almost sure to lack one or more men. That many of the errands had concerned the farm on the Pawtuxet Road, and that few of the sailors had ever been seen to return from that place, was not forgotten; so that in time it became exceedingly difficult for Curwen to keep his oddly assorted hands. Almost invariably several would desert soon after hearing the gossip of the Providence wharves, and their replacement in the West Indies became an increasingly great problem to the merchant.

By 1760 Joseph Curwen was virtually an outcast, suspected of vague horrors and daemoniac alliances which seemed all the more menacing because they could not be named, understood, or even proved to exist. The last straw may have come from the affair of the missing soldiers in 1758, for in March and April of that year two Royal regiments on their way to New France were quartered in Providence, and depleted by an inexplicable process far beyond the average rate of desertion. Rumour dwelt on the frequency with which Curwen was wont to be seen talking with the red-coated strangers; and as several of them began to be missed, people thought of the odd conditions among his own seamen. What would have happened if the regiments had not been ordered on, no one can tell.

Meanwhile the merchant's worldly affairs were prospering. He had a virtual monopoly of the town's trade in saltpetre, black pepper, and cinnamon, and easily led any other one shipping establishment save the Browns in his importation of brassware, indigo, cotton, woollens, salt, rigging, iron, paper, and English goods of every kind. Such shopkeepers as James Green, at the Sign of the Elephant in Cheapside, the Russells, at the Sign of the Golden Eagle across the Bridge, or Clark and Nightingale at the Frying-Pan and Fish near the New Coffee-House, depended almost wholly upon him for their stock; and his arrangements with the local distillers, the Narragansett dairymen and horse-breeders, and the Newport candle-makers, made him one of the prime exporters of the Colony.

Ostracised though he was, he did not lack for civic spirit of a sort. When the Colony House burned down, he subscribed handsomely to the lotteries by which the new brick one—still standing at the head of its parade in the old main street—was built in 1761. In that same year, too, he helped rebuild the Great Bridge after the October gale. He replaced many of the books of the public library consumed in the Colony House fire, and bought heavily in the lottery that gave the muddy Market Parade and deep-rutted Town Street their pavement of great round stones with a brick footwalk or "causey" in the middle. About this time, also, he built the plain but excellent new house whose doorway is still such a triumph of carving. When the Whitefield adherents broke off from Dr. Cotton's hill church in 1743 and founded Deacon Snow's church across the Bridge, Curwen had gone with them; though his zeal and attendance soon abated. Now, however, he cultivated piety once more; as if to dispel the shadow which had thrown him into isolation and would soon begin to wreck his business fortunes if not sharply checked.

The sight of this strange, pallid man, hardly middle-aged in aspect yet certainly not less than a full century old, seeking at last to emerge from a cloud of fright and detestation too vague to pin down or analyse, was at once a pathetic, a dramatic, and a contemptible thing. Such is the power of wealth and of surface gestures, however, that there came indeed a slight abatement in the visible aversion displayed toward him; especially after the rapid disappearances of his sailors abruptly ceased. He must likewise have begun to practice an extreme care and secrecy in his graveyard expeditions, for he was never again caught at such wanderings; whilst the rumours of uncanny sounds and manoeuvres at his Pawtuxet farm diminished in proportion. His rate of food consumption and cattle replacement remained abnormally high; but not until modern times, when Charles Ward examined a set of his accounts and invoices in the Shepley Library, did it occur to any person—save one embittered youth, perhaps—to make dark comparisons between the large number of Guinea blacks he imported until 1766, and the disturbingly small number for whom he could produce bona fide bills of sale either to slave-dealers at the Great Bridge or to the planters of the Narragansett Country. Certainly, the cunning and ingenuity of this abhorred character were uncannily profound, once the necessity for their exercise had become impressed upon him.

But of course the effect of all this belated mending was necessarily slight. Curwen continued to be avoided and distrusted, as indeed the one fact of his continued air of youth at a great age would have been enough to warrant; and he could see that in the end his fortunes would be likely to suffer. His elaborate studies and experiments, whatever they may have been, apparently required a heavy income for their maintenance; and since a change of environment would deprive him of the trading advantages he had gained, it would not have profited him to begin anew in a different region just then. Judgment demanded that he patch up his relations with the townsfolk of Providence, so that his presence might no longer be a signal for hushed conversation, transparent excuses of errands elsewhere, and a general atmosphere of constraint and uneasiness. His clerks, being now reduced to the shiftless and impecunious residue whom no one else would employ, were giving him much worry; and he held to his sea-captains and mates only by shrewdness in gaining some kind of ascendancy over them—a mortgage, a promissory note, or a bit of information very pertinent to their welfare. In many cases, diarists have recorded with some awe, Curwen shewed almost the power of a wizard in unearthing family secrets for questionable use.

During the final five years of his life it seemed as though only direct talks with the long-dead could possibly have furnished some of the data which he had so glibly at his tongue's end.

About this time the crafty scholar hit upon a last desperate expedient to regain his footing in the community. Hitherto a complete hermit, he now determined to contract an advantageous marriage; securing as a bride some lady whose unquestioned position would make all ostracism of his home impossible. It may be that he also had deeper reasons for wishing an alliance; reasons so far outside the known cosmic sphere that only papers found a century and a half after his death caused anyone to suspect them; but of this nothing certain can ever be learned. Naturally he was aware of the horror and indignation with which any ordinary courtship of his would be received, hence he looked about for some likely candidate upon whose parents he might exert a suitable pressure. Such candidates, he found, were not at all easy to discover; since he had very particular requirements in the way of beauty, accomplishments, and social security. At length his survey narrowed down to the household of one of his best and oldest ship-captains, a widower of high birth and unblemished standing named Dutee Tillinghast, whose only daughter Eliza seemed dowered with every conceivable advantage save prospects as an heiress. Capt. Tillinghast was completely under the domination of Curwen; and consented, after a terrible interview in his cupolaed house on Power's Lane hill, to sanction the blasphemous alliance.

Eliza Tillinghast was at that time eighteen years of age, and had been reared as gently as the reduced circumstances of her father permitted. She had attended Stephen Jackson's school opposite the Court-House Parade; and had been diligently instructed by her mother, before the latter's death of smallpox in 1757, in all the arts and refinements of domestic life. A sampler of hers, worked in 1753 at the age of nine, may still be found in the rooms of the Rhode Island Historical Society. After her mother's death she had kept the house, aided only by one old black woman. Her arguments with her father concerning the proposed Curwen marriage must have been painful indeed; but of these we have no record. Certain it is that her engagement to young Ezra Weeden, second mate of the Crawford packet *Enterprise,* was dutifully broken off, and that her union with Joseph Curwen took place on the seventh of March, 1763, in the Baptist church, in the presence of one of the most distinguished assemblages which the town could boast; the ceremony being performed by the younger Samuel Winsor. The *Gazette* mentioned the event very briefly, and in most surviving copies the item in question seems to be cut or torn out. Ward found a single intact copy after much search in the archives of a private collector of note, observing with amusement the meaningless urbanity of the language:

> Monday evening last, Mr. Joseph Curwen, of this Town, Merchant, was married to Miss Eliza Tillinghast, Daughter of Capt. Dutee Tillinghast, a young Lady who has real Merit, added to a beautiful Person, to grace the connubial State and perpetuate its Felicity.

The collection of Durfee-Arnold letters, discovered by Charles Ward shortly before his first reputed madness in the private collection of Melville F. Peters, Esq., of George St., and covering this and a somewhat antecedent period, throws vivid light on the outrage done to public sentiment by this ill-assorted match. The social influence of the Tillinghasts, however, was not to be denied; and once more Joseph Curwen found his house frequented by persons whom he could never otherwise have induced to cross his threshold. His acceptance was by no means complete, and his bride was socially the sufferer through her forced venture; but at all events the wall of utter ostracism was somewhat worn down. In his treatment of his wife the strange bridegroom astonished both her and the community by displaying an extreme graciousness and consideration. The new house in Olney Court was now wholly free from disturbing manifestations, and although Curwen was much absent at the Pawtuxet farm which his wife never visited, he seemed more like a normal citizen than at any other time in his long years of residence. Only one person remained in open enmity with him, this being the youthful ship's officer whose engagement to Eliza Tillinghast had been so abruptly broken. Ezra Weeden had frankly vowed vengeance; and though of a quiet and ordinarily mild disposition, was now gaining a hate-bred, dogged purpose which boded no good to the usurping husband.

On the seventh of May, 1765, Curwen's only child Ann was born; and was christened by the Rev. John Graves of King's Church, of which both husband and wife had become communicants shortly after their marriage, in order to compromise between their respective Congregational and Baptist affiliations. The record of this birth, as well as that of the marriage two years before, was stricken from most copies of the church and town annals where it ought to appear; and Charles Ward located both with the greatest difficulty after his discovery of the widow's change of name had apprised him of his own relationship, and engendered the feverish interest which culminated in his madness. The birth entry, indeed, was found very curiously through correspondence with the heirs of the loyalist Dr. Graves, who had taken with him a duplicate set of records when he left his pastorate at the outbreak of the Revolution. Ward had tried this source because he knew that his great-great-grandmother Ann Tillinghast Potter had been an Episcopalian.

Shortly after the birth of his daughter, an event he seemed to welcome with a fervour greatly out of keeping with his usual coldness, Curwen resolved to sit for a portrait. This he had painted by a very gifted Scotsman named Cosmo Alexander, then a resident of Newport, and since famous as the early teacher of Gilbert Stuart. The likeness was said to have been executed on a wall-panel of the library of the house in Olney Court, but neither of the two old diaries mentioning it gave any hint of its ultimate disposition. At this period the erratic scholar shewed signs of unusual abstraction, and spent as much time as he possibly could at his farm on the Pawtuxet Road. He seemed, it was stated, in a condition of suppressed excitement or suspense; as if expecting some phenomenal thing or on the brink of some strange discovery. Chemistry or alchemy would appear to have played a great part, for he took from his house to the farm the greater number of his volumes on that subject.

His affectation of civic interest did not diminish, and he lost no opportunities for helping such leaders as Stephen Hopkins, Joseph Brown, and Benjamin West in their efforts to raise the cultural tone of the town, which was then much below the level of Newport in its patronage of the liberal arts. He had helped Daniel Jenckes found his bookshop in 1763, and was thereafter his best customer; extending aid likewise to the struggling

Gazette that appeared each Wednesday at the Sign of Head. In politics he ardently supported Governor Hopkins against the Ward party whose prime strength was in Newport, and his really eloquent speech at Hacher's Hall in 1765 against the setting off of North Providence as a separate town with a pro-Ward vote in the General Assembly did more than any other one thing to wear down the prejudice against him. But Ezra Weeden, who watched him closely, sneered cynically at all this outward activity; and freely swore it was no more than a mask for some nameless traffick with the blackest gulfs of Tartarus. The revengeful youth began a systematic study of the man and his doings whenever he was in port; spending hours at night by the wharves with a dory in readiness when he saw lights in the Curwen warehouses, and following the small boat which would sometimes steal quietly off and down the bay. He also kept as close a watch as possible on the Pawtuxet farm, and was once severely bitten by the dogs the old Indian couple loosed upon him.

In 1766 came the final change in Joseph Curwen. It was very sudden, and gained wide notice amongst the curious townsfolk; for the air of suspense and expectancy dropped like an old cloak, giving instant place to an ill-concealed exaltation of perfect triumph. Curwen seemed to have difficulty in restraining himself from public harangues on what he had found or learned or made; but apparently the need of secrecy was greater than the longing to share his rejoicing, for no explanation was ever offered by him. It was after this transition, which appears to have come early in July, that the sinister scholar began to astonish people by his possession of information which only their long-dead ancestors would seem to be able to impart.

But Curwen's feverish secret activities by no means ceased with this change. On the contrary, they tended rather to increase; so that more and more of his shipping business was handled by the captains whom he now bound to him by ties of fear as potent as those of bankruptcy had been. He altogether abandoned the slave trade, alleging that its profits were constantly decreasing. Every possible moment was spent at the Pawtuxet farm; though there were rumours now and then of his presence in places which, though not actually near graveyards, were yet so situated in relation to graveyards that thoughtful people wondered just how thorough the old merchant's change of habits really was. Ezra Weeden, though his periods of espionage were necessarily brief and intermittent on account of his sea voyaging, had a vindictive persistence which the bulk of the practical townsfolk and farmers lacked; and subjected Curwen's affairs to a scrutiny such as they had never had before.

Many of the odd manoeuvres of the strange merchant's vessels had been taken for granted on account of the unrest of the times, when every colonist seemed determined to resist the provisions of the Sugar Act which hampered a prominent traffick. Smuggling and evasion were the rule in Narragansett Bay, and nocturnal landings of illicit cargoes were continuous commonplaces. But Weeden, night after night following the lighters or small sloops which he saw steal off from the Curwen warehouses at the Town Street docks, soon felt assured that it was not merely His Majesty's armed ships which the sinister skulker was anxious to avoid. Prior to the change in 1766 these boats had for the most part contained chained negroes, who were carried down and across the bay and landed at an obscure point on the shore just north of Pawtuxet; being afterward driven up the bluff and across country to the Curwen farm, where they were locked in that enormous stone outbuilding which had only high narrow slits for windows. After that change, however, the whole programme was altered. Importation of slaves ceased at once, and for a time Curwen abandoned his midnight sailings. Then, about the spring of 1767, a new policy appeared. Once more the lighters grew wont to put out from the black, silent docks, and this time they would go down the bay some distance, perhaps as far as Namquit Point, where they would meet and receive cargo from strange ships of considerable size and widely varied appearance. Curwen's sailors would then deposit this cargo at the usual point on the shore, and transport it overland to the farm; locking it in the same cryptical stone building which had formerly received the negroes. The cargo consisted almost wholly of boxes and cases, of which a large proportion were oblong and heavy and disturbingly suggestive of coffins.

Weeden always watched the farm with unremitting assiduity; visiting it each night for long periods, and seldom letting a week go by without a sight except when the ground bore a footprint-revealing snow. Even then he would often walk as close as possible in the travelled road or on the ice of the neighbouring river to see what tracks others might have left. Finding his own vigils interrupted by nautical duties, he hired a tavern companion named Eleazar Smith to continue the survey during his absences; and between them the two could have set in motion some extraordinary rumours. That they did not do so was only because they knew the effect of publicity would be to warn their quarry and make further progress impossible. Instead, they wished to learn something definite before taking any action. What they did learn must have been startling indeed, and Charles Ward spoke many times to his parents of his regret at Weeden's later burning of his notebooks. All that can be told of their discoveries is what Eleazar Smith jotted down in a none too coherent diary, and what other diarists and letter-writers have timidly repeated from the statements which they finally made—and according to which the farm was only the outer shell of some vast and revolting menace, of a scope and depth too profound and intangible for more than shadowy comprehension.

It is gathered that Weeden and Smith became early convinced that a great series of tunnels and catacombs, inhabited by a very sizeable staff of persons besides the old Indian and his wife, underlay the farm. The house was an old peaked relic of the middle seventeenth century with enormous stack chimney and diamond-paned lattice windows, the laboratory being in a lean-to toward the north, where the roof came nearly to the ground. This building stood clear of any other; yet judging by the different voices heard at odd times within, it must have been accessible through secret passages beneath. These voices, before 1766, were mere mumblings and negro whisperings and frenzied screams, coupled with curious chants or invocations. After that date, however, they assumed a very singular and terrible cast as they ran the gamut betwixt dronings of dull acquiescence and explosions of frantic pain or fury, rumblings of conversation and whines of entreaty, pantings of eagerness and shouts of protest. They appeared to be in different languages, all known to Curwen, whose rasping accents were frequently distinguishable in reply, reproof, or threatening. Sometimes it seemed that several persons must be in the house; Curwen, certain captives, and the guards of those captives. There were voices of a sort that neither

Weeden nor Smith had ever heard before despite their wide knowledge of foreign parts, and many that they did seem to place as belonging to this or that nationality. The nature of the conversations seemed always a kind of catechism, as if Curwen were extorting some sort of information from terrified or rebellious prisoners.

Weeden had many verbatim reports of overheard scraps in his notebook, for English, French, and Spanish, which he knew, were frequently used; but of these nothing has survived. He did, however, say that besides a few ghoulish dialogues in which the past affairs of Providence families were concerned, most of the questions and answers he could understand were historical or scientific; occasionally pertaining to very remote places and ages. Once, for example, an alternately raging and sullen figure was questioned in French about the Black Prince's massacre at Limoges in 1370, as if there were some hidden reason which he ought to know. Curwen asked the prisoner—if prisoner it were—whether the order to slay was given because of the Sign of the Goat found on the altar in the ancient Roman crypt beneath the Cathedral, or whether the Dark Man of the Haute Vienne Coven had spoken the Three Words. Failing to obtain replies, the inquisitor had seemingly resorted to extreme means; for there was a terrific shriek followed by silence and muttering and a bumping sound.

None of these colloquies was ever ocularly witnessed, since the windows were always heavily draped. Once, though, during a discourse in an unknown tongue, a shadow was seen on the curtain which startled Weeden exceedingly; reminding him of one of the puppets in a show he had seen in the autumn of 1764 in Hacher's Hall, when a man from Germantown, Pennsylvania, had given a clever mechanical spectacle advertised as "View of the Famous City of Jerusalem, in which are represented Jerusalem, the Temple of Solomon, his Royal Throne, the noted Towers, and Hills, likewise the Sufferings of Our Saviour from the Garden of Gethsemane to the Cross on the Hill of Golgotha; an artful piece of Statuary, Worthy to be seen by the Curious." It was on this occasion that the listener, who had crept close to the window of the front room whence the speaking proceeded, gave a start which roused the old Indian pair and caused them to loose the dogs on him. After that no more

conversations were ever heard in the house, and Weeden and Smith concluded that Curwen had transferred his field of action to regions below.

That such regions in truth existed, seemed amply clear from many
things. Faint cries and groans unmistakably came up now and then from
what appeared to be the solid earth in places far from any structure; whilst
hidden in the bushes along the river-bank in the rear, where the high
ground sloped steeply down to the valley of the Pawtuxet, there was found
an arched oaken door in a frame of heavy masonry, which was obviously an
entrance to caverns within the hill. When or how these catacombs could
have been constructed, Weeden was unable to say; but he frequently pointed
out how easily the place might have been reached by bands of unseen
workmen from the river. Joseph Curwen put his mongrel seamen to diverse
uses indeed! During the heavy spring rains of 1769 the two watchers kept
a sharp eye on the steep river-bank to see if any subterrene secrets might
be washed to light, and were rewarded by the sight of a profusion of both
human and animal bones in places where deep gullies had been worn in
the banks. Naturally there might be many explanations of such things in
the rear of a stock farm, and in a locality where old Indian burying-grounds
were common, but Weeden and Smith drew their own inferences.

It was in January 1770, whilst Weeden and Smith were still debating
vainly on what, if anything, to think or do about the whole bewildering
business, that the incident of the *Fortaleza* occurred. Exasperated by the
burning of the revenue sloop *Liberty* at Newport during the previous
summer, the customs fleet under Admiral Wallace had adopted an increased
vigilance concerning strange vessels; and on this occasion His Majesty's
armed schooner *Cygnet*, under Capt. Charles Leslie, captured after a short
pursuit one early morning the scow *Fortaleza* of Barcelona, Spain, under
Capt. Manuel Arruda, bound according to its log from Grand Cairo,
Egypt, to Providence. When searched for contraband material, this ship
revealed the astonishing fact that its cargo consisted exclusively of Egyptian
mummies, consigned to "Sailor A. B. C.", who would come to remove his
goods in a lighter just off Namquit Point and whose identity Capt. Arruda
felt himself in honour bound not to reveal. The Vice-Admiralty Court at
Newport, at a loss what to do in view of the non-contraband nature of the
cargo on the one hand and of the unlawful secrecy of the entry on the other

hand, compromised on Collector Robinson's recommendation by freeing the ship but forbidding it a port in Rhode Island waters. There were later rumours of its having been seen in Boston Harbour, though it never openly entered the Port of Boston.

This extraordinary incident did not fail of wide remark in Providence, and there were not many who doubted the existence of some connexion between the cargo of mummies and the sinister Joseph Curwen. His exotic studies and his curious chemical importations being common knowledge, and his fondness for graveyards being common suspicion; it did not take much imagination to link him with a freakish importation which could not conceivably have been destined for anyone else in the town. As if conscious of this natural belief, Curwen took care to speak casually on several occasions of the chemical value of the balsams found in mummies; thinking perhaps that he might make the affair seem less unnatural, yet stopping just short of admitting his participation. Weeden and Smith, of course, felt no doubt whatsoever of the significance of the thing; and indulged in the wildest theories concerning Curwen and his monstrous labours.

The following spring, like that of the year before, had heavy rains; and the watchers kept careful track of the river-bank behind the Curwen farm. Large sections were washed away, and a certain number of bones discovered; but no glimpse was afforded of any actual subterranean chambers or burrows. Something was rumoured, however, at the village of Pawtuxet about a mile below, where the river flows in falls over a rocky terrace to join the placid landlocked cove. There, where quaint old cottages climbed the hill from the rustic bridge, and fishing-smacks lay anchored at their sleepy docks, a vague report went round of things that were floating down the river and flashing into sight for a minute as they went over the falls. Of course the Pawtuxet is a long river which winds through many settled regions abounding in graveyards, and of course the spring rains had been very heavy; but the fisherfolk about the bridge did not like the wild way that one of the things stared as it shot down to the still water below, or the way that another half cried out although its condition had greatly departed from that of objects which normally cry out. That rumour sent Smith—for Weeden was just then at sea—in haste to the river-bank behind the farm; where surely enough there remained the evidences of an extensive cave-in.

There was, however, no trace of a passage into the steep bank; for the miniature avalanche had left behind a solid wall of mixed earth and shrubbery
from aloft. Smith went to the extent of some experimental digging, but
was deterred by lack of success—or perhaps by fear of possible success. It
is interesting to speculate on what the persistent and revengeful Weeden
would have done had he been ashore at the time.

By the autumn of 1770 Weeden decided that the time was ripe to tell others
of his discoveries; for he had a large number of facts to link together, and
a second eye-witness to refute the possible charge that jealousy and vin-
dictiveness had spurred his fancy. As his first confidant he selected Capt.
James Mathewson of the *Enterprise*, who on the one hand knew him well
enough not to doubt his veracity, and on the other hand was sufficiently
influential in the town to be heard in turn with respect. The colloquy took
place in an upper room of Sabin's Tavern near the docks, with Smith present
to corroborate virtually every statement; and it could be seen that Capt.
Mathewson was tremendously impressed. Like nearly everyone else in the
town, he had had black suspicions of his own anent Joseph Curwen; hence
it needed only this confirmation and enlargement of data to convince him
absolutely. At the end of the conference he was very grave, and enjoined
strict silence upon the two younger men. He would, he said, transmit the
information separately to some ten or so of the most learned and prominent
citizens of Providence; ascertaining their views and following whatever
advice they might have to offer. Secrecy would probably be essential in any
case, for this was no matter that the town constables or militia could cope
with; and above all else the excitable crowd must be kept in ignorance,
lest there be enacted in these already troublous times a repetition of that
frightful Salem panic of less than a century before which had first brought
Curwen hither.

The right persons to tell, he believed, would be Dr. Benjamin West,
whose pamphlet on the late transit of Venus proved him a scholar and
keen thinker; Rev. James Manning, President of the College which had
just moved up from Warren and was temporarily housed in the new King

Street schoolhouse awaiting the completion of its building on the hill above Presbyterian-Lane; ex-Governor Stephen Hopkins, who had been a member of the Philosophical Society at Newport, and was a man of very broad perceptions; John Carter, publisher of the *Gazette*; all four of the Brown brothers, John, Joseph, Nicholas, and Moses, who formed the recognised local magnates, and of whom Joseph was an amateur scientist of parts; old Dr. Jabez Bowen, whose erudition was considerable, and who had much first-hand knowledge of Curwen's odd purchases; and Capt. Abraham Whipple, a privateersman of phenomenal boldness and energy who could be counted on to lead in any active measures needed. These men, if favourable, might eventually be brought together for collective deliberation; and with them would rest the responsibility of deciding whether or not to inform the Governor of the Colony, Joseph Wanton of Newport, before taking action.

The mission of Capt. Mathewson prospered beyond his highest expectations; for whilst he found one or two of the chosen confidants somewhat sceptical of the possible ghastly side of Weeden's tale, there was not one who did not think it necessary to take some sort of secret and coordinated action. Curwen, it was clear, formed a vague potential menace to the welfare of the town and Colony; and must be eliminated at any cost. Late in December 1770 a group of eminent townsmen met at the home of Stephen Hopkins and debated tentative measures. Weeden's notes, which he had given to Capt. Mathewson, were carefully read; and he and Smith were summoned to give testimony anent details. Something very like fear seized the whole assemblage before the meeting was over, though there ran through that fear a grim determination which Capt. Whipple's bluff and resonant profanity best expressed. They would not notify the Governor, because a more than legal course seemed necessary. With hidden powers of uncertain extent apparently at his disposal, Curwen was not a man who could safely be warned to leave town. Nameless reprisals might ensue, and even if the sinister creature complied, the removal would be no more than the shifting of an unclean burden to another place. The times were lawless, and men who had flouted the King's revenue forces for years were not the ones to balk at sterner things when duty impelled. Curwen must be surprised at his Pawtuxet farm by a large raiding-party of seasoned privateersmen and given one decisive chance to explain himself. If he proved a madman, amusing himself with shrieks and imaginary conversations in different voices, he would be properly confined. If something graver appeared, and if the underground horrors indeed turned out to be real, he and all with him must die. It could be done quietly, and even the widow and her father need not be told how it came about.

While these serious steps were under discussion there occurred in the town an incident so terrible and inexplicable that for a time little else was mentioned for miles around. In the middle of a moonlight January night with heavy snow underfoot there resounded over the river and up the hill a shocking series of cries which brought sleepy heads to every window; and people around Weybosset Point saw a great white thing plunging frantically along the badly cleared space in front of the Turk's Head. There was a baying of dogs in the distance, but this subsided as soon as the clamour of the awakened town became audible. Parties of men with lanterns and muskets hurried out to see what was happening, but nothing rewarded their search. The next morning, however, a giant, muscular body, stark naked, was found on the jams of ice around the southern piers of the Great Bridge, where the Long Dock stretched out beside Abbott's distil-house, and the identity of this object became a theme for endless speculation and whispering. It was not so much the younger as the older folk who whispered, for only in the patriarchs did that rigid face with horror-bulging eyes strike any chord of memory. They, shaking as they did so, exchanged furtive murmurs of wonder and fear; for in those stiff, hideous features lay a resemblance so marvellous as to be almost an identity—and that identity was with a man who had died full fifty years before.

Ezra Weeden was present at the finding; and remembering the baying of the night before, set out along Weybosset Street and across Muddy Dock Bridge whence the sound had come. He had a curious expectancy, and was not surprised when, reaching the edge of the settled district where the street merged into the Pawtuxet Road, he came upon some very curious tracks in the snow. The naked giant had been pursued by dogs and many booted men, and the returning tracks of the hounds and their masters could be easily traced. They had given up the chase upon coming too near the town. Weeden smiled grimly, and as a perfunctory detail traced the footprints

back to their source. It was the Pawtuxet farm of Joseph Curwen, as he
well knew it would be; and he would have given much had the yard been
less confusingly trampled. As it was, he dared not seem too interested in
full daylight. Dr. Bowen, to whom Weeden went at once with his report,
performed an autopsy on the strange corpse, and discovered peculiarities
which baffled him utterly. The digestive tracts of the huge man seemed
never to have been in use, whilst the whole skin had a coarse, loosely knit
texture impossible to account for. Impressed by what the old men whispered
of this body's likeness to the long-dead blacksmith Daniel Green, whose
great-grandson Aaron Hoppin was a supercargo in Curwen's employ,
Weeden asked casual questions till he found where Green was buried.
That night a party of ten visited the old North Burying Ground opposite
Herrenden's Lane and opened a grave. They found it vacant, precisely as
they had expected.

Meanwhile arrangements had been made with the post riders to intercept
Joseph Curwen's mail, and shortly before the incident of the naked body there
was found a letter from one Jedediah Orne of Salem which made the coop-
erating citizens think deeply. Parts of it, copied and preserved in the private
archives of the Smith family where Charles Ward found it, ran as follows:

"I delight that you continue in ye Gett'g at Olde Matters in your
Way, and doe not think better was done at Mr. Hutchinson's
in Salem-Village. Certainely, there was Noth'g butt ye liveliest
Awfulness in that which H. rais'd upp from What he cou'd
gather onlie a part of. What you sente, did not Worke, whether
because of Any Thing miss'g, or because ye Wordes were not
Righte from my Speak'g or y^r Copy'g. I alone am at a Loss.
I have not ye Chymicall art to followe Borellus, and owne
my Self confounded by ye VII. Booke of ye Necronomicon
that you recommende. But I wou'd have you Observe what
was tolde to us aboute tak'g Care whom to calle up, for you
are Sensible what Mr. Mather writ in ye Marginalia of——,
and can judge how truely that Horrendous thing is reported.
I say to you againe, doe not call up Any that you can not put
downe; by the Which I meane, Any that can in Turne call up

somewhat against you, whereby your Powerfullest Devices may not be of use. Ask of the Lesser, lest the Greater shall not wish to Answer, and shall commande more than you. I was frighted when I read of your know'g what Ben Zariatnatmik hadde in his ebony Boxe, for I was conscious who must have tolde you. And againe I ask that you shalle write me as Jedediah and not Simon. In this Community a Man may not live too long, and you knowe my Plan by which I came back as my Son. I am desirous you will Acquaint me with what ye Blacke Man learnt from Sylvanus Cocidius in ye Vault, under ye Roman Wall, and will be oblig'd for ye Lend'g of ye MS. you speak of."

Another and unsigned letter from Philadelphia provoked equal thought, especially for the following passage:

"I will observe what you say respecting the sending of Accounts only by y^r Vessels, but can not always be certain when to expect them. In the Matter spoke of, I require onlie one more thing; but wish to be sure I apprehend you exactly. You inform me, that no Part must be missing if the finest Effects are to be had, but you can not but know how hard it is to be sure. It seems a great Hazard and Burthen to take away the whole Box, and in Town (i.e. St. Peter's, St. Paul's, St. Mary's, or Christ Church) it can scarce be done at all. But I know what Imperfections were in the one I rais'd up October last, and how many live Specimens you were forc'd to imploy before you hit upon the right Mode in the year 1766; so will be guided by you in all Matters. I am impatient for y^r Brig, and inquire daily at Mr. Biddle's Wharf."

A third suspicious letter was in an unknown tongue and even an unknown alphabet. In the Smith diary found by Charles Ward a single oft-repeated combination of characters is clumsily copied; and authorities at Brown University have pronounced the alphabet Amharic or Abyssinian, although they do not recognise the word. None of these epistles was ever delivered to Curwen, though the disappearance of Jedediah Orne from Salem as recorded shortly afterward shewed that the Providence men took certain quiet steps. The Pennsylvania Historical Society also has some curious letters received by Dr. Shippen regarding the presence of an unwholesome character in Philadelphia. But more decisive steps were in the air, and it is in the secret assemblages of sworn and tested sailors and faithful old privateersmen in the Brown warehouses by night that we must look for the main fruits of Weeden's disclosures. Slowly and surely a plan of campaign was under development which would leave no trace of Joseph Curwen's noxious mysteries.

Curwen, despite all precautions, apparently felt that something was in the wind; for he was now remarked to wear an unusually worried look. His coach was seen at all hours in the town and on the Pawtuxet Road, and he dropped little by little the air of forced geniality with which he had latterly sought to combat the town's prejudice. The nearest neighbours to his farm, the Fenners, one night remarked a great shaft of light shooting into the sky from some aperture in the roof of that cryptical stone building with the high, excessively narrow windows; an event which they quickly communicated to John Brown in Providence. Mr. Brown had become the executive leader of the select group bent on Curwen's extirpation, and had informed the Fenners that some action was about to be taken. This he deemed needful because of the impossibility of their not witnessing the final raid; and he explained his course by saying that Curwen was known to be a spy of the customs officers at Newport, against whom the hand of every Providence shipper, merchant, and farmer was openly or clandestinely raised. Whether the ruse was wholly believed by neighbours who had seen so many queer things is not certain; but at any rate the Fenners were willing to connect any evil with a man of such queer ways. To them Mr. Brown had entrusted the duty of watching the Curwen farmhouse, and of regularly reporting every incident which took place there.

The probability that Curwen was on guard and attempting unusual things, as suggested by the odd shaft of light, precipitated at last the action so carefully devised by the band of serious citizens. According to the Smith diary a company of about 100 men met at 10 p.m. on Friday, April 12th, 1771, in the great room of Thurston's Tavern at the Sign of the Golden Lion on Weybosset Point across the Bridge. Of the guiding group of prominent men in addition to the leader John Brown there were present Dr. Bowen, with his case of surgical instruments, President Manning without the great periwig (the largest in the Colonies) for which he was noted, Governor Hopkins, wrapped in his dark cloak and accompanied by his seafaring brother Esek, whom he had initiated at the last moment with the permission of the rest, John Carter, Capt. Mathewson, and Capt. Whipple, who was to lead the actual raiding party. These chiefs conferred apart in a rear chamber, after which Capt. Whipple emerged to the great room and gave the gathered seamen their last oaths and instructions. Eleazar Smith was with the leaders as they sat in the rear apartment awaiting the arrival of Ezra Weeden, whose duty was to keep track of Curwen and report the departure of his coach for the farm.

About 10:30 a heavy rumble was heard on the Great Bridge, followed by the sound of a coach in the street outside; and at that hour there was no need of waiting for Weeden in order to know that the doomed man had set out for his last night of unhallowed wizardry. A moment later, as the receding coach clattered faintly over the Muddy Dock Bridge, Weeden appeared; and the raiders fell silently into military order in the street, shouldering the firelocks, fowling-pieces, or whaling harpoons which they had with them. Weeden and Smith were with the party, and of the deliberating citizens there were present for active service Capt. Whipple, the leader, Capt. Esek Hopkins, John Carter, President Manning, Capt. Mathewson, and Dr. Bowen; together with Moses Brown, who had come up at the eleventh hour though absent from the preliminary session in the tavern. All these freemen and their hundred sailors began the long march without delay, grim and a trifle apprehensive as they left the Muddy Dock behind and mounted the gentle rise of Broad Street toward the Pawtuxet Road. Just beyond Elder Snow's church some of the men turned back to take a parting look at Providence lying outspread under the early spring stars. Steeples and gables rose dark and shapely, and salt breezes swept up gently from the cove north of the Bridge. Vega was climbing above the great hill across the water, whose crest of trees was broken by the roof-line of the unfinished College edifice. At the foot of that hill, and along the narrow mounting lanes of its side, the old town dreamed; Old Providence, for whose safety and sanity so monstrous and colossal a blasphemy was about to be wiped out.

An hour and a quarter later the raiders arrived, as previously agreed, at the Fenner farmhouse; where they heard a final report on their intended victim. He had reached his farm over half an hour before, and the strange light had soon afterward shot once into the sky, but there were no lights in any visible windows. This was always the case of late. Even as this news was given another great glare arose toward the south, and the party realised that they had indeed come close to the scene of awesome and unnatural wonders. Capt. Whipple now ordered his force to separate into three divisions; one of twenty men under Eleazar Smith to strike across to the shore and guard the landing-place against possible reinforcements for Curwen until summoned by a messenger for desperate service, a second of twenty men under Capt. Esek Hopkins to steal down into the river valley behind the Curwen farm and demolish with axes or gunpowder the oaken door in the high, steep bank, and the third to close in on the house and adjacent buildings themselves. Of this division one third was to be led by Capt. Mathewson to the cryptical stone edifice with high narrow windows, another third to follow Capt. Whipple himself to the main farmhouse, and the remaining third to preserve a circle around the whole group of buildings until summoned by a final emergency signal.

The river party would break down the hillside door at the sound of a single whistle-blast, then waiting and capturing anything which might issue from the regions within. At the sound of two whistle-blasts it would advance through the aperture to oppose the enemy or join the rest of the raiding contingent. The party at the stone building would accept these respective signals in an analogous manner; forcing an entrance at the first, and at the second descending whatever passage into the ground might be discovered, and joining the general or focal warfare expected to take place within the caverns. A third or emergency signal of three blasts would summon the immediate reserve from its general guard duty; its twenty men dividing equally and entering the unknown depths through both farmhouse and stone building. Capt. Whipple's belief in the existence of catacombs was absolute, and he took no alternative into consideration when making his plans. He had with him a whistle of great power and shrillness, and did not fear any upsetting or misunderstanding of signals. The final reserve at the landing, of course, was nearly out of the whistle's range; hence would require a special messenger if needed for help. Moses Brown and John Carter went with Capt. Hopkins to the river-bank, while President Manning was detailed with Capt. Mathewson to the stone building. Dr. Bowen, with Ezra Weeden, remained in Capt. Whipple's party which was to storm the farmhouse itself. The attack was to begin as soon as a messenger from Capt. Hopkins had joined Capt. Whipple to notify him of the river party's readiness. The leader would then deliver the loud single blast, and the various advance parties would commence their simultaneous attack on three points. Shortly before 1 a.m. the three divisions left the Fenner farmhouse; one to guard the landing, another to seek the river valley and the hillside door, and the third to subdivide and attend to the actual buildings of the Curwen farm.

Eleazar Smith, who accompanied the shore-guarding party, records in his diary an uneventful march and a long wait on the bluff by the bay; broken once by what seemed to be the distant sound of the signal whistle and again by a peculiar muffled blend of roaring and crying and a powder blast which seemed to come from the same direction. Later on one man thought he caught some distant gunshots, and still later Smith himself felt the throb of titanic and thunderous words resounding in upper air. It was just before dawn that a single haggard messenger with wild eyes and a hideous unknown odour about his clothing appeared and told the detachment to disperse quietly to their homes and never again think or speak of the night's doings or of him who had been Joseph Curwen. Something about the bearing of the messenger carried a conviction which his mere words could never have conveyed; for though he was a seaman well known to many of them, there was something obscurely lost or gained in his soul which set him for evermore apart. It was the same later on when they met other old companions who had gone into that zone of horror. Most of them had lost or gained something imponderable and indescribable. They had seen or heard or felt something which was not for human creatures, and could not forget it. From them there was never any gossip, for to even the commonest of mortal instincts there are terrible boundaries. And from that single messenger the party at the shore caught a nameless awe which almost sealed their own lips. Very few are the rumours which ever came from any of them, and Eleazar Smith's diary is the only written record which has survived from that whole expedition which set forth from the Sign of the Golden Lion under the stars.

Charles Ward, however, discovered another vague sidelight in some Fenner correspondence which he found in New London, where he knew another branch of the family had lived. It seems that the Fenners, from whose house the doomed farm was distantly visible, had watched the departing columns of raiders; and had heard very clearly the angry barking of the Curwen dogs, followed by the first shrill blast which precipitated the attack. This blast had been followed by a repetition of the great shaft of light from the stone building, and in another moment, after a quick sounding of the second signal ordering a general invasion, there had come a subdued prattle of musketry followed by a horrible roaring cry which the correspondent Luke Fenner had represented in his epistle by the characters "Waaaahrrrrr-R'waaahrrr." This cry, however, had possessed a quality which no mere writing could convey, and the correspondent mentions that his mother fainted completely at the sound. It was later repeated less loudly, and further but more muffled evidences of gunfire ensued; together with a loud explosion of powder from the direction of the river. About an hour afterward all the dogs began to bark frightfully, and there were vague ground rumblings so marked that the candlesticks tottered on the mantelpiece. A strong smell of sulphur was noted; and Luke Fenner's father declared that he heard the third or emergency whistle signal, though the others failed to detect it. Muffled musketry sounded again, followed by a deep scream less piercing but even more horrible than those which had preceded it; a kind of throaty, nastily plastic cough or gurgle whose quality as a scream must have come more from its continuity and psychological import than from its actual acoustic value.

Then the flaming thing burst into sight at a point where the Curwen farm ought to lie, and the human cries of desperate and frightened men were heard. Muskets flashed and cracked, and the flaming thing fell to the

THE CASE OF CHARLES DEXTER WARD

ground. A second flaming thing appeared, and a shriek of human origin was plainly distinguished. Fenner wrote that he could even gather a few words belched in frenzy: "Almighty, protect thy lamb!" Then there were more shots, and the second flaming thing fell. After that came silence for about three-quarters of an hour; at the end of which time little Arthur Fenner, Luke's brother, exclaimed that he saw "a red fog" going up to the stars from the accursed farm in the distance. No one but the child can testify to this, but Luke admits the significant coincidence implied by the panic of almost convulsive fright which at the same moment arched the backs and stiffened the fur of the three cats then within the room.

Five minutes later a chill wind blew up, and the air became suffused with such an intolerable stench that only the strong freshness of the sea could have prevented its being noticed by the shore party or by any wakeful souls in Pawtuxet village. This stench was nothing which any of the Fenners had ever encountered before, and produced a kind of clutching, amorphous fear beyond that of the tomb or the charnel-house. Close upon it came the awful voice which no hapless hearer will ever be able to forget. It thundered out of the sky like a doom, and windows rattled as its echoes died away. It was deep and musical; powerful as a bass organ, but evil as the forbidden books of the Arabs. What it said no man can tell, for it spoke in an unknown tongue, but this is the writing Luke Fenner set down to portray the daemoniac intonations: "DEESMEES JESHET BONE DOSEFE DUVEMA ENITEMOSS." Not till the year 1919 did any soul link this crude transcript with anything else in mortal knowledge, but Charles Ward paled as he recognised what Mirandola had denounced in shudders as the ultimate horror among black magic's incantations.

An unmistakably human shout or deep chorused scream seemed to answer this malign wonder from the Curwen farm, after which the unknown stench grew complex with an added odour equally intolerable. A wailing distinctly different from the scream now burst out, and was protracted ululantly in rising and falling paroxysms. At times it became almost articulate, though no auditor could trace any definite words; and at one point it seemed to verge toward the confines of diabolic and hysterical laughter. Then a yell of utter, ultimate fright and stark madness wrenched from scores of human throats—a yell which came strong and clear despite the depth from which it must have burst; after which darkness and silence ruled all things. Spirals of acrid smoke ascended to blot out the stars, though no flames appeared and no buildings were observed to be gone or injured on the following day.

Toward dawn two frightened messengers with monstrous and unplaceable odours saturating their clothing knocked at the Fenner door and requested a keg of rum, for which they paid very well indeed. One of them told the family that the affair of Joseph Curwen was over, and that the events of the night were not to be mentioned again. Arrogant as the order seemed, the aspect of him who gave it took away all resentment and lent it a fearsome authority; so that only these furtive letters of Luke Fenner, which he urged his Connecticut relative to destroy, remain to tell what was seen and heard. The non-compliance of that relative, whereby the letters were saved after all, has alone kept the matter from a merciful oblivion. Charles Ward had one detail to add as a result of a long canvass of Pawtuxet residents for ancestral traditions. Old Charles Slocum of that village said that there was known to his grandfather a queer rumour concerning a charred, distorted body found in the fields a week after the death of Joseph Curwen was announced. What kept the talk alive was the notion that this body, so far as could be seen in its burnt and twisted condition, was neither thoroughly human nor wholly allied to any animal which Pawtuxet folk had ever seen or read about.

Not one man who participated in that terrible raid could ever be induced to say a word concerning it, and every fragment of the vague data which survives comes from those outside the final fighting party. There is something frightful in the care with which these actual raiders destroyed each scrap which bore the least allusion to the matter. Eight sailors had been killed, but although their bodies were not produced their families were satisfied with the statement that a clash with customs officers had occurred. The same statement also covered the numerous cases of wounds, all of which were extensively bandaged and treated only by Dr. Jabez Bowen, who had accompanied the party. Hardest to explain was the nameless odour clinging to all the raiders, a thing which was discussed for weeks. Of the citizen leaders, Capt. Whipple and Moses Brown were most severely hurt, and letters of their wives testify the bewilderment which their reticence and close guarding of their bandages produced. Psychologically every participant was aged, sobered, and shaken. It is fortunate that they were all strong men of action and simple, orthodox religionists, for with more subtle introspectiveness and mental complexity they would have fared ill indeed. President Manning was the most disturbed; but even he outgrew the darkest shadow, and smothered memories in prayers. Every man of those leaders had a stirring part to play in later years, and it is perhaps fortunate that this is so. Little more than a twelvemonth afterward Capt. Whipple led the mob who burnt the revenue ship *Gaspee*, and in this bold act we may trace one step in the blotting out of unwholesome images.

There was delivered to the widow of Joseph Curwen a sealed leaden coffin of curious design, obviously found ready on the spot when needed, in which she was told her husband's body lay. He had, it was explained, been killed in a customs battle about which it was not politic to give details. More than this no tongue ever uttered of Joseph Curwen's end, and Charles Ward had only a single hint wherewith to construct a theory. This hint was the merest thread—a shaky underscoring of a passage in Jedediah Orne's confiscated letter to Curwen, as partly copied in Ezra Weeden's handwriting. The copy was found in the possession of Smith's descendants; and we are left to decide whether Weeden gave it to his companion after the end, as a mute clue to the abnormality which had occurred, or whether, as is more probable, Smith had it before, and added the underscoring himself from what he had managed to extract from his friend by shrewd guessing and adroit cross-questioning. The underlined passage is merely this:

> *I say to you againe, doe not call up Any that you can not put downe; by the which I meane, Any that can in turn call up somewhat against you, whereby your powerfullest Devices may not be of use. Ask of the Lesser, lest the Greater shall not wish to Answer, and shall commande more than you.*

In the light of this passage, and reflecting on what last unmentionable allies a beaten man might try to summon in his direst extremity, Charles Ward may well have wondered whether any citizen of Providence killed Joseph Curwen.

The deliberate effacement of every memory of the dead man from Providence life and annals was vastly aided by the influence of the raiding leaders. They had not at first meant to be so thorough, and had allowed the widow and her father and child to remain in ignorance of the true conditions; but Capt. Tillinghast was an astute man, and soon uncovered enough rumours to whet his horror and cause him to demand that his daughter and granddaughter change their name, burn the library and all remaining papers, and chisel the inscription from the slate slab above Joseph Curwen's grave. He knew Capt. Whipple well, and probably extracted more hints from that bluff mariner than anyone else ever gained respecting the end of the accursed sorcerer.

From that time on the obliteration of Curwen's memory became increasingly rigid, extending at last by common consent even to the town records and files of the *Gazette*. It can be compared in spirit only to the hush that lay on Oscar Wilde's name for a decade after his disgrace, and in extent only to the fate of that sinful King of Runazar in Lord Dunsany's tale, whom the Gods decided must not only cease to be, but must cease ever to have been.

Mrs. Tillinghast, as the widow became known after 1772, sold the house in Olney Court and resided with her father in Power's Lane till her death in 1817. The farm at Pawtuxet, shunned by every living soul, remained to moulder through the years; and seemed to decay with unaccountable rapidity. By 1780 only the stone and brickwork were standing, and by 1800 even these had fallen to shapeless heaps. None ventured to pierce the tangled shrubbery on the river-bank behind which the hillside door may have lain, nor did any try to frame a definite image of the scenes amidst which Joseph Curwen departed from the horrors he had wrought.

Only robust old Capt. Whipple was heard by alert listeners to mutter once in a while to himself, "Pox on that——, but he had no business to laugh while he screamed. 'Twas as though the damn'd——had some'at up his sleeve. For half a crown I'd burn his ——house."

ACKNOWLEDGMENTS

I would like to thank the following people, without whom this book would never have been possible.

Lawrence Ellsworth, whose *Big Book of Swashbuckling Adventure* inspired me to compile this anthology and who introduced me to:

Philip Turner, Lawrence's agent and now mine as well, who guided my faltering steps as I took the rough idea and crafted it into a proposal we could both be proud of before passing it to:

William Claiborne Hancock of Pegasus Books, who guided the manuscript through to publication.

Thanks are also due to:

Jamie Paige Davis, my wife, my love, my friend, and my fellow author, who somehow managed to keep putting up with me through some trying times that accompanied my work on this book;

ACKNOWLEDGMENTS

Richard Iorio II of Rogue Games, whose historical-horror tabletop game *Colonial Gothic* first sparked my interest in the period;

Hammer Films and Universal Pictures, whose films I devoured on my parents' black-and-white TV during my youth;

And, of course, the writers, from Increase Mather to H. P. Lovecraft, who established the Colonial period as the natural home of American Gothic fiction. My compliments and thanks to you all!

ABOUT THE EDITOR

Graeme Davis has worked as a writer and editor in the games industry since 1986. His best-known work includes Games Workshop's critically acclaimed *Warhammer Fantasy Roleplay* tabletop game and the mobile strategy game *Kingdoms of Camelot: Battle for the North*, which topped the iOS and Android charts in 2012. He has also published a small (but hopefully, growing) amount of fantasy, horror, and adventure fiction.

Born in England, Davis grew up surrounded by the crumbling castles and drafty mansions of the English Gothic, many of which he visited with his parents or on school outings. He developed a fondness for Universal and Hammer horror films that has stayed with him ever since, along with a taste for authors such as Vernon Lee, M. R. James, and Montague Summers. He studied archaeology at Durham University in the United Kingdom, where he also spent far too much time playing *Dungeons & Dragons* and other fantasy role-playing games.

He lives in Colorado with his wife, Jamie Paige Davis, who is also an author.